HUW'S LEGACY

Book Three of the Evans Family Saga

C.J. PETIT

C.J. PETIT

Printed in the United States of America

First Printing, 2019

ISBN: 9781670023100

TABLE OF CONTENTS

HUW'S LEGACY...1
PROLOGUE..5
CHAPTER 1..9
CHAPTER 2..35
CHAPTER 3..65
CHAPTER 4..106
CHAPTER 5..148
CHAPTER 6..188
CHAPTER 7..215
CHAPTER 8..252
CHAPTER 9..290
CHAPTER 10..319
CHAPTER 11..363
CHAPTER 12..395
CHAPTER 13..431
EPILOGUE..478

C.J. PETIT

PROLOGUE

September 12, 1866

"Well, I'll be damned!" exclaimed Bryn as he sat on Maddy looking across the landscape.

There was no one nearby to hear his expletive other than his buckskin gelding, but it didn't matter. He hadn't expected Jim Peacock to provide an honest description of the land, but he hadn't quite done it justice.

————

On the long ride from O'Fallons in Nebraska Territory, the end of track for the Union Pacific, he and the counterfeiter had become better acquainted. They weren't exactly friends, but Bryn had been impressed with the small man's skills and inventiveness and had grown fond of the short man.

When they'd set up camp about sixty miles north of Denver, Jim had asked about the bribery charge when he'd offered Bryn four pouches of gold dust to let him go back in Omaha. He believed that he could beat the counterfeiting charge, but the bribery charge would almost certainly guarantee that he would serve a long stretch in the territorial prison, something that wouldn't be a pleasant experience for a man of his size and gentle demeanor.

Bryn knew that he was the only one who could testify about the bribe attempt and was already on the fence about even mentioning it to U.S. Marshal Al Esposito when Jim made a second, more subtle bribery attempt.

Naturally, by the time they were in the camp, Bryn had explained that he'd be looking for someplace to start his horse ranch after he dropped Jim Peacock at the Denver County jail. That piece of information led to Jim's decision to suggest a mutually beneficial arrangement.

As he thought that he'd never be caught as a counterfeiter because he'd already sold his press and plates, he'd added land speculation to his money-making enterprises, but not just the open plains that comprised eastern Colorado. He bought land southwest of Denver, closer to the Rockies, and sold some of it at exorbitant prices to the hopeful prospectors who would arrive searching for the gold that seemed to be everywhere, just not in the land they were buying from Jim Peacock.

The land sales were actually more dangerous for Jim than the counterfeiting, and some of the disgruntled purchasers had threatened him with bodily harm after they realized that they'd been had, so Jim had been convinced to buy the land back from them, at a reduced cost, of course.

So, as they sat before the campfire, Jim had casually asked Bryn if he'd be willing to drop the charge of attempted bribery if he sold him some of his land at a good price. He wanted real cash desperately to hire a good attorney rather than use a court-appointed defender and as far as Jim was concerned, it wasn't really a bribe.

Bryn knew that he was going into the gray area of the law, but at the same time, he really didn't want to send Peacock into a place that would be nothing more than a death sentence.

Before he'd picked up the counterfeiter from the Douglas County jail for transport to Denver, he'd told Dylan that he might not tell Al Esposito about the attempted bribe for the same reason that he hadn't charged Jack Mitchell with attempted murder of a U.S. Deputy Marshal, that there was no point in sending the man to prison. Jim Peacock was far from a dangerous man and didn't deserve the harsh punishment that the bribery charge would bring. Dylan had agreed with him and said it was his call.

So, that night Dylan had given Jim Peacock three hundred dollars in cash, which was less than half of his original asking price for four sections of land just eight miles southwest of Denver. Bryn would have to trust the man that he actually owned the property and that he wouldn't be accused of accepting a bribe. It was a serious gamble, but Bryn believed that Jim Peacock was so afraid of being incarcerated in the territorial prison that he wasn't about to lie.

———

When they arrived in Denver, before he dropped Mister Peacock off with Al Esposito, he took the man to the land office where they seemed to know him quite well. It turned out that he actually owned quite an extensive area of land and the four sections was only a small part of his holdings. Bryn wondered if the land he was buying was actually the worst of the entire area. The maps didn't include any topological features but did show the main water locations. The land he was buying did have a blue line squiggling through it, but he had no idea how big the creek or stream was.

They did the transfer then after he had the deed in his pocket, they left the land office and headed to the offices of the United States Marshal.

After dropping off his prisoner, Bryn left the gold that Mister Peacock had with him and explained to Al Esposito both the real and borderline bribery issues. Al was far from upset about

Bryn's decision, but was tickled pink to know that Bryn would soon be moving nearby.

Bryn then sent a telegram to Erin and Dylan that he'd arrived safely and that he'd bought the land for the horse ranch but didn't provide any details. He expected to return in four days.

———

Now he sat in the saddle and looked at his future home. There were no buildings, of course, and the nearest road to the property was almost a mile east, but it was still accessible and the blue squiggle on the map turned out to be a wide creek that flowed from the foothills of the Rockies and crossed the property before turning north where it probably emptied into the Platte River.

Once his surprise had subsided, he walked Maddy onto his land and spent hours exploring the four square miles of property. There were a few areas that could be used as pastures and a small box canyon that would provide protection for the horses in bad weather. He'd already been told of the horrendous winds and snows that would arrive as early as late October, and the canyon was a welcome surprise.

As he rode along the ground, he already imagined where he'd have their new house built and then pictured a large barn and corral for their horses. He hadn't seen any mustang herds but had been told that there were some south of his new ranch site.

He walked Maddy to his new creek, dismounted and let the gelding drink as he stood with arms folded, scanned the spectacular Rocky Mountains to the west and smiled.

"Erin," he said aloud, "this is where we'll raise our children."

CHAPTER 1

June 2, 1867
Wilkes-Barre, Pennsylvania

Kyle knew that this was his last chance. It was do or die and everyone was watching. He couldn't fail, not again.

He stepped up and gripped the heavy bat as he stared out at the pitcher. He hadn't had a hit past the infielders all day and Spike Smith was a hard thrower who liked to intimidate anyone who faced him.

He heard the encouraging shouts of his teammates as he dug in with his old work boots and heard even more insults and jeers from the team on the field and their supporters.

The boys from work floor hadn't beaten the more athletic team made up of the office workers from the Vulcan Iron Works in almost two years and this was as close as they'd come. It was for a good reason, too. If one of the laborers showed skill with the bat or could hurl the ball, he'd suddenly find himself in a cushy office job. Kyle wasn't that good, but he needed to get this hit. Billy Arnold was on second and Toad Williams was on first, but there were two out and they trailed by two runs.

He knew that hitting a home run was unlikely, if not impossible. All he could hope to do was to get wood on the ball and make it safely to first base and let hard-hitting Chuck Smith do his job.

Kyle glared out at Spike and could see the confidence in his hard, brown eyes that were backed up with an added glint of malice.

"C'mon, Spike!" he yelled, "Let's see what you've got!"

Spike knew the power he had in his right arm and so did Kyle as he made his windup and then let the baseball fly.

Kyle dropped to the dirt as the ball zipped past his eyes and their catcher, Rusty Booker caught the ball then laughed as he tossed it back to Spike.

Kyle stood, dusted off the seat of his pants then actually crowded the plate almost daring Spike to throw another one at his head. He was betting his precious noggin that the last thing that the pitcher would want was to send him to first base and let Chuck bat with the sacks full.

After swinging the bat twice, he steadied it on his shoulder, then brought it ready to swing as Spike began his windup.

As soon as he released the pitch, Kyle knew that his gamble had paid off as the ball raced for the outside of their homemade plate that was more round than square.

He swung much more softly than he'd done earlier and felt the bat's sweet spot meet the ball. The ball was already soft from overuse, so it wasn't going to go far, but he just needed it to go where the defenders weren't.

Kyle dropped the bat then sprinted for first base not even looking where the ball was headed.

After he stomped on the first base bag, he finally glanced to his left and was stunned to see the ball still rolling between the center and right fielders.

Without hesitation, Kyle then angled to his left and began racing toward second base as he heard the shouts of his team exhorting the runners to score while the opposing players yelled for the outfielders to get the ball back into the infield.

He glanced over his shoulder as he sprinted toward second and saw the right fielder grab the baseball just as he reached the base and should have stopped, but something compelled him to keep going, so he put his head down and began to race for third, not hearing another sound as he concentrated on the bag and the third baseman who had his hands out to receive the thrown ball from the fielder.

Just before he reached the bag, the ball bounced into the third baseman's hands and Kyle knew he'd have to slide but would probably be out. But just as he prepared to hit the dirt, their third baseman made a monumental mental error when he gleefully slammed his foot on the bag before he turned and left the base with the ball held above his head as he bounced around ready to accept the congratulations of his teammates, believing that he had just made the third out and the game was over.

Kyle could have just slid into the bag knowing that his hit had probably just tied the game, but he didn't. He wanted to win this one now rather than risk a tie and go into extra innings.

He barely slowed after using the base as a pivot point and raced for home plate as the third baseman was being vociferously informed of his error and his entire team began shouting for him to throw home to the waiting catcher.

Kyle had the catcher in his sight and when he was halfway home, he saw the baseball take one long bounce then settle into the catcher's waiting maws as he spread his legs across the base path to block the plate.

Rusty Booker was their catcher for one good reason, he was huge. He was only eighteen, but he was already well over six feet and weighed almost two hundred and fifty pounds. His hands were enormous and incredibly strong and the only reason he was on the office workers team was that the Iron Works' vice president of finance had hired him as a custodian so he could play on his son's team.

Kyle was giving up almost a hundred pounds, but he never gave a second thought to what he was going to do in those last thirty feet before trying to score the winning run. Everyone on the field and watching from the makeshift stands expected him to try to bowl over the enormous catcher, but that would be painful and probably cost him a broken bone or two, so he instantly came up with a much different idea.

Ten feet before the expected collision with Rusty, Kyle dropped into a slide and watched Rusty drop his hands to make the tag. As he slid in a large cloud of dust, Kyle let Rusty ram the baseball onto his stomach, but at the same time, yanked up his right knee into the catcher's exposed crotch.

Rusty screeched in pain as he fell then even as Kyle slammed his left hand on home plate as he slowed to a stop, he looked back and watched as the baseball trickled away.

Kyle popped up and was mobbed by his teammates while the other team began complaining about the viciousness of the slide and said it was nothing less than cheating.

They could complain all they wanted, but everyone knew that his slide wasn't nearly as bad as some of the other shady techniques that the office team had used over the years.

"Let's go and have some beer!" shouted Chuck Smith as he pounded Kyle on the back.

"I'd better not," Kyle replied, "I've got to go and see my mother. She's ailing."

"When you tell her you won the game, maybe it'll make her feel better," Chuck replied as he grinned.

"Maybe," Kyle said before he dusted off his britches again, then said, "I'll see you at work tomorrow, Chuck."

After leaving the field, Kyle began the long walk home. The Vulcan Iron Works dominated the western end of Wiles-Barre, but most of the laborers lived on the southern end of the town while the field where they played their Sunday games was on the north side.

He regretted leaving his mother to play the game, but she had insisted and now he was glad that she had. He wanted to make her proud of him although he knew that she always was.

Kyle and his mother lived alone in a tiny dwelling that was stuck between two normal-sized houses. It had one main room and a kitchen. Each rain revealed new holes in the roof and when the cold weather arrived, the winds would find all of the cracks in the wall. It had been his home for as long as he could remember and because his father had abandoned them years ago, he was their only source of income with his job on the foundry floor. He hadn't had much schooling and almost all he'd learned had come from his mother. Luckily, his ignorance wasn't that unusual, and his friends' situations were hardly much better. Most had begun work before they were ten and those who had attended formal school had never passed the second year.

Kyle had turned seventeen in January and knew that his future wasn't going to change much. His only concern now was for his ailing mother. She'd been losing weight for months, and her appetite was almost gone. Now she was so weak that she couldn't even walk to the privy. He had become her nurse and help her use the chamber pot. He'd long since gotten over the embarrassment.

Kyle reached the house after walking for forty minutes, opened the door and turned to the left to see his mother in her narrow bed.

Bess smiled at him from across the small and asked, "Did you win?"

Kyle walked to the head of the bed, smiled back and excitedly replied, "We were losing in the bottom of the ninth with two outs and I got a hit that won the game!"

"I'm so proud of you that you finally beat those boys, Kyle. I didn't think I'd see the day that you came out on top in one of those contests."

Kyle had hoped that his enthusiastic reply would lift her spirits, but he could tell that even as she smiled, it was at best a momentary state.

He then asked, "Would you like some broth now, Mom?"

Bess looked up at her son and said, "In a moment, Kyle. Go get a chair and sit down so I can talk to you."

Kyle nodded then stepped back into the kitchen, grabbed a chair set it near the bed and sat down. He felt an overwhelming sense of dread just by looking into her pain-filled eyes.

After he was sitting nearby, Bess took a deep breath, tried not to grimace from the pain then said, "Kyle, I know that you don't want to hear this, but I'm not going to be with you much longer."

"Mom, you've got to go back to see the doctor! Please! You don't have to die!"

She raised her thin right index finger then said, "Sssh. Sssh, now. Let me say this. It's the hardest thing I've ever had to do, Kyle. Don't make it harder."

Kyle fought back tears as he just nodded.

Bess then continued, saying, "I wasn't fully honest with you when I returned from Doctor Turnbull. I didn't want you to worry more than you already did. He told me that I had a cancer inside my stomach and that it was too big to cut out and that it would cost more money than we had. He told me that I had six months to live, but I'm not sure that I can last that long. Eating is becoming very painful and the monster that is growing inside me is getting stronger as I'm growing weaker. I've made my peace with God and that's the best I can do. Now you can understand why I haven't asked to see the doctor again, but it wasn't really a difficult decision for me."

"But what about the medicine he gave you?" Kyle asked desperately.

"The medicine is laudanum and it's for the pain, not to make the cancer go away. Nothing can do that. I'm sorry for deceiving you, Kyle, but I believe it was the right thing to do. Now please let me tell you what I had never expected to tell you before it's too late."

Kyle just nodded as he looked into his mother's tired blue eyes.

"When I first learned of my cancer, I wrote a letter to you that explains many things that I've never told you because I thought that you would never need to know. That's all changed now and you have to know about your father."

Kyle's sadness instantly morphed into anger as he muttered, "That bastard left you, Mom! He should have stayed and taken care of you."

Bess took another breath, then replied, "No, Kyle, Tom Nolan wasn't your father. I married him after you were already in my womb. It's all in the letter, but your real father was named Huw Evans and I loved him very much."

Kyle was stunned at the revelation, but quietly asked, "But he left you too? Why? Didn't he love you?"

"He loved me as much as I loved him, but fate can be cruel. I didn't know that I was carrying you when he was killed in a mine collapse in Carbondale. I was devastated to hear the news and thought that I would die from my broken heart. Then a few weeks later, I discovered that I was pregnant and was overjoyed to know that I was carrying Huw's child. You brought me back to life, Kyle, when I thought that I'd never be happy again. When I told my parents that I was pregnant, my father demanded to know who the father was and after I told him that he was Huw Evans, he became enraged."

"Why? Wasn't he a good man?"

"He was the best man I've ever met, but my father thought that I was protecting the real father by saying that a dead man was responsible. But you also must understand that Huw's family was Welsh, and my father was an English Welsh-hater. No one in either of our families knew we were seeing each other and that made it difficult for us, but we both knew it was right. Huw was saving money so we could leave Carbondale and get married. He gave part of his pay each month to me and the rest to his mother. He was going without so we could be together. We were so close that we finally became intimate and then disaster struck.

"When I said that Huw Evans was your father, my father was angry for two reasons. He thought that I was blaming a dead man and a Welshman at that. He assumed that I wouldn't tell him the real father's name because he was another Welshman or even worse, an Irishman, so he banned me from the house. I think that he expected me to run off with my imaginary lover, but I had no place to go, so I took the money that Huw had given to me and came to Wilkes-Barre."

"Why couldn't you go to Huw's family?"

"I was afraid, Kyle, it was as simple as that. I knew how much his mother and family grieved over his loss and I was convinced that if I suddenly arrived at their doorstep and announced that I was carrying Huw's child, they wouldn't even believe me. I thought that I'd be met with cold indifference at best, so I left.

"When I arrived in Wilkes-Barre, I had to find a husband quickly, so I married Tom Nolan because he showed an interest. He didn't know I was pregnant, and I had no intention of telling him. When you were born just seven months after we were married, he had his suspicions, and even asked me if you were his son, so I lied, Kyle. I told him you were because I was afraid that he'd just leave, and I wouldn't be able to care for you anymore."

"Why did he leave?"

"As you grew, you were so obviously different from him in almost every way possible that it became more apparent to him that you weren't his son. Then there was the other indication, when after five years of marriage, I never conceived again. I tried to convince him that I was barren or that something else was wrong, but he finally understood that he was the reason I had never had another child. After that first year, he'd been dallying with other women and some of them were unmarried, yet none had become pregnant. He realized when you were six that he was probably impotent."

"Impotent?"

"That's when a man cannot father children. Once he came to that conclusion, he called you a bastard and simply left. He took the household money, but he never knew about the money that Huw had given to me. I worked as a nanny, housekeeper and took in sewing and other home jobs to get by rather than spend Huw's gift."

"Why are you telling me at all, Mom? It doesn't change anything."

"You needed to know, Kyle. You needed to know," she said weakly before adding, "I'm tired now and need to rest."

As she closed her eyes, Kyle nodded, then leaned over and kissed her forehead before standing and walking the short distance back into the kitchen.

On the small cookstove that also served as the only heat source in the cold weather, was a pot that was half full of a beef soup that provided him with food and his mother with her broth.

He opened the firebox door, crumpled up some old newspapers, then used his flint box to spark a flame before tossing on some dry twigs. Once the fire was going, he added two of the eight split logs onto the fire and knew that he'd have to get more wood soon.

After closing the firebox door, he slid the iron cover from the pot, then took the heavy wooden spoon and began to stir the soup. The contents of the soup varied depending on what food he could find at the best price. He'd been doing all of the shopping before the winter set in and it took him a while to find the best bargains.

Since he'd begun working at the Vulcan Iron Works in '60, when he'd turned nine, his salary had followed a hilly course. He was paid twelve dollars a month at first, but as workers began to leave to fight in the war, his pay climbed to eighteen and then twenty-four dollars a month as he grew bigger and did the work of a full-grown man.

Then the war ended, and his salary dropped back to eighteen dollars a month before it settled to its current sixteen as the returning soldiers looked for work. He still counted himself fortunate to have a job when so many of the veterans couldn't find work. The factory was churning out six locomotives a month during the last half of the war, but then the demand dropped for a year or so. Now demand was picking up again, but his salary wasn't going to go any higher.

As the soup began to heat, he thought about what his mother had told him and wondered why she had waited until now to make her confession. It sounded as if she wasn't ashamed of his real father, so once his temporary father had gone, there was no reason for her to keep it a secret any longer. *Why had she not told him years ago?*

He still couldn't understand her reasoning by the time the soup was getting hot enough to smell. It wouldn't have made any difference to him if she had told him when he was just a boy.

He ladled some of the soup's meat and vegetables into his bowl, then set it aside before he added some water to the soup, put the cover back on the pot, and slipped a spoon into the bowl.

Kyle set the bowl on the table, filled a glass with water from the pitcher and sat down to have his lunch. He'd probably finish off the soup tomorrow morning and make more tomorrow night when he returned from work.

As he chewed the soft, day-old meat and veggie mush, he tried to imagine his mother's distress when she left Carbondale and found it difficult. They'd managed reasonably well once he'd begun working at the ironworks but knew how hard it must have been for her before then. The man she married and believed to be his father, Tom Nolan, wasn't a very good provider. He rarely had a steady job and spent much of his pay on himself. Kyle had been too young and ignorant to realize just how close to becoming an orphan he must have been those first few years, and an orphaned bastard at that.

He finished his soup then stood and washed the bowl, spoon and glass before returning to the stove and stirring the soup before sliding it onto the warming plate. He was about to start searching for the letter his mother had written when he barely heard her call to him, so he walked the eighteen feet to her bedside and sat down.

"Are you ready for your broth now, Mom?"

"In a moment, Kyle. May I have some water first?"

Kyle didn't reply, but just reached over to her nightstand and picked up the glass of water that he kept full by her bedside when he wasn't there. She kept it beside her half-full bottle of laudanum. She could reach the glass and the medicine, but he knew it was difficult for her.

Once he had the glass in his hand, he helped her into a sitting position then let her take the glass and watched as she took just two small sips before handing the glass back to him.

He lowered her gently back to the pillow, set the glass back on the nightstand and waited.

"Kyle, the letter I wrote to you is under my bed, near the wall, but there's no need to read it yet. You can read it after I've gone to meet Huw, your real father."

"Mom…" he began.

"Sssh! It's going to happen, Kyle, and you must be ready for it. What you do after I'm gone is up to you. You can stay here and work in the factory with your friends, or you can leave and find your real family."

"You're my only family, Mom," Kyle said softly.

"No, I'm not. Since I've been here, I've been following the news from Carbondale closely because I thought that I'd be able to send you to your Evans uncles and grandparents, Huw's parents and brothers. One day when you were just a young boy, I was walking to the greengrocer and was startled when I thought I saw Huw walking down the street.

"I boldly stopped the young man and asked his name. He was very polite and told me that he was Dylan Evans, Huw's younger brother by several years. He told me that he was getting ready to leave on a steamboat. He looked a lot like you do now, Kyle, and was just about your age, too."

"Did you tell him about me?"

"I couldn't, Kyle. I was married to Tom Nolan, remember?"

"Oh."

"In 1860, I learned that there had been a major explosion and cave-in at a mine in Carbondale and all of the Evans men, except for Dylan and the youngest boy, Bryn, had been killed. After that, I lost track of the family and thought it didn't matter any longer. That changed in '63 when I read a newspaper story about a local boy, Bryn Evans, who had won the Medal of Honor in a skirmish in Mississippi. It said that his older brother, Dylan Evans, was the United States Marshal in Nebraska Territory."

"Why are you telling me this, Mom? It doesn't matter to me. You are my family, not two men living in the wilderness."

"I won't be your family much longer, Kyle. I'm just telling you because I wanted you to understand that you aren't alone. You could have an entire family living out west and they could provide you with a new home and a new life after I'm gone."

"Mom, I'm staying with you and besides, they wouldn't want a bastard son suddenly showing up at their door. I'd be thrown clear back to Pennsylvania."

Bess took a long breath and with a stronger voice than Kyle thought she had within her, said, "No, they won't, Kyle. My Huw was so gentle and kind and in that brief time that I talked with Dylan, I could tell he was no different. I'm just giving you a choice that you didn't know that you had, nothing more."

Kyle nodded, but knew he'd never leave Wilkes-Barre. If his mother died, he'd want to visit her grave every day. He had no one else.

His mother finally sighed after using almost all of her energy then whispered, "I'd like the broth now."

"I'll be right back, Mom," Kyle said before he rose then walked to the kitchen and ladled some broth from the soup into the same bowl he'd just used before placing the same spoon in the bowl and returning to her bedside.

She only took four tablespoons of broth before she lay back down, closed her eyes and quietly said, "Thank you, Kyle. You're a good son."

Kyle didn't reply because it wasn't necessary as his mother had drifted off to sleep right after she spoke. He set the bowl of broth on the nightstand as he looked at her still-troubled face. She should be having a peaceful sleep but even now, he knew that she was in pain. Despite his insistence, she'd been using the laudanum sparingly because she didn't want to spend the fifty cents for another bottle. That was when he thought it was also working to make her better, now he wished she'd just take it to make the pain go away.

He sat looking at her for another ten minutes before he rose, then carried the broth back to the kitchen and tossed it out the back door.

———

The next morning, before sunrise, he'd helped her use the chamber pot, given her some more broth then after quickly washing, he kissed her goodbye and hurried out of the house to make the walk to the Vulcan Iron Works.

As he jogged along with the other workers, he wished that he could have stayed with her rather than spending the day helping to rivet heavy iron plates onto new locomotives, but he knew that he had no choice.

What had made it more difficult this morning was that when he'd kissed her goodbye, she had tears in her eyes for some reason. She didn't say anything that was different, but those few trickles of moisture had bothered him.

He could hear the noise on the factory floor before he went through the wide doors and then headed for his position at the second half-assembled locomotive.

He waved at Chuck Smith, who didn't smile or wave back, which surprised him then before he could ask why, Will Cochrane, his foreman rapidly approached him.

"Kyle, come over here," Will said when he was close.

"Yes, sir," he replied as he turned toward the foreman.

Kyle could see anxiety and a touch of anger in his foreman's eyes when he stopped and looked at him as the loud banging and shouts of workers echoed across the floor.

"Kyle, the boss wasn't too happy with what you did yesterday at the baseball game. Now I was there and me and a lot of the other fellers were laughing ourselves silly when you made that slide into home, but I guess Rusty Booker complained to his father and they're all saying that you cheated."

"Boss, you know that they do worse than that!"

"I know, and it ain't right, but the boss told me to fire you. I'm sorry."

Kyle was stunned. It was just a game!

"Can't I go and talk to him?"

"Nope. He said he didn't want any cheaters working for him. At least that's the excuse he used. We all kinda figured he's just mad 'cause his hand-picked boys finally lost to a bunch of floor monkeys."

Kyle nodded then turned to leave when Will stopped him, then pulled out a thick brown envelope and handed it to him.

"The boys took up a collection."

Kyle accepted the heavy envelope slipped it into his light jacket pocket and shook the foreman's hand before saying, "Thanks."

As he slowly walked out of the immense factory, he wondered where he could find a job now. He really didn't have any other skills and he'd just been a laborer on the factory floor. He doubted if the envelope held enough cash to pay the ten dollar a month rent on the house. He'd need to find another job, but with all of the veterans still out of work, if he was lucky enough to find a job, he'd probably have to work for less money.

He didn't go straight home but stopped at the wharf to see if anything was available then after not finding any work, he headed for the warehouses. He struck out there as well, so he decided that he'd try again tomorrow, but at least he'd be able to take care of his mother now.

Kyle began to wish that he had just stayed on third yesterday rather than make that race home. Going home sounded so comforting in normal usage but this time, it had just the opposite effect. Now he was going home without a job because of it.

He tried to put his mind in a better state as he neared the small house but wasn't any less frustrated as he opened the door and turned to see how his mother was doing.

"Mom?" he asked quietly as looked at her.

His mother didn't reply or even move, and he felt a stab of pain rip into his chest as he stepped quickly to her bedside.

"Mom?" he asked again only more loudly.

He dropped to his knees next to her bed and only then realized that she wasn't breathing.

"Mom!" he shouted even as he pressed his hand to her cold chest feeling for any sign of life.

Kyle dropped his head and felt the explosive level of grief and loss pervade his entire being as his tears filled his eyes and he shook uncontrollably.

He stayed in agonizing sorrow for almost five minutes without a single rational thought filling his mind as he knelt beside the bed.

Finally, he sniffed wiped his eyes and his running nose on his sleeve then stood slowly and looked down at his mother's body. She was already cold, and he didn't know how that was possible. He'd only been gone for two hours, so she had to have died right after he'd left the house.

A horrifying thought invaded his mind and he whipped his eyes to the nightstand. He didn't know anything about medicine, but the bottle of laudanum was empty now. He wasn't sure if she'd accidentally taken too much or if it was her intention. He didn't even know how much of the drug would be too much. He supposed that it didn't matter in the end. He'd lost the only person who meant anything to him, and he would never think any less of her.

Kyle then folded the blankets over his mother's body covering her peaceful face. He was grateful that her eyes had been closed as he didn't know if he could have maintained his sanity if he'd seen her dead blue eyes looking at him.

He didn't know where he could take her body, so he turned and left the house to go to Doctor Turnbull's office. He'd been the one who had given her the laudanum after telling her that she had months to live.

———

Doctor Turnbull was surprisingly compassionate and told him that he'd send the undertaker to the house and didn't even ask how she'd died. Kyle had been surprised to find that his mother had already paid for her own burial during the same visit when he'd given her his diagnosis.

He returned to the house and left the door open before taking a seat by the bed then waiting for the mortician.

As he sat beside his mother's covered body, he looked at the bed and said softly, "You told me just yesterday that I had a family out west, but I didn't think it mattered at all. Now I'm not so sure. Did you know that they would fire me after I left this morning, Mom?"

He knew that he'd never get an answer at least not in this life. His mother wasn't a churchgoer, but she was a good, caring woman who believed in God and that He would allow her to spend everlasting life with Him. Maybe even now, she had been joyfully reunited with his real father; a man he'd never met.

The mortician, Herbert Milton, arrived with his assistant twenty minutes after Kyle had returned to the house and expressed his well-practiced and often used condolences. He then told him that Doctor Turnbull had already provided the particulars for her burial marker and that Kyle could visit the site in the town cemetery in four hours.

"Thank you," Kyle said softly before they carried his mother out of the house.

After they'd gone, he felt as if he should have been the one to take her to the waiting hearse, but then finally accepted the cold fact that his mother was no longer inside that blanket, so it didn't matter.

He looked at the empty bed, then walked to the nightstand, took the glass of water and the empty laudanum bottle then walked into the kitchen where he set them in the small sink before sitting at the table.

He then pulled out the heavy brown envelope and dumped its contents onto the table. Most of it was silver and the majority were copper coins. When he totaled their donations, he arrived at $8.82. It may not have sounded like a lot, but for the boys on the factory floor to part with the dimes, nickels, and even pennies, was like the bosses handing him a gold double eagle. There was the household money in an old baking powder tin, but he didn't know how much was in there, or what he planned on doing now. At least now that he wasn't working, he had time to think.

He laughed aloud at the irony. He had time to care for his mother, but she no longer needed his care. He could work, but no one would hire him. He was seventeen and was lost.

Then he remembered the letter that his mother had told him about just yesterday, so he stood, walked to the bed and dropped to his belly.

He reached under the narrow bed, felt the paper envelope then slid it out into the light and carried it back into the kitchen.

HUW'S LEGACY

There was nothing written on the outside of the envelope, probably so he wouldn't open it if he found it accidentally, even though he was somewhat remiss in his cleaning duties since his mother had taken to the sickbed.

He slipped his index finger under the loose flap popped it open and slid the pages from inside.

When he unfolded it, he was surprised to see three twenty-dollar notes float onto the floor. He didn't care about the cash now, but quickly began reading the letter.

My Dearest Son,

I know that I've told you about your real father before I pass because I will choose the time that I leave this world. It is the last thing that I can control in my life.

Doctor Turnbull told me that I could last as long as six months, but the pain would be excruciating. I could bear my own pain, but I couldn't bear to watch yours as you witnessed my suffering.

I'm sorry to have left you alone in this hard world, but it was never my choice. I'm just happy to have seen you grow into a man who would make your father proud. I'm sure that even now, we're both looking down at you as your read this and he's telling me that he couldn't have hoped for a better son.

I should have told you about your real family – the Evans. I know that there are no more family members in Carbondale, but you have a grandmother and two uncles living in Nebraska Territory. As your uncle Dylan is the United States Marshal, he should be the easiest to find, and I sincerely hope that you do make that long journey.

It won't be easy, and you won't have the resources to make it quickly, but I genuinely believe that if you walk into your Uncle Dylan's office and tell them you are Huw's son, then you will be accepted. You do look so much like the young Dylan that I met years ago that they should have no doubts to your claim. You won't be asking for anything more than to belong.

If Dylan or Bryn does have a question at all, tell them that the only reason they never worked in the mine was because their father and your grandfather, Lynn Evans, had promised his wife, Meredith, that after Alwen was born, any more boys would be hers. Huw told me that story and it was why Dylan and Bryn probably worked in the pump house and not in the mine.

I've enclosed the money that Huw gave to me when we were going to leave Carbondale and marry. I never let Tom Nolan know that it existed, so now it will help you in whatever you decide to do. You won't find any mementos of our love in my things for the obvious reason that Tom Nolan would have become enraged if he'd found them.

Whether you decide to stay and work in the ironworks or do something else, your father and I will watch over you and do whatever we can do to protect you.

Always remember that you were the focus of all of my love since I lost your father and will never stop loving you.

I hope that you can find the happiness that I shared with my Huw and that your happiness will last for your entire life.

Your loving mother

Kyle felt his tears dripping onto the dry wood of the small table as he slowly folded the letter and slipped it back into its envelope. It was the only thing he'd ever have to remind him of his mother other than the vibrant memories that he hoped would never fade.

He then stood and picked the baking powder tin from the shelf and dumped its contents onto the table with the rest of the money.

When he finished adding it up, he had $83.15 to start the rest of his life. It was a lot more than most boys his age had, and after reading his mother's letter, he understood that he had a family now, too. They may have been more than a thousand miles away, and it might take him a year to get there, but he'd leave Wilkes-Barre tomorrow and start walking west.

Kyle left the kitchen and walked to his corner of the front room where he had his cot, a used crate for his clothes, and his prized possession, an unfinished baseball bat that he'd been working on since last October. He picked up the heavy maple staff that was still too long for a bat and the taper wasn't right yet either, but what had marked it as such an effective candidate for a bat was that at one end of the forty-two-inch-long, three-inch thick maple branch was that at the thick end was a large knot. He hadn't shown it to any of his friends yet and wasn't sure that he'd even be allowed to use it in a game as the knot would almost be cheating.

Now he thought that it would make an ideal walking stick for his long trek across half the continent. There would be many streams to cross and he suspected that the almost-bat would give him the support he'd need to safely cross them.

He took out his trusty pocketknife, a birthday gift from his mother three years ago, and stared at the bat. He hated to desecrate the wood, but if he intended to use it as a walking stick, it had to have a handle of sorts on the end without the heavy knot. So, as he sat in the quiet house, he began to use the point of the smaller blade to drill a hole near the thinner end of the maple bat.

The simple labor allowed him to let his mind steady and make other plans for the journey. He had two shirts and another pair of britches but suspected that his boots wouldn't survive the miles of use. They'd be good enough for a while, but he'd replace them when it became necessary. He had two jackets, the light one he was wearing now and the heavy, winter coat hanging by the doorway with his dark blue woolen scarf and his old felt hat. He'd need gloves when the weather grew cold, but they could wait probably when he had to buy his new boots.

He'd use the two pillowcases for his baggage and take both of the remaining blankets and all of the towels. He'd need to travel light, so he wouldn't bother taking anything heavy from the kitchen. There wasn't much food in the house anyway.

Kyle didn't have a gun for hunting or protection, but had become skilled in snaring rabbits and squirrels, and his pitching arm had developed to the point where he could pick off a curious rabbit at thirty feet with a rock more than half the time.

He knew that he'd have to work his way across the country, and asking for jobs would be new to him, but he'd have to do it even if he stayed in Wilkes-Barre.

Even as he finished the hole through his bat's handle, Kyle began to feel a sense of excitement about starting the journey of discovery and meeting all sorts of different people. He hoped that his new, expanded horizons would make him a better man by the time he reached Omaha, assuming he made it. He had no illusions of the dangers he would face but felt as if he was ready.

He blew the shavings from the hole, then inserted some heavy cord through it before creating a four-inch loop and tying it off with a double knot. He slipped it over his right hand, wrapped it around his wrist then began clumping across the wooden floor. It was heavier than a walking stick should be, but Kyle had hopes that one day, he'd still be able to use it to hit a baseball.

———

June 4, 1867

It was almost mid-morning when Kyle had his two pillowcase travel bags hanging over his left shoulder and his heavy coat and scarf over his right as he left the only home he ever knew.

He'd put most of the money in one of his spare socks in the front pillowcase but kept three dollars and some change in his light jacket's left pocket.

He reached the cemetery after just ten minute then walked to the only grave that hadn't been overgrown with grass yet, stopped and looked at his mother's marker. It was simple, yet he knew that he couldn't afford to have a granite stone carved. Maybe when he was older, he could come back and have it replaced.

All the simple wooden cross had written across it was:

BESS ANN EVANS OCT 11, 1838 ~ JUNE 3, 1867

Kyle smiled as he read the name. His mother had given it to Doctor Turnbull and wondered if she'd told him the reason for its use on the marker.

He removed his hat before he softly said, "Goodbye, Mom. I'm leaving now and I hope that you were right about my real family. I'm sure that you'll be watching when I find them."

He then took in a deep breath, pulled his hat back on then turned and stepped away from the gravesite and soon left the cemetery and began heading for the road leading west out of Wilkes-Barre.

CHAPTER 2

June 8, 1867
Double E Ranch Southwest of Denver

Bryn pulled Maddy to a stop, stood in his stirrups, then turned and smiled down at Erin as she sat in the wagon's seat.

"Well, there it is, Erin. Our new home."

Erin had been so excited on the drive from Denver that she had almost expected to be disappointed, but as she looked at the ranch houses, enormous barn and large corral that already housed more than a dozen horses, she found herself anything but disappointed.

"It's so perfect!" she exclaimed as she beamed up at her husband.

Katie Mitchell said, "Let's go, Mister Evans, I'm getting hungry."

Bryn laughed then said, "Your sister is the one who always seems to be hungry, Katie, and we all know why."

Erin patted her huge bump and said, "Grace needs her nourishment, husband."

Bryn was grinning as he sat back in the saddle and started Maddy down the shallow decline toward the ranch house.

It had taken him longer than he'd expected to bring his family to their home after he bought the land almost two years earlier. When he'd returned to Omaha, he'd told his excited wife and the rest of his family of the property and his plans to have a house and barn built on it before they moved there in the spring of '67.

He'd contracted for the house, barn and corral before he'd left, and they would all be ready before the snows arrived. That meant he'd be making frequent trips back to Denver to check on its progress and to get it ready for occupation with furniture and other necessities. The trip from Omaha to Denver by train and then stagecoach took five days in each direction, so he'd spent a lot of time on the road, but it was worth it.

In November, he'd received a letter from Griff Hughes in which he lamented the loss of his wife, Alice, but that he'd remarried quickly. His new wife wasn't pleased with his plan to move to the wilds of Colorado with his friend and had laid down the law. He apologized and hoped that his new situation didn't affect Bryn's dream of starting his horse ranch.

Bryn had replied expressing his condolences for his loss and explaining that he'd miss having Griff join him, but it wouldn't have an impact on the ranch.

His expected late spring departure had been delayed slightly by the arrival of Dylan and Gwen's fifth child, Brian Lynn Evans. The long span after Bethan's birth before Gwen delivered Cari was matched by the extended time before the family welcomed Brian into the fold. Everyone, especially the parents, had wondered if there would be any more offspring.

Such was not the concern with Bryn and Erin. As she had said when he first left to escort Mister Peacock to Denver, it appeared that she would be in perpetual pregnancy as she conceived shortly after Ethan Lynn Evans was born in March of '66.

Normally, having a new nephew added to the Evans clan wasn't enough of a reason for keeping him from leaving, but Bryn had decided to stay because Katie was learning the skills necessary to be a midwife and would be the one to help Erin with their next child. He wanted to see how she did and wasn't that surprised that Katie had performed admirably in her new role.

Katie functioned as a nanny and housekeeper in Omaha and would do the same in Denver, helping her sister and her sister-in-law with their chores and considered it penance for her decision to not become a nun.

Katie had found it somewhat difficult to adjust to her new social status as a marriageable young woman after moving to Dylan and Gwen's house, and used her relatively remote location to shift into the new, unexpected path more gradually.

When Bryn had finally made it back to his ranch, he threw himself into making it ready for Erin and his family. Rather than building a bunkhouse, he had a second, smaller house built for his expected hired hand. He wasn't planning on creating a big ranch, despite its size. He was still a Deputy U.S. Marshal and had mixed in his duties with the creation of the ranch. Dylan was still his boss when he began the transition, but once he moved Erin, the children and Katie to the new ranch, he'd be officially transferred to Marshal Al Esposito's Denver office.

By the time the winter weather had moved in, the horse ranch was ready with the notable absence of horses. That was remedied in the spring when he'd hired a full-time wrangler named Flat Jack Armstrong. He was closing in on fifty years old and had spent more time with horses than humans. His nickname came from his abnormally large and decidedly flat feet, but he was an affable sort and was pleased with his new job because it meant that he'd have someplace to hang his hat in his declining years and spend it with horses.

Bryn and Flat Jack had first traveled south where they found a small herd of mustangs, and then took a week to get them cornered and roped. They brought the eighteen animals back to the ranch in late April, and Bryn had left them with Flat Jack to break into riding animals.

On his last trip, he'd finally brought the horses that Dylan had saved for him since he went off to war, and now he was ready to bring Erin, the children and Katie to the new ranch.

As he rode ahead of the wagon, he couldn't help but feel a growing sense of satisfaction and pride. There was still a lot of work to be done, but this was now home.

———

June 9, 1867

Kyle had maintained a reasonably steady pace for the first few days of his long hike and had averaged more than twenty-five miles by pacing himself. He soon discovered several shortcomings and it wasn't until he'd reached Williamsport that he was able to remedy them at a new enterprise called an army surplus store.

He imagined that the proprietor had paid almost nothing for the shelves of excess army equipment that filled his store after the war, and even though his prices were reasonable, Kyle was sure that he was making a considerable profit.

After he'd wandered the store, he found the items that he wanted and some that he hadn't realized he needed until he saw them. The first were a canteen and a slicker then he added a small, two-man tent and a proper knapsack before buying some solid infantry boots. The items that he didn't expect to buy were an army hatchet, a sewing kit and the biggest surprise, a small kit with fishing line and hooks. Why it was even in the store was a mystery.

The entire purchase cost him $7.15 of his limited funds and had taken a good amount of negotiation to get it that low. Nonetheless, he felt better prepared after leaving the biggest town on his walk so far.

He'd managed to avoid spending money for food thus far but knew it couldn't last much longer. He had nine hundred miles still before him and knew that he'd have to find someplace to stay over the winter and hopefully make some money.

There had been many small towns along the well-traveled roadway, and he'd met many travelers going in the opposite direction and had been given rides on freight and farm wagons going west, which had saved his failing work boots.

He'd been grateful for the good weather and now that he had his new slicker, felt that it could pour if Mother Nature felt the need to weep. With his new boots on his feet and his U.S.-emblazoned knapsack over his shoulders, he felt ready for whatever awaited him. He still had his pillowcase travel bags, so he knew that he must have looked a sight as he walked west out of Williamsport that afternoon.

His maple baseball bat-walking stick had served him well, although its weight might have seemed excessive to some. His biggest enemy was the growing heat of the coming summer even in northern Pennsylvania, and it was that concern that had made the purchase of the canteen so imperative.

Kyle was an hour out of Williamsport and was thinking about his mother and his unknown relatives in Nebraska, which was now a state, and he wondered if that change would have any impact on his uncles.

He was smiling at the concept of such things as he was still very doubtful of his mother's claim that he would be accepted by the Evans family. He was still Kyle Hugh Nolan on his birth certificate, but until his mother had told him of his birth father, he hadn't recognized the significance of his middle name. Maybe that and the date of his birth would help them believe his story. But even if they didn't, Kyle still was convinced that he'd made the right decision to leave Wilkes-Barre. He suspected that work would be much easier to find somewhere out West.

Kyle was thumping his way along the roadway with the hot afternoon sun in his face when he spotted two fellow pedestrians heading east about a mile away. It wasn't anything to be concerned about, but he still checked behind him for more traffic. There wasn't any, but that wasn't unusual either. This late in the afternoon, most commercial vehicles had already reached their destinations.

So, he continued his steady pace without any real worries. Everyone he'd met on his journey had been pleasant and some had been downright generous and helpful. He expected no different from the two men approaching him.

When they were four hundred yards away, he still wasn't concerned in the least. They were strolling at a reasonable pace and conversing loudly with occasional breaks of laughter, and some of it may have been after they'd spotted him, which he could understand. He was loaded down with his heavy coat and scarf on one shoulder, his two pillow travel bags hung over his left while he had a knapsack and tent strapped to his back. He knew that he must look like a scruffy Santa Claus as he made his way along the road.

When they were close, they waved and the taller of the two shouted, "Howdy!"

Kyle replied, "Afternoon. You boys headed for Williamsport?"

The shorter man guffawed and replied, "Well now, where else would we be goin'?"

Kyle laughed then replied, "I guess that was kind of stupid to ask."

The taller man just laughed and when they were just fifteen feet away, they stopped and he asked, "Where are you headed? You're pretty loaded down there, boy."

"I'm heading west to find my uncles."

"Do they live in Pennsylvania?" he asked.

"Nope. I think they live in Nebraska somewhere."

"You're walkin' all the way there?"

"Yes, sir, and I'd like to spend the time to tell you the story, but I have a long way to go."

"Good enough. We'll be on our way, and good luck."

Kyle nodded then said, "Have a good time in Williamsport," before resuming his interrupted journey.

Nothing they had said or done was any different than other travelers he'd encountered, but even as they passed him, Kyle felt the hairs on the back of his neck tingle.

He took three more long strides then even as he turned to look behind him, he spotted the taller of the two men with his knife drawn above his head and about to ram it into his back as his shorter partner advanced holding his own blade at waist level.

Kyle had no time to avoid the tall man's blow and felt the heavy blade punch into his new knapsack before he jerked away, and the big knife dropped to the ground. The leather covering wouldn't have stopped the sharp knife on its own, but inside, the two heavy blankets that now wrapped his old work boots did. The force of the blow knocked Kyle off balance and would have sent him to the ground where the second man would have finished him if it wasn't for his maple walking stick that instantly became his baseball bat-club.

He stumbled one step forward as his pillowcase travel bags and his heavy coat dropped to the ground then grabbed his walking stick with his left hand as his right already had a firm grip thanks to the wrist cord.

The first man had gone to his knees after his killing blow had failed and was scrambling to his feet as the second man made his attack at the surprisingly unharmed victim.

Kyle swung his heavy maple weapon harder than he'd ever managed on the ball field, hearing the whoosh of the thick wood rush through the air before he felt it connect with a sickening crack on the shorter man's left shoulder. His knife may have been in his right hand, but when his left humerus was shattered by the force of that big knot at the end of Kyle's bat. He howled in pain and dropped his knife, even as his partner regained his feet and lunged to regain his dropped knife while Kyle was stepping back to gain distance from his attackers.

The tall man ignored his partner's screams as he grasped his blade while Kyle brought the staff above his head and screamed, "Leave me alone!"

The tall man hesitated for just moment as he let his hand get a better grip on his knife and then took one step back and stared at the boy glaring at him. It took him just a few seconds to realize that any possible gain wasn't worth having his head bashed in.

He lowered his knife and slid it into its sheath on his belt before saying, "Alright, kid. Just let me help my friend and we'll keep goin'."

"Leave his knife on the ground and just go," Kyle growled as he kept his club ready to strike.

His partner was just moaning as he tried to keep his broken arm from moving as the tall man said, "It's his knife, boy."

"And it was my back that you tried to stick yours into. Just leave it!"

His partner finally spoke when he said, "Let's go, Elmer. It ain't worth it and I need to get my arm fixed."

Elmer gave Kyle one long glare before turning and waiting for his injured companion to begin walking.

Kyle kept his club held over his head as he watched them leave, expecting the tall one to turn and hurl his knife at him. He didn't convert his weapon back into a walking stick until they were a good hundred yards away.

He finally set the knotted end on the ground and continued to keep them in sight until he was satisfied that they wouldn't return then stepped over to the dropped knife and picked it from the ground.

It was an eight-inch blade with a razor-sharp edge that would have made short work of any part of his body that it touched. The other man's knife was probably just as well sharpened, and the thought of how close he'd been to meeting his mother again so soon sent a chill down his spine. Even as he examined the knife, he realized that he'd been fortunate that neither of them had a pistol. His bat was a good defensive weapon against a knife-wielding thief but wouldn't do much good if the man could stand twenty feet away and shoot him. Even that revelation didn't inspire him to buy one. He'd never fired one before and wasn't about to waste the money to learn.

He slid his knapsack from his back and stared at the two-inch gash right under the S in the US. It had been so very close.

He took some time to empty the knapsack and check the damage and what he found chilled him again. His old boots had suffered damage that rendered them beyond repair by even the most skilled cobbler. They'd saved his life, and maybe they deserved better treatment, but Kyle simply tossed the useless footwear off the road then wrapped the knife in one of the slashed blankets before returning it to the knapsack.

Kyle took a long drink from his new canteen before restoring his standard packing to his back and shoulders and after looking once more to the east, finally resumed his walk.

The incident had only one significant impact on Kyle. It awakened him to the real dangers that he would face over the next year. He hadn't been completely unaware of the dangers, but now the threats were very real. He had always been an optimist and believed the best of other people until proven otherwise. He hoped that he wouldn't change, but he knew that he had to be leerier of any strangers and the even bigger danger posed by thieves armed with pistols.

Because it was almost summer, the daylight lasted well past eight o'clock, but well before sunset, Kyle left the road and walked north until he felt his campsite wouldn't be seen by anyone from the roadway.

He set up a cold camp this time and didn't bother erecting his new tent because he was still spooked by the recent attack. He ate the last of the rabbit from yesterday's successful rock toss and knew that he wasn't as well prepared as he should be. He was lucky to still be alive to see tomorrow's sunrise, and he had to be better. Having the big knife was an improvement in his capabilities, but his bat was still his best defense. He'd just been awkward in its use and could have used it much more effectively.

So, after he finished his cold, greasy rabbit and crackers, he finished the water in the canteen before filling it in the nearby stream then picked up his walking stick that would probably never be used as a baseball bat and tried to picture the fight.

It didn't take long to realize each of his mistakes, beginning with turning his back on two strangers when there was no one else around. Several times in the brief encounter, he'd lost his balance and had to use the bat to keep from falling. He now understood that balance was the key to survival, but not just balance with the walking stick, balance with everything in his new life.

Kyle removed his shirt to keep it reasonably clean then for the next forty minutes, he practiced swinging and stopping the heavy maple rod, but never quite achieved anything close to real balance. He'd almost fallen a few times in his exercises and cursed each time.

After he finished and stood breathing heavily with sweat dripping across his skin, he knew that he'd have to modify his walking stick. The hole and wrist loop that made it easier to use as a walking stick made it terribly imbalanced when used as a defensive weapon. He then removed the cord from his wrist and moved his hands further down the staff, as if he was preparing to bunt the baseball. Most of the weight was still on the longer end, but just having those four inches behind his hands seemed to make an enormous difference.

He began to repeat the same swinging and stopping motions and started to modify each swing, making it shorter and more compact to make it easier to stop or change direction. When the knotted end had slammed into the left arm of the shorter attacker, he had felt the power of the bat and even then, he understood that it was more than necessary to stop the man. He could have hurt him with a much shorter blow and not lost his balance.

Kyle was still very awkward in his movements by the time he finished and knew that he'd have to improve.

As he set his walking stick on the blanket while he let his sweat dry, he wondered if one of the more embarrassing things that his mother had taught him would be useful. When he was thirteen, she told him that soon, he'd be going to socials and dances to meet girls and needed to know how to dance. He'd been appalled at the idea because he was so clumsy and gangly that he knew that the girls would laugh at him, but she had insisted. So, at least twice each week, she hummed waltzes as she guided him around the small room and praised him for his growing skill.

He'd never gone to any socials or dances because he was even more awkward around girls than he had been when he first started to dance and was usually too tired after a long day on the factory floor anyway, but at least the dance lessons helped when he played baseball. He even had begun to look forward to those nights where he danced with his mother, and he was equally sure that she enjoyed them as well. She had been his only dance partner.

After washing in the stream and donning his dry shirt, he lay on the blanket and looked up at the bright band of the Milky Way. He was still unsure about undertaking the lengthy journey into the unknown, but he knew that out there, among those stars, his mother and his real father were smiling at him. Maybe she had been the one to have him decide to keep his old boots in his knapsack.

He smiled as the night sky filled his eyes and said, "I know that it was my decision to keep the old work boots, Mom, but I'll say 'thank you' anyway. Tomorrow, when I try my exercises, I'll dance."

———

Erin lay close to her husband and asked, "Do you really think that not even having a boy's name will give us a girl?"

Bryn chuckled as he caressed his wife's large bump and replied, "It worked for Dylan and Gwen, and they had a boy's name ready this time and look what happened."

Erin laughed and said, "Brian is a cute little boy, Bryn. I think they chose that name because it's so close to yours. I think they're breaking from the Welsh names."

"As well we should. Some of them do have an odd ring about them and some are impossible to spell. I still recall standing in front of that enlistment table and having to spell my name for the recruiter."

"I like your name, and I like the name we've chosen for our daughter, Grace Lynn. I've always liked it and I've never met a shrew or a biddy with that name."

"I've never met any woman named Grace, to be honest. Our daughter will be the first."

"After Mason and Ethan, I think we're making progress."

"What do you think of Flat Jack?"

"He's a good man and I think your sons will love him when they get older. He tells some tall tales that keep things interesting."

Bryn laughed and said, "I don't think they'll love him just when he begins one of his tales, but they sure are interesting. How's Katie adjusting?"

"She's happy to be with us and I know that she's doing better now that she's away from Omaha. I think she was worried that our parents might somehow take her back and send her to the convent anyway."

"When is your other brother, Daniel, going to be a priest?"

"He's going to be ordained in September. Where he goes is up to the bishop."

"Did he want to be a priest, or was he just driven into it by your parents?"

"Dan was happy to be going to the seminary, and I think if he didn't have a true calling, he would have snuck away on his own. He's a stubborn Irishman just like all of us."

"I know you are, my wife, but I haven't seen it in Katie yet."

"Give her a chance, Mister Evans, and you'll discover just how Irish she is. Katie has red hair too, so that should be a warning to any young man that woos her."

"Do you think we should bring her into Denver to meet young men?"

"Give her time, Bryn. You've got to remember that for most of her life, she'd been being prepared to go to the convent. She needs to find herself."

"Yes, ma'am. I just wanted to be sure."

Erin then asked, "Before we left, Gwen mentioned that the governor might want to appoint his own United States Marshal. Can he do that?"

"I'm not sure. A territorial or state governor nominates a man for the position and sends his recommendation to the president, who always signs it. I know that Dylan would still be a U.S. Marshal, but I don't have a clue if the governor can ask for another one. A lot of it is politics, too. Governor Butler is a Republican and with a Republican president in office, he might be able to get his way. It would be an unusual situation, but if there's one arena where the unreal happens at a high rate, it's politics."

"So, it could happen?"

"I suppose it could. If it does, I can't imagine Dylan staying in that office with a political hack wearing the badge. Maybe he and Gwen could move to Denver and work with Al Esposito. I know that Al would be happy to have him here. We're short a few deputies as it is, and Dylan would be a real asset, but that would be a decision by the Marshals Service."

"It would be wonderful to have Gwen and all of the family nearby again."

"You haven't been gone that long, Mrs. Evans."

Erin didn't reply but swatted her husband's naked behind. She knew how much Gwen was fretting about the impact that a new marshal would have on their family life. Dylan wouldn't abide having to give up control of the office to someone who probably only wore the badge because he had donated to the governor's campaign or was the nephew of a friend. If that happened, they'd leave their family home on the hill and go elsewhere.

Dylan was still subject to reassignment by the head of the U.S. Marshals Service, but Gwen knew that he wouldn't accept just any assignment. Gwen had told Erin that she believed that if this all happened, he might be assigned to the Dakota Territories because of his familiarity with the Crow Indians. She had even told him that she and Dylan still owned a bank in Fort Benton, which had stunned Erin. She'd also said that if they ordered Dylan to the Dakotas, she didn't know if he'd take the job or resign. It was that possible sequence of future events that had created Gwen's and now Erin and Bryn's concerns.

She and Bryn were just getting settled into their new life in Colorado, while Dylan and Gwen might be facing a more unplanned change in theirs.

————

Before he regained the road the next morning, Kyle spent thirty minutes practicing with his bat using his waltz steps to provide a smoother, practiced motion and immediately discovered that the familiar beats also provided a consistent timing for his moves with the heavy stick. It may not have been ballet, but it was a considerable improvement from his first clumsy practice the night before.

By nine o'clock, he was well on the road and making good time. His stomach was growling as he'd skipped any form of breakfast to practice, but having an empty stomach wasn't an uncommon state since he'd left Wilkes-Barre. He'd been so pernicious in his spending that he'd avoided leaving a dime at any of the eating places in the towns he'd passed through.

He knew that he'd have to change that because as much as he hated to admit it, he was still a growing teenager. He knew he was close to six feet tall and the last time he'd weighed himself on the scale at the feed and grain, he'd barely passed a hundred and sixty pounds. He doubted if he was within five pounds of that weight anymore.

Kyle resolved to start spending some of his cash to eat a substantial meal at least once every three days, but then he knew that he'd have to stop at a farm along the way to offer to work for food and a place to stay. It was far from uncommon for young men to arrive at a farmhouse door and make the offer and most farmers not only expected it but appreciated the extra labor for minimum cost. Having a strong back to help plow, seed, weed and harvest the crops was always welcome. It was just a question of the young man who knocked on the door. If he appeared to be of sound character, he would be permitted to stay, but if he was of questionable nature, he'd be denied entrance.

As he walked, Kyle felt his growing beard and his overly long hair and knew that he probably presented a less than acceptable appearance. When he stopped for the night, he'd cut his hair and then shave in the morning. He'd have to shave every morning in the chance that he'd have to stand before a door and ask for some work.

During that day's long walk, he was passed by other pedestrians, riders, and wagons and shortly after noon, was lucky to get a ride on a wagon that was going to the next town of Linden.

He bought his big meal at Rosco's Diner in Linden and found it difficult to finish the entire plate of roast pork and gravy. He packed the two biscuits before paying his twenty-five cents and leaving the eatery.

As he left Linden heading west, he felt better, but somewhat lethargic and downright sleepy from having a full stomach.

He was forty minutes out of town when he suffered a very different kind of attack. For the last twenty minutes, his stomach had started a rebellion. He felt a growing sense of nausea and thought that walking was the best medicine. It was a hot day and he believed that he could sweat out the stomach problem.

Now he knew that no amount of exercise would purge his increasing nausea, so he turned north off the roadway and began to jog quickly into the dense overgrowth of trees and bushes.

Kyle barely had time to drop his load to the ground when he doubled over and wretched, hurling the twenty-five-cent lunch across the ground. He remained in that position for another five minutes, vomiting every bit of his stomach's contents until there was nothing left. He continued to dry heave for another few minutes, before he stepped away from his mess and, breathing heavily, he slowly sat down on a downed tree trunk.

"So much for gaining weight," he said aloud then started to laugh.

He reached down, picked up his canteen then rinsed out his mouth as well as possible, but couldn't quite clear the sour taste.

He wanted to just rest, but knew he couldn't do it here, so he loaded his things onto his shoulders and back then started walking again. His legs were still shaky as he reached the roadway but wanted to gain as much distance as possible from his mess.

Less than an hour later, he could go no further, so he turned back off the road and headed into the woods. He dropped his things to the ground and let his staff fall. He was exhausted and all he wanted to do was sleep, but he didn't.

After laying out his two blankets, he set his things in a reasonable order, then sat down and retrieved the sewing kit from his backpack. It had a pair of small scissors inside, so he pulled them free of the small leather folder and began to cut his hair. He knew it was far from what even an inept, blind barber could do, but he just wanted it shorter.

When he was finished, he felt his scruffy whiskers and knew that the longer he put off shaving, the worse it would be, so despite his weariness, he took out his shaving kit and headed for a nearby pond.

As he whipped the brush through the cup to make the lather, he saw a fish leap from the nearby water, snare a nearby dragonfly then splash back into the depths. He was surprised because he thought that fish only ate during the morning hours. That dragonfly must have been too much temptation for the small mouthed bass.

He wasn't going to do anything about it today, but tomorrow morning, he'd see if he could put that fishing set that he'd bought at the army surplus store to good use.

Kyle finished his shave then washed his face in the cool water before returning to his campsite. He didn't have nearly the number of nicks that he'd expected and the sour taste in his mouth was finally fading. His stomach felt like an empty pit, which it was, and he was still tired, but shaving had somehow made him feel human again.

As the sun faded, he found a long branch and as he cleared it of its branches with his pocketknife, he munched down the two biscuits, hoping that they weren't going to make him sick again.

By the time Kyle had slipped one of his two blankets over him, he wondered what other discoveries lay ahead, good and bad. One thing he'd learned was to ask folks in towns about the quality of food in the eateries, or maybe he'd just buy a tin of beans at the greengrocer. He really didn't want to go through that horrendous loss of lunch again.

———

The sun was barely showing through the trees when Kyle dropped his first line into the pond. He'd easily found a large patch of damp earth that had yielded a virtual hotel inhabited by large worms and selected a few to use as temptation for his breakfast.

He'd formed his own bobber for his fishing line out of a dry piece of oak bark and now watched it closely for any sudden movement when the fish below the surface investigated the wiggling worm.

He wished it could have been further from shore but didn't have long to wait before the bark twitched, making small ripples then suddenly disappeared in a small whirlpool. He yanked the pole back and was rewarded when it bent as the fish fought. It only took a few seconds to walk his breakfast back to the shore and was pleased at the size of his catch. The perch was probably about two and a half pounds and would be enough for him to fill his empty stomach.

———

An hour later, a satisfied Kyle returned to the road. He'd cut and roasted the fish over his fire using the same branch he'd used as a pole. It wasn't the most ideal method, but after he'd sprinkled some salt on the fish, it was actually quite tasty. It wasn't going to make him sick either.

He continued his journey, reaching the large town of Lock Haven in early afternoon, and after checking with some of the townsfolk, had his lunch at Mary's Café. For the next hour after leaving the town, he monitored his stomach as much as the road and found trouble with neither.

———

For three more days, Kyle continued his journey, shaving each morning and either trapping or catching his dinner and breakfast. He'd only stopped in Mt. Pleasant for a full meal, and anticipating being in Ohio in another week, but circumstances changed his plans.

He was about an hour past Brookville when he spotted a wagon rolling behind him, so he stepped aside to let it pass and ask if he could ride along.

As the wagon neared, the driver, a bearded man wearing overalls and a shabby straw hat waved to him and slowed the wagon.

"Need a ride, son?" he asked.

"I'd appreciate it, sir," Kyle said as he reached the wagon, then after leaving his walking stick in the empty bed, he began stripping off the rest of his load and laying it in the back.

When he was free of his encumbrances, Kyle climbed onto the wagon's seat and watched as the farmer snapped his reins and the wagon lurched forward with its two-mule power.

"My name's Karl Neuman. What's yours?"

Kyle paused for just a heartbeat and replied, "Kyle Evans."

"It looks like you're heading a far way there, son. You're too young to have fought in that blasted war, so what's got you on the road?"

"My mother died and told me that I had uncles in Nebraska, so I'm going there to meet them. They're the only family I have."

Karl turned to look at him and exclaimed, "*You're going all the way there on foot?*"

"Yes, sir, unless I can catch rides from friendly folks like yourself."

"That's gonna take some amount of walking, Kyle. I figure even if you kept going during the winter, you might make it by springtime."

"No, sir. I don't think it'll take that long. I figured that it's about another eight hundred miles to Omaha, and I've been walking about twenty miles a day, so I should get there before the leaves turn."

"That's if you don't get hurt or sick. You seem a bit skinny already."

"I'll admit to that, sir, but I aim to get there. It may be a waste of my time, but it's all I have now."

"Well, I'll make you an offer, Kyle. Why don't you stay with my family for a while to get some meat on your bones? My wife, Erna, is a right fine cook and so are my three girls. I kinda need some help after I lost two of my boys in war and only have my youngest, Ernst, still with us. He's only twelve and does what he can, but I need some strong hands to help with some of the big jobs."

"I've never been on a farm before, Mister Neuman. I've only worked in a locomotive factory in Wilkes-Barre."

"That doesn't matter much, Kyle. I need a strong back and you won't need to know what to sow or when to harvest. If you think you can make it to Omaha in forty days, then spending a couple of weeks with us won't hurt much."

Before he'd even left Wilkes-Barre, Kyle knew that he'd have to work and earn some money or at least have a steady diet for a time, and this did seem like an ideal situation, although he suspected that there was no money in it.

"Alright, Mister Neuman, I'll stick around and help."

Karl smiled at him and replied, "I appreciate it, Kyle."

Kyle smiled back then turned his head forward wondering what Mister Neuman's farm looked like. He'd seen many of them as he passed through the Pennsylvania countryside and some were still showing the effects levied by the war even in the untouched areas that had never seen armies passing through. Manpower had been sucked from the farms leaving some almost derelict while others seemed quite prosperous.

When Karl pointed out his farmhouse on the north side of the roadway ahead, Kyle wasn't sure which category it earned. The house needed a good whitewash and the barn had some boards missing, but the fields were well ordered, and he could see women hanging laundry. As he let his eyes scan the fields, he spotted someone he assumed was Ernst Neuman hoeing between the growing stalks of wheat. He wondered why Karl had gone into town alone, but it wasn't important.

As Karl Neuman turned down the access road, the women hanging laundry all turned and waved, but resumed hanging the wash.

"That's my Erna and our girls hanging the laundry and Ernst is weeding. I'm sure he'll be heading over here soon enough when he sees you."

Any reply that Kyle might have made was interrupted by a loud bellow from the barn, which generated a laugh from Karl.

Kyle asked, "You have cows?"

"That's Bertha. She's always complaining about something, but Sophie is much friendlier. We have some chickens in back, too. I take some milk and eggs into town every couple of days."

Kyle still wondered why he'd gone to town alone but didn't ask as the wagon trundled closer to the house.

As Karl had predicted, Ernst came trotting from the wheat field as the wagon came to a stop but waited for his father to make the introduction.

Karl set the handbrake then climbed down as Kyle clambered to the ground from the opposite side then quickly walked around the back of the wagon to meet Ernst.

Karl then looked at his son and said, "Ernst, this is Kyle Evans. I found him walking on the road and asked him to give us some help for a little while."

Ernst grinned then offered a hand to Kyle as he said, "I'm glad to meet you, Mister Evans. I know papa can't get some of the big jobs done with just me."

Kyle smiled back as he shook Ernst's hand and replied, "Call me, Kyle, Ernst, and I'll be happy to help."

Karl then said, "Ernst, can you take wagon to the barn, unharness the mules and wash out the milk cans. I need to introduce Kyle to your mother and sisters."

Ernst nodded then as he climbed into the driver's seat and said, "I'm sure that my sisters will be very happy to meet Kyle," before he laughed, snapped the reins and got the wagon rolling toward the barn.

Only when Kyle looked back at the wagon did he notice two milk cans that had been lashed to the back of the wagon seat alongside a large, empty basket and he understood why Karl had gone into town. Somehow, the fact that he hadn't noticed the two big cans bothered him. He should have been aware of his surroundings.

He was still staring at the wagon when he heard Karl say, "Erna, this is Kyle Evans. He's on his way to Nebraska to find his family, but he'll be staying with us for a while. I promised him that you'd put some meat on his bones while he was here."

Kyle then turned his eyes back to Mrs. Neuman and was somewhat surprised to see a handsome, smiling woman with sparkling blue eyes. He'd always heard that those of German descent were more taciturn, if not perpetually angry.

"Well, I'm sure that I will, Karl. I can see that he needs it, too," she said as she looked at Kyle then asked, "Do you mind if I call you Kyle?"

"No, ma'am," Kyle replied already with a hint of a blush which was about to grow.

Erna Neuman then turned slightly and held out her hand as she said, "These three very pretty young ladies are our daughters, Elsa, Gertrude and Lisa."

Erna may have been expressing parental pride in her girls' appearance, but she wasn't wrong.

As each of the young women introduced themselves to Kyle, he could scarcely tell them apart except for their slight difference in height. He knew there were other differences in their faces but was sure that he'd misidentify them over the next few days.

Erna watched each of her girls as they talked to Kyle and had to wonder if her husband hadn't made the offer expecting that he'd be able to talk the young man into staying and marrying one of their daughters.

Each of them was highly sought by the young men in town, and Elsa was close to an agreement with Leonard Hooper, a miller's son. Gertrude was between boyfriends at the moment and Lisa had attracted the attention of a much older boy, Michael Lowry, but Karl disapproved of the young man. He had already been married and divorced before he was nineteen and then had his father pay the three-hundred-dollar fee to have another man take his place with the 48th Pennsylvania. His father was a state judge and seemed to accumulate his family's wealth without any apparent source.

Erna wasn't sure of Kyle's age but had instantly recognized his gentle nature. Men like Michael Lowry didn't blush when they were introduced to young women and Kyle's ears were the shade of pickled beets.

After the awkward introductions, at least for Kyle, Karl said, "Let's go inside and have some coffee, Kyle, and I'll tell you what I need done."

"Yes, sir," Kyle replied then gave the Neuman women a short wave before following Karl up the porch steps while the four women walked back to finish hanging the wash.

Once inside, Karl asked, "What do you think of my girls?"

"They're all very pretty, Mister Neuman."

"How old are you, Kyle?" he asked when they reached the kitchen.

"I just turned seventeen in March."

"Really? You look older," he said as he poured the lukewarm coffee into two cups.

"I've always looked older, but it never helped me much. I've always been so skinny and tall that the older boys thought it was okay to beat me up, even if I was three or four years younger than they were."

As they took a seat at the large table, Karl set a cup before Kyle and asked, "Did you always get beat up?"

"No, sir, just when I was young. I had a reach advantage over the older boys by then and could jab at them with impunity, so they left me alone."

Kyle sipped the coffee, avoided grimacing at the bitterness, then asked, "What do you need done, Mister Neuman?"

"Lots of things. I have a windmill that's lost a blade and too many gaps in the walls of the barn. I'm sure that you noticed that the house needed a good coat of whitewash, too. Then there are the other jobs that are always there."

"I'll do all that you need me to do, Mister Neuman."

Karl smiled and asked, "You said you lost your mother a little while ago. Where is your father?"

"He ran off when I was six and I haven't seen him since. My mother only told me about my uncles and their families the day before she died. She had a cancer in her stomach."

"I'm sorry for your loss, Kyle. I know how much Erna grieved after the army sent those two telegrams about our boys. Our house should have been painted black for a few months after the joy was swept from inside its walls. They died within two weeks of each other from the diphtheria that had swept through their camp."

"I can understand how much of a shock it must have been for you, Mister Neuman. Even though I refused to accept it, I was prepared for my mother's death because she was getting so thin and weak. I can't imagine how bad it must have been for your family to get the news so suddenly."

"We were ready for the bad news and had been preparing ourselves for those damned telegrams since the boys left. But when the messenger showed up on our doorstep, we still were shaken. Luckily, the army only sent one telegram for Karl and Willie. I don't know how much worse it would have been to receive one then a second just two weeks later."

Kyle just nodded and then sipped his coffee again, not noticing the bitterness.

Karl then blew out his breath, smiled at Kyle and asked, "So, Kyle, have you had any adventures on your journey?"

Kyle was just as pleased as his host to change the topic and began his only exciting story; the encounter with the two assailants.

He was halfway through the tale when Erna and her daughters entered the house and he stopped in mid-sentence.

"Karl, surely you didn't give Kyle some of that old coffee! Where are your manners?"

"Right where they were when you married me, Mrs. Neuman. I left my manners and my bachelorhood at the altar of the Second Lutheran Church."

Erna laughed as she dumped the old coffee into the sink and her daughters all took seats at the table.

Karl then said, "Kyle was telling me how he was waylaid by two men on the road and held them off with his walking stick."

Erna set the empty coffeepot on the cookstove then sat down and asked, "Would you mind starting over, Kyle? I'd love to hear the story. It's so dreadfully boring here."

Kyle smiled and replied, "That surprises me, ma'am. I can't imagine that you would ever allow it to reach that state."

Erna and her daughters all laughed while Karl just grinned and watched. Gertie was Kyle's age and Lisa wouldn't turn sixteen until August. He was most concerned about Lisa and her growing infatuation with that divorced 'gentleman', Michael Lowry.

Michael would arrive at the farm unannounced and would tell Lisa all the words a young girl liked to hear, and Karl knew that it was only a matter of time before he won her. What really chafed him was his and Erna's decision to let their children choose their own mates and so far, it hadn't been a problem. He had been counting on his daughters' respect for their parents and devotion to their mother to guide them in their choices but now, he wasn't sure it mattered.

Whether Kyle Evans knew it or not, he would be the best weapon to deflect Michael Lowry's intentions.

Kyle had been surprised to find himself so comfortable with Mrs. Neuman until he realized how much she reminded him of his mother. She seemed to be as full of life as his mother had been before the cancerous monster had taken her from him. That revelation aside, he knew that he would have to limit his stay at the family farm if he ever hoped to meet his father's brothers. If he hadn't already committed his mind to go to Omaha to find them, he might have decided to stay and get to know one of the Neuman girls better.

CHAPTER 3

June 16, 1867

There wasn't much sun that Sunday but there wasn't any rain either as Dylan and Gwen sat on the front porch watching their boys' horseplay in the front yard. Even Bethan was involved and was almost indistinguishable from her brothers except for her long, pony-tailed hair. The newest nanny, Mrs. Alba March, was in the house with napping three-year-old Cari and their newest addition to the family, two-month-old Brian Lynn.

"What are you going to do if the president approves the governor's request?" Gwen asked.

"I can't work with that man, Gwen. What makes it worse is that even though I'd be the senior marshal, I'm certain that he'd treat me like a green deputy. It's not a matter of pride…well, maybe some, but I know that sooner or later, he'll do something that I know is wrong and I'll lose my job if I do anything about it."

"We're fine with money, Dylan, and we still have that bank in Fort Benton. I think we should sell it anyway. We're never going back there."

"Don't be too sure. If the president approves Claggett's appointment, then they can send me anywhere, but I'd rather take off my badge than take you and our children back there, Gwen."

Gwen smiled at Dylan but understood what an awkward situation he'd be in if Edgar Claggett was made the U.S. Marshal for Nebraska. She knew that it was almost a foregone conclusion, but still held out a glimmer of hope that it either wouldn't happen or that they'd reassign Dylan to someplace better. She just couldn't picture her husband without the badge on his chest.

"Well, we'll just have to wait…"

Gwen's reply was interrupted by the sound of pounding hooves on the road and as they watched, three riders galloped past the end of their drive leaving a mammoth cloud of dust.

Before he understood the reason for their haste, Dylan rose and said, "Get the children inside and get the shotgun."

Gwen didn't say a word as she stood and trotted down the porch steps to the yard and walked quickly to the four children who had all turned to watch the racing horses.

"Inside! All of you!" she exclaimed as she reached the youngsters.

Lynn, Al and Garth all began to protest, but Bethan could see the fire in her mother's eyes and shouted, "Don't argue!" before trotting toward the porch.

While Gwen rounded up the children, Dylan ran inside the house and headed for his office where he quickly grabbed his gunbelt, strapped it on then took one of his new Winchesters from its rack and left the office.

He passed Gwen and the children as he left the house and waited on the porch. He didn't have to wait very long when he saw two riders moving south along the road at a fast pace, but short of a gallop. He recognized the lead rider's horse, so he knew that Sheriff Pete Pawlowski was on the chase.

Dylan stepped down from the porch and headed for the barn to saddle his new primary ride, a tall, dark chestnut gelding he'd named Crow. Ewan and Randy, his previous mounts were still both healthy, but Ewan was still Gwen's horse and Randy was older and had become an occasional ride.

He quickly saddled Crow, slipped his new repeater into its scabbard and stepped into the saddle. He knew that Pete Pawlowski was a capable lawman, but there had only been two lawmen trailing those three outlaws and the second had to be one of his less than competent deputies. Dylan doubted that Pete would have sufficient support if he caught up with the three bad men. What they had done to warrant the rare hot pursuit didn't matter.

He sent Crow down his drive at a medium trot and turned south toward Bellevue. Pete was already out of his jurisdiction when he passed Dylan's house and entered Sarpy County, not that it made much of a difference, but it was one more reason for Dylan to join the chase.

The real reason was that Dylan was getting a bit bored with the constant paperwork and lack of fieldwork. He'd assigned himself a few of the hard jobs since moving up to the position, but it was never enough. Dylan had to be part of the action and knew it was a fault in his character but didn't care.

He had Crow at a fast trot as he shot down the incline toward Bellevue and couldn't see anyone on the road ahead, which didn't surprise him as it was a Sunday afternoon, but not seeing the sheriff or the troublemakers did bother him.

He reached level ground and slowed when he approached the main street of the town and pulled to a stop once he entered Bellevue. *Where did they go?* Sunday afternoon aside, the street was eerily empty of traffic as if the entire town was still asleep.

He turned back toward the Missouri River, a thousand yards to the east and saw where most of the folks were and felt like smacking his head when he recalled being told about the town picnic. He didn't know if the riders had all passed through town riding west or not, but he needed to make sure that the folks were safe, so he turned Crow to the east and nudged him to a slow trot.

The docks on the Missouri were fairly small and could only serve a single riverboat at a time, but to the south of the docks, they'd created a town park complete with a bandstand. There was no band playing today and as Dylan scanned the scene, he noticed that almost all of the people were standing in one mass and staring at the bandstand, but there was no music. He let Crow continue for another hundred yards before he pulled him to a stop to try and understand what was happening.

There were a number of horses, buggies and wagons scattered around the park, but he soon spotted Pete Pawlowski's mottled gray mare among the ones near the bandstand. It took him another minute to get the basic gist of what was happening when he spotted a drawn revolver among the small group in the bandstand then identified the sheriff and his deputy with his hands up.

He couldn't hear what was being shouted by the man holding the pistol, but the entire situation was extremely dangerous and would be a difficult nut to crack. There were dozens of innocent bystanders and he wondered why none of them had run away which was the normal tendency for folks when they see guns drawn.

Dylan scanned further past the standing audience and when he looked almost due south, he spotted one of the three men standing with a repeater pointed at the crowd. The one with the pistol must have warned the unarmed citizens that they'd be shot if they tried to run.

He had more questions than he could even ask but now, he needed to come up with a plan to stop this and he still couldn't come up with anything that would prevent the loss of innocent lives.

Then almost on cue, his danger state took over and he noticed that the one with the repeater was about a hundred yards from the bandstand and just as quickly a plan blossomed in his mind, but knew he had to act fast.

He turned Crow to the north and left the road at a slow trot. He descended into the other side of the road to the low ground. The roadway had to be elevated because of the frequent Missouri flooding when the low ground near the docks was doomed to be underwater for at least a few weeks of the year. He was going to use that topography to his advantage knowing that they couldn't see him as he drew closer to the river and the warehouse. He'd have to leave Crow near the dock and circle around behind the bandstand on foot and hoped that none of the townsfolk pointed him out when he was visible.

Dylan dismounted two hundred yards from the dock then led Crow to the warehouse and tied him off before quickly trotting along the riverside of the building and headed south toward the bandstand now less than a hundred yards away.

He cocked the hammer to his Winchester knowing there was a cartridge already in the chamber and quickly duck walked toward the bandstand. He was beginning to pick up the voice of one of the two outlaws who had the sheriff and his deputy under their pistols and knew that there wasn't much time.

Then he heard something that gave him more hope when the man shouted, "You'd better hope that Charlie gets back here with the money, or we'll kill a whole bunch of ya!"

Dylan realized that the reason they were all standing like that was that two of the outlaws held the entire group hostage while one of them took the Bellevue Bank president, Lee Kline, to his bank to open the vault. They must have been in the bank already when he'd ridden into town which meant he'd be returning soon.

With that revelation, Dylan picked up the pace and then as he approached the back of the bandstand without being noticed, he began to believe that he'd pull this off.

His danger state kept everything clear to him as he looked at the backs of the men on the bandstand just fifteen feet away. He slowly stood, leveled his Winchester at the man with the pistol and let his sights steady on the man's head. If he shot any lower at this range, his .44 would go through the man and strike a civilian or the sheriff.

Once he was satisfied, he said in a slightly louder than normal voice, "Mister, I've got a rifle sighted on the back of your head. If you so much as twitch, you'll never know what hit you and your brains will be blown all over the bandstand."

Teddy Baxter was startled by the nearby voice and almost pulled his trigger but hesitated long enough to regain his composure then without turning, he said, "I'll still shoot this bastard if you do and my brother will lay waste to those folks."

Dylan had to give him credit for not losing his control but replied, "I don't care about the sheriff and once you pull that trigger, you're a dead man and then I'll take out your partner before he can do too much damage. I'll get Charlie, too. I've done it before."

"Who the hell are you?" Teddy asked even as he tried to come up with a way out.

"It doesn't matter. It's your choice. You can either drop the pistol and live another day or you can pull your trigger and never hear the sound of your pistol."

Teddy still hadn't come up with anything that could get him out of the mess and despite the prospect of hanging, he didn't want to die right now, not that way. The thought of his head exploding with everyone watching was too disgusting for him to imagine.

He slowly released his hammer and asked, "Now what?"

Dylan said, "Pete, I want you and all the others to stay put like nothing has changed. Got it?"

The sheriff replied, "Got it."

Dylan then said, "Drop the pistol, but don't move. I've got my Winchester still aimed at your head."

Teddy closed his eyes and let his Colt thump to the bandstand's wooden deck hoping that the man didn't shoot.

Before the pistol even hit the floor, Dylan was bent at the waist and climbing the back steps to the bandstand using the standing men as cover. Once he was on the floor, he kicked the Colt away from the outlaw who was still standing with his eyes closed.

He didn't have time to ask how this had happened but stood behind the gun-less gunman and looked out at the crowd, recognizing many of the folks, including his sister-in-law, Arial and her husband Steve. Apparently, no one had even noticed his arrival yet as their eyes were all either on the ground or looking into the heavens as they prayed. The only one who was looking in his direction was the second outlaw and his repeater a hundred yards away.

Dylan was still in his danger state as he looked at the man and noticed that his muzzle was swaying back and forth, probably as a warning, but it also meant that he wasn't ready to fire. Then he switched his attention to the road, knowing that Charlie would be returning soon with Lee Kline and the money from his bank's vault. He had to act now to get the second one and he had to gamble.

If he waited for the last man to appear, then it would make things dicey having two armed outlaws to deal with and one with a repeater aimed at a crowd of innocents. His danger mind told him that the last one wouldn't be that surprised by a Winchester report because the man keeping the crowd under control might have to fire a warning shot or shoot a running spectator.

To make this work, Dylan would have to be absolutely confident in his marksmanship, but at a hundred yards at a tall man who wasn't moving, it wasn't that much different than the target practice he still did almost daily behind his barn.

He stepped slightly to the right knowing that it was likely that his target would spot him but quickly brought his sights to bear on the man and squeezed his trigger.

Harry Baxter hadn't seen Dylan at all as he reveled in the feeling of power with the fear of death that he created in more than a hundred people. He'd never felt so alive as he shifted his sights back and forth at their backs.

Then just as he was swinging his uncocked Winchester back toward the center, he caught a bright flash from the bandstand and for the briefest of moments, he was confused, but the bullet and the sound arrived at the same time ending his confusion as the .44 ripped into his upper gut on the left side and punched into his stomach.

Harry screamed and dropped to the ground and curled into a ball as he clutched his middle.

Dylan shouted, "Pete, I've got to get out there!" then yanked his pistol from his holster, handed it to the sheriff and raced down the front steps of the bandstand.

Sheriff Pawlowski had been startled by the Winchester's nearby blast but had recovered quickly accepted Dylan's pistol and then snatched Teddy Baxter's pistol from the floor and handed it to his deputy.

Dylan didn't know what was happening behind him at the bandstand as he weaved through the stunned crowd at a fast trot. He wanted to get to the wounded man to make sure he wasn't capable of shooting.

Just as he neared the sobbing man, his peripheral vision picked up movement to the north on the roadway. He immediately came to a stop, levered in a new round then brought his Winchester level and aimed at the approaching rider.

Charlie Baxter had been pleased with the banker's cooperation but not surprised. What had pleased him was the unexpectedly large haul that resulted from their improvised plan. He hadn't done an exact count but knew it was over three thousand dollars.

When he first heard the shot as he rode alone back to the park after having left the banker tied up in his own fault, just as Dylan had expected, Charlie thought that Harry had fired a warning shot and then when he heard the loud scream, he believed that Harry had shot one of the townsfolk as a warning.

So, as he neared the park, he didn't even have his Winchester out of its scabbard when he looked for Harry and was stunned to see a man with a rifle pointing at him and Harry on the ground.

Charlie experienced three seconds of total confusion as he shifted his eyes from Harry to the bandstand then snapped out of his confusion and snatched his repeater from its scabbard.

Dylan had been waiting for some reaction from the rider and wasn't at all surprised that he chose to fight. He didn't know if it was out of brotherly loyalty or that he knew he was going to hang anyway and wanted to go down fighting. It didn't matter when Dylan squeezed his trigger and felt the Winchester ram into his right shoulder.

Charlie was swinging his repeater level as he sat in the saddle, but never had a chance to fire the gun when Dylan's .44 ripped into his right shoulder shattering the joint and then ricocheting through his subclavian artery.

Charlie howled in pain as he fell to the roadway and after his jarring landing on the same shoulder that had been destroyed by Dylan's shot, passed out as his life's blood bubbled from the severed artery.

Dylan knew that Charlie wasn't going anywhere then turned and stepped back to Harry and picked up his unfired Winchester.

"We'll get you to a doctor, but I don't think you're going to make it, mister."

Harry never heard Dylan's voice over his own cries of pain, and it didn't matter anyway as he knew he was going to die.

Dylan then stripped Harry of his gunbelt, hung it over his shoulder then started walking to the road to check on the last brother.

When he arrived, he found Charlie dead, so he slid Harry's Winchester into Charlie's scabbard before picking up Charlie's repeater and sliding it into his bedroll. After removing Charlie's gunbelt, he rolled it and slid it into the right saddlebag and when he tried to put Harry's in the left, he found it filled with cash, so he put it in with the other pistol.

By the time he'd taken hold of Charlie's horse, the crowd had realized that the danger was over, and he could hear the cries of relief, joy and anger at the men who had put their lives at risk.

He didn't want to go through the crowd, so he turned left and exited the road to take the same back route to the bandstand. He could retrieve Crow along the way.

When he led the two horses to the back of the bandstand, he spotted Sheriff Pawlowski waiting for him as his prisoner was under the control of his deputy.

"Glad you bailed me out on this one, Dylan," the sheriff said as he drew close and handed Dylan back his pistol.

"What the hell happened?" he asked as he slipped his Smith & Wesson home.

"Stupid happened," he replied as he took Charlie's horse's reins.

"These three are the Baxter brothers. We arrested them a few days ago in Elkhorn when Teddy Baxter, the one who isn't shot, got into a tussle over a woman and shot her boyfriend. Then his brothers decided to help when some of the boyfriend's pals took offense and by the time we got there, there were two dead and another one wounded. We surprised them and brought them back to the county jail. They were going to trial on Wednesday for murder and I'm kind of surprised that you didn't hear about it."

"I knew about it, but I'm just surprised that you're telling me that it's the same boys. Can I guess that the reason that they're no longer in jail is the stupid part of this?"

Pete let out a breath, nodded and replied, "You got that right. It was Sunday and Bob Swanson had the desk. Before noon, a young woman comes in and says that she wants to talk to Teddy Baxter. Now Bob isn't the sharpest nail in the pouch, but even he should have known better than to open that cell with no one else there. But he said that the woman smiled at him and whispered that she'd be forever grateful if he'd let her talk to her brothers. They don't even have a sister, by the way. So, Bob thinks that he's gonna get lucky and is all too happy to open the cell and let the woman visit her brothers."

Dylan was close to smiling as he visualized the scene despite the results of Deputy Swanson's mistakes.

"As soon as Bob unlocks the cell, the woman smiles at him again then takes his hand and lays it on her breast. Bob, of course, turns to look at her and that's the last thing he remembers until we woke him up in the empty cell."

"How'd they get mounted and so well-armed?"

"I'm embarrassed to admit those are our weapons. They took the guns from our office and walked around back to our barn where they took some of the horses. Luckily, they didn't take mine."

"What happened to the woman?"

"I have no idea. She might have taken the train out of town for all I know. I haven't had time to investigate anything else yet. Henry here stopped by the jail to talk to Bob just after they left and found him in the cell, and it's been chaos since then. We grabbed our weapons and chased after them."

"I saw them and then you and Henry go past, which is why I saddled Crow and chased after you. I figured you could use the help, but how did the rest happen?"

"We were about a thousand yards behind them when they reached Bellevue, and I don't know if they saw the crowds near the river or not but instead of heading west through town, they rode into the park. Teddy Baxter, the oldest, told Harry to drop off to the side when they left the road and we didn't see him. We shot right past him as there was panic among the townsfolk. Then we spotted Harry with his repeater pointed at the folks and he shouted for us to put up our hands or he'd fire into the crowd. We really didn't have any choice.

"Then Teddy took over and started ordering folks to behave or they'd be shot. He had me and Henry come up to the bandstand and took our pistols. Once he had us disarmed and his pistol at our backs, he sent Charlie with Lee Kline to open his vault. We were like that for almost ten minutes before you showed up. We never even knew you were there."

"I rode along the other side of the road. Charlie's saddlebags have the money he took from the bank, but I don't know what he did to Lee, so I'll head over there now and check on him. Can you handle the rest?"

"We'll do that, Dylan and I'll never be able to thank you enough. I can't believe that the governor appointed a new marshal."

"Politics, Pete."

"I know, but you'll still be a U.S. Marshal, so what happens when the new guy shows up in your office?"

"I'll shake his hand and leave. Where I go will be up to headquarters. If I don't like where they send me, then I'll hand in my badge and go somewhere I want to go."

"I hope it doesn't come to that, Dylan."

"Neither do I," he replied as he removed the saddlebags, removed the two pistols and gave them to the sheriff then hung the cash-filled saddlebags over his own before mounting Crow, saluting and wheeling the gelding to ride back the way he came away from the meandering crowd.

As he reached the road and headed for the bank, he recalled that Sheriff Pawlowski had said 'when' not 'if' the new man would arrive. He guessed that the rumor mill had already made the president's decision, even if he hadn't approved the appointment yet.

After finding and releasing the bound bank president, he returned the saddlebags full of his stolen cash and graciously accepted his thanks before leaving the bank, mounting Crow and riding out of town.

His welcome home was much more appreciated just by the sight of Gwen and the children on the porch waiting for him as he turned down their long drive. He could see the shotgun in his petite wife's arms and smiled at the sight knowing that any man who threatened her or her children and doubted that she had the will to use the scattergun wouldn't live long.

———

Dylan spent a while telling his family of the picnic shootout as he unsaddled Crow but didn't mention the comments about his probably replacement. As far as he was concerned, it was out of his control until he received official notification. After that, he and Gwen would decide what to do.

———

Kyle had been working at the Neuman farm for a few days now and had become accepted by the family especially Ernst, who obviously missed his older brothers.

He was living in the barn's loft, which suited him perfectly. Each morning, he'd wash and shave using an old pot then he'd join the family for breakfast. It took him a while to get accustomed to the amount of food that he consumed, but still didn't go overboard because he knew it was only temporary and he didn't want his stomach to get used to it.

The other unusual aspect of his morning routine was that while he was shaving, he could hear one of the Neuman girls milking the cows. He never knew which one was handling the daily chore but welcomed the sound as they either sang or hummed as their hands worked the cows' teats. He was glad that he'd never have to learn how to milk a cow as he wasn't planning on acquiring the skill as part of his new life's work.

After breakfast, he'd join Karl in getting the heavier jobs done. The first was to repair the windmill. Karl could probably have done it himself, but he confessed to a fear of heights. That task had taken just four hours and after a big lunch, they started work on repairing the barn's many gaps which would take a couple of days.

Each night, after dinner, Kyle would return to his loft and spend some time working with his staff to improve his techniques. He'd learned that swinging the heavy bat wasn't necessarily the best approach as he'd have that momentary loss of balance after it struck, no matter how well prepared he was. He found that if he swung it underhanded like a pendulum and delivered a jab that he could still maintain control even after the heavy knot at the end of the bat did its damage.

It was on a warm Thursday evening when he was in his loft and sweating from his swings and jabs, all to the rhythm of a Strauss waltz, when he was interrupted.

"What are you doing up there, Kyle?" a female voice asked from the barn floor beneath his wooden loft floor.

He wasn't sure which of the Neuman girls had asked, so he replied, "Just exercising."

"I could hear you grunting, but your footsteps sounded as if you were dancing."

"I was just practicing with my bat."

Lisa then walked to the back of the barn and began to climb the ladder to the loft.

Kyle heard the creaks of the ladder and almost panicked. It was her family's barn and he couldn't tell her not to come into the loft, so he dropped his bat and quickly stepped over to his shirt and was hastily pulling it on when he saw Lisa's head pop out of the cutout.

"Don't be embarrassed, Kyle," she said as she continued to climb and then stepped onto the loft floor.

"I'm not, Lisa. Why did you come up here? That could get me in trouble with your father," he said as he began fumbling with his buttons.

She laughed and said, "No, it wouldn't. Besides, the loft doors are wide open, so they can see inside from the house. That's why I knew you were doing your exercises. You do them every night, don't you?"

"I need to get ready for the rest of my journey."

Lisa sat on an upside-down crate that doubled as Kyle's table and asked, "Are you still planning on leaving soon?"

"I have to, Lisa. The only real family I have is out in Nebraska and they don't even know that I exist."

"Do you think that they'll be happy to see you?"

"To be honest, I don't know, but I have to find out."

"Why?"

Kyle was startled by the simple question and stared at her questioning blue eyes for a few silent seconds before replying, "I'm not sure. Part of me is curious and another part of me really wants to meet my uncles."

C.J. PETIT

"But there's still the chance that they'll be ashamed to know that you're their nephew."

"I know that, but if that happens, it really doesn't change anything. I'll just stay out West and find something to do. A lot of men are heading that way."

"You're only seventeen, Kyle."

"My age doesn't matter, Lisa. I've been working and taking care of my mother since I was nine. It made me grow up faster inside. Now I just need to put on some weight, so my outside catches up."

Lisa laughed and said, "I think you look quite manly, Kyle."

Kyle blushed and replied, "I'm too skinny."

"No, you're not. You're sleek and have strong muscles. You just don't have any fat."

Kyle's blush deepened as he asked, "Do you always talk like this?"

"No, I really don't. I just was trying to let you know that I didn't think you were skinny at all."

"Well, thank you. Is there anything else that you needed to talk about?"

Lisa reached over, picked up his canteen then tossed it to Kyle.

After he caught it, he pulled off the cap, took a long drink, then sealed it again before he surprised Lisa and lobbed it back to her.

Lisa snared it then laughed and returned it to his pile of things before saying, "You caught me by surprise when you threw it back."

"I figured that any girl who said the things that you just did would be able to catch a canteen. It was almost empty anyway."

He then picked up his bat and as he sat on his cot, she said, "That doesn't look like a walking stick."

Kyle then spent some time explaining its original purpose and how he'd modified it for use on the trip but hoped to use it in a baseball game eventually. That led to further questions about baseball and eventually led to his last game that had cost him his job.

By the time Lisa finally left the loft, Kyle felt that growing uneasiness that either Lisa or one of her sisters would prevent him from leaving the Neuman farm.

————

Lisa's visit wasn't repeated the next night, and Kyle appreciated it, but then on Saturday evening things took an unusual twist.

After a normal day of work and more food, Kyle was in his loft preparing to begin his exercises when he heard a buggy approaching the house. He hadn't seen any other visitors since he'd been on the farm, so he stepped over to the loft doors and peered down at the arrival. He knew that it would probably be a gentleman caller, as it seemed to be a common topic of conversation at the table.

He knew the names of each of the prospective boys who were visiting the Neuman girls and had understood the dislike that Karl and Erna had for Michael Lowry, the man who was wooing Lisa. That knowledge had made her visit to the loft more uncomfortable, almost as if her father had suggested that she go to the barn.

Kyle stood shirtless at the loft doors as Michael Lowry stepped out of the buggy and walked to the porch steps. He was a dapper young man wearing a nice, gray suit and wore a beaver hat and Kyle wondered how hot he was under that wool jacket, vest, shirt and undershirt.

Kyle stepped back into the loft a few steps so he wouldn't be so obvious, but waited to watch him exit with Lisa, just out of curiosity.

It was another ten minutes before the door opened and Michael Lowry exited the house, but without Lisa on his arm. Kyle wasn't sure if that was normal or not, but didn't wait around to see him drive away, so he turned and headed deeper into the loft to begin his exercises.

He'd picked up his bat, set his hands and started his dance without swinging the bat until he was loose as the daily hard work made his muscles stiff.

Kyle was in the middle of a slow counterclockwise spin when he heard the loud creak as a rung on the loft ladder protested. He thought that Lisa might be coming up to explain what had happened with her beau, so he quickly set the bat on his cot and reached for his shirt as he heard more creaks and smiled.

He had just shoved his right arm through the sleeve when a head appeared in the hole and he was startled to see Michael Lowry's face and he wasn't smiling. Why he had come to visit was a puzzle, but Kyle instantly knew that it had something to do with Lisa.

Michael continued to climb as Kyle quickly forgot about dressing and with his shirt hanging on his right arm, he asked, "Who are you and what are you doing up here?"

"My name is Michael Wilson Lowry and you know why I'm here," he snarled as his torso cleared the opening.

Kyle reached down to his cot, grasped his bat and moved back toward the open loft doors as he watched Michael step onto the loft floor. He still thought he was safe when Michael reached under his suit jacket and pulled out a pistol.

"I have no idea why you're here, mister. I've only been here for a week and I'm not planning on staying."

"That's not what I was just told by her father. I'm here to make sure that you leave Lisa alone. She's my girl and you have no business spending any time with her."

Kyle could see the anger in his eyes and knew that he'd have to calm him down, so he dropped his bat believing that Michael would see him as less of a threat then put his palms out in front of him.

"I've only talked to her once, mister, and I'm not about to spend any time with her."

Kyle's protests didn't seem to lessen Michael's anger much and Kyle began to think that dropping his bat was a bad idea.

After a few tense seconds, Kyle asked, "Are you going to shoot me? Do you think you can get away with it?"

Michael smiled then replied, "Maybe I will, because I know that I can get away with it. I'll just tell the judge, my father, that you threatened me with your club, and I had to shoot you in self-defense. The sheriff won't care because you're a nobody; just a boy passing through."

"And you think that it won't bother Lisa that you're a murderer?"

His question obviously had an impact on Michael who slowly lowered the pistol but said, "I'm warning you, mister. Stay away from Lisa. If you don't, the sheriff will come visiting and you'll be arrested and tossed in jail."

Kyle glared at him and said, "Because you'll file a complaint that I've committed some heinous crime."

Michael was still smiling as he replied, "Maybe it won't be so heinous, but it'll land you a few years behind bars."

He then slid his pistol back into his holster that Kyle hadn't seen under his jacket turned and began climbing back down the ladder.

Kyle turned then walked to the loft doors and watched him climb into his buggy and drive off. He didn't doubt that Neuman eyes had watched him enter the barn and yet none had left the house to help. That realization made Lowry's claim that he was a nobody strike home. He'd just started to feel like part of the family and now he understood that the only family he had wasn't in Pennsylvania. He then pulled off his shirt and began his exercises as if there had been no interruption.

As he danced, swung and stabbed with his bat, he thought about Michael Lowry's second threat, that he could send the sheriff to arrest him if he paid any more attention to Lisa. He didn't doubt that it was a genuine warning either and it left him in an almost impossible situation. Having the sheriff act as his personal bully and with his judge father backing up his claim, he knew that Lowry's threat would be easily accomplished.

His sweat was spraying across the loft floor ten minutes after he started, but his growing anger at the futility of his position drove him harder. He didn't like being manipulated and he felt that he was being pushed by all sides.

When he finished his workout, he was physically spent, but his spirit had calmed. He had resolved to just continue his journey, as he was planning on doing anyway. It may have been earlier than he'd planned, but maybe he needed the kick in the pants to get going. He just hoped that Lisa's jealous suitor didn't go running to the sheriff before he had a chance to leave the county.

After he stopped sweating, he donned his shirt and began to pack his things. He had just wrapped the attacker's knife in a towel when he stopped and thought that he should tell Mister Neuman that he was leaving. Just packing up and disappearing was rude if not cowardly.

So, he ran his fingers through his light brown hair to make it less disastrous then climbed down the ladder to the barn floor and headed toward the house.

There was light coming from the front room window, so he turned toward the house then hopped past the two steps onto the porch and knocked on the front door.

He heard loud footsteps and the door was ripped open and for just a moment, he saw an angry Karl Neuman before he saw Kyle and instantly smiled and said, "Oh, it's you, Kyle. Come in."

Kyle didn't move but said, "It's alright, Mister Neuman, I just wanted to let you know that I decided to resume my journey and I'll be leaving in the morning."

Karl's surprise was evident as he asked, "Why so sudden?"

"I just think it's time for me to go. I do appreciate you letting me stay here, but I need to be moving west again."

"Does this have anything to do with Michael Lowry's visit?"

Kyle shuffled his feet and after a brief pause, he replied, "It does, but I think it would be better for me and your family if I left."

Karl glanced back inside then stepped onto the porch and closed the door as Kyle grew more uncomfortable.

"Kyle, why did his visit bother you? Are you becoming fond of Lisa?"

Kyle's eyes shot wide as he shook his head and quickly answered, "No, no, sir. That's not it at all. It's just that he came to see me in the barn after leaving the house and we had words."

"What did he say?"

Kyle chose his words carefully when he replied, "He was just jealous for some reason and I don't understand why he would be."

"That was my fault, Kyle. When he came to ask Lisa to join him on a buggy ride, she demurred, and he became more insistent. I came into the room and told him to leave, but he said that Lisa would never find a better man to call on her and I pointed to the barn and said there was a better man staying in my hay loft.

"He looked at Lisa then at me and left without saying a word. We didn't think for a moment that he'd go to see you. We were all in the sitting room talking about what had happened and didn't even see him leave in his buggy. I'm really sorry for what happened, Kyle, and there's no reason for you to leave."

Kyle felt better knowing that the family hadn't seen Michael Lowry go into the barn, but it didn't affect his decision. He knew that a man like Lowry would follow through on his threat just out of spite.

"I still need to go, Mister Neuman. I don't want to cause any trouble, and you know that he'll cause your family grief if I stay."

"Kyle, I can understand your concern, but I don't believe it could get any worse. He seems infatuated with Lisa, and quite honestly, I don't know why he keeps returning. Lisa liked him at first, but he became so possessive that he frightened her. He just won't take 'no' for an answer, and there's nothing I can do about it."

"Do you think he's a danger to your family?"

"I'm not sure. He's only been a problem since April, so he might stop visiting."

"Well, I'll think about it, Mister Neuman."

"I wish you'd stay, Kyle."

Kyle nodded then turned and stepped off the porch then headed for the barn with his mind a chaotic jumble. Despite Mister Neuman's assurances, he doubted that Michael Lowry would give up so easily. He'd seen the seething anger and jealousy in the man's eyes as he held his pistol, yet the cold threats were more indicative of the man's obsession with Lisa.

Kyle had the feeling that if he actually won her somehow, he'd grow tired of her quickly and move on, leaving Lisa ruined and heartbroken just as he had probably done with his divorced wife. He wondered what the circumstances were in that situation and was curious if his father had been the one to grant the divorce.

After he reached his loft, he continued his packing and thought about what he should do. He'd still need to leave, but the thought of that jealous bastard making Lisa and her family's life miserable bothered him. He was certain that his departure wouldn't change the man's behavior.

He stripped and lay stretched out on his cot in the warm air and stared at the dark barn roof just four feet above his head. He had to come up with some way to leave and after he did, to let the Neuman family live in peace.

———

The next morning, he was washed, shaved and dressed when he heard one of the daughters singing as she milked the cows, so he waited until she finished then climbed down the ladder.

"Good morning, Elsa," he said as he walked toward the cows.

Elsa smiled and said, "Good morning, Kyle. Father said you might be leaving."

"Not yet," he replied as he grasped the handles of the two full pails of warm milk.

Elsa stood, stretched her back then slid the milking stool aside and followed Kyle out of the barn.

When they entered the kitchen, Kyle could tell that they were somewhat surprised to see him, but happily so.

He set the milk pails down and joined them at the breakfast table where he was soon peppered by questions about Michael Lowry's visit with none coming from Lisa. He didn't mention the threats or the pistol but could see the concern in their eyes yet couldn't get a real read on Lisa's emotions as she kept her eyes on the table as she ate.

With the Lowry incident answered and behind them, Karl asked if Kyle wanted to join them when they went to church in Brookville. He hadn't asked before, probably out of courtesy, but Kyle declined, saying that he wasn't a churchgoer. The real reason was that he was concerned that he would run afoul of Michael Lowry.

After he returned to the barn, he harnessed the wagon while the family dressed in their Sunday best, so when they left the house, the wagon was parked out front and ready to transport them into Brookville.

Kyle helped Elsa and Gertrude onto the bed but let Karl help Lisa just to maintain his self-imposed barrier. He didn't want to give Michael Lowry any excuse, not that he needed one.

After waving to the family as they rolled down their access road, he turned and walked back to the barn and climbed into the loft. Once there, he finished his packing, but left the sharp knife on his cot with his bat. He wasn't expecting a visitor, but he didn't want to be caught by surprise again either.

Ninety minutes later, he was sitting on his cot, using his pocketknife to smooth his bat's handle when he heard the distant sounds of hoofbeats. He set the bat down, closed the pocketknife and as he stood, he slipped it into his pocket.

Kyle slowly approached the open loft doors, peeked outside but didn't see anyone and began to think that he imagined the

91

sound. But he had learned from his experience on the road with his two attackers not to disregard any potential threats, so rather than brushing it off, he returned to his cot and picked up his bat. Then he looked at the knife, picked it up and carefully slid it under his belt at the small of his back. He had to be careful about how he moved, or he could slice open his own behind, but figured that he wouldn't leave it there very long if that brief sound of hoofbeats was just a passing rider.

He stood silently in the center of the loft listening for any sounds but only heard the shuffling of the cows below him and the squawking of the chickens in their nearby coop. He was ready to relax when one of the cows mooed and the sudden loud sound startled him and almost made him laugh. Then he heard it. It was a loud creak from the ladder and he knew that he was about to have an unwelcome visitor.

Kyle thought about moving close to the opening to the barn floor but suspected that Lowry already expected him to do that and had his pistol pointed at the spot, so he backed toward the open loft doors as he readied his bat.

Michael Lowry's head popped out of the hole and was immediately followed by his right hand clutching his pistol. No words were passed as he continued to rise as if from the grave and soon stepped onto the loft floor.

"Put down the club, boy."

Kyle lowered his bat to the floor but kept his eyes on Lowry.

Michael took two steps from the opening then said, "I warned you, boy. You didn't leave and I'm not going to warn you again."

Kyle glared at him but said calmly, "This isn't very smart, Lowry. You'll hang for this."

Michael laughed then said, "I told you, that's not going to happen. The sheriff will just take my word for whatever I tell him."

"I don't care about your damned sheriff. After you threatened me, I wrote a letter to my uncle in Omaha and told him what happened. He's never met me, so it was a long letter. If anything happens to me then he'll come, and you'll regret ever hearing the Evans name."

"What do I care about your uncle in godforsaken Omaha? That's half the continent away and he'll get thrown in jail if he comes here and makes trouble."

Kyle smiled and said, "Oh, did I forget to mention that my Uncle Dylan is a United States Marshal? He's got jurisdiction all across this land and the power to arrest judges and sheriffs, too. Now are you still planning on pulling that trigger?"

Michael stared at Kyle unsure if he was bluffing or downright lying, so he asked, "If he's so important, then how come you're walking and have to work for food? Why didn't he just wire you some money so you could take the train?"

"Like I said, he doesn't know me yet. He doesn't even know that I exist, nor does my other uncle, United States Deputy Marshal Bryn Evans. When Marshal Evans gets my letter, he may try to contact me and send me train fare but right now, you should just be smart and leave me alone."

Michael still wasn't sure. If the kid was bluffing or lying, he was doing a good job.

"I'll leave you alone, but only if you're on the road before I leave."

Kyle really hadn't expected him to give in but suspected that he might try to waylay him on the road later and then just hide his body, so even if there was a real investigation into his disappearance then no one would know where he'd gone.

"Alright. I'm almost finished packing, so I'll be on the road in ten minutes."

"Stay right there and wait for me to get on the ground. I'll mount my horse and wait to watch you leave. The Neumans won't be back from church for another two hours, so don't think of stalling."

"Okay."

Kyle watched Michael back to the opening and after glancing for the ladder, he began to climb down always keeping his eyes and his pistol on Kyle.

Once his head disappeared, Kyle quickly slid the knife from his belt and tossed it to his bunk. It took him just five minutes to get ready to leave, but it was awkward to climb down the ladder as heavily loaded as he was, so he had to drop his bat to the barn floor before making his descent.

Even as he clambered down the rungs, he wondered how he could avoid being shot in the back as he walked down the road. He knew that Lowry would have to avoid being seen following him by other travelers but would have to act soon as he'd soon be leaving Jefferson County and entering Clarion County which would negate his protection.

He picked up his staff and looped the cord around his wrist before stepping out into the bright June sunshine and soon spotted Michael astride his horse sitting at the entrance road.

Kyle didn't stare at him as he cut diagonally across the front yard and headed for the westbound road but did cast the occasional glance to make sure that he wasn't aiming his pistol. He didn't think it was likely, but he'd learned the danger of not being prepared and wasn't ready to be shot yet.

He reached the road and began taking long strides without looking behind him but listened for any approaching hoofbeats. The road ahead was empty, and he was just as sure that there were no riders or wagons on the road behind him either. It was a Sunday morning, so there was no commercial traffic and most folks were either in church or taking the opportunity to sleep late.

After three tense minutes, Kyle finally turned to look behind him and saw an empty road. He should have been relieved, but it bothered him. He could see a good mile down the road, yet it was empty of riders and dust clouds, and he suspected that Michael Lowry had disappeared into the heavily forested areas that bordered both sides of the road. The question was which side he had chosen, but he quickly guessed that he would be on the right because it was the side of the Neuman farm.

Kyle suddenly shifted to the right then hurried off the road and soon entered the deep forest, feeling safer once he was hidden by the trees. He didn't know where or even if Michael Lowry was among the trees but suspected he was somewhere between him and the farm, so he continued until he was about a hundred feet into the forest. He found a thick oak and quickly dropped his knapsack and belongings behind a tree and took a few seconds to cover them with the dark blue slicker he'd bought at the army surplus store before hurriedly returning to another stout old oak and planting his back against the wide trunk.

He held his maple bat in his hands as he listened for the sound of an approaching horse and hoping that he didn't hear it at all. He'd much rather just continue walking without incident, but it wasn't up to him anymore.

He wasn't in his hidden position more than three minutes when he heard a loud crack when something snapped a decent-sized branch in two. The sound had come from his left, but he couldn't judge the distance. The crack was soon followed by a low thump rather than the more recognizable regular hoofbeats of a walking horse but was soon found by a second and a third before Kyle realized that the soft, mulch-covered soil was masking the approach of a shoed horse.

He raised his bat straight up until it rested against the tree trunk and waited.

————

Michael had his Smith & Wesson Model 2 in his hand as he looked to his right to the road and tried to spot Kyle through the trees. He'd seen him walk far enough away before he rode around the Neuman farmhouse to enter the trees then had to cut back toward the road so he could track him. He thought he'd spotted him once, but only for a second as the tree trunks blocked his vision. He'd shifted closer to the road and now had a better line of sight, but still couldn't see the kid.

He knew that as long as he hid the body, no one, not even his uncle, if he really existed, would ever find it. Even if they investigated, his butler would give him an iron-clad alibi. Now all he needed to do was find him. *Where was he?*

As he passed by a large oak, his eyes were still focused on the roadway until he heard a grunt and as he whipped his head to the right, he found Kyle swinging his bat at his right knee.

Before Michael could even think of turning his pistol to his right, the heavy bat struck but missed.

Kyle had misjudged the speed of the horse and instead of slamming his knotted maple bat's head into Michael Lowry's knee, the heavy wood rammed into his saddle skirt just two inches behind the joint. He knew he'd missed but had put so much effort into the swing, he realized that he'd never get a chance to take a second.

Yet his surprising attack and the sudden jolt of pain startled Michael's gelding causing him to rear, throwing his rider onto the moist Pennsylvania soil before he bolted away into the trees.

As Michael landed on his back in a loud whump onto the soft dirt, Kyle knew that he had to take advantage of the brief stroke of good luck, so he regained control of his bat raised it over his head and stepped quickly toward Lowry.

Michael still had his pistol in his hand and once he overcame the shock of being thrown, he spotted Kyle as he neared and was bringing his sights to bear when Kyle's bat whistled downward.

It came down to a fraction of a second between the bullet leaving Michael's pistol or Kyle's bat striking home and it was the maple knot that won when it cracked into Michael's right knee, square on his kneecap.

Michael screamed when the electric jolt of pain that blasted from the injury into his brain and he never even pulled his trigger from his reflex reaction to the shock. His pistol dropped to the ground and was quickly snatched by Kyle as he stood over Michael Lowry with his bat now returned to its use as a walking stick.

As Michael wailed in agony, Kyle glanced at the pistol in his hand, the first time he'd ever held a gun of any kind. He noticed that it had Smith & Wesson Model 2 imprinted on its side and that the grip was a nice cherry with a script MWL carved into the wood.

Lowry was still rolling on the ground, so Kyle slid the pistol under his belt then left him to hunt for his horse wondering what he should do next. He really would like to have the horse but knew that Michael would probably have him arrested for horse theft. He even began to seriously contemplate finishing him off and burying him somewhere, but that idea didn't last long.

It took him a few minutes to track down the horse and after he took the reins, he had to admit he was handsome animal. There was no problem finding Michael again as he still was announcing his location with either cries of pain or curses.

When Michael spotted Kyle leading his horse back, he stopped his wailing and cursing long enough to ask through gritted teeth, "Are you going to kill me and take my horse now?"

Kyle tied off the reins on a nearby branch then approached Lowry but stopped ten feet away just in case he had another pistol somewhere.

"No, I'm not going to steal your horse, Lowry. I'm going to put you back in the saddle and you can ride back to town and see a doctor. But before I do, I want you to understand a few things.

"I wasn't lying about my uncle being a U.S. Marshal, although I was bluffing about the letter. I'll write that letter when get to the next town though. I'll keep your pistol just to prove that you were trying to kill me, and I'll take any spare ammunition you have too. I'm still going to leave because I had intended to anyway, but I'll make one last promise to you.

"I'll write a letter to Karl Neuman when I get to Omaha and tell him what happened. If he writes back that you set one toe on his farm or even said a word to Lisa again, I'll have my uncles come back here and arrest you for attempted murder and probably get your crooked judge father and the sheriff fired."

"You can't do that!"

"No, I can't, but my uncles can. Now if you want me to help you onto your horse, you'll leave all your spare ammunition and cash on the ground then you can return to Brookville."

"You're robbing me?" he exclaimed.

"Not exactly. You're paying me to leave, Lowry."

Michael wanted to argue, but his knee was extraordinarily painful, so he opened his jacket unbuckled his gunbelt and let it drop before sliding his wallet out of his inside jacket pocket and tossing some bills onto the ground.

"Satisfied?" he snarled.

Kyle didn't answer but set his bat on the ground then untied the gelding and led him to where Michael still lay in obvious pain.

This was going to be the most dangerous part. Kyle would have to help him onto his horse and would be vulnerable to a sudden sucker punch or kick from his good leg. He lifted Michael to his feet and as he stood on his left leg, Kyle grabbed his belt and hoisted him higher so he could get his left boot into the stirrup and swing his injured knee over the horse's back.

Michael screamed again as his injured leg cleared his saddlebags and then dropped it to the right side of the saddle but didn't use the right stirrup.

He glared once more at Kyle before setting his horse off at a walk and soon disappeared into the trees.

Kyle waited for a few minutes then picked up the bills and counted seventy-five dollars.

"Who goes off to murder someone with this much money in his pocket?" he asked himself aloud.

After stuffing the bills into his pocket, he picked up the gunbelt and strapped it around his waist before slipping the pistol into the holster. He noticed the leather strip near the top and quickly understood its purpose, so he hooked the hammer loop in place and headed back to his things.

It was just thirty minutes after taking that first swing that Kyle returned to the road. Before he headed west, he glanced back in the direction of the Neuman farm and hoped that Lisa would find someone who treated her well.

———

Just before he reached Brookville, Michael passed the Neuman family as they left town to return to the farm. He didn't even look at Lisa as he rode past, blaming her for what had happened. As far as he was concerned, she could rot in hell.

When he reached his house, he had the butler help him down,then explained to his father that he'd been out riding, and his horse had been spooked by a bobcat. When he drew his pistol to shoot it, his horse had thrown him, and he'd struck his knee on a rock. He managed to climb back in the saddle but had no idea where his pistol had gone. No one questioned his story despite his missing gunbelt.

———

After Michael had passed the family without so much as a tilt of his hat, Karl turned to his wife and asked, "Where do you think he's coming from?"

"I'm sure he went to pay Kyle another visit."

Ernst quickly asked, "You don't think he did anything to him, do you?"

"We'll see when we get back, but I won't be surprised if he's gone. If he is, I'm going to wait a few weeks then write a letter to him in care of his uncle in Omaha. If I don't get a reply then I'll write another to his uncle directly and see if he'll investigate his disappearance."

"Do you think that Michael could have killed Kyle?" Lisa asked.

"I don't know what that man is capable of doing, but I know that I never want to see his face on our farm again," her father answered sharply.

When they reached the farm, it didn't take them long to realize that Kyle had gone. The question was if he'd gone on his own, or if his body had been dragged into the nearby woods and buried.

———

Kyle didn't write or mail a letter to his uncle when he reached the next town but did splurge on a big meal before resuming his long walk. As he plodded along, he took out the pistol and knew that someone would have to tell him how it worked, or he'd be stuck with the six bullets that were in its chambers. He didn't even know how to make those bullets come out of the muzzle. He knew he had to pull the trigger, and after a while figured out that he had to pull the hammer back first.

Once it was pulled back, he discovered that he didn't know how to put it back without firing a bullet, and although he didn't want to waste one, he had to fire it once to let the hammer return. He had the ones that were still in the gun and there were eight more in loops on the gunbelt. When he stopped at a bigger town with a gunsmith, he'd stop and ask how to use the pistol, including how to release the hammer, and then buy some more ammunition. If nothing else, the gun would make hunting easier.

He aimed the cocked pistol at a nearby tree and pulled the trigger. He didn't know if he hit the tree, but the pistol did give him a greater measure of security as he returned it to the holster and pulled the leather strap over the hammer.

———

"When is Claggett taking over, boss?" Thom Smythe asked.

"Soon, I guess, but I don't know the exact date."

"This just ain't right, Dylan," Fred Atchison snapped.

"It's just politics, Fred. The governor wants his own man in the job and probably had to pay off some favors. It's not that unusual."

"That doesn't make it right," Benji Green said with more than a hint of disgust.

"What are you going to do, boss?" Fred asked.

"I'll just wait for my orders from the head of the service in Washington. If I don't like them, I'll hand in my badge."

Thom said, "You'll never be anything but a lawman, boss. Why don't you join Bryn and head out to Denver? I'm sure Al would love to have you work with him and you'd get to go on more jobs, too."

"I've thought of that. I'd be willing to step down to a deputy marshal again and work for Al, but we'll see. But regardless of what I do, you'll all have to stay here and continue to be the good lawmen that you are."

"What does Gwen think about all this?" Benji asked.

"She tries to put on a brave face, but I know she's worried about leaving. Her mother and all of her sisters are here. At least if we went to Denver, she'd have Erin and Katie to keep her company."

Fred asked, "How long before you get word from the big boss in Washington?"

"They already know that the president appointed Claggett to the job and they can't have two U.S. Marshals in the same office, so I'm sure it'll be soon."

Thom grinned and said, "Maybe they'll send you back East so you can sit around in one of those fancy offices and tell us what to do."

Dylan laughed and replied, "That would be the death of me."

———

That night after all of the children were asleep, and Mrs. March had returned to the other house, Dylan sat with Gwen at the kitchen table sharing coffee. He could tell that she was distraught by the news that they'd both expected for months now, but now it was looming ever larger in their future and even she couldn't hide her worries any longer.

Gwen sighed then said, "I'll miss our home, Dylan. Ever since we built it, it's been our home. It's where we've raised our children and even where we welcomed Bryn and Erin's babies."

"I can always turn in my badge. John has already told me that he'd love to have me join his salvage company. With my experience in steam engines and even driving his salvage tug, I could fit right in."

Gwen smiled at her husband as she squeezed his hands then said, "You can never be anything but a lawman, Marshal Evans. I've known that for years and you reinforced that belief when you returned from that almost disaster at the town picnic in Bellevue. Your eyes were alive as you told us what had happened. Don't deny it, sir. You love what you do."

Dylan smiled back, kissed Gwen's fingers then replied, "I'll admit it. I had begun to feel left out when I had to do so much paperwork and assign deputies to do jobs that I wanted to do. That was an opportunity to do what I do best."

"Then no more talk about quitting your job. Unless they give you an assignment that is completely hideous, we'll go to wherever they send us."

Dylan nodded and let his eyes wander across his wife's face before stopping in her big brown eyes. He found it hard to believe that she was twenty-seven and was about to have her fifth child. He still saw the same face he'd seen on the foredeck of the *Providence* with those ridiculous pigtails drooped across her shoulders. He knew that she was a mature woman now, but she was still so full of the life that seemed to be hoarded by the very young.

CHAPTER 4

June 30, 1867

Kyle guessed that he had finally entered Ohio when he spotted a road sign announcing that he was now in Columbiana County but didn't specify the state. He had been keeping his steady pace since the confrontation with Michael Lowry and had half-expected to have him or some crooked lawman to come charging down the road behind him for the first few days after the incident. But the only other traffic he'd encountered on the road were the familiar wagons of farmers and freighters, riders, coaches and buggies and a steady parade of fellow pedestrians walking east.

He'd smiled and waved or greeted them all and had been given a few rides on the wagons going in his direction, so he was very pleased with his progress. He still hadn't had anyone show him how to use the pistol yet, but he hadn't found any gunsmiths along his travels either.

The unexpected infusion of Michael Lowry's cash did allow him to indulge in regular meals every other day when he passed through a town. He felt stronger and his nightly exercises had continued to improve his skill with his bat even though it was now a secondary weapon. He had the pistol and had at least figured out how to release the hammer on his own. He still hadn't taken another shot yet as he wanted to know how to reload the pistol before he started using ammunition.

After stopping for lunch in Enon which was a good-sized town, he asked the waitress if there was gunsmith nearby and she told him that they didn't have a real gunsmith, but Landry's Hardware sold guns and the owner knew a lot about them. So, after paying the twenty cents for his meal and leaving his first tip of a nickel, he gathered his belongings and headed down the main street for Landry's Hardware.

Once inside, he stopped and looked at all of the tools and materials and wished he could carry some with him. A shovel or a full-sized axe might be useful, but they were also heavy and out of the question. The army hatchet he had in his backpack was heavy enough.

The proprietor had noticed him enter and was amused at the sight of the heavily loaded young man and waited for Kyle to approach the counter. He just had the look of someone who had no idea what he wanted.

Kyle finally stepped to the counter and leaned his bat against the wooden shelf before he slipped his revolver from its holster and asked, "I was given this pistol, but I haven't a clue how to use it. Can you show me? I need some more ammunition, too."

Ed Landry picked up the pistol and said, "This is a Smith & Wesson Model 2 and it uses a .32 caliber rimfire cartridge. I sold my last one a month ago, but still have a box of cartridges. It's kind of rare because it doesn't use percussion caps. Let me show you."

Kyle could tell that the man was more than pleased to demonstrate his knowledge of the weapon and listened intently as he showed him how the pistol loaded and talked about the difference between a cartridge pistol and one that used percussion caps and powder. The impromptu lesson lasted longer than Kyle had expected, but he was still glad that he'd stopped in.

When Mister Landry finally finished, he handed the pistol back to Kyle and then reached under his counter and set the box of twenty-four rimfire .32 caliber cartridges on the counter.

After Kyle paid the dollar and twenty cents for the ammunition, Mister Landry said, "You seem to be traveling a long way, son. Where are you headed?"

"Nebraska. I have family there."

His eyebrows rose as he asked, "You're walking all the way to Nebraska?"

"Yes, sir. I should get there in another five or six weeks."

"Why don't you take the train or a stage?"

"I can't afford it."

"You can always buy a horse or a mule. You can get one pretty cheap now that the war's over."

"I'd just have to take care of it anyway. I'll be okay."

Ed shrugged then said, "You must get kind of lonely out there on the road."

"It's not so bad."

"Want a friend to take along?"

Kyle looked back at him curiously and asked, "What do you mean?"

"If you don't want to ride, then maybe you could walk with a four-footed friend. My dog had puppies last September and they're eating me out of house and home. I've gotten rid of three of them, but I still have two left and my wife won't let me just let them loose. I'd appreciate it if you'd take one with you."

Kyle was ready to turn down his offer but asked, "How big are they?"

"Right now, they're about knee-high, but I think when they're finished growing, they'll be almost to your waist. Their father is about that size and the last two are males."

"Can he keep up with me? I walk about twenty-five miles a day."

"If you can walk that far, the dog will keep up and have energy to spare."

"Can I see them?"

Ed grinned then said, "Follow me."

An hour later, Kyle was walking out of Enon with his new friend trotting alongside. He joined Kyle happily after Mister Landry had given him some beef jerky to give the dog as incentive. He'd also sold Kyle a larger knapsack that replaced his damaged army surplus backpack and swallowed all of his possessions except the tent without a problem. It even had loops of cord on the back so he could attach the tent to the back.

It had taken him a little while to adjust to the different load, but once he was used to it, he found it much more comfortable. It freed both of his arms and finally allowed him to get his heavy jacket off of his shoulder. He knew that it would only get hotter now and having a heavy woolen jacket on his right shoulder wasn't helping.

The dog was a mixed black and brown coloring and his ears were pointed. He had a big, bushy tail that was curled upward and seemed friendly enough, at least as long as Kyle kept giving him small pieces of jerky.

They were about two hours out of Enon when Kyle looked down at his companion and said, "I suppose you want a name now. What should I call you?"

The dog looked up at him as he continued to trot alongside but didn't comment.

"No preferences?" Kyle asked before saying, "I guess I'll just have to choose one for you. Give me a few minutes."

As Kyle continued to walk and come up with a name, he had to admit that just having the dog nearby filled a need to communicate even if it was a monologue.

Three minutes later, he glanced back down at the dog and asked, "How about Lobo? I heard someone tell me that it means 'wolf', but I don't remember who it was. You look like a wolf but not so scary. Is Lobo okay?"

The dog didn't bark or even wag his tail, but Kyle figured his lack of a response was as good as a yes, so he stuck with the name.

———

That evening, after he set up his camp in the nearby woods, he went on the hunt with Lobo and hit a gray squirrel with a rock and gave him to the dog while he continued searching for a rabbit.

Forty minutes later, he was roasting his rabbit over the fire as Lobo sat nearby staring at the fragrant meat. As he turned the rabbit on his trimmed branch, Kyle understood that Lobo would probably eat as much as he did, and he'd have to modify his hunting and fishing to make sure they both had enough. He could have just abandoned Lobo but once he'd given him a name, he had accepted him as a friend and friends didn't do that to each other.

———

The next morning, Kyle snared another rabbit and two squirrels before leaving the camp and reached the road to continue the journey across the country. He still had Ohio, Indiana, Illinois and Iowa to cross and was beginning to fully grasp the enormity of the land that spread out before him. He'd just crossed most of Pennsylvania and it had taken him almost a month. He couldn't understand why he hadn't made more progress and was mulling the problem as he strode along the roadway with Lobo.

He was talking aloud as he kept returning to the basic math. He had nine-hundred miles to reach Omaha when he left Wilkes-Barre, and wasn't even to Columbus, Ohio yet. He'd examined some maps along his way and knew that Columbus was about four hundred miles from Wilkes-Barre, so he should have been there a week ago at the latest, even accounting for the time he'd spent at the Neumans. *Why was he so far behind his estimated schedule?*

It wasn't until he reached the town of Louis that it hit him. The roads weren't exactly straight and the miles that were listed on the big maps were using a scale of miles that were measured with a ruler. He smacked his forehead when he realized that he wouldn't arrive in Omaha for another two months, assuming he didn't stop to work or have any other calamities.

After a big lunch in Louis, he and Lobo hit the road again. He'd stopped at a general store to load up on jerky for both himself and Lobo as a filler between meals.

It was later that afternoon when the first signs of another delay arrived. It wasn't much at first, but after giving Lobo his jerky, he popped one into his mouth and when he swallowed, he felt a burn in his throat. It didn't bother him too much, but when he took a drink of water from his canteen, it was difficult to swallow, and he knew that his sore throat was probably the start of a summer cold.

By the time he set up camp that night, his nose was running, and he felt lousy. He was sneezing and coughing but thought that a good night's sleep would be all the medicine he would need.

He rolled up under one of his blankets and didn't bother eating as Lobo laid down at his feet seemingly content with a handful of jerky.

———

The night's sleep was hardly enough medicine and wasn't even a good night's sleep. He'd woken up from his stuffy nose and congested chest several times and found it difficult to go back to sleep.

When the sun rose, he really didn't want to slip out from under the blanket, but he didn't have a choice. So, he threw it off cursing at the cold as if it would help then walked into the bushes and relieved himself before returning to the camp and taking out more of the jerky for Lobo.

He sat back down on his blanket feeling miserable and wanted to just lie back down, roll up under the blanket and sleep until the cold was over. But the drive that had made him leave Wilkes-Barre and then the Neuman farm was still there. It was strong enough to push him back to his feet before he belted on his pistol, pulled his backpack onto shoulders then slung his canteen on his left shoulder and picked up his walking stick.

Kyle soon reached the road and managed a shuffling gait as he headed west with the morning sun on his back. He glanced down at a happy Lobo and was ready to curse him for being so healthy but realized it wasn't his fault, so he just kept walking.

———

For three days, Kyle endured the blasted cold and he knew that he was losing weight because he still had little appetite. He'd stopped in one town and had a light supper but had to force down even the small amount of food. He took most of it with him in a small tin container that he had to buy from the eatery. But once he had the container, he thought it would be useful when he decided to start eating again, assuming that he would.

He finally reached the large town of Newark on the Fourth of July and was feeling good enough to sit down for a full meal. He still put half of it into his tin, but left the diner feeling better.

There were fireworks in the sky as he set up a camp just a mile west of town and Lobo didn't care for them one bit as he huddled close to Kyle for protection.

"What are you going to do if we really get into trouble, Lobo?" he asked his cowering canine companion.

Lobo seemed to understand the question, or at least the accusatory tone and picked up his head and just stared at

Kyle almost as if to say he wasn't a coward, he just didn't like loud noises.

———

With his chest and sinuses clearing, Kyle set out on the morning after the holiday in good spirits. He was almost to Columbus and in another four days, he should be into Indiana leaving just two more states to cross after he reached Illinois.

It should have depressed him knowing that he still had so many more miles to travel, but the fact that he would soon be leaving his second state and that neither Indiana nor Illinois was as wide as Ohio and that Iowa wasn't as wide as the part of Pennsylvania he'd conquered actually buoyed his optimism. He began to see the light at the end of the long, dark tunnel.

———

In the Omaha office of the United States Marshal, Dylan shook Edgar Claggett's hand as he smiled at the short man. He couldn't have been five and a half feet tall as he smiled back. Dylan was sure that the new marshal's handshake was as disingenuous as his own well wishes had been when he expressed his confidence that his replacement would do a good job.

The deputy marshals that were still in Omaha crowded the office and none really disguised their unhappiness with the change, but the new marshal didn't seem to notice or at least didn't care.

"So, do you have your new assignment yet, Dylan?" Edgar asked.

"Not yet. I guess they'll give me some time to get you settled in the job."

"Well, that's not necessary. I'm sure my deputies can do that. You just take some time to get ready for your new job. I'm sure that it will be a step up. The governor told me that you've done a fine job."

Dylan wanted to scream at the man but smiled and said, "Well, I'll just ride back to the house and wait for my assignment."

He then gave a short salute to the deputies grabbed his floppy flat leather hat and left the office. Once outside, he dropped his smile and headed for Crow who was still saddled after the ride into town. He hadn't expected to stay at the office even though he was sure that the head of the service was holding his new assignment for a week to let his replacement learn the job. Dylan just had no respect for the man and all he could hope was that he wouldn't get any of his deputies killed.

————

When he returned to the barn, he unsaddled Crow and left him in his stall before heading to the house.

As he opened the back door, he found Mrs. March baking cookies for the children and smiled as he said, "You're spoiling them, Alba."

Alba smiled back and said, "They're wonderful children, Dylan, and deserve to be spoiled as if you and Gwen don't spoil them enough."

"Speaking of my wife, where is she hiding?"

"She's feeding Brian in your bedroom."

Dylan nodded then pulled off his hat, headed down the hallway and just rapped on the door before swinging it open and stepping inside.

"Afraid I might see something that I shouldn't, Mrs. Evans?" he asked with a grin as he closed the door.

"Seeing these things is what produced this insatiable baby boy at my breast, Mister Evans. You're back early, so can I guess that the transfer of the marshal position went as you had anticipated."

Dylan sat on the bed next to Gwen and replied, "Pretty much. He didn't want to hear anything from me, so he said a very phony 'good luck' before the door spanked my behind on the way out. It's just as well, I suppose. I would probably have said something that I shouldn't have soon enough."

"So, now we just sit and wait for your assignment?"

"Yes, ma'am. I'm Alba's temporary assistant nanny until I get my official notification."

"Do you have any idea where they'll send you?"

"I've heard rumors but nothing official or even a serious whisper."

"What rumors?"

"They're going to be cutting up Dakota Territory again after chopping it out of Nebraska Territory. I don't know how they're planning on doing it, but I know it's just a matter of who gets what. One of the rumors is that they'll be slicing the western half of Dakota Territory and creating at least two more. There isn't much out that way but with the Union Pacific leaving

Nebraska soon and entering Dakota territory, they know that there will be new towns springing up along the route.

"Once they decide where to build a station for watering and coaling those trains, there will be an explosive growth in population and trouble just like what happened in North Platte. This time, they want to get ahead of the game and get law in there quickly."

"And there will be almost nothing there if they send you that way?"

"Not much, but once the trains arrive, a town will appear almost overnight. That's the real reason for the transcontinental railroad. They want to start towns out West."

He could tell that Gwen wasn't happy about it, so he said, "Let's not worry about it before we find out where they want to send me. We can always make my assistant nanny position permanent."

Gwen laughed as she pulled Brian free and set him on her shoulder to burp him. She was suddenly almost sure that they would send Dylan to a new town and had no idea what to expect if they did.

———

Even as Dylan was expressing his guess about a possible new assignment, the same question was being asked in the private office of another U.S. Marshal in Denver.

"What have you heard, Al?" Bryn asked as he looked at Marshal Al Esposito.

"Not much. But now that weasel is in charge in the Omaha office, I'd guess that they'll send Dylan west to follow the

Union Pacific. After the North Platte disaster, the Congress expressed their desire to the Marshal's Service that they didn't want a repeat in another town. The funny thing is that the railroad is lobbying for the same thing yet they're the ones who furnished the trains to bring the saloons and whores into North Platte that got those Irishmen all worked up."

"Now don't go knocking the Irish, Al. I'm married to a wonderful Irish lass and her pretty sister is Irish as well."

"Erin is a wonderful lady, Bryn, but you'll have to admit that her countrymen are serious about their drink."

"I'll grant you that, but how accurate do you think that rumor is?"

"Better than most, I think."

"I don't know if he'll leave Omaha, but if he does, at least it'll be a lot closer to us. I just hope that it's not too bad. I just want him and Gwen to see the ranch. Erin is still astounded by it and even in her current condition, she insists on exploring the property on horseback. She always takes either Katie or Jack with her, or I wouldn't let her go."

Al grinned and said, "I'm sure that if you ordered her to stay in the house, she'd just bow her head and say, 'yes, sir'."

Bryn laughed before saying, "You have me there. I guess all we can do is wait."

Al then reached into his box, pulled out a sheet of paper and said, "This was delivered this morning from the Excelsior Hotel."

Bryn took the paper and after he read the short note asked, "Do you know what he wants?"

"Nope, but he specifically asked for you. I'm not sure if there's a crime involved, so if you want to toss it in the trashcan, I'd agree with you."

"I know he's a swindler and a conniver, Al, but I actually like the man and not because he practically gave me the land for my ranch. I can't imagine what trouble he's got himself into since he was acquitted on the counterfeit charges. He had more than enough cash to leave Denver and begin some other scheme in San Francisco or somewhere else."

Marshal Esposito leaned back and grinned before he said, "Well, I guess you'd better head over to the hotel and find out. It might prove to be interesting."

Bryn was smiling as he stood and replied, "I'm sure it will be at least interesting but probably just as confusing."

After grabbing his hat, Bryn left the big office, mounted Maddy and trotted down the streets of Denver heading for the plush Excelsior Hotel. He had no idea why Jim Peacock would even be staying at a hotel. He thought that he had bought a house and settled down into the legal, albeit shady, life of a businessman. He hadn't talked to him in the past few months, and the fact that he was living in a hotel suggested that he hadn't completely reformed not that Bryn really expected that he would.

He soon reached the hotel, dismounted and tied off Maddy at one of the brass hitching posts along the right side of the stone building. He then walked across the granite entrance, climbed the stone steps and entered the lobby.

Peacock's short note didn't say which room he was using, so Bryn approached the desk showed the clerk his badge and asked, "Can you tell me which room Mister James Peacock is in?"

"He's in room 212, but he's not in at the moment."

"Do you know when he'll be back?"

"I'm not certain. He was escorted out of the hotel just two hours ago by a band of rather unkempt gentlemen."

Bryn's lawmen sense kicked in and he asked, "How many men?"

"Eight, I believe."

"Did you hear them talking at all?"

"It was a bit confusing to be honest, Marshal, but I did hear something about 'claims' and 'payback'. They seemed a bit angry at Mister Peacock."

"Were they armed?"

"I noticed that at least two were wearing pistols."

"Thank you. You've been a great help," Bryn said before turning and walking quickly across the lobby and exiting the hotel.

Once aboard Maddy, he headed west out of Denver and soon turned south toward his ranch. He was almost positive that the eight men were some of the miners who had bought claims from Jim Peacock and must have finally realized that there was no gold on the property.

He had bought a total of sixteen sections of land from another land speculator who had anticipated finding gold on the large tract but had never found a single nugget. Mister Peacock then had it surveyed into single acre plots and sold each acre as a claim to some of the hoards who had arrived in the area after the Pike Peak gold rush. He'd even admitted to Bryn that he had seeded some of it with gold dust. Apparently, some of the land purchasers were unhappy with him but the land they'd paid to work was all south of his four sections. It was still a large area to search, but Bryn knew that he'd only successfully sold the claims to the string of acreage nearest the mountains. He was guessing that the deceived miners had taken Peacock to one of those useless mines to extract their pound of flesh now that they hadn't extracted an ounce of gold.

He had Maddy moving at a good clip as he approached his ranch and could see Flat Jack Armstrong out with the herd but kept going. He had another two miles before he reached the end of his property and the rest of Peacock's land began.

When he was near the southeastern corner of his ranch, he angled Maddy to the west and had to maneuver around the rugged landscape that was already beginning to rise into the Rocky Mountain foothills. It was what had impressed him and then Erin when he'd first inspected his new ranch land.

Bryn had another three miles of the rocky terrain to pass through before he reached the edge of Jim Peacock's property, but the miners could be another two hours away if their failed claims were on the far south of the large swath that he'd bought.

He angled slightly to the south when he was within a mile of the western edge of the tract and just as he did, he spotted a conspicuous disturbance in the rocky soil. He turned Maddy to follow the tracks and soon spotted recent horse droppings and knew that he was trailing the miners. He just hoped that they didn't shoot or hang Jim Peacock before he arrived. So. He pulled his Winchester from his scabbard as he kept Maddy at a walk. He didn't dare go any faster as the ground was so uneven and covered with large stones and sharp rocks.

After another ten minutes, Bryn spotted their horses in the distance but didn't see anyone. He kept his eyes on the saddled horses and wondered where they had gone but soon had a good idea where they had taken Jim Peacock when he spotted the mouth of a small cave that had been hidden by the horses. It was probably a mine shaft that some hopeful miner had spent years digging as he searched for his impossible fortune. He just didn't know what they were doing to the man who had cheated them out of their dreams.

He pulled Maddy to a stop about a hundred yards from the other horses, dismounted then tied him off at a sorry excuse for some sort of pine tree before he began walking toward the mine.

The horses didn't seem to care that he was there, but he soon picked up voices echoing from the mine shaft that couldn't have been more than fifty feet deep. Jim Peacock must still be alive because he could hear a higher-pitched voice making all sorts of offers over the more agitated voices of the miners.

As Bryn approached the shaft's mouth, he knew he couldn't fire into the mine shaft but suspected that if he announced himself, he might draw the fire of one of the miners for interrupting their vigilante trial.

He really wanted to draw them out of the mine shaft without any gunfire at all, and it didn't take long for him to come up with a plan.

He turned away from the mine and headed back to the horses, just fifty feet away. When he was close, he untied them from the rope that had been strung between two boulders then stepped away from the horses and angled toward the side of the mine shaft.

Once he was in position, he grabbed a head-sized rock then tossed it toward the horses and said loudly, "Damn it, Al! Get the horses and let's go!"

The horses didn't move as he'd hoped they would, but he heard the rush of feet and cursing from the mine as the miners burst into the sunlight and after shielding their eyes, they all just stared at the horses.

"*Where are those horse thieves?*" one of them exclaimed as he looked at the string of horses.

Bryn then leveled his cocked Winchester at the group and shouted, "United States Deputy Marshal Bryn Evans! Put your hands in the air and you'll all live to see the sun rise tomorrow."

Eight faces turned towards him and as soon as they saw the badge and the repeater, sixteen hand jammed into the thin Colorado air.

"Alright, now I want the four of you wearing gunbelts to use your left hand to release the buckle and let them drop. Slowly, now."

Each of the armed miners did as he ordered before he had them step fifteen feet back.

Once they were disarmed, he approached the miners who displayed a mix of anger, disappointment and fear then picked up their gunbelts and hung them over his shoulder one at a time.

He kept his Winchester pointed at the miners as he shouted into the shaft, "Peacock, this is Deputy Marshal Evans, can you walk out of there?"

Peacock's reply echoed, "No. I'm tied up."

Bryn looked at the miners, spotted one who had more fear than anger in his eyes then pulled his pocketknife and said, "You. Go into the mine and cut him free. If he doesn't' walk out of there without a scratch, then I'll charge you all with assault in addition to kidnapping."

The man stepped forward accepted the pocketknife, took one short glance into Bryn's eyes then trotted into the mine.

Once he'd entered the dark hole another miner said, "We were just takin' justice for what he did to us, Marshal. You can't arrest us."

"I most certainly can arrest all of you. If you had a grievance with Mister Peacock, and I'm sure that you do then you have legal ways to resolve them. But you kidnapped him instead and that's a crime. Did you know that?"

Another miner said, "What do you mean? We just took him here to teach him a lesson and get our money back."

"You took him out of the hotel against his will and that's kidnapping. You boys will all be facing long prison sentences for kidnapping and the desk clerk saw you take him away, so we have an eyewitness. You haven't got a chance in court."

"That just ain't right!" the first miner exclaimed, "He's the one who done the crime!"

"So, you're telling me that you didn't go to the Excelsior Hotel this morning and take him here against his will?"

The man began to open his mouth to argue but stopped and just stared at Bryn knowing that he and his fellow miners didn't stand a chance in a courtroom.

Bryn, on the other hand, knew that they stood a very good chance of acquittal in the courtroom. A jury would hear their argument that Jim Peacock had swindled them by selling them land that he knew didn't have any gold and their lawyer would probably bring up Jim's counterfeiting past even though he hadn't been convicted. He couldn't imagine any jury that wouldn't side with the miners. He'd only brought it up as a bargaining chip to keep Jim Peacock safe until someone else he'd swindled decided to take revenge.

As they stood in the blinding Colorado summer sun, Jim Peacock finally gingerly exited the mine shaft with the miner who handed the pocketknife back to Bryn before joining his fellow kidnappers.

Peacock stopped and said, "Thanks, Bryn. I didn't think they'd come to my hotel to get me, and I'm really glad that you tracked us down in time. They were going to tie me up and just leave me there to die."

As the miners watched and listened closely, Bryn asked, "Alright, Jim, now I want to know exactly what you did that made them so angry, and don't sugar coat it."

Jim thought briefly about glossing over his shenanigans but knew it was fruitless to bother as Bryn knew him better than anyone else after that long ride across Nebraska and Colorado.

"I sold each of them the claim rights to an acre of land and I guess none of them found any gold. They found out that none of the miners who'd bought claims from me had found any after working it for a couple of years and then they kind of banded together. They approached me at my house and demanded their money back, so I offered to settle with them. I offered them each fifty dollars for their claims, but they didn't want half. They wanted all of it back. We argued and they said they'd be back to get all of their money, so I moved to the hotel and sent the note just in case. They found out where I was and took me here. I offered them seventy dollars, but they refused and finally decided to leave me there to die."

Bryn sighed then looked at the miners and asked, "Is that the truth?"

Their spokesman replied, "Pretty close."

Bryn then took his eyes off the miners turned to Peacock and whispered, "Good God, Jim! Couldn't you even give them the money? Is your life worth four hundred dollars? You've got thousands in the bank once you were acquitted on that counterfeiting charge."

Jim shrugged and whispered back, "I didn't think they'd really do it and besides, I've got most of my money tied up in another land deal up north near Boulder."

"You're finally leaving Denver?"

"My house is on the market. It was getting too difficult to stay here. I just didn't expect them to show up. Can you get me out of this fix?"

Bryn paused before saying, "One last time, Jim. Don't make me come up to Boulder and bail you out again."

Without waiting for his expression of thanks, Bryn turned to the miners and said, "After talking to Mister Peacock, who I arrested a couple of years ago, I have no doubt that he did take advantage of you. Now I'm willing to let the kidnapping charge go with the promise that you'll forget about seeking revenge."

"What about our money?" the spokesman demanded.

"Really? You really believe that you deserve to be reimbursed for being fooled and then being fortunate enough to ride away after committing a crime? We all make mistakes in our lives, boys, and you made one when you bought your claims sight unseen. It's not the worst mistakes I've ever seen, so don't make another one. Just ride away and be grateful that you're still free men."

Bryn wasn't sure that they had all bought what he was selling but one at a time, they began moving toward their horses. As the gun-owners passed Bryn, each collected his gunbelt and strapped it on before mounting.

Bryn still had his cocked Winchester ready in case they decided to take a pot shot, but none of them even looked back as they led their horses down the rocky slope.

When the last one was out of sight, Bryn turned to Jim Peacock and said, "Before I left the office, my boss told me that whatever you'd gotten yourself into was probably interesting, and he wasn't wrong. Now tell me honestly, are you really moving to Boulder?"

"No, I'm moving to Central City. I bought the mineral rights to half of a mountain nearby and I think it'll give me a huge return on my investment. I just didn't want them to know where I was going."

"And do you really have all of your money tied up?"

Jim grinned and said, "Well, not all of it. Do you want to buy my house, Bryn? I can give you a good deal."

"No, thanks, Jim. We're happy with our ranch house that we built on the land that you practically gave to me."

"It didn't matter to me, Bryn. The sale of those claims had pretty much died off by then and I was stuck with it. Your three hundred dollars allowed me to hire a good attorney and beat that counterfeiting rap. And without the bribery charge, I was able to get back to work. Can we see your ranch on the way back? I didn't get a good look at it on the ride in for some reason."

Bryn laughed and said, "Let's go," then asked, "Out of curiosity, how many of those one-acre claims did you sell?"

"I sold forty-six, and those eight were the last ones. They never owned the land anyway. I just sold them the mineral rights. You don't think they'll bother me again, do you?"

"No, I don't think so. But if they do, just run to the office and I'll arrest them for kidnapping and at least hold them until you leave for Central City. Just don't keep making it a habit to have me keep bailing you out, Jim."

"I'm not making any promises, Bryn. I really owe you for this one."

"Just doing my job, old pal."

Jim grinned at Bryn as they angled their horses to the north.

————

After he introduced Jim Peacock to Erin, Katie, Flat Jack and the children, he showed him around the ranch. Then he escorted him back to the hotel before returning to the office to make his report and regale Marshal Esposito and the other deputies with the story. He may have saved Jim Peacock's life but to Bryn it smacked more of a comedy than a tragedy.

————

While his uncles were both experiencing very different issues hundreds of miles away to the west, Kyle and Lobo were walking at a good pace on that compass heading.

He was feeling almost human again after the short but wicked summer cold and as he walked with Lobo trotting beside him, he still waved and greeted passersby and began to notice that after they returned his greetings, they'd let their eyes focus on his furry friend even after they'd passed. He realized that even as placid as Lobo was, they all seemed to have an almost instinctual fear of the dog even though he wasn't fully grown.

That realization gave him a chance to relax a bit and then he decided that he should really teach Lobo some basic commands to make him stay where he needed him to stay rather than follow him into stores or diners as he'd try to do twice.

The other thing he had to do was to learn how to fire the pistol accurately. He still hadn't taken a second shot with the gun, but he'd been under the weather and the last thing on his mind was target practice. He also didn't want to waste ammunition, so he thought that after he set up camp for the night, he'd do some hunting with his gun rather than rocks.

He could bring down larger game with the pistol but didn't want to kill anything that big because he couldn't use all the meat even with Lobo consuming most of it. A rabbit or squirrel would be almost impossible to hit with a bullet even if he knew how to shoot, so that limited his choice of targets; not too big and not too small or too fast.

Kyle exited the road just twelve miles east of Columbus and entered the ever-present forest. He found a nice stream, dropped his bat and shrugged off his new, very heavy backpack before he pulled the pistol to do some hunting. He already knew which mid-sized animal would become his and Lobo's supper providing he found one.

It was after seven o'clock, but there was still plenty of early summer sunlight as he and Lobo made their way through the brush. He had the pistol in his hand but not cocked as he scanned the small area of open ground.

He and his dog searched for twenty minutes before he spotted his unsuspecting prey waddling across a fairly wide break in the foliage thirty feet away. He cocked the hammer of the pistol and just as he prepared to fire, Lobo barked. If it had been any other wild creature, it would have bolted for the protection of the nearby bushes, but the large possum simply collapsed onto its side let its tongue flop out of its mouth and lay still.

Kyle almost thought it unfair as he steadied his sights on the apparently dead opossum and squeezed the trigger. The pistol bucked in his hand as the .32 caliber bullet reached its target almost instantly and sent a shower of dirt into the air a good foot above the possum's head.

The possum suddenly seemed to understand that playing dead wasn't such a good idea then bounced to his feet and tried to race into the bushes after all, but Lobo was much faster. As soon as the possum returned to life, Lobo shot away from Kyle and in less than ten seconds reached the marsupial and did what the human's gun had failed to do.

He walked triumphantly back to Kyle with the dead possum in his jaws letting him know that at least he knew what he was doing.

Kyle was surprised when Lobo dropped the possum at his feet rather than taking it back to their camp and just devouring it wholesale. He picked their dinner from the ground turned and began walking back to the campsite with Lobo just a foot beside him.

———

As Kyle roasted the good-sized possum over the campfire, he assumed that Lobo had developed a taste for the salted, roasted meat over the bloody raw variety. It was the only reason he could fathom for the dog's behavior.

After they'd both eaten their fill, Bryn took a few minutes to clean and reload the pistol as Mister Landry had shown him. He knew that it wasn't a terrible first shot, but it wasn't great either. It didn't matter much because he didn't think that he'd need to use the pistol in self-defense now that he had Lobo.

With their supper over, Kyle thought it was time for some basic training for Lobo and started with the easiest command by teaching him to sit. As he had hoped, the dog understood the order quickly and after just a few minutes, he would sit on command. He rewarded Lobo with a piece of jerky when he got it right. Then he moved onto the very similar command of 'stay' which he also learned after just a few minutes.

Kyle called it quits after those two commands and spent another thirty minutes on his own exercises with his bat. For the first time, he finished the exercise with an imaginary baseball game where he stood at the plate and used his knotted maple bat to hit a ball that flew high over the head of the center fielder stunning everyone who witnessed the mammoth clout.

He was still grinning as he sat on the blanket and looked up at the sky but when he couldn't see any stars, he realized that it might be wise to set up his tent for the first time. He'd been very fortunate that he hadn't even had to use his slicker since he bought it weeks ago. When it had rained, he'd been in the

Neuman's barn and once he'd gone, the cloudy days hadn't dropped a single drop on his head. He thought he was due for a deluge.

He'd just hammered home the last stake with the back of his hatchet when the first rumble of thunder reached his ears. He hadn't seen the flash of lightning that had produced it, so he knew he had a few more minutes before the storm arrived.

Lobo joined him in the tent after he'd pulled his backpack inside when the lightning flashed, and the thunder increased in volume and frequency. The first heavy drops soon followed and before long, the tent's roof echoed with the pounding of the downpour.

He'd set up the tent on the sloping ground near a large maple tree that blocked most of the rain, but it still was an impressive display as the wind pushed the rain under the dense foliage to reach the tent, but the slope kept the water from reaching the inside.

As the storm raged above, Kyle petted his dog and said, "I'm glad I bought the tent, Lobo. We'd be soaked right now if I hadn't. You seem to be a lot braver with the thunder booming outside, too."

Lobo was already wagging his tail because Kyle was rubbing his head, so Kyle wasn't sure if he appreciated the compliment.

———

The next morning, the sunlight streamed through the trees as Kyle and Lobo exited their small refuge and after taking care of nature's needs and a quick breakfast of jerky and crackers, Kyle thought a bath was long overdue. He'd almost used a tonsorial parlor in Newark, but Lobo insisted on following him inside, so he'd lost the opportunity.

He stripped then took his clothes with him as he headed for the swollen stream. The water was brisk but not as cold as he expected as he waded in with his bar of soap. He spent a good ten minutes scrubbing the dirt and grime from his body and washed his hair before taking his dirty clothes with him into the stream and washing them with the same soap.

After rinsing and wringing his clothes, he left the stream and walked back to the tent where he hung the damp clothes on branches and dressed in his clean clothes. He didn't realize how long he'd worn the same outfit until he began washing the filthy clothes. He'd worn the same clothes since he left the Neumans.

As he dressed, he wondered how they were doing and if Michael Lowry had taken his threat seriously. He hoped that he didn't return to frighten Lisa because he admitted to himself that he had already been getting very fond of her. It was that dangerous fondness that had added to his decision to leave, regardless of Michael Lowry's threats. He just didn't think he was either old enough or secure enough to even think about seeing a girl.

———

It wasn't until mid-morning that Kyle and Lobo reached the road and continued west. They stopped in the city of Columbus where Kyle used his 'stay' command to keep Lobo waiting while he had a big lunch but put some of the chicken into his food tin for his dog. He then stopped at a large greengrocer and bought some tins of beans and a small pot in addition to the customary jerky and crackers. He bought some smoked pork this time too. It was a heavy addition to his pack, but he was growing accustomed to the weight and was already excited to be so close to Indiana.

They left Columbus just after noon and were again making good time. There was a lot more traffic on the busy road near the city, so he wasn't worried in the least about being waylaid. He had his pistol and he had Lobo trotting alongside which added to his sense of security.

But he soon discovered that having Lobo also had one great disadvantage as the frequent offers of free rides by freighters and farmers driving in his direction evaporated when they spied the growing dog. He wasn't even a year old yet, but his back was already even with Kyle's knee.

He didn't really care that much about the lost opportunities to avoid walking. Granted, the rides were faster than he could walk and saved him wear on his new boots which were already pretty worn, but he felt that the companionship and protection that Lobo offered were well worth the loss of a few miles.

He hoped to reach London by this evening and then tomorrow, he'd get as far as Xenia. He'd pass through Dayton before noon the following day and that night, he'd camp in Indiana. The thought that he was getting closer to his destination added a bounce to his step. He still had no idea what to expect when he finally arrived in Omaha, but the very name was becoming synonymous with hope. He began to think of each of the byways he walked with his traveling baseball bat as 'The Road to Omaha'.

———

In Omaha, Marshal Claggett handed an envelope to the man he had replaced. The return address was the headquarters of the United States Marshal Service in Washington.

Ed Claggett asked, "Are you going to open it, Dylan?"

Dylan wasn't about to give him the satisfaction, so he replied, "Later. I'll open it at home so Gwen can read it at the same time."

Ed was disappointed but managed to hide it behind his politician's smile as he said, "Well, good luck."

Dylan didn't wait for Ed to offer a phony handshake but quickly turned and left the office as his former deputies watched. He knew that he should say something to them, but he had time and expected that at least the old-timers would come to the house and ask where he was going.

He mounted Crow and headed south out of Omaha leaving the sealed envelope in his saddlebags. He really didn't want to know until he was sitting with Gwen and the children. Lynn and Alwen were both ten now, Garth was nine and Bethan was eight, so they would all understand what was happening. Four-year-old Cari would take her cue from her brothers, sister and cousin while three-month-old Brian would just burp.

He turned down the drive and felt a bit queasy as he looked at the two houses, barn and corral that he'd probably have to sell now. He'd kept a stoic front when Gwen had confessed how much she'd miss the home where they'd raised their children, where Bryn and Erin had found each other, married and raised their own brood, but it had touched him deeply. He was actually torn between his love for his vocation and his love for this home. He really was close to believing that he should hand in his badge and work with John at his salvage company.

Dylan dismounted took the envelope from his saddlebags and tied Crow at the front hitchrail before stepping onto the porch. The door swung open before he reached it and Gwen stood before him with Brian in her arms.

"Did it come?" she asked.

He held out the envelope and replied, "I haven't opened it yet. I wanted you with me when I did."

Gwen nodded then waited for Dylan to enter before he put his arm around her waist and walked into the parlor. He wasn't a bit surprised to find all five children sitting on the floor looking up at him. Alba March was sitting on a chair waiting for the news as well. When Thom Smythe had ridden out that morning and told him that an official letter had arrived at the office, they all knew what the letter contained. It was more than just a notification of assignment; it was their future.

He walked with Gwen to the couch and after she sat down with Brian on her lap, he looked at the curious eyes of his children, including his nephew, Alwen, whom he considered his son now and would adopt him legally before they left Omaha, if they left.

"I guess it's time to find out where the big boss thinks we should live," he said with a smile that he didn't feel.

He took out his pocketknife extended the bigger blade, slipped it under the flap and sliced it open then extracted his orders.

There were two sheets. The first was a letter from the head of the service commending him for his exemplary performance but bemoaning the politics that had forced his hand. Dylan read the letter aloud to his attentive audience and thought that the big boss was actually sincere in his praise and disgust with having to deal with politicians. He also added a short postscript that said he would talk to the president about the appointments that were becoming an even bigger headache.

After he finished reading, he slid the first letter aside and stared at the second sheet which contained the notice of his new assignment. It wasn't exactly as he'd expected, but it was close. They had just created a new town called Cheyenne City in Dakota Territory along the route that the Union Pacific would take.

Even though it was just a place on the map a few weeks ago, they were already building the town. What was odd about his orders was that because there was already a U.S. Marshal in Yankton, the Dakota Territorial capital. He was technically being made an 'at-large' U.S. Marshal, meaning he could set up and operate wherever he chose. If they carved out another territory, which the boss expected to happen soon then he would become the resident U.S. Marshal for the new territory. It was an unusual set of orders.

He stared at the sheet for another thirty seconds before he raised his eyes and said, "It's hard to explain but essentially, they want me to go west and follow the Union Pacific to a new town called Cheyenne City. He says that I'm to be an 'at-large' marshal and can go where I'm needed, but if I read it right, he really expects me to go to Cheyenne City and set up there."

Then he turned to Gwen and asked, "What do you think?"

Gwen had steeled herself for the news and quickly replied, "We'll go where you go, Dylan. We can make a new home there and the best part is that Bryn and Erin would be about a hundred miles away. I imagine that pretty soon there will be a railroad to Denver, and it'll be just like having them as next-door neighbors."

Dylan was somewhat surprised by her answer and asked, "Are you sure, Gwen?"

"I'm sure. What happens next?"

"The first thing I have to do to go to out there and evaluate the situation. I'll return in a couple of weeks and let you know what I find. If it's too bad, I'll turn down the assignment. I'm not going to yank you and the children away from home if it's a bad place. The boss in Washington is pretty sure it'll be in a new territory pretty soon too."

"If they make it a territory, can't this happen all over again?"

"I get the idea from the postscript that the boss in Washington is getting fed up with these rubber stamp approvals that put politicians in law enforcement positions. That's not that big a problem back east where most of their work is paperwork anyway but out here, it can cost folks their lives. If he tells the president that those are voters that are being lost, he might win his argument.

"Regardless of what he does, we can only bet the hand we're dealt, Gwen. Remember what it looked like here when we arrived? Omaha was a hectic, dangerous town that was small and unruly, and it's just a bit unruly now. I'll just have to go out there and see what it's like."

"You're right, of course. We'll talk when you get back. Maybe we can build a new house with two bathtubs, one on each floor."

Dylan smiled at Gwen and could see the growing excitement over the change replace her wariness and concern. He still had no idea what to expect when he arrived in Cheyenne City.

He then looked at his brood on the floor and said, "It looks like we might be moving to Cheyenne City. It's about five hundred miles west of here and when you all come, you'll be riding in a train."

The children were already excited by the sense of adventure and the thought of going on a train was the impetus for them to pop to their feet and begin to jabber to each other about the move. Little Cari had no idea why they were all bouncing around but joined them in their excitement, nonetheless.

Alba asked, "Am I coming if you move, Dylan?"

"Only if you want to, Alba. It's your choice, but I know that Gwen and the children would miss you if you didn't join us."

Alba smiled in relief and replied, "Thank you, Dylan."

With the family settled, Dylan rose and said, "I'm going to head back to Omaha, and I'll be back in a few hours."

Gwen stood turned slightly to keep Brian from getting squashed in the middle and stepped onto her tiptoes as she kissed her husband.

"We have a lot of planning to do, just in case."

"Yes, ma'am," Dylan replied as he turned and headed for the door.

————

Dylan's first stop after arriving in Omaha was to send his two telegrams, one east and one west. The one he sent to Washington said that he was heading to Cheyenne City and depending on what he found, he'd either accept the at-large position or resign. The other was to Bryn telling him the same thing.

Then he stopped at the office to tell the deputies where he was going and to leave the not-too-subtle hint that if he set up the office in Cheyenne City, he'd be looking for some deputies. He knew that his most trusted deputies were all married, and if they decided to join him, they'd have to convince their wives, and he really didn't want to strip the Omaha office of their most trusted men anyway.

When he left, the new boss seemed more than just a bit irritated by his comments even though Dylan's own decision to stay in Cheyenne City was far from certain. If he did turn in his badge, he'd already decided that he couldn't work for John in the salvage business. He'd head to Denver and work for Al Esposito again rather than leave the life of a lawman. He hadn't told Gwen about that backup decision yet and would only bring it up if the trip west turned into a disaster.

His next stop was at his mother's house on 12th Street, the one he'd bought for her and John along with the salvage business. As he rode toward the house, he tried to get a handle on the passage of time since he'd made that deal with Mrs. Reynolds. He was going to be thirty years old next summer and his mother would be turning fifty. *Where had the time gone?*

She was still a strong, lively woman but John was beginning to slow down and show his age. He was already fifty-four and had put on some weight. Luckily, he didn't have to do any physical labor as his hands were becoming arthritic.

He stopped in front of the house, dismounted and tied off Crow before stepping quickly down the walkway climbed the porch steps and soon knocked on the door once before going inside.

"Mom?" he asked as he entered the foyer and removed his hat.

"In the parlor, Dylan," she replied.

He turned left into the parlor and found his mother stitching a flannel baby nightdress.

She smiled up at him and said, "Erin is following Gwen's suggestion and hasn't even thought of a boy's name. She is adamant that she'll be having little Grace Lynn next month. So, did you get the news?"

Dylan took a seat across from her and replied, "Yes, ma'am. We might be moving to a new town called Cheyenne City in a few months. I'll be going there shortly to check on the place and either take the assignment or turn in my badge."

Meredith set her needlework down and asked, "Dylan, may I make a request that I've already discussed with John?"

"You want to join us if I decide to stay there?"

His mother smiled and replied, "I don't want to lose all of my grandchildren, Dylan. John is getting tired of just going to the office every day and seems to reminisce too often about that run up to Fort Randall on the *Gray Hawk* before it became the *River Warrior*. I think the change would do him good and I want to watch my grandbabies grow up."

"I think Gwen and the children will be delighted to have you and their Grandpa John come with us. That's assuming we move."

"You'll never know how touched he was when Lynn was the first to call him grandpa. I think it was only then that he really felt as if he was part of the family."

"I'll be leaving for Cheyenne City in about a week, so we'll need to iron out what you and John want in the way of a house. If you want to have a new one built, I can have it done on an adjoining lot to ours."

Meredith beamed as she exclaimed, "That would be wonderful!"

Dylan smiled back and said, "And the best part is that Cheyenne City would be just a two-day coach ride north of Denver and soon, they'll build a railroad between them and it'll just take you four hours to visit your other grandchildren and meet Grace Lynn. Gwen told me that she'll feel guilty if Erin has a boy."

His mother was still glowing when she answered, "That baby wouldn't dare be another Evans male. She'll be Grace Lynn or stay there."

Dylan laughed then stood stepped over to his mother, kissed her on her forehead and then turned and left the house. He had a lot to do before he went to Cheyenne City.

He hadn't been at all surprised by his mother's request. When he talked to John yesterday, he'd asked a few questions about his possible new assignment that suggested that he and his mother had already decided that they'd be leaving Omaha with Gwen and the children.

He was really pleased that if he moved, they would be living nearby because he was so accustomed to having his mother close after leaving her in Carbondale back in '54 and not seeing her for more than five years. The chance that he'd be breaking that bond again might be a deciding argument for turning down the assignment and his badge. But now that she and John would be coming along, it made the situation he found when he reached the new town as the only real obstacle.

After stopping to send a second telegram to Bryn with their mother's decision, he rode south to the house to let Gwen know about his mother's request.

————

Two hours later, Bryn received the two telegrams while he was still at the office in Denver and then walked into Marshal Esposito's office without knocking.

Al looked up and asked, "What's the news, Bryn?"

"As we all expected, he's being sent to Cheyenne City and then he sent another telegram to let me know that our mother and her husband are going to be joining him if he takes the job."

"When is he getting there?"

"He's going to a preliminary investigation in a week or so, but if he decides to go the rest of the family won't follow until the Union Pacific reaches Cheyenne City."

"From what I hear, that won't be until November. I know they're kind of unhappy with the Union Pacific around here because they first expected that they would send the transcontinental rails this way because of the terrain west of here. When that didn't happen, they demanded that local Denver investors pay to have a spur sent down from Cheyenne City. They've been negotiating with some Kansas railroad to run a line to Kansas City and then up to Cheyenne City, but that's run into roadblocks, too. I think it'll be a while before there are any tracks heading north, but it'll happen."

"It'll be a good thing for Denver when it does. It's growing pretty fast now, but if they get a railroad, it'll explode. We've got our hands full now with the miners and the scum that try to take their gold and silver, and I can't imagine how bad it'll get when the railroad arrives."

"Well, at least we don't have to get involved too much in the county work, that's Sheriff Wheeler's job."

"I hope Dylan gets help up there soon. I imagine it's going to be a real mess when the railroad reaches Cheyenne City and then winters there. It'll be North Platte all over again."

"That's why they're sending Dylan. He's the best I've ever met. No offense."

Bryn smiled and said, "I agree with you, Al."

"You're not leaving me if he takes that job, are you?"

"No, sir. My home is here with Erin and our horse ranch. I'm a little worried about her sister, Katie, though."

"She's not in trouble with some boy, is she?"

"No. It's just the opposite. She was convinced that she'd be going to the convent for so long that she's almost afraid of boys and men. We thought that she'd be happy to be free of the commitment and she is, but she's still incredibly shy about seeing boys. I thought she'd be over it by now."

"How old is she?"

"She'll be twenty in December."

"She's not exactly a spinster, Bryn."

"I know, but Erin is worried that she might become one."

"After meeting her, I'd be shocked if that happens. She'll be okay."

"Well, I'm going to head back to the ranch and let them know about Dylan. Anything big going on?"

"Just the usual. There's more noise out of Golden about their sheriff that might require our attention. One of the citizens wrote me a letter saying that Sheriff Latimore Brown was getting chummy with a man named Cornbread Funk who's the owner of two gambling house saloons and a brothel."

"That's not unusual, Al."

"I know, but according to the complaint, Latimore is intimidating miners and ranch hands into only visiting his partner's establishments. The man who wrote the letter might just be angry because his saloon is losing a lot of business and he might have to shut down, but he said that the other saloon owner is having the same problem. If those other two close their doors, then Sheriff Brown's pal will have a monopoly and who knows what that will mean."

"Is that any different than some smaller towns with only one saloon?"

"Only if we have a lawman making it that way so he can line his pockets."

"Do you want me to go up there and investigate the problem?"

"Not yet, but if I send you up there, I want you to take backup. Cal Burris could use the experience."

"Let me know, boss. I'm out of here."

Bryn left Marshal Esposito's private office then passed through the front office glancing at Deputy Cal Burris sitting at the desk. He'd only been hired three months ago but had been a deputy sheriff in Douglas County for two years before joining them. He wasn't quite twenty-one yet and looked it. Bryn wasn't sure of his skills, but it wasn't his choice if Al wanted to send him along.

He mounted Maddy turned south and headed out of town for the Double EE ranch.

———

Kyle had spent most of the day in Dayton now that Lobo would wait outside. He bought some more clothes including a second pair of boots, had a haircut, shave and a real bath before having a full meal at a nice diner. He packed his food tin with the extra meat he'd ordered for Lobo before leaving the restaurant and resuming his walk late in the afternoon.

His journey was getting practically monotonous now that he felt so protected. He greeted passing strangers and waved at wagons as they rolled past without any real concern for possible dangers. He was depending on Lobo to warn him of anyone that presented a threat.

Since the violent thunderstorm, he'd only been sprinkled with one summer shower that was actually refreshing and he hadn't had to set up the tent each night. He'd still only fired the pistol at a target once, his missed shot at the immobile possum. He just didn't see the need to improve his accuracy or familiarity with the revolver.

The other reason for his decision not to use the gun was that he'd run the numbers in his head before reaching Dayton and realized that with the infusion of Michael Lowry's cash, he could afford to eat regularly in each of the towns they passed through and still have more than half of his money left when he reached Omaha. That computation also allowed him to spend the eight dollars and change for his clothes, boots and other necessities in town.

Even though he'd left Dayton late in the day, he and Lobo still walked another three hours before setting up camp.

As he handed Lobo the meat he'd saved from his lunch, he stared west and knew that by noon tomorrow, he'd be in Indiana. He was almost halfway there, and it wasn't even the middle of July. At this rate, he'd reach Omaha before September and the very thought made him excited yet a bit nervous, too. Despite what his mother had told him, he still wasn't convinced that his uncles would be pleased with his arrival.

So, as he sat by the fading light, he took out his most prized possession, his mother's letter, then carefully unfolded the page and read her last words to reinforce his commitment to the journey. He wasn't sure if he'd ever return to Wilkes-Barre to give his mother a proper gravestone, but he wasn't sure if she really wanted one. He just knew that she was finally able to proclaim to anyone finding her resting place that she was Bess Evans and the wife of her beloved Huw.

CHAPTER 5

July 13, 1867

Kyle had just passed through Greenfield the day before and knew that the real city of Indianapolis was just a few miles ahead. The road traffic had been steadily increasing over the past few days and his restored sense of safety had diminished as some of the men began to study him despite Lobo trotting beside him. He assumed it was just because there were so many people in the city that there were bound to be more disreputable types, so he increased his vigilance marking those who were armed as the greater danger.

But even with that added scrutiny, he didn't believe anyone would bother him, at least not with so many witnesses on the road. If he didn't have Lobo with him, he might have considered staying in a hotel or rooming house for the night when he reached Indianapolis, but he didn't want to be separated from his friend.

It took him over an hour to pass through the city, but that included a stop at a street vendor selling sausages. He bought four of them, ate one and gave one to Lobo before he put the remaining two into his stuffed backpack for their dinner.

It was late in the afternoon when he finally left the outskirts of Indianapolis behind and entered the familiar countryside. He had noticed that ever since he left Pennsylvania, the wooded areas had been thinning and wondered if the trees would stop altogether when he reached Omaha. He'd read about the Great Plains and had seen one drawing in a newspaper that showed what appeared to be a sea of grass without a tree in sight and wondered if that's what it really looked like.

The road traffic was slowing down because of the time of day, so when he spotted a stream off to the right, he turned into the less dense trees and followed the stream into a reasonably hidden area.

After setting up his campsite, he gave Lobo his sausage and began munching the last one as he sat on his blanket. It still had the hole in it from the knife of the attacker and he noticed that the rip had been growing. He'd fix it tomorrow because he was already tired because he had picked up the pace after leaving Indianapolis not wanting to attract too much attention from any of the unfriendly crowd.

As he sat on the blanket, he pulled out the pistol and began to examine the gun. He recalled Mister Landry's explanation of how it worked and for the first time, tried to visualize the process. He cursed his lack of education that left him confused about the mechanics and explosive process that made it a weapon and believed that he never would remedy his ignorance.

Still, he removed the cartridges and then examined the .32 caliber rimfires. Mister Landry had explained the difference between it and a much more common percussion cap pistol and had grasped its significance. But now as he stared at the brass cartridge, he began to visualize the firing pin striking the rim of the cartridge, igniting the powder and sending the bullet down the barrel. With the gun empty, he stared down the barrel and saw the grooves that made the bullet spin to improve accuracy. Kyle then reloaded the pistol, slid it into his holster and after securing it with the hammer loop, felt better about having the Smith & Wesson. Tomorrow, he'd begin to practice with the pistol. He couldn't waste much ammunition, but he wanted to get better.

———

After Bryn had unsaddled and brushed Maddy, he walked to the back of the house and entered the kitchen where as he had expected, he found Erin waiting for him at the table. Katie was taking some biscuits out of the oven as he hung his hat and closed the door.

Erin looked at his face and asked, "What's wrong, Bryn?"

He shook his head and replied, "Nothing. Everything's fine."

Katie glanced at her brother-in-law and could see why Erin had asked the question, but she didn't comment.

"Something is bothering you, husband. So, let's hear it."

Bryn sat down then waited for Katie to join them at the table before saying, "It's not bad, Erin, it's just, well, unexpected."

"What is?"

He reached inside his vest, slipped out a thick envelope and slid it across the table as he replied, "This is."

Erin stared at Bryn for a couple of seconds then picked up the envelope and extracted several folded sheets of paper. When she unfolded them, she found a half-sheet on top that read:

You saved my life, Bryn. None of this matters to me, but I hope you find them useful.

Jim

As she slid the note to the table, Bryn said, "They're the deeds to his house in Denver and the twelve sections of land to the south that he'd been selling to miners after telling them there was gold to be found."

"But how can he do that if he sold it?"

"He sold them an acre each, but only as mineral claims, so once they vacated the claim, they have nothing. They're all gone now."

"What will we do with a house in Denver? This is our home."

"We'll hold onto it for a while then think about selling it later. I just don't know what we'll do with all that land. This is plenty for what we need."

"We already have two sons who might need their own places, and we'll have a daughter next month, too. Then Katie could have her own house after she's married, or maybe she'd rather live in Denver."

Katie softly said, "Don't worry about me, Erin. I like it here."

Erin smiled at her younger sister and said, "Let's not worry about it right now. Okay?"

Katie nodded but knew that she'd have to accept her new future soon. She'd only been to Denver a couple of times and had been embarrassed when young men looked at her, so she began to keep her eyes on the ground before her to avoid their stares. She wasn't about to change her mind and run to a convent because Father Duffy had explained that if there was any doubt in her mind, she didn't have the calling. Still, her new life would require her to get over her shyness.

————

Kyle was on the road early and the road traffic kept increasing as he and Lobo made their way west. It was already hot by mid-morning and he knew that by noon, they'd have to slow their pace in the overbearing heat.

He could feel the sweat soaking his back and his hair was matted down on his head long before they reached the middle of the day. They had just passed through Avon where he'd refilled his canteen and let Lobo lap some of the water from the trough when he lost his canine friend.

When the sun was almost directly overhead and blasting its fiery heat down on them, Kyle glanced at Lobo and asked, "Do you want to rest for a while, pal?"

Lobo's tongue was hanging down as he looked up at him without supplying an answer and Kyle laughed. He hadn't gotten an answer to any of his other questions and was glad that he hadn't but just before he turned his eyes back to the road, Lobo froze.

Kyle stopped and watched as Lobo closed his mouth, turned to the right side of the road and stared at the trees. Not knowing what had attracted Lobo's attention, Kyle gripped his bat in both hands, expecting a wolf or bobcat to pop out of the woods. But Lobo's hackles weren't up, and he wasn't growling but just staring with keen interest into the forest.

Then he barked once and remained unmoving. After a short pause he barked again and just a moment later, Kyle heard another bark from inside the trees. Lobo then sprang away from Kyle and shot into the woods.

"Lobo! Come back! Here, Lobo!" Kyle shouted as his companion disappeared into the foliage.

Kyle set his bat back on the ground and just stared at the trees, debating about following to find Lobo or just staying put to wait for his return. He decided to wait because he didn't know what was waiting in the forest. It could be a pack of gray wolves, but he doubted it. He was pretty sure that Lobo was too smart to invade their territory. He expected that he'd picked up the scent of a female in heat, so he expected that after Lobo satisfied his urges, he'd just come trotting out of the trees with a dog grin on his face.

He stood sweating in the Indiana road for another thirty minutes breaking up the broiling afternoon with periodic calls for his friend, but Lobo never emerged from the trees. As much as he wanted to wait, he finally turned and began walking west again assuming that Lobo would be able to track him easily when he decided to rejoin him.

He'd passed through the town of Easton by mid-afternoon but had just been nibbling on jerky rather than stopping for lunch. He'd been glancing behind him every couple of minutes hoping to see Lobo trotting down the road, but all he saw were the eastbound riders and wagons.

He'd emptied his canteen before he reached Danville, which was a much bigger town, so he refilled it at the community pump then sat on a bench in a small park right in the middle of town. He had his bat leaned against the bench seat and his weighty backpack beside him as he stared back east.

He'd only had Lobo with him for a few weeks but knew that he'd miss him. Granted, all of their conversations had been one-sided but just being able to say things without feeling like a loon had made the long days' walks pass more easily.

He sat on the bench until late afternoon then hung his backpack in place and picked up his bat before walking to a small diner where he had a full meal. He still wasn't going to waste his money for a room, so after he left the restaurant, he took one last long look east then turned and slowly began to walk westward. He found it hard to keep up his accustomed pace with the combination of the heat and Lobo's loss, but he still strode west for another four hours putting nine more miles behind him.

By the time he was setting up for camp near a good-sized pond, he'd given up on Lobo and felt the sense of loss as he assembled his tent. After the furnace of the day there had been a rapid buildup of clouds to the west and he suspected that he'd soon be visited by another thunderstorm.

After his full supper, he didn't bother eating the leftovers in his tin and would save them for his breakfast. But rather than practicing with his pistol, or even doing his exercises with his bat, he stripped and hurled himself into the pond. The cool water cleansed his body and revived his spirit, and as the clouds grew thicker, he swam and dove in the water until he finally stepped out onto the muddy bank and trotted back to his tent, secretly hoping to find Lobo waiting inside. There was no waiting dog, so Kyle slowly dressed then pulled his backpack and bat into the tent with him and lay on his back as the first rumbles of thunder echoed across Indiana.

"I hope your new girlfriend isn't a bitch, Lobo," he said aloud as he stretched out with his fingers locked behind his neck then snickered at his joke.

There was lightning and thunder over the next hour, but the rain must have fallen elsewhere as his campsite remained dry. Tomorrow, he'd resume his journey but without companionship. He'd pick up the pace too. He had about another sixty miles left in Indiana, then he'd be in Illinois. He wanted to cross that border in three days.

Before he slept that night, a new thought crept into his mind for the first time and he'd do an accounting of his remaining cash tomorrow to see if it was possible.

———

Gwen was lying on her back leaving a gap between her and Dylan not because she was upset but the stifling heat made snuggling distinctly uncomfortable.

"If we go, are we bringing all of the horses with us, or will you be taking them on one of your earlier trips?"

"I'll ride Crow, but I'll take one of the geldings for a pack horse next week. We'll move the others after I have our house and barn built. You do understand that this is all speculation, don't you?"

"I know, Mister Marshal. But if we go, will we be taking Peanut, too?"

Dylan laughed and replied, "Of course, we are. I made that boy a promise to take care of him, and we will. Besides, I think our young wildlings would revolt if we didn't. Even Cari thinks of him as a pet. I'll admit that he is cute."

Gwen giggled lightly then said, "I know that there's still a chance that you'll turn the job down, but I kind of wish that you didn't."

Dylan stared at his wife and asked, "Gwen? Are you serious? I thought you loved it here."

"I do, but even though I'd miss this place, I find that I'm already excited about Cheyenne City. It would be like our early days when it seemed as if everyone was out to get us."

"I don't think it will reach that level again, sweetheart. We have enough firepower to keep anyone from even thinking about it. You're getting pretty good with that Model 1, too. I'll order some more cartridges when I get back."

"Leave it to you to start talking about guns on your last night in bed with your wife for a few weeks."

Dylan rolled onto his side, smiled at Gwen and said, "The night isn't over, Mrs. Evans."

———

The morning sun promised another scorcher as Kyle sat on a log near his tent and counted his remaining wealth. He'd been so miserly over the past six weeks that he'd never made an accurate count.

He'd left Wilkes-Barre with around eighty dollars then he'd added the seventy-five from Michael Lowry, and for some reason, he had never bothered adding the two. He'd mostly been spending the silver that the men on the factory floor at the ironworks had given him and hadn't used many of the banknotes at all. Now as he spread the cash on the blanket before him, he realized that he still had over a hundred and thirty dollars.

He had no idea how much a ticket to Omaha would cost on a train or a coach, but the thought was there now. When he reached Terre Haute, he'd stop and ask. He'd be willing to spend eighty dollars of his fortune if it could get him most of the way to his destination, but if it would only get him into Iowa, then he'd stick with his original plan.

After stowing most of the cash in one of his socks in the backpack, he dismantled the tent, attached it to the straps on the backpack then buckled on his gunbelt, lifted the backpack onto his shoulders and secured it with the front strap then grabbed his bat and left the pond campsite.

He soon reached the road and after one last hopeful glance to the east for Lobo, he turned west and stepped off at a fast pace knowing he'd have to slow when the heat arrived in earnest. He wanted to reach Greencastle by the evening and then tomorrow, he'd stop in Terre Haute and maybe he'd ride to Omaha the following day.

Despite Lobo's absence, he found that the idea that he might reach his destination a lot earlier than he'd anticipated gave him renewed energy and he was soon walking at a fast pace as he crossed Indiana.

———

In Denver, Bryn and Cal Burris sat across from Marshal Esposito as he explained the ongoing problem in Golden.

"I received a second letter, this time it was from the mayor of Golden. He didn't add anything new but because he's the elected official of the town, he made a formal request for assistance. Sheriff Brown is the county sheriff, so he has no authority over the man, but we have to at least investigate the issue. If necessary, you'll need to remove him from office pending review by a county judge. If you think the county judge is corrupt, then let me know."

"Okay, boss. Did you get any background information about the deputies in that office?" Bryn asked.

"I know that he's got four deputies, but I don't know if they're looking the other way, helping or just worried about keeping their jobs."

"Do you think he knows that we're coming?"

"Play it safe and assume that he does. I wouldn't be surprised if the mayor didn't warn him that he'd better behave, or he'd write to us."

"Okay, boss. We'll get going. I'm going to swing by the house and pick up my spare pistol and let Erin know that I'll be gone for a few days. I'll be back in a couple of hours."

Cal Burris then said, "I'll be ready to go when you get back, Bryn. How long will it take to get there?"

"We should arrive in early afternoon. It's only about twenty miles or so."

Cal nodded then he and Bryn rose and left Al's office.

As Bryn rode south to the ranch to tell Erin, he was concerned about two things: Cal's lack of experience and the potential for being ambushed before they arrived in Golden. He had to operate on the assumption that there would be hidden assassins somewhere along the route, but still thought it was unlikely. The sheriff may be corrupt, but Bryn found it hard to believe that he'd arrange for shooters to kill two United States Deputy Marshals.

———

Erin was packing some sandwiches for Bryn as Katie listened while he explained the situation in Golden. He didn't express his discomfort with his partner or the potential for ambush, but he suspected that Erin already reached both conclusions. She knew Cal Burris and the dangers that corrupt men in power posed, but she didn't let on that she understood. She just listened as she laid the sliced ham onto the bread.

Katie did ask, "Is it going to be dangerous, Bryn?"

He glanced at his sister-in-law and replied, "Honestly? I don't know. It's not an uncommon situation, but it depends on the sheriff. I've only met him once, and that was about a year ago. He seemed pleasant enough, but people sometimes have two very different faces."

Katie nodded but didn't comment. It was one of the reasons she'd shied away from social gatherings. She simply didn't know whom to trust because she was so ignorant when it came to understanding motives. Erin and Bryn were both very good at seeing what was behind others' eyes, and she knew that she just had a bad habit of taking the first impression as the real person. The possibility of finding a lurking monster behind a smiling mask added trepidation to her awkward shyness.

Erin asked, "Do you think you'll be back tomorrow?"

Bryn replied, "I hope so, but it could be the day after."

She handed him the cloth bag with the four sandwiches, then kissed him before he said, "Well, I've got to get back and pick up Cal."

"Good luck, Deputy Evans," Erin said as she smiled.

"Good luck, Bryn," Katie echoed.

Bryn kissed Katie on the forehead before leaving the kitchen then heading outside and mounting Maddy.

After taking the reins, he looked down at Flat Jack and said, "Keep my family safe, Jack, and tell Katie to make sure that Grace Lynn doesn't make her appearance before I return."

Jack laughed and replied, "I'll do that, Bryn. I'm not ready to be a midwife anyway."

Bryn grinned at Jack, saluted and then wheeled Maddy about and headed back to Denver. Erin's advanced pregnancy was going well but the lack of an experienced midwife gave him some concern. Katie had assisted in two childbirths but hadn't actually been the one who managed the delivery. He knew that she was capable, but he wanted Erin to have the best care possible when she finally had their daughter.

When he thought of her insistence about the baby's sex because she hadn't allowed a single boy's name to be considered, he smiled. It wasn't as if it had been like his parents, who had five sons and no daughters. He and Erin had only produced two boys so far, and as Dylan and Gwen now had two daughters, he thought that the odds favored a little girl anyway.

But as he drew closer to Denver, he had to shift his mind back to the job at hand. He had his new Winchester in his right-hand scabbard and a shotgun in his left. He had picked up his spare Smith & Wesson Model 2 but was only wearing one. His badge was behind his vest as he reached the outskirts of the town and headed for the office.

By the time he and Cal were riding out of Denver, it was almost noon.

———

Dylan sat on the hard bench seat of the passenger car as the Union Pacific train rolled west across the plains of Nebraska. The Great Plains had been likened to an ocean of grass by poets and newspapermen and it wasn't far from the truth. There were hills and the occasional clump of trees where there was water nearby, but the regular arrivals of enormous grass fires kept the trees from spreading too far away from the creeks, streams and ponds. He hadn't been as far west as Cheyenne City before but knew that the topography of the land wasn't much different until it reached the start of the Continental Divide. He'd been told that there were more sources of water and larger forests but even with the rolling hills, the landscape was still essentially part of the Great Plains. It was why the Union Pacific had chosen this route. Their surveyors had followed the path that would be the easiest and cheapest topography to lay their tracks.

When he'd bought his ticket, the station manager had told him that the end of track was now somewhere between Julesburg, Colorado before it twisted back toward Kimball, Nebraska. He'd joked that when folks heard that the tracks had reached Colorado, they thought it was already finished, but it had just kissed the northeastern corner of the territory as it followed the flattest land before curving back into Nebraska. He said that, depending on how much track they'd laid since his last update, Dylan would probably have between seventy and eighty miles to go before he reached Cheyenne City.

Crow and his pack horse were in the stock car and the train had already passed through Grand Island. He should reach the end of track late in the evening but wasn't going to stay. He'd leave as soon as he retrieved his horses and take advantage of the summer sun to get a few miles behind him.

He expected to be in Cheyenne City in two days and then he'd find out whether or not to stay. Secretly, he hoped it was as bad as Omaha had been when he first started working with Marshal R.J. Garrison. He hated to admit that he missed the excitement, but he did, and he was sure that Gwen knew it too. Her comment last night had surprised him, but after he thought about it, he realized that she missed the excitement of their early years as well.

Even though he'd only left her and the children a few hours ago, he already missed her. He'd been separated from her much longer before but somehow, knowing he was still going away from her made the separation more intense.

————

Bryn and Cal were riding at a medium trot as they headed for Golden. Bryn had instructed Cal to be on the lookout for a possible ambush, so it made for a quiet ride as both lawmen scanned the surrounding landscape for potential drygulch sites and there were a lot of them as the road twisted and curved around natural obstacles.

The road traffic was sporadic, but as the roadway in both directions was rarely visible for more than a few hundred yards, it seemed to be almost empty.

When they were about an hour out of Golden and hadn't had any issues, Bryn turned to Cal and said, "Drop back until you can't see me, then follow at this pace. If anyone is waiting, they'll be closer to town and I don't want us both to get caught by surprise. If you hear gunfire, come in carefully and pick up the gunsmoke."

"Alright, Bryn," Cal replied as he pulled his gray gelding to a stop.

Bryn didn't look back as he continued at the same pace and soon had to make a sharp turn around a large granite outcrop, so he knew that Cal should start following.

He still didn't anticipate any problems and expected to see Golden soon, when he felt a familiar tingle on the back of his neck and slid into his danger zone wondering what had trigged it. There had to be something that he'd missed but now, with his heightened awareness, he let his surroundings pop into vivid detail. He still didn't find anything that could have caused the sensation which meant it had to be behind him.

He quickly swiveled in the saddle as he yanked his pistol from his holster and was barely bringing it to bear when he spotted two men standing with their pistols pointed at him just forty feet away.

By the time he was drawing back his hammer both men fired simultaneously, and he felt one of their bullets buzz closely past him instantly, but neither of them stuck him as Maddy had turned with him.

Bryn needed to put the fear of God in the assassins but didn't want to waste a round to get them to duck. He took an extra moment to settle his sights before he fired his first shot, then shifted the muzzle less than in inch to his left and fired again.

His first .32 had nicked the shorter man on the right side of his chest but the surprise of being hit made him lower his pistol as his left hand reached automatically to assess the damage.

His partner wasn't so lucky. Just as he was ready to fire his next shot, Bryn's second bullet arrived and drilled into his left lower gut just above his pelvis. He grunted, bent at the waist and dropped his pistol as blood began to soak his sweaty shirt.

Bryn had them under his pistol as he trotted Maddy toward the men and Cal trotted around the outcrop with his pistol drawn.

"Keep them under cover while I have a little talk with them."

"Okay, Bryn," Cal said as he pulled his horse to a stop before the rocks they had used as a killing platform.

Bryn dismounted, but kept his pistol cocked and ready as he climbed onto the enormous flat rock. He snatched the downed man's revolver, tossed it into the road then said, "Drop the pistol, mister. Don't give me an excuse to shoot you."

The short man scowled at Bryn but dropped his pistol as he still held onto his chest's flesh wound which was barely bleeding.

Bryn just kicked the second pistol toward Cal and listened as it rattled across the rock and then dropped to the ground before he asked, "Do you know who we are?"

"We were just gonna rob you, that's all."

"Well, then I guess it's all right. We'll just tie you both up here then pick you up on the way back to Denver after we finish our job in Golden. It won't be but a few hours."

The gut-shot man curled in a ball on the rock exclaimed, "You can't leave me here! I'll die!"

"You were both planning on killing me, so why should I do you any favors."

"You gotta help me. You're a lawman and that's the law."

Bryn looked back at the short man and asked, "How would he know that?"

"You look like you carry a badge. That's all."

"Do you see a badge?"

He shrugged and hoped that they did tie him up. He knew that he'd have a decent chance to escape once they arrived in

Golden and met up with the boss. He didn't care about his partner.

Bryn then looked down at the bleeder and said, "Your pal over there doesn't care if you live or die, mister. Now that bullet I put into you is only a .32 caliber, so if you get treated soon, you'll probably live. If you tell me everything, I'll forget about charging you with attempted murder of a United States Deputy Marshal and take you to Golden to see a doctor."

Bryn was expecting the short man to threaten his fellow would-be assassin, so as soon as he snarled, "Don't you...", Bryn sideswiped him on the damaged side of his chest with his pistol with the barrel finding the back of his hand first.

As he howled, Bryn said, "Tell me the truth now, mister. You were sent by Sheriff Brown to stop us from reaching town. Is that right?"

"Yeah. I'm Sy Hartman and that's Joe Utz. We're two of his deputies and he told us you were going to arrest us all because of what he's been doing."

"Okay, Sy, here's the way this is going to work. I'm going to help you back onto your horse after we tie up Joe and hide him behind this big rock. We'll ride into Golden, but I want you to show us a back way into town and we'll take you to the doctor to get patched up. On the way, you'll tell me everything you know. Is it a deal?"

"Yeah, but hurry!"

————

With Cal handling binding and moving Joe to his temporary open-air cell, Bryn checked Sy's wound and after cleaning it with water from his canteen, he cut off one of Sy's sleeves and used it as a bandage before helping him into his saddle.

As he'd worked on his prisoner, Sy began talking and Kyle almost had a hard time keeping up. It was as if Sy couldn't wait to make his confession and gushed non-stop even after they started toward town.

Sy explained that the sheriff's threatening guiding of clients to Cornbread Funk's sinful enterprises was just part of the sheriff's abuse of power. He also had what amounted to a protection racket for other businesses which had begun with the competing saloons. He said that he and another deputy, Jimmy Gabbart, had been there before Sheriff Brown really hit his stride, but he'd hired two other men, Joe Utz being one of them, who were more thugs than deputies. The other thug deputy was named Arnie Popovich.

"Why did he send you rather than the other thug?" Bryn asked.

"He never sends them together. He sent me because, well, because I'm weak and he knows that I'll do what he says rather than stand up for myself. I didn't even aim at you. I fired high. I wish you woulda hit Joe instead."

Bryn nodded and even before the first sign of Golden appeared ahead, he knew that he had to come up with a plan. Sy had given him the basic layout of the town, and Cal would escort him to the doctor's office which was luckily on a side street on the eastern side of Golden.

The trouble was the other thug deputy and the sheriff himself. It was early afternoon and most sheriffs would be in the office but according to Sy, he rarely was there.

Then he recalled Dylan's approach when a gang of four men had taken over the ferry over the Elkhorn River and thought that might be the best way to handle the sheriff. He hoped that the sheriff didn't remember what he looked like after that brief meeting, but having the shotgun along with the Winchester did make him stand out, so he pulled to a stop and when Cal halted alongside, he disconnected the shotgun's scabbard from his saddle and handed it to Cal.

"Hang onto this, Cal. After we split, I'm going to ride into town and have a beer at The Big Nugget."

"Why?"

"I figure Sheriff Brown will arrive and suggest that I visit one of Cornbread's establishments. If not, I'll have to hunt him down. After you drop off Sy, just ride back around and enter the town from the east. You should find me when you spot Maddy."

"Okay, Bryn. I hope this works."

Bryn nodded as he rode ahead of Cal and Sy then turned south as soon as he reached the busy town. There was plenty of road traffic and he wasn't sure that he hadn't been spotted but stayed with his original plan and after riding south for two blocks, turned back east.

The Big Nugget was six blocks into the town on the main street, but he wanted to approach from the west, so he trotted Maddy for nine blocks before heading back to the main road. Once he turned east, he had the sun at his back and had a much clearer view of the activity.

He soon spotted The Big Nugget and angled for the saloon. He didn't see the sheriff or his deputy nearby but dismounted and tied off Maddy before stepping across the boardwalk and through the batwing doors.

As he entered the almost deserted barroom, Bryn was initially disappointed that he hadn't been stopped but as he crossed the empty floor, he realized that he had struck pay dirt and may have gotten the better break when he heard heavy boot steps approaching from the right, turned and saw a large man with a badge who he hadn't noticed when he entered.

He turned his eyes back to the bar as if he wasn't interested then stopped at the bar and said, "Beer," before he dropped a nickel on the rough bar.

The bartender didn't move to draw his order as he looked at the big deputy who had just reached the bar.

"You're a stranger here, ain't ya?" asked the deputy he knew had to be Arnie Popovich.

"Yup. Just got here and fancied a nice cold beer. It's mighty hot out there."

"If you want a beer, mister, you ain't gonna drink it here. You need to head down to The Bighorn or The Ace High. They're a lot better than this place."

Bryn finally turned to look at the deputy and replied, "I'm already here and it looks like I got the place all to myself, too. You can head over to one of those places if you want."

"Do you see this badge, mister? I'm not askin' you to go there, I'm tellin' you to leave. If you want a beer, you ain't gonna get it here."

Bryn put his palms out before him as he said, "I'm sorry there, Deputy. I didn't see the badge. You got a law about where a guy can get a drink?"

Arnie was getting irritated and Bryn knew that he may have gone too far already, so before the deputy replied, he asked, "Say, Deputy, do you know a lawman named Joe Utz? I knew him when we were young'uns and I heard he was up this way."

His question disarmed Arnie for a moment before he asked, "You know Joe?"

Bryn grinned as he answered, "Sure. We go way back. Did you ever ask him how he got that scar on the right side of his chest?"

Arnie was confused as he'd never seen a scar but really didn't want to be seen staring at another man when he had his shirt off, so he wasn't sure if Joe had a scar or not.

"How'd did he get it?" he finally asked.

Kyle laughed and said, "Well, when we were joshing each other, I pretended I had a pistol in my hand and pointed my finger at him and yelled 'bang!'. He pretended to be shot and grabbed his side, but forgot he had an open pocketknife in his hand. He was mad at first, but then he looked and saw he'd only sliced himself a bit and thought it was funny."

Arnie laughed and slapped a heavy hand on Bryn's shoulder as he exclaimed, "That sounds like something that stupid bastard would do."

Bryn was still grinning when he quickly jerked his right knee into the junction of Arnie's big thighs and as he grunted and bent over at the waist, Bryn rammed his right elbow into the back of his neck sending him crashing to the floor.

Arnie was still writhing in pain as he grabbed his crotch, but before he could even think about standing, Bryn launched a hard kick into the back of Arnie's head silencing him.

He then turned to the bartender and said, "I'm United States Deputy Marshal Bryn Evans. I'm going to tie this so-called lawman up and drag him to your storeroom. When I come back, can I have that beer?"

The bartender was all grins as he loudly replied, "Yes, sir!"

Bryn quickly dragged the heavy, unconscious deputy across the floor to the nearby storeroom and once inside, stripped him of his gunbelt and then his badge before tying him up with his own pigging strings. He then gagged him so he couldn't shout a warning and exited the storeroom closing the door behind him before he headed back to the bar.

He handed the gunbelt to the bartender and said, "Hang onto this," before he upended his cold beer.

After quenching his thirst, he asked, "Where can I find Sheriff Brown at this time of day?"

"He'd be in The Bighorn. Do you know what he looks like?"

"I do, but I've never met Cornbread Funk. Where does he hang out?"

"He's usually at The Ace High, and he's easy to spot. He wears a black suit with a red vest. Are you really gonna take them out?"

"I'd rather arrest them both, but we'll see how they react."

When Bryn finished his beer, he wiped the foam from his lips with his sleeve before he headed back across the saloon floor debating about which of the two saloons to visit next. He soon stepped out into the glaring afternoon sun and stopped on the boardwalk to look for Cal.

After not seeing his partner, he mounted Maddy and turned him east to go to The Bighorn after deciding to confront the sheriff first. He expected that once Cornbread lost his backing, he'd be more reasonable.

When he stopped before the much larger saloon, he could already hear the sounds of a much busier establishment as men called for the roulette wheel's ball to land on their numbers or the wheel of fortune to stop on their choices. Knowing that it was so crowded could be a problem or an advantage depending on what he found inside.

After dismounting, Bryn tied off Maddy and released his pistol's hammer loop. He'd reloaded the pistol since leaving Joe behind the rock and had even added a sixth cartridge, which he rarely did. Sheriff Brown may have only hired two thug deputies, but that didn't mean he wouldn't have more supporters in his saloon. If he had more than five, Bryn knew he had a problem. The biggest problem might be the bartender, who probably had a shotgun under the bar. A lot depended on whether or not the sheriff recognized him.

Bryn took one last glance to the east didn't see Cal then stepped through the much nicer doorway and entered The Bighorn Saloon. It took a few seconds for his eyes to adjust to the shadows, but after he walked a few feet into the large room, he quickly began scanning for the sheriff. He wasn't hard to locate when his loud laughter overpowered the other sounds and Bryn turned to the left side of the floor and found Sheriff Brown standing at the craps table beside the man in control of the dice who had just obviously rolled a seven and lost a sizeable wager.

Once he'd identified the sheriff, Bryn continued his scan and lingered his attention on the bartender, who was looking in the other direction. The room was so full that Bryn found it difficult to decide who might be a problem and who would be just a spectator. There was also a very real risk of dead innocents if there was gunfire. He had to find a better way.

He turned and slowly walked back through the doorway and stepped back out into the not-so-harsh light under the saloon's porch then glanced east and finally spotted Cal heading his way.

They met before the adjacent barber shop and Bryn said, "I took care of the other bad deputy and left him tied up in one of the competitor's saloons. The sheriff is inside, but it's too crowded. How's Sy?"

"He never shut up, even while the doctor was checking him out. Doc says he'll be okay, by the way."

"Good. We may need his testimony. Let's head over to the jail. The only one left who could be there is the last deputy, Jimmy Gabbart."

"Okay, Bryn. This oughta be interesting."

Bryn stepped off the boardwalk with Cal as he replied, "And then some."

The jail was two blocks west of the barber shop and across the street, so after the short walk, Bryn and Cal entered the open door. Even with the two windows and front door open, it was stifling inside and as they entered, they spotted Deputy Sheriff Jimmy Gabbart fanning himself with his hat.

"What can I do for you fellers?" he asked as he continued to try to cool himself.

Kyle walked to the desk, opened his vest and showed him his badge as he said, "I'm United States Deputy Marshal Bryn Evans and this is Deputy Marshal Cal Burris."

The deputy's hat stopped in mid-sweep as he stared wide-eyed at the two lawmen then slowly said, "They didn't get you."

"You knew about their attempt to ambush us?" Bryn asked.

"Sy told me when he left with Charlie this morning. Where's Sy?"

"He's at the doctor's office with one of my bullets in his gut. He'll be okay. Why didn't you ask about Joe Utz?"

"I hate the bastard. Him, Arnie and our thieving sheriff are making their own little empire."

"Well, Deputy, the emperor has no clothes because Joe Utz is tied up and sweating in the sun where he set up his ambush and Arnie is bound and gagged in the storeroom in The Big Nugget. I just visited The Bighorn and spotted the sheriff, but it's too crowded, so I need to get him out of there, and I'll need your help."

"How?" asked an obviously nervous Jimmy Gabbart.

"Nothing bad. I just want you to go over to the saloon and tell the sheriff that Joe Utz needs to talk to him at the jail. If he asks why Joe couldn't come himself, just shrug and say you don't know because Joe didn't give a reason, but he was all grins."

Jimmy thought about it for a few seconds then nodded and rose from the chair pulled on his hat and left the jail.

After he'd gone, Bryn said, "When the sheriff comes through that door, I'll be waiting off to the side in case the deputy is in front. You'll be in that small room on the right with your pistol cocked and the door open. As soon as I have the sheriff under control, we'll toss him in a cell. Then we'll go from there."

"Okay, Bryn," Cal said as he drew his Colt New Army and headed for the room.

Bryn pulled his Smith & Wesson and walked to the wall near the door. There was a window behind him, so it was possible for the sheriff to spot him, but he was hoping that the sheriff would be too focused on hearing the news from Joe Utz and wouldn't bother looking.

The room seemed to be getting hotter by the second as Bryn stood pressed against the wall and sweat trickled down his forehead and soaked his shirt. He began to think about Cornbread Funk. He had no doubt that the saloon owner was involved in the ambush attempt but knew it would be hard to prove. He knew that he and Cal had met the objectives of the mission, but he suspected that after the sheriff and his boys were taken out of Golden, Cornbread would find a replacement within a week.

Bryn was almost startled when he heard a loud voice saying, "Joe had better have a damned good reason for dragging me over here!"

He quickly cocked his pistol as he heard Jimmy Gabbart reply, "He sure seemed pleased about something, boss."

The footsteps drew closer and soon Deputy Gabbart passed by and Sheriff Latimore Brown walked entered behind him pulling off his hat.

Just as the sheriff came to an abrupt stop, Bryn stepped behind him with his pistol and said, "Sheriff Brown, I'm United States Deputy Marshal Bryn Evans and you are under arrest for conspiracy to murder a Federal agent. Put your hands in the air or I'll put a bullet in your back."

Sheriff Brown, the moment he'd seen the empty desk, knew that he'd been duped, but it was too late to do anything other than to thrust both hands above his head.

Bryn said loudly, "Cal, come on in," then pulled the sheriff's pistol from his holster and waited for Cal to reach them.

When he did, Bryn handed him the sheriff's revolver then said, "Walk slowly to your first cell, Mister Brown. You're no longer sheriff of this county or anything else."

Latimore didn't say a word as he marched to the open cell and just sat on the hard cot as Cal slammed the door closed.

Cal then turned to Bryn and asked, "What's next? Do we get the other deputy out of the storeroom?"

"Not yet. Let's head over to The Ace High and have a chat with Mister Funk. I want to let him know that we've got our eyes on him."

He then turned to Deputy Sheriff Gabbart and said, "Can you find the mayor and bring him here, Deputy?"

"Yes, sir," he replied then trotted out of the room.

Once he was gone, Bryn said, "I don't think either of the deputies would stand up to Cornbread after we're gone. The mayor's going to have to find a stronger man to be sheriff."

Cal nodded, but didn't answer before they both walked out of the jail and turned north toward The Ace High. As they walked, Bryn transferred his badge to the outside of his vest and then Cal did the same.

They entered the large saloon and gambling house and Bryn paid no attention to the eyes that began turning their way in waves as the word passed among the gamblers and drinkers. Cal was watching and wondered if there were any of Cornbread's friends among them, but still walked alongside Bryn.

Bryn headed for the only door at the end of the bar and without knocking, turned the knob and entered. Cal hesitated, thinking that Bryn probably wanted him to stand guard, but then figured that if he'd wanted him to stand and watch the saloon floor, he would have told him to do so and entered the office.

Just as Kyle passed through the doorway, he saw Cornbread Funk look up at them and just as he was about to protest, he saw their badges and just stared at the two lawmen.

Bryn quietly said, "Surprised to see us still breathing, Mister Funk?"

Funk smiled and replied, "Now, why would I be surprised?"

Bryn had his answer but unless the sheriff or Joe Utz gave him up before the trial, there was nothing he could do about it.

"I've been told that you know everything that's going on in Golden and figured you probably have heard rumors that the sheriff sent two of his deputies to ambush me and my partner east of town."

"You're mistaken, Marshal. I didn't even know you were coming. Why are you here?"

"We received a complaint that Sheriff Brown was running a protection racket and we were sent to investigate and if proven true, to remove him from office and arrest him. But now we're taking him and his deputy back to Denver for trial in a Federal court for attempted murder of Federal officers. As you seem to be the most prominent citizen in Golden, I'm just letting you know. Of course, we'll still monitor the situation closely. You can never tell about new sheriffs."

The smile never left Cornbread's face as he leaned back and replied, "No, you never know what's inside a man when he gets a chance to make some real money, do you?"

Bryn smiled back then asked, "You know, Mister Funk, I've only known two men who used 'Cornbread' as a nickname, and both of them were Confederate prisoners. The first time I heard it, I asked the man and he said it was pretty common in the deep South, but yours is the first I've heard out here. Are you from the South originally?"

"Does it matter?"

"Just curious."

"I grew up on a plantation in Georgia and was given the nickname by my colored nanny."

"You don't have much of an accent."

"I never did. I suppose you were a Yankee soldier and maybe were with that bastard Sherman when he razed my home state."

"I was a captain when they mustered me out in '63 because of a severe wound, so I never was able to have the pleasure of burning down your plantation. How many slaves did you have?"

Cornbread's smile was gone before he slowly answered, "Forty-six. Not that I cared. So, you're one of those bleeding-heart abolitionists who rode into battle to free the Negroes. Do you feel happy now that they're all homeless or are so poor that they have to work for almost nothing?"

"What happened to them before the war or what's happening now is beyond my control, Funk. What you're doing now, however, is within my control. The fact that you were a slave owner only increases my desire to see you rot in prison. Golden is only a four-hour ride from Denver and when they complete the railroad, it'll be an hour. I'll make a point of making unannounced visits from time to time and I hope you make a mistake."

"You're welcome to visit as often as you'd like, Marshal, but you'll never find any evidence of wrongdoing on my part and you'll go to your grave a disappointed man."

Bryn shrugged then said, "As long as you behave yourself, Funk, I won't be disappointed at all. We're going to get the sheriff out of jail now and then we'll take him to trial in Denver. I wonder what he'll say if we offer him a plea bargain. I don't think he'll want to spend thirty years in prison. They really don't like crooked lawmen in there."

He gave Cornbread a short salute then turned on his heels, waited for Cal to precede him out the door and closed it behind him before they crossed the barroom floor under the scrutiny of every man in the place.

Once outside, Bryn said, "Let's get back to the jail and prepare to move quickly. I don't want to give Cornbread enough time to set up another ambush."

"Is that why you made him so mad?"

"I'm impressed that you noticed that, Cal. He managed to hold it back pretty well, but he was seething behind that relatively calm façade. And yes, that's why I pushed him. Judging by the sheriff's lack of response after we put him in his cell, he's expecting Cornbread to prevent us from taking him to Denver and after our short time with Joe Utz, I'm sure that he won't talk either. That being said, I don't think that Cornbread can take that chance."

"Did you really get shot so bad that the army sent you home?"

"Yup. It was friendly fire, too. I'll tell you about it later," he replied as they reached the jail and stepped inside.

Mayor Don Thomas was waiting with Deputy Gabbart when they entered the room and asked, "What happened to the other deputies?"

Bryn took off his hat wiped his brow and replied, "Sy is over at the doctor's office with a bullet wound in his gut but will be okay and Joe Utz is tied up about three miles east of town where he set up the ambush. The other one, Arnie What's-his-name, is bound and gagged in the storeroom at The Big Nugget. We just talked to Cornbread Funk, and I let him know that we'd be watching him, so I'm pretty sure he'll try to stop us from getting the sheriff to Denver for trial, so we need to go quickly."

Mayor Thomas asked, "Can't you stay for a day, at least? It's going to be pretty bad around here after you're gone."

"It's going to be worse if we stay, Mayor. I can't charge Arnie with anything that rises to Federal crime level, so I'll leave it up to Deputy Gabbart what to do with him. As far as I'm concerned, you can leave him in that storeroom. I'm not pressing charges against Sy because he cooperated and didn't even aim his pistol at us. That leaves the sheriff and Joe Utz."

He then looked at Deputy Gabbart and asked, "Can you saddle the sheriff's horse?"

The wide-eyed deputy nodded then trotted out of the room.

After he'd gone, Bryn said, "I think he's an honest man, Mayor, but I don't believe he has the sand to stand up to strong men like Cornbread. Do you have anyone else you can appoint to be the new sheriff?"

The mayor slowly shook his head and replied, "I can't think of anyone who's that confident and still honest. There's a lot of gold flowing through town and the temptation for corruption is too great."

Before Bryn could say anything, Cal suddenly asked, "How much does the job pay?"

The mayor looked at him and answered, "We were paying him a hundred dollars a month and paid for his room and board at Tippy's Boarding House."

Cal then glanced at Bryn before looking back to the mayor and saying, "I'll take the job, Mayor. I'm only making sixty dollars a month as a deputy marshal and have to ride all over the place. I'd like to settle down."

The mayor then looked at Bryn who said, "He's a good man, Mayor, but I'll probably get an earful from Marshal Esposito for losing him."

The mayor grinned then shook Cal's hand and said, "You've got the job, Marshal. But how can you stay if you're going back to Denver?"

Bryn answered, "He'll help me get the sheriff and Joe Utz halfway there, and then I'll go on alone."

Then he looked at Cal and asked, "Are you sure? Things will still be tough for a while."

Cal nodded then replied, "I'm sure. I want to be in charge, and I know I'm ready."

Bryn shook his hand then said, "Okay, let's get ready to move my prisoner, Sheriff."

Cal grinned then he and Bryn headed for the jail.

————

After walking the ex-sheriff out the back door and securing him to his horse, Bryn and Cal headed east using side streets. Bryn didn't expect that Cornbread would have had enough time to mount a serious effort to prevent their departure but wasn't taking any chances.

Once they cleared the town, Bryn asked, "Are you really sure that you're making the right decision, Cal? You'll have to depend on Gabbart until you can hire another deputy, and the mayor didn't know of any candidates for that job either."

"I'm sure, Bryn. Like I said, I always wanted to be in charge, and I know that I'll never get to be a U.S. Marshal like you will. This is my chance."

"Well, that being said, you've got to watch your back at all times. Don't assume that Funk will just take my warning to heart."

"I know. Just tell the boss why I had to take the job and let him know that I still think he's the best."

Bryn smiled and replied, "That's only because you never met my brother."

"Before we get to Joe, tell me about how you got shot in the war."

Bryn began his narrative, not skipping over the reason he'd been sitting alone in the dark outside the camp where he'd been shot by his own picket. He didn't feel even the least bit of angst when he told Cal about the blue letters and the shocking revelation of reading his brother's telegram letting him know that Arial was getting married that very day.

"Do you miss her at all?" Cal asked.

"No. I have Erin and I can't tell you how grateful I am that I didn't get that telegram before she married, not that it would have made a difference in her decision. She grew up while I was gone and has her own life now. I'm so incredibly happy with Erin and that's all that's important."

They reached the rock and found Joe Utz on his back sound asleep. After rousing him, Bryn gave him half a canteen of water while Cal brought up his horse and after another twenty minutes getting Joe ready for the ride to Denver, they finally had him in the saddle and secured.

Bryn then turned to Cal and said, "I've got it from here, Cal. Good luck with the job and send me a telegram when you're settled in. If you need any help, let us know right away."

Cal replied, "I intended to do that, Bryn. I hope those two enjoy their time in prison," then waved and turned west for Golden.

Bryn watched him ride away and hoped that he'd be all right. He may have wanted to be in charge, but Bryn wasn't sure if he'd even make it to Golden. He knew that he wouldn't have been able to talk him out of it, but it still bothered him to watch Cal leave.

After Cal disappeared around a bend, Bryn said, "Okay, gentlemen, let's head back to Denver," then set Maddy to a slow trot.

———

After leaving his two prisoners in the county jail, Bryn rode back to the office in the early evening and found Marshal Esposito waiting for him with a telegram in his hand.

"What does this mean? Cal said he made it back and has everything under control."

Bryn smiled then proceeded to explain the day's work. The marshal was indeed unhappy about losing Cal but understood that the added income and the opportunity to be the boss was too much to overcome. It would leave the office a bit shorthanded for a while but like Bryn, Al Esposito was concerned that Cal had bitten off more than he could chew.

———

As Bryn rode back to the ranch, he knew that he had a lot of stories to tell Erin and the rest of the family. What he'd never even told Erin was that he'd secretly hoped that he'd be able to introduce Katie to Cal and maybe something would come of it, but he wasn't about to let Katie go to Golden. He knew what a mess that town would be until they rid themselves of Cornbread Funk.

————

Kyle was exhausted as the heat had seemed to suck out the last of his energy, but he had reached Greencastle and the sun was still in the sky. Tomorrow, he'd be able to make it to Terre Haute and maybe he'd take a coach or a train the rest of the way if it met his budget restraints.

As he trudged into Greencastle, he was debating about getting a room when he spotted the train station on his right and thought that he should ask how much a ticket cost just to answer the question. He simply had no idea what it would be.

He stepped onto the platform and walked to the ticket window where he gratefully let his backpack slide from his shoulders and set it on the floor then leaned his bat against the wall.

"What can I do for you, young feller?" the man behind the barred window asked.

"I was wondering how much a ticket would cost to get to Omaha. Does the train even go to Omaha from here?"

"Yep, but you'll have to switch trains. Can I guess that you want to know the price of a standard fare? You aren't travelin' first class, I'm guessin'."

Kyle grinned and replied, "Yes, sir. I haven't been walking first-class since I left Pennsylvania in June."

"You been walkin' all the way from Pennsylvania and were plannin' on walkin' another six hundred miles?"

"Six hundred? I've got another six hundred miles? I thought I was more than halfway there."

"Sorry to disappoint you, son. But let me check the fare for ya."

He slid his finger down a chart and then said, "Standard fare to Omaha is $47.45. Can you handle that?"

Kyle nodded then slowly asked, "Can you tell me how much it would have cost me to buy a ticket to Omaha from say, Columbus, Ohio?"

"Well, we don't go that far, but if I had to guess, you'd pay about eighty dollars altogether."

Kyle wasn't sure if he would have paid it anyway, but it still annoyed him that he hadn't bothered to check earlier, so he scrounged for his cash and paid for a standard fare ticket to Omaha.

As the ticket agent slid the ticket across the shelf, he said, "Your train leaves here at 11:10 tonight and is scheduled to arrive in Omaha the day after tomorrow at 9:25, but don't be surprised if it's late. The Illinois Central is a bit cheap about getting their locomotives serviced."

Kyle nodded as he slipped the ticket into his pocket along with his change before pulling his backpack onto his shoulders and picking up his staff.

He glanced at the station's big clock and saw that he had four hours before his train departed if it was on time. He decided he'd make use of the time to clean up and fill his stomach, so he headed for the Robert House Hotel just a block away.

After paying a dollar for a room, he climbed the stairs then entered room 205. Once inside, he set his things down, removed his gunbelt and hung it over the bedpost and then left the room to use the bathroom at the end of the hall.

Twenty minutes later, he felt energetic and clean as he returned to the room where he dressed in clean clothes and strapped on his gunbelt. He left his backpack and bat in the room then walked downstairs to the hotel restaurant.

He felt out of place as most of the other diners were properly clothed for dinner, but he needed to eat before the long train ride. He ordered a big steak to celebrate his change in mode of transportation, and after it arrived and he began to eat, he almost cut a piece aside for Lobo just out of habit. As he cut and chewed, he wondered where Lobo was and if he and his girlfriend were still together.

After paying fifty cents for his big dinner, he left the dining room and climbed the stairs. The clock behind the check in desk read 9:40, so he figured he may as well head to the train station and wait on the platform.

———

It was pitch dark when Kyle felt the passenger car lurch and begin its movement west. As he sat on the thinly padded seat, staring out into the shadows, he whispered, "Well, Mom, in two days, maybe I'll meet my uncles and they'll be as good as you said they would be. If not then at least I'll be able to start a new life with you and my real father watching. I hope you're happy now, Mom."

CHAPTER 6

Dylan spotted the first buildings of Cheyenne City in mid-morning and was surprised by the amount of construction, but disappointed at the same time. He knew that his expectations had been too high or maybe just too optimistic. There hadn't even been a town here just weeks before, but once the Union Pacific had ordained it as a major stop on its route the influx of new residents had almost materialized from the earth. Yet even as he rode into what would probably become the main street, he didn't bother looking for a place to stay.

Gwen may have expressed her desire to regain some of the excitement of their earlier times together, but he couldn't bring his children to such a place. It wasn't the wildness that he knew would be coming, it was the lack of all those things that young children needed and had become accustomed to having.

He followed the telegraph wire to the new station and dismounted. Once inside, he sent a lengthy telegram to Washington letting the head of the service know that he was regretfully resigning from the United States Marshals and wished him good luck in his fight to remove politics from the position.

After he paid for the message, he left the small office, stepped into the saddle and headed back east following his own trail. He hadn't sent a telegram to Gwen because he wanted to tell her in person. When he returned, he'd ask her about his idea of joining Al Esposito in Denver as a Deputy Marshal.

As Crow left Cheyenne City behind, he wondered if he had made the right decision. He was sure, just by seeing how much work had been done in just a few weeks that Cheyenne City would be a real town within a year and that many other families would soon arrive and live in the same conditions. He just hoped that Gwen and his mother would understand.

Before Dylan stopped to set up camp for the night, his resignation would ignite a flurry of telegrams racing across the country.

———

In the Omaha U.S. Marshal's office, it wasn't a telegram that was causing some puzzled faces, it was a regular letter that didn't make much sense.

"What do you make of this?" Thom Smythe asked Benji Green as he held up an envelope.

"Do you know any of the Evans named Kyle?"

"Nope, and I know all of Dylan's and Bryn's youngsters, too."

Thom looked back at the envelope that had just been delivered to the office and said aloud, "Mister Kyle Evans, care of United States Marshal Dylan Evans, Omaha, Nebraska. It was sent by some feller named Neuman back in Pennsylvania."

Benji said, "Dylan and Bryn are from Pennsylvania. Maybe he's kin."

"I don't think so. They didn't leave any family back there."

"What do you want to do with it? What if it's important? Do you want to give it to Gwen or his mother?"

Thom tossed it into the box on the desk and said, "Let it sit for a few days then if nothing else happens, I'll take it over to his mother."

Benji nodded and said, "That sure is queer."

––––––

Even as Thom was tossing the letter into the box on the desk, the addressee was having a late lunch at the railroad restaurant in Dubuque. The train hadn't broken down, but it was still behind schedule. Kyle wasn't sure that it was going to make it the next three hundred miles.

He'd gotten some sleep on the train overnight but was still tired. Initially, he'd found train travel a bit hard on his stomach with the constant rolling of the passenger car, but he'd gotten past that discomfort. He still found it boring but knew that it was saving him weeks of travel. He still found it hard to fathom that after almost two months of walking, he still hadn't reached the halfway point. He was very pleased that he'd stopped to ask about the ticket because if he'd kept walking, he wouldn't arrive until late September if not later.

After having his hasty meal, he trotted back to the train platform and boarded the train again. He walked down the aisle to a different seat at the back of the car so he could rest his head on the back wall. Snoozing with his head against the window had literally been a pain in the neck.

Ten minutes after sitting down, the train left Dubuque and continued westward across Iowa. He was sitting on the bench with his backpack beside him serving as a support to keep his bat from moving as it was wedged between the window and the backpack.

He'd discovered late last night that if you were planning on sleeping, it wasn't a good idea to leave your things on the outside. A boy, who was probably just two or three years younger than him had started rummaging through his backpack and only when he knocked over the bat, did Kyle awaken and caught him red-handed with the knife in his hand. Kyle hadn't done anything but glare at the boy, who said that he was just looking for a towel to wash his hands before he dropped the knife back into the open backpack and hurried back to the front of the car to join his sleeping family.

After the boy had gone, Kyle quickly checked his pistol then did a quick inventory of his belongings. It took him longer than he'd expected because he hadn't really done a neat job of packing and wasn't even sure of what was inside anymore.

He'd also moved his pistol to the left side, so no one could just lift it easily from the holster although that wasn't very likely.

As Iowa rolled past, he noted the ever-decreasing number of trees. There were still quite a few, but nowhere close to what there had been in Pennsylvania. He guessed that's where the state got its name, Penn's Woods. He had no idea what Nebraska meant, but he had a feeling that it was probably Indian for, 'What's a tree?"

———

Over the next few hours, the train stopped at small stations when there was a signal that a passenger needed to board or it needed to take on water and coal. It always stopped at the bigger towns like Independence, Waterloo, and Webster and stayed long enough to let the passengers eat or use the rest facilities. At Dodge City, Kyle had to switch trains to head south, but was grateful that the tired locomotive had gotten him this far.

The new train seemed faster, but he guessed it was just wishful thinking. He was sound asleep when the train shifted west again toward Omaha, so when he awakened with the dawn, he was lost about his location. He'd have to leave the train to make use of the station's privy at the next stop because he'd tried the rolling privy at the front of the passenger car and had at first been mesmerized by watching the track's crossties whizzing past the opening, but found that it was only acceptable if he had to empty his bladder.

It wasn't until the train slowed and he read ANITA on the water tower that he was able to get a better idea of how much longer he'd be aboard the train. There was a timetable posted at the front of the car near the water barrel and Anita was just three hours and twenty minutes from Omaha.

After his rush from the train to use the privy, he returned just as the train's whistle announced its departure. The train would take on water and coal at the next big stop at Atlantic, and if there were no more passengers boarding after that, it wouldn't stop again until it reached Council Bluffs.

As the train picked up speed, he wondered if it would be faster to leave the train in Council Bluffs and walk across the bridge to Omaha but wasn't sure if there was a bridge for non-train traffic across the Missouri River, so he decided he'd just stay put.

It was when he was debating making a premature exit that the realization that he was finally nearing his destination struck him. It had been nothing but a goal since he'd started walking out of Wilkes-Barre almost two months ago yet now it was here. In just three hours, he'd be stepping off the train into a place and a life that he couldn't envision. He stared outside at the passing countryside and wondered what his life would be tomorrow.

———

As the train crossed the Missouri River, Kyle looked for other bridges and didn't see any, at least on the south side of the train. He'd crossed the Mississippi River before Dubuque, and now was crossing the second of America's great rivers. He thought the Mississippi was wider, but the Missouri looked faster and deeper.

He was still staring back at the brown water as the engineer pulled the whistle and the brakeman began his race from car to car to spin the brake wheels to help halt the momentum of the rolling mass.

Even with the brakes being applied, when the locomotive reversed its drive wheels as it arrived at the station, the cars still accordioned into each other in a loud series of shuddering bangs.

After it stopped, Kyle waited for the other passengers to start queueing to exit the passenger car before he rose, hung his backpack over his shoulders then his canteen before he picked up his bat and left his bench.

It was a cloudy but still hot day as he stepped onto the platform and after taking a few steps to clear the way, he stopped and scanned the town. It was bigger than most towns and the large station was busier than any other he'd seen in his travels, but understandably so. The Union Pacific funneled all of its supplies and materials through Omaha as it drove west. They had timber mills along the way for the crossties, but the rails, spikes and most of the other finished materials and equipment had to start here.

Kyle took in a deep breath then stepped across the platform and turned west into Omaha. He then asked a passerby if he knew where the U.S. Marshal's office was, but it turned out he was a recent arrival as well, so he turned into the first business, a haberdashery, and asked the proprietor. After turning down his special offer for a new bowler hat, Kyle thanked him for his help then left the shop and continued west.

As he walked, the amount of traffic of all sorts, wheeled, hooved and pedestrian amazed him. There were a few men still wearing old Union or Confederate uniforms probably seeking jobs on the transcontinental railroad. He imagined it must have been much more noticeable right after the war fizzled to an end and the veterans of the war had no jobs or homes waiting for them.

But now it was time to find his uncle, United States Marshal Dylan Evans, and the rest of his surroundings slipped out of focus as he concentrated on the building across the street on the next block.

Kyle almost ran afoul of a hearse of all things, as he crossed the busy thoroughfare but aside from a very unseemly shout from the undertaker, he was none worse for the wear as he stepped onto the boardwalk then continued walking west.

When he reached the open doorway, he stopped let out a long breath then grasped his walking stick and entered the large office.

As he did, several faces turned to him, and each belonged to a man with a badge.

One of them asked, "What can I do for you, son?"

Kyle replied, "I need to see the marshal."

Before the deputy could respond, a short, older man turned from reading a paper and asked, "I'm the marshal. What do you want, boy?"

Kyle stared at the marshal and felt his stomach drop. *This man was his Uncle Dylan?* Since the first step that he'd taken on the long journey, he'd anticipated that his uncles would look something like him, assuming his mother had told him the truth. Yet the marshal looked like a weasel and there wasn't a single physical characteristic that they shared.

The irritated marshal again asked the dumbfounded Kyle, "What do you want to see me about?"

Thom Smythe plucked the envelope from the desk box, then said, "Your name wouldn't be Kyle, would it?"

Kyle pried his eyes from the marshal's face looked at the smiling deputy and replied, "Yes. How did you know?"

Thom stepped close to Kyle, placed his hand on his shoulder then turned him toward the door before saying, "Let's go outside."

Both Ron Smith and Benji Green, the other two longtime deputies had been stunned when they saw Kyle, and only when Thom escorted him from the office did Benji say, "I can't believe it. If he isn't an Evans, then neither is Dylan or Bryn."

Once outside, Thom held out the envelope and said, "This arrived a couple of days ago and had us all wondering who the hell Kyle Evans was. The second you walked through the doorway I knew the answer."

"Why?"

"If you mixed Dylan and Bryn, subtracted a few years and a few pounds, then I'd see you."

Kyle accepted the envelope without looking at the address as he asked, "Then the marshal isn't my Uncle Dylan?"

Thom's eyebrows rose as he replied, "No. He's the new marshal, courtesy of our new governor. Dylan went out to Cheyenne City a few days ago to check out his new assignment. He should be back in a week or so. Can you clear up a mystery for us? You said that he's your uncle, but neither he nor Bryn had ever mentioned anyone named Kyle, much less a nephew."

"I didn't know they were my uncles until just before my mother died in June. I don't have any other family, so I came here to meet them. I don't expect anything from them, but my mother said I should come here."

"Well, Kyle, your Uncle Bryn is out in Denver and Dylan isn't back yet, but I'm sure that there's someone else who would like to meet you."

Kyle was relieved to hear that the marshal wasn't related but didn't know if there were more Evans living in Omaha.

"Who is that?" he asked.

"Come with me. It's only two blocks."

Kyle nodded then turned and began walking back east again before they turned south at the next corner. With each step, the questions sprouted in his mind and he appreciated the deputy marshal's silence. The fact that one uncle was already living in Denver and the other was moving to a place that he'd never heard of had already thrown his long-anticipated, imaginary welcoming into the mental waste bin.

The deputy soon turned down the walkway of a large house and Kyle felt shabby. He hadn't shaved in two days and his clothes were dirty but at least they weren't as bad as they'd been for most of his journey.

They mounted the porch steps, crossed the large, varnished porch and the deputy knocked loudly on the heavy front door.

Kyle was staring at the dark red paneled door with some level of trepidation when it suddenly swung open and he saw the smiling face of an older woman and somehow immediately knew who she was.

Meredith smiled at Thom Smythe then as she said, "Well, Thom what brings you…", she glanced at Kyle and stopped in mid-sentence.

Her mouth fell agape, and her right hand quickly flew to cover her astonishment as she stared into Kyle's hazel eyes.

Thom watched her reaction with a big smile on his face then turned to look at Kyle and saw a similar recognition as they both continued to silently stare at each other.

After twenty seconds, Thom said, "Mrs. Wittemore, this young man just arrived in our office. I believe that you and he have much to talk about."

Meredith didn't look at Thom as she whispered, "Yes. I believe we do."

Thom knew it was time to leave, so he just did an about face and hurried from the porch knowing that he'd find out more later.

Meredith then said, "Won't you come in?"

Kyle nodded then replied, "Thank you, ma'am," before entering the foyer as his grandmother closed the door.

She then asked, "Are you hungry?"

Kyle almost giggled at the question but replied, "No, ma'am. I'm fine. My name's Kyle, by the way."

"Let's have a seat in the parlor, Kyle, and you can unload your heavy pack."

"Thank you, ma'am. I've gotten so used to carrying it that I almost don't notice it anymore."

Meredith walked into the parlor ahead of Kyle but stole glances back at him several times before taking a seat.

Kyle slid his canteen to the carpeted floor then unstrapped his backpack and carefully set it down before leaning his bat against the backpack and sitting down on a chair to face his grandmother. He didn't understand why he'd made that instant connection, but there was now no doubt in his mind that he was an Evans. He was curious why the deputy had addressed her as Mrs. Wittemore.

"You'll have to excuse me for reacting as I did, Kyle, but as soon as I saw your face, it was a shock. I felt as if I had gone back in time and was talking to my son Dylan before he left Carbondale or when I spoke to Bryn. You have Dylan's hazel eyes, but Bryn's hair color and cheekbones. You're still yourself, of course, but the resemblance is remarkable. Now you must clear up the mystery that has me totally befuddled. Are you my grandson?"

Kyle nodded then replied, "Yes, ma'am. My mother, her maiden name was Bess Ann Nelson, was from Carbondale and it wasn't until just before she died on the third of June that she told me about my real father. She wasn't going to tell me until I was eighteen, but she was ill with a cancer in her stomach and knew she wouldn't last that long.

"She told me that my real father was Huw Lynn Evans, and they were going to run away and marry, but he died in a mine collapse. She didn't find out she was pregnant with me for a month afterwards and her father expelled her from their home. She moved to Wilkes-Barre and quickly married a man named Tom Nolan. He deserted us when I was around six."

"Bess Nelson? I remember her but only vaguely. I had suspected that she and Huw were seeing each other, but never asked about it. Why didn't she come to us after she was sent away?"

"She said that she was afraid that you might blame her somehow because you were all so upset about Huw and that you might do what her father did and accuse her of using his death to cover the identity of the man who had fathered me."

Meredith shook her head slowly and said, "That's such a tragedy, Kyle. If she had come to the house, I would have welcomed her with open arms. Did you know that Colwyn's son, Alwen, is living with Dylan now? We would have accepted her and you with no less love or devotion. But it doesn't change anything now. You're here with your family now."

Kyle dropped his eyes to the carpet and said, "This is strange and uncomfortable for me. Everything is so different, and I feel as if I don't belong here. Ever since I was a boy, all I knew was my mother, the two rooms we called home and the factory floor at the ironworks. I thought it would be wonderful if I actually found that I had a family, but I feel so out of place. I could be just a stranger off the street pretending to be your grandson."

Meredith smiled then said, "Look at me, Kyle."

He raised his eyes and once he looked at her, she accessed her motherly and grandmotherly voice and said, "Now, Mister Evans, enough of this! You do not need to prove who you are. I knew you were an Evans the moment I laid eyes on you. Yes, you're uncomfortable, but no less so than any young person in your situation would be. Now young man, before we do anything else, I will show you to your room where you can put away your things. I'll heat water for your bath and after you're clean and shaved, we'll have lunch with my husband to discuss what we'll do after that. Is that clear?"

Kyle couldn't help but to return her smile as he heard his mother's firm voice in hers and replied, "Yes, ma'am."

"Good. Now, let's get you into your room," she said as she rose.

———

An hour later, a freshly shaved Kyle sat at the kitchen table with his grandmother as he explained more about his life and the journey from Pennsylvania when the door opened and he heard a loud voice ask, "Where are you, wife?"

Meredith shouted back, "In the kitchen, Mister Wittemore."

She intentionally didn't mention Kyle's presence but wanted to see his reaction when he entered the room. She wasn't disappointed.

John Wittemore quickly stepped into the kitchen and as soon as he spotted Kyle, he stopped in mid-step, stared at him for a few brief seconds then looked back at his wife.

"You didn't tell me that we had a visitor, Mrs. Wittemore, and I'm sure that you have a reason for doing so."

As John took off his hat, Meredith said, "John, this is Kyle Evans. He's my grandson and just arrived from Pennsylvania. He didn't know he was Huw's son until early June."

John did a doubletake before saying, "No wonder I was a bit confused when I saw him."

He then reached out and shook Kyle's hand as he said, "I'm sure I'll hear your story in great detail, but I stopped by for lunch and expect to be fed."

Meredith laughed before standing then as she walked to the cold room, she said, "I was going to feed Kyle anyway, so I suppose I can fix something for you as well, husband."

John kissed her before joining Kyle at the table and saying, "Did she tell you why she's Mrs. Wittemore now?"

"No, sir. I just arrived a little while ago and I had to wash and shave first. I was just explaining how I got here."

"I married your grandmother after your grandfather and their other two sons died in a mine explosion seven years ago."

Kyle asked, "How is that possible? I thought my father died in a mine collapse before I was born."

"Your father must have been Huw, and he died in a different accident more than ten years before that. We lost Alwen and Colwyn in the bigger one."

Kyle didn't know how to respond to the revelation, so he just nodded.

The extended lunchtime was a constant question and answer period where Kyle learned much about his new family, including the current homes of both uncles and the number of cousins, including the expectant arrival of Grace Lynn in Denver.

But even as he had his questions answered and provided his own responses, Kyle found that there was so much more he needed to know, and it would take weeks if not months to adjust to his new life. He still had no idea what he would do or where he would live, but the warm welcome by his grandmother and her husband eliminated many of his concerns.

———

As Kyle was getting acquainted with his grandmother, a telegram arrived at the Denver U.S. Marshal's office. It was marked personal for Marshal Al Esposito, so the messenger had to hand it to the marshal directly.

Al looked at the message in his office, smiled and said to himself, "Well, now this is good news."

He then left the office and sent his reply back to Washington but didn't let his deputies know about the message yet, especially not Bryn. He wanted confirmation before he said a word.

———

Dylan reached the new end of line for the Union Pacific earlier than he'd expected as they were laying track at an incredible rate over the flatlands of western Nebraska and Dakota Territory. He guessed that they were twenty miles closer to Cheyenne City than they'd been when he left the last end of track three days ago.

He bought his ticket and horse transports for Crow and the pack horse before waiting at the watering station for the train to be ready to leave. It wasn't a scheduled train, but one of the working trains to advance the tracks westward. There was a passenger car to bring in more workers as well as two stock cars, but they'd be almost empty on the return trip. They'd pick up passengers that were heading back to Omaha, but he knew that there wouldn't be many.

Just two hours after arriving, Dylan was sitting in the lone passenger car by himself as the train roared eastward at a faster speed than a regular train would make. The bosses wanted that supply train back in Omaha to reload and send back as quickly as possible.

As the landscape flew by, Dylan wondered if he'd made the right decision to turn in his badge rather than move Gwen and the children to Cheyenne City. He'd been weighing that choice since he'd walked out of the telegraph office, and still wasn't convinced that it was the right one. He was also unsure of how Gwen would react to the news. The only thing that was sure to him was that he'd have another twenty hours of travel ahead of him before he talked to her but doubted that he'd be any closer to an answer before then.

———

Kyle tried to insist to his grandmother and Mister Wittemore that he could pay for his new clothes, but neither of them listened. After they had spent over two hours during their extended lunch, his grandmother had insisted that they go to the clothing store and fill all of the drawers in his new dresser.

After they finished shopping, John returned to work, then Kyle changed into some of his new clothes, but still wore his comfortable boots before Meredith inspected his appearance.

"Very nice, Mister Evans," she said as she tugged on his shirt sleeve.

"Can you harness a buggy?" she asked.

"Yes, ma'am."

"Good. Behind the house is a small barn with two horses and the buggy. Use the black gelding and when you've finished, come back into the kitchen and let me know it's ready."

"Um, may I ask where we'll be going?"

"We are going to meet your Aunt Gwendolyn and your six cousins."

Kyle nodded then turned and left the house to harness the buggy feeling as if he had been sucked into a whirlwind. Everything was happening so fast that he felt as if he barely had time to catch his breath.

———

The drive to Dylan and Gwen's home was a continuation of constant questions and answers as Meredith handled the reins.

As they climbed the last hill, Kyle asked, "What will I do now? I can't just sit around."

"That's up to you. When Dylan returns, which could be tomorrow or two weeks from now, he'll give you some ideas. John will have suggestions, too."

"I've never been on a boat before."

Meredith smiled and said, "Neither had John until we stepped aboard the *Providence* with Kyle and Alwen to make the trip here in '60."

"And now he owns a shipping salvage company? How did that happen?"

"That is a long story that is best told by Dylan and John, but mostly by Dylan. Here's the turn," she said as she tugged the right rein and the buggy made the turn into the long drive.

Kyle hadn't been prepared for the two houses, large barn or the extensive corral that still held a dozen horses, even after Bryn's animals had moved to his Double EE ranch outside of Denver.

"Uncle Dylan lives here?" he asked in awe then added, "Who lives in the second house?"

"Originally, Dylan and Gwen built it for her mother and sisters then after they all married and left, one of Dylan's deputies and his family lived there before his wife persuaded him to move back to Omaha. Since then, it's housed Bryn, then his wife Erin and their family, and now it's empty. Mrs. March, Gwen's nanny, lives in the big house."

"You said she might be moving to Cheyenne City soon. Will they sell everything?"

"I'm sure they will. And we'll sell the house and salvage business if they do because we've already asked Dylan if we could join them. Cheyenne City is only about a hundred miles north of Denver, where Bryn has his big ranch."

"I thought he was a deputy marshal."

"He is, but his ranch is just four miles southwest of Denver. From the way he describes it, I hope I get to see it. It's right at the foothills of the Rocky Mountains."

As she pulled the buggy to a stop before the house, Kyle said, "I haven't seen any real mountains since I left Pennsylvania."

Meredith set the handbrake, laughed then said, "From what I hear, you still haven't seen real mountains, Kyle."

As Kyle clambered out of the buggy, he spotted a herd of children racing out of the barn leaving a good-sized dust cloud in their wake.

Meredith exited and said, "There are most of your cousins, Kyle. There are two smaller ones in the house."

Kyle stood and waited for the youngsters who seemed to have turned their run into a contest as the boys jockeyed for position while the only girl trotted behind patiently.

Then just ten yards before they reached Kyle, the girl swung to the outside and shot past her brothers as if they were standing still and was giggling as she reached their grandmother and the tall young man standing beside her.

Eight-year-old Bethan drew to a sudden stop and instead of looking at her grandmother, she stared at Kyle and said, "Hello. I'm Bethan. You look like my dad and Uncle Bryn. Did anyone tell you that before?"

Kyle smiled down at Bethan and replied, "Yes, ma'am. Ever since I got here, folks have been telling me that very thing."

The boys had all plowed to a stop nearby as Bethan asked her question and all three of them stared up at Kyle with the same curious expression.

Meredith then said, "This is your cousin Kyle. He just got here from Pennsylvania and he didn't know that your father was his uncle until two months ago."

"Really?" asked Garth, "How come it took so long?"

"Let's go inside and introduce Kyle to your mom."

"Okay," Lynn said as he started for the porch.

Bethan smiled up at Kyle then took his hand and tugged him along behind her brothers.

Kyle stepped off and glanced at his smiling grandmother. Somehow, the reaction of his young cousins, especially Bethan, had washed away much of his awkwardness.

As Bethan towed him through the front door, Kyle spotted a middle-aged woman holding a baby and for just a heartbeat thought she was Gwen and almost greeted her as such.

But no sooner had he realized his mistake when a laughing little girl raced into the room and Gwen chased her from the hallway with her hands out in front of her with tickle-threatening fingers.

She was laughing herself as she stopped and smiled at Meredith then turned her eyes to Kyle and her big smile evaporated as she stared at him.

Kyle was now used to the reaction, so he smiled and said, "I'm Kyle, and I'm pleased to meet you Aunt Gwendolyn."

Gwen stepped closer to Kyle then stopped and slowly said, "It's uncanny. I felt as if I had just seen Dylan for the first time on the deck of the *Providence*. How old are you, Kyle?"

"I'll be eighteen in January."

"Dylan was eighteen when we met and except for some small differences and your hair color, you could be his twin brother."

Cari was standing beside her mother staring up at Kyle and said, "You look like my daddy."

Kyle looked down at her round face and said, "And you look like a princess."

Cari grinned then looked back at her mother and said, "He said I'm a princess, Mommy, just like daddy does."

Gwen then shook her head slightly and said, "I'm sorry for being so distracted, but I'm sure that you can understand. Let me introduce you to my offspring and then we can talk."

Gwen went down the line, saying, "This is Lynn Robert, our oldest, he's ten now. Alwen Lynn is ten too, but even though he's technically our nephew, we treat him as our son and slap his behind just as vigorously as the other boys when he misbehaves. Then we have Garth Lynn, who is nine, eight-year-old Bethan Ann, and then that short one holding onto my skirt with a death grip is almost-four-year-old Cari Efa."

Then she turned to Mrs. March and said, "This is Alba March, my good friend and my invaluable helper to keep control of the brood. She's holding Brian Lynn, who was born on April the second."

Kyle acknowledged each of the children in turn then greeted Mrs. March.

Gwen then took charge and maneuvered the children down the hall to the kitchen as Kyle followed Mrs. March and Meredith.

It was almost a repeat of the long lunch that he'd had with his grandmother and John Wittemore earlier, except that he learned more about his uncles and his Aunt Erin. The children insisted on asking their own questions, and the boys were especially interested in his use of the bat as a weapon. He hadn't told them of its intended purpose for hitting a baseball because there were so many other things to talk about.

When it was getting close to suppertime, Meredith said she and Kyle had to return to the house, but they'd be back tomorrow.

Before they left, Meredith asked, "Do you think that Dylan is going to move? He seemed to be less certain about it than I'd expected."

"I know. I told him that I really wouldn't mind at all and that I was missing the excitement of our earlier days. I felt that I'd put extra weight on his shoulders when I had originally said that I'd miss our home here. I wanted him to make the decision without having that worry. We'll just have to see what happens when he returns."

"I'm certain that he doesn't want to work with John in the salvage business and even John is getting a bit tired of the job."

"All we can do is wait, Mom," Gwen said before she turned to Kyle then surprised him when she stretched on her tiptoes and kissed him on the cheek.

"It's wonderful that you came to join us, Kyle. I can't wait to see Dylan's expression when he meets you."

"I look forward to meeting him, too."

He then had to shake each of his cousins' hands before following Meredith out of the house.

As they rode back toward Omaha in the evening sun, he asked, "You said that you weren't sure that Uncle Dylan would go to Cheyenne City. Doesn't he have to go where they send him?"

"He does, but if he doesn't want to go, he can turn in his badge. If he does, then I don't know how he'll react. I imagine he'll just try to find a job as a sheriff somewhere. He was born to be a lawman and I don't think he'll be satisfied doing anything else."

Kyle nodded as the buggy rolled over the second hill. As they reached the valley before the last hill, Meredith told Kyle the story of how Erin's brother and his friend had trapped Bryn to the east and were about to shoot him when Dylan arrived just because of the weather and he had to prepare for Bryn and Erin's wedding the next day.

Kyle studied the terrain where the incident had occurred over three years earlier and tried to recall what he had been doing back then. It wasn't hard to imagine as each of his days was exactly like the other except for Sundays. He'd get up in the dark, help his mother as best he could then after breakfast, he'd go to work at the ironworks and return in the dark during the cold months and with the sun setting when the days were longer.

Every day blended into the next and it wasn't until his mother began experiencing the early signs of her cancer that anything changed and only then, it had changed for the worse. Now maybe things would be better. If his first day in Omaha with his new family was any indication, they would be much better.

―――――

Al Esposito didn't get a reply to his telegram by the time the office closed, so he didn't tell anyone of its contents, but would tell Jean and knew that she'd be ecstatic with the news. She'd be going home.

―――――

Dylan left the passenger car as it took on coal and water in North Platte. He could already hear the loud ruckus in the distance that had earned the town its unsavory, and well-deserved reputation. There weren't any gunshots, but he wouldn't have been surprised if there had been. He knew that there was a sheriff and two deputies in town, yet it still seemed almost as wild as it had been before the Union Pacific moved on after that long winter.

He then looked back west and hoped that his decision not to accept the position didn't turn Cheyenne City into another hell hole. He knew that North Platte would probably settle down as more farmers immigrated and homesteaded around the town, but its reputation would take a lot longer to change.

The train's whistle announcing its departure startled him, but he quickly turned and jogged back across the platform and hopped onto the passenger car's metal steps.

Once he was in his seat, he pulled out his pocket watch. He had set it using the clock at the Union Pacific's massive station in Omaha, and saw the hands pointing to almost exactly eight o'clock. It was just about three hundred miles to Omaha, so at the supply train's speed, he should be arriving in town just in time for breakfast where he'd break the news to Gwen. Then after getting her approval, he would wire Al Esposito and ask if he'd like a new deputy.

———

"Something's going on with Al and I don't know what it is," Bryn said as he sat across from Erin at the kitchen table.

"What do you mean?"

"I don't know. He received a telegram and then left for a while. He didn't tell us what was in it because it was marked personal, but he was trying to act as if he wasn't excited but doing a bad job of it. He never was much of a poker player."

"What do you think it was?" Katie asked.

"I have no idea, but he was acting so queer all afternoon that we all began to wonder. At first, we thought it had something to do with Cal Burris and Golden, but that didn't last long because he was so damned chipper the rest of the day. It was like he found out that Jean was going to have another baby, or he just had an unknown rich uncle die and leave him a gold mine."

"Do you think he'll tell you tomorrow?".

"I hope so. If he doesn't, he'll have four U.S. Deputy Marshals lash him to his chair until he confesses."

Flat Jack laughed and said, "That'd be a sight. Then he'd fire all of your butts and you'd have to stay out here and help me with the horses."

Bryn grinned and replied, "There are worse sentences, Jack. How's the buckskin mare doing?"

"I'm a bit worried about her. She shoulda foaled last month, but she's still getting bigger, so maybe I just got my dates wrong."

Erin laughed and said, "That's what I keep saying. Grace Lynn is kicking up a storm and wants out."

Katie then said, "I'm ready whenever she is, Erin."

Bryn looked at Erin's younger sister and hoped she was right. He still wished that he had an older midwife with more experience in the house when she went into labor, but Erin has insisted that Katie would handle it well.

As he looked at Katie, he thought that if she never married, it would be a tragedy. She was such a delightful young woman and despite her Irish stubbornness, she was every bit as much fun to have around as his wife. Still, he'd learned his lesson about matchmaking even before he contemplated trying to inject Cal into her life. He still believed Gwen when she had told him that there had been no matchmaking on her part when she hired Erin as her nanny. Erin certainly hadn't enlightened him either.

———

As Kyle lay on top of his quilts in the overly stuffy house despite the bedroom window being wide open, he wondered if fate had somehow worked its will to have him arrive here just when his new Uncle Dylan was returning from Cheyenne City. Maybe he was supposed to join him there to help him as the new town grew. Perhaps that was where his future lay, in the western part of Dakota Territory.

He smiled as the idea washed over him. He'd never ridden a horse and had barely learned how to fire a gun, yet here he was imagining himself helping a United States Marshal tame a wild, growing town out in the middle of nowhere. If anyone had suggested that it was even remotely possible as he stepped to the plate in that baseball game at Wilkes-Barre, he would have thought they were candidates for the crazy house. But now he thought that maybe it was his destiny. If it was, it was a destiny that would take time and a lot of education and training.

He was well aware of his overwhelming ignorance in almost everything. All he'd learned after the third year at school had come from his mother, and yet she taught him so much, including how to dance.

As he looked at his bat leaning on the wall near the window, he thanked her for those lessons, and decided that he'd still need to keep practicing even after he learned to ride and shoot his pistol. Maybe he wouldn't ever need the bat as a weapon again, but he'd learned that the balance that he was close to perfecting during his waltzing practices would serve him well in other confrontations; confrontations that he was certain would be in his future.

CHAPTER 7

The train slowed as it approached the already bustling yard in Omaha and Dylan stood before it came to a stop. There were six passengers in the car now and all of them had to exit the train before it was serviced, turned around and loaded for another trip to end of track.

The sun was barely above the horizon as he stepped out onto the platform then headed for the large stock corral to collect Crow and the packhorse.

Just fifteen minutes later, he was winding his way over the tracks to take a shortcut to the south road to his house and once he reached the hardpacked roadway, he didn't have to guide the gelding who seemed to be anxious to return to his home barn.

The sun was higher in the sky as he turned down the long drive and looked at his home through the eyes of a stranger. He tried to imagine someone else living where he and Gwen had spent so many wonderful and some difficult days together and found it almost painful. He began to think that maybe he should forget about even bringing up the idea of leaving their home to join Bryn. He was beginning to believe that Gwen's comments about being excited about going to Cheyenne City weren't necessarily how she felt.

He rode directly to the barn and dismounted then spent twenty minutes unsaddling and caring for the two horses before leaving them in their stalls. He threw his saddlebags over his shoulder then with his Winchester in his right hand he headed for the house.

There was already smoke coming from the cookstove pipe, which was to be expected in a home with so many youngsters and a four-month-old baby. He may have been drifting into a funk as he headed home, but the thought of seeing Gwen and the children again brightened his spirit as he picked up his pace to the back porch.

Dylan hopped onto the porch without the assistance of the steps and swung the door open before anyone was able to reach the inside knob.

"Dylan!" Gwen exclaimed, "You're back already!"

Dylan smiled as he approached her then scooped her into his arms and kissed her as if they were newlyweds as he held her above the floor ignoring the childish giggles from the table.

He set Gwen down and said, "We need to talk."

"We do, sir. But sit down and we'll feed you while you tell me what's so important."

Dylan filled a cup with hot coffee then took his appointed seat at the head of the large table after Lynn Robert made a hasty exit from the chair.

"Gwen," he asked, "before I say anything, I want to ask if you were serious when you told me that you were excited about possibly moving to Cheyenne City."

Gwen turned and let Mrs. March handle the eggs as she asked, "Why is it important? Did you turn the job down?"

Dylan wasn't surprised that she'd already guessed the reason he'd asked, so he answered, "I sent a telegram to the boss in Washington before I left Cheyenne City. I'll go into the office in a little while and see if they've received confirmation of my resignation yet."

"Why did you do it, Dylan? I know that it wasn't the best assignment in the world, but you're a lawman and I didn't want you to give up the badge because you didn't like the place."

"I know, sweetheart, but it was just so new and didn't have anything that young children needed. I don't think they even thought about a school yet."

"Alba and I can teach them at home, Dylan. It's how children have learned since the dawn of time."

"I know, Gwen, and I wish you weren't so disappointed. I really believed that you wouldn't be happy there."

Gwen stepped closer rested her hand on his shoulder then smiled and said, "I'm not disappointed, Dylan. I could never be disappointed in anything you do. I'm just sad that you had to give up something that was so important to you just to make me and our children happy."

Dylan nodded then took a sip of his coffee rather than continue the difficult conversation, but it didn't matter.

Garth then asked, "We're not going now?"

Before Dylan could reply, Gwen exclaimed, "Sssh! Enough questions. We have to tell your dad about our news now. Don't we?"

The non-move forgotten, each youngster broke into a grin as Dylan looked up at his smiling wife and asked, "What news?"

"Yesterday, your mother brought a visitor to the house and I introduced him to each of his cousins."

Dylan blinked as he rummaged through the family tree and was still lost after a few seconds, so he asked, "Which cousin was he? Was it one of your sisters' children?"

"No, sir. He is your brother's son."

Now Dylan was seriously confused as he shook his head and said, "They already met Bryn's sons and they're all in Colorado."

"No, he isn't Bryn's son, and obviously he isn't Colwyn's because Alwen is sitting right there. He's Huw's son, Kyle, and he arrived yesterday from Pennsylvania."

Gwen was enjoying herself immensely as she watched her husband squirm.

She finally sat in the chair beside him and said, "I'm sorry for doing it this way, Dylan, but I'll admit that I had some fun watching your face."

"Tell me who he is and why he suddenly showed up in our lives. Are you sure he's not a fraud?"

"Oh, no. He's definitely an Evans. When I first saw him, I was speechless. He looked so much like you were when I first saw you. Your mother felt the same way and after he told her the story, it all made perfect sense."

"But how is that even possible? Huw died in that mine collapse and never even married."

"You don't need to be married to father a child, Mister Evans. Kyle explained that his mother and Huw were planning on eloping because her father hated the Welsh. I guess they were close to leaving Carbondale when he died, and she discovered she was pregnant soon afterwards. Her father sent her away, so she went to Wilkes-Barre where she quickly married, then seven months later, she gave birth to Kyle. She didn't tell him until she was dying of stomach cancer. We're the only family he has now, Dylan."

"Did he show you any proof?"

Gwen smiled and replied, "When you see him, sweetheart, you won't need to read any piece of paper."

Bethan then exclaimed, "He looks just like you, Dad, only skinnier."

Dylan ran his fingers through his hair then asked, "Where is he staying?"

"He's with your mother and John right now. Personally, I think he'd be more comfortable living in the second house."

"We'll talk about that after I get back from the office. I'll swing by and visit mom too, just to see him."

"That should convince you. Now before I feed you, tell me what your plans are now that you're no longer a United States Marshal? We're still in good shape for money, so you have options."

"I haven't decided yet, but I need to get the confirmation of the boss's acceptance of my resignation. He should have sent it already because I wired it three days ago."

"Take your time, husband," Gwen replied before she rose, kissed him on the cheek then returned to the stove to help Alba with the breakfast.

Dylan sat sipping his coffee almost oblivious to the chattering of the children as they told stories about their new cousin. He caught snippets that reached his mind as it still tried to come to grip with the impact it could have on their lives.

As Gwen set his plate before him, he asked, "How old is he, Gwen?"

"He'll turn eighteen in January. He looks a bit older, though, despite his need to put on some pounds. He's almost as tall as you, so he's a bit taller than Bryn already. He had Bryn's shade of light brown hair, but your hazel green eyes. It really is astonishing to look at him, Dylan."

Dylan nodded then began to eat his food. If this Kyle was almost eighteen, then he could be handy to have around now that he was the only adult male in the house. He'd always been a bit concerned when he left Gwen alone with the children even though she was reasonably proficient with her .22 caliber pistol and the shotgun. Mrs. March never learned to use either but had a stiff spine and could stare down most men.

He decided to reserve judgement until he met the boy. He knew he'd be able to get a good idea of his character after just a short examination. It was one of the advantages of dealing with the lower echelons of men for ten years.

———

Kyle walked with John toward the docks still scanning the busy town. John wanted to show him the operation and his two salvage tugs, the *River Warrior* and the smaller *Saving Grace*. Both had been overhauled in the spring and were in excellent shape, which had proven to be a good investment when there had been eleven extractions of stuck riverboats and two losses over the past four months.

The second boat to drop below the Missouri was the *Adirondack* and the cargo alone had netted John an incredible eleven thousand dollars. As successful as the business was, he was getting tired of working and wanted to spend some time with Meredith just enjoying his last years. The arthritis in his hands was just the first stage of the disease which had now progressed to his hips and knees. He wasn't sure that Cheyenne City was where he wanted to go, but Meredith wanted to be near Dylan, and Bryn would be just a day away and he always did anything he could for her. He was hoping that she'd at least decide they should move to Denver rather than the unknown town of Cheyenne City.

When they reached the docks, they boarded the *River Warrior*, and John did more than just show him the tug itself, he explained the reason for the two swivel guns on the bow and then showed him where they could attach the rope-cutting blade if the Indians tried to float another boom across the Missouri to stop them.

Naturally, Kyle was intrigued by all of the stories that John and his grandmother had told him about his uncles since he'd arrived, and after talking to Gwen, he had an inkling that there were many more tales, and some were even more exciting.

After a much shorter tour of the *Saving Grace*, which had no Evans history behind it, they walked to the warehouse, passed through the bustling, full warehouse floor then entered John's small office in the back.

"Is all of that out there from things that you've salvaged from sunk riverboats?" Kyle asked as he sat down.

"Yes, sir. We sell most of it to merchants right after we bring it ashore. After we unload, this place is like an Arab marketplace. It slows down after a couple of days and the rest kind of leaves piecemeal. Sometimes, folks come in and buy just a thing or two."

Kyle wanted to ask more but didn't want to sound as if he had only appeared because he wanted a handout.

John then leaned back and asked, "What do you want to do, Kyle?"

Kyle shrugged then answered, "I don't know yet. All I've ever done is manual labor on the factory floor at the ironworks. I really don't have any skills. I'm not that smart, either."

"I don't see that. Why don't you think you're smart?"

"Maybe I didn't say that right. I meant that I don't know much."

"That's ignorance, Kyle, and we can help you a lot there. There's no rush anyway. When Dylan returns from Cheyenne City in a little while, we'll have a better idea of what lies ahead."

"That's what my grandmother said."

"Why don't you head back to the house and tell her that I need to stay here for lunch today. I'm expecting the carriagemaker to stop by and look at the wheels from the last salvage job."

"Okay, Mister Wittemore," Kyle said as he stood then waved and headed out the door.

As he walked to the exit, he glanced at the piles of all manner of items that were stacked on shelves or just on the floor itself. He figured you could build a house with the things that were inside.

After he stepped back into the bright morning sun, he turned left and headed back to 12th Street having to dodge wheeled and horse traffic as he made his way to the safety of the boardwalk.

He'd barely made it when he had to stop and let a rider pass then glanced up at the tall man in the saddle who had pulled his horse to a stop and stared down at him.

If it had been any other man, he would have just jogged around his horse quickly expecting a kick for getting in his way, but as soon as he saw the man's face, he knew that it wasn't just any man, he was his Uncle Dylan.

"Are you Kyle?" Dylan asked as he looked down.

"Yes, sir. You must be my Uncle Dylan. Gwen said you weren't coming back for a week or so."

Dylan then swung his right leg around Crow's butt and stepped down before he replied, "I got back early this morning."

Before he could say anything else, a buckboard driver shouted from behind, "Move that nag! You're blocking traffic!"

Dylan waved then led Crow to the side of the roadway and waited for Kyle to join him. He had to admit that there was no doubt that he was an Evans, but only had Bryn's face to use in comparison.

"Where are you headed?" Dylan asked.

"I was returning to your mother's house. Mister Wittemore just showed me his business."

Dylan nodded then said, "Tell my mother that I'll be stopping by after I head over to the office."

"May I come along? I don't have anything else to do."

Dylan nodded and replied, "Sure. It'll only be a few minutes anyway."

After he'd turned Crow and started leading him back down the road with Kyle walking beside him, Dylan asked, "Why did you come all the way from Pennsylvania?"

"After my mother died, I had no one else and when she told me who my real father was, it was more curiosity than anything else."

"Didn't you have a girlfriend or some pals?"

"No girlfriend and my friends were just co-workers at the factory."

Dylan glanced at Kyle and felt a measure of sympathy for the young man. He'd seen countless boys start work before they were ten and what little free time that they had was absorbed by doing chores at home. They had no real life available to them because they had no spare time at all. He'd been fortunate because there were so many men in the family, yet for more than ten years, Kyle had been the sole source of income and support for his mother. It must have been a real burden to know that you couldn't afford to get sick or injured and then fail in what you felt were your duties.

Dylan then said, "I'm going to the office to turn in my badge. I turned down the assignment to Cheyenne City, but I need to receive the confirmation from my boss in Washington to make it official. It should be in the office now, so all I'll need to do is drop off the badge, shake my old deputies' hands then we can head over to my mother's and give her the news."

Kyle was surprised that Dylan had told him and asked, "Why did you tell me? I just met you and I could be a scam artist."

Dylan smiled at him and replied, "That was my first thought when Gwen told me that you had just appeared out of the blue, but then she said I'd have no doubt about your story once I met you. She was right. I thought I was looking at Bryn the moment I saw your face."

"Everyone tells me I look more like you."

"Well, I don't spend a lot of time looking in the mirror. How'd you know it was me in the first place? You've never seen Bryn."

"Your mother showed me a tintype of Bryn from the war and then had me look in the mirror."

"That explains that. We'll talk more later, but it's time for me to end my career with the United States Marshals Service."

Dylan tied off Crow then walked through the open door of the office with Kyle following.

He'd barely crossed the threshold when Thom Smythe spotted him and exclaimed, "What are you doing back so soon? We weren't expecting you for two weeks."

Dylan walked closer to the desk pulling off his badge as he stepped across the office floor then stopped and said, "I sent my resignation to the big boss three days ago. I came to drop off my badge, assuming that I received a telegram confirming that he'd received and accepted my resignation."

Thom just stared at Dylan in stunned silence as all five feet and six inches of Marshal Edgar Claggett stepped into the room.

"I was wondering why we received this. We don't get many personal telegrams to the office," he said as he held up a sealed sheet of paper.

Dylan was technically still a U.S. Marshal, so he couldn't slap the sly grin off the man's face but knew he wouldn't have done it anyway. The man was too small and wasn't worth the effort.

Marshal Claggett handed the sheet to Dylan who just took it from his hand before dropping his badge on the desk.

He then shook Thom Smythe's hand and walked to each of the other deputy marshals who were present to shake theirs then turned to Kyle and said, "Let's go and tell my mother, Kyle."

Kyle nodded and turned as Dylan strode behind him. After they reached Crow, Dylan just crumpled the sheet in his right hand and tossed it onto the boardwalk in front of the office before he began to untie Crow.

Kyle watched the crushed paper ball bounce onto the wood and then after Dylan turned away, he reached down and caught it before the breeze took it away.

"Aren't you even going to read it?" he asked.

Dylan turned with his reins in his hand and said, "There's no point, Kyle. It'll only put me in a bad mood. You can read it if you want. You can read, can't you?"

"Yes, sir," Kyle replied but was hesitant to open the personal message.

Dylan saw his reluctance and said, "I'm ordering you to read it, Mister Evans. Then you can do whatever you want with it."

Kyle unsealed the telegram unfolded the sheet and began to read the first telegram he'd ever seen, and it was a long one that covered almost the entire page.

As he read his eyebrows rose before he slowly said, "Uncle Dylan, you might want to tie off your horse and read this."

Dylan looked at Kyle but didn't bother tying the reins again before he ripped the telegram from Kyle's hand and turned it to the written side to see what had inspired Kyle. As he read, his mind wasn't believing what his eyes were telling him. *And he'd almost thrown the telegram away!*

"Bless you, Kyle!" he exclaimed then added, "Let's go back inside!"

Kyle was grinning as he followed his excited uncle into the office again and as he watched, he saw the astonished faces of the lawmen in the room stare at him as Dylan stormed to the desk, snatched his badge from desktop and pinned it on.

Thom was the first to speak when he asked, "They didn't accept your resignation?"

Dylan was grinning as widely as Kyle when he replied, "Nope. He said that he had to replace one of his assistant marshals at the headquarters in Washington, then that rippled down through the service and when he got my telegram, he'd already sent one to the head of the Kansas City office, notifying him of his promotion."

"You're going to Kansas City?" asked Beni Green.

"No, sir. The new head of the Kansas City office will be Marshal Al Esposito. I'll be taking his place in Denver. Can you believe it? I'll be working with Bryn again after all."

The deputies all crowded around Dylan and shook his hand, pounded him on the back and expressed their congratulations as Kyle watched with a great deal of satisfaction knowing that he'd prevented a family disaster already. It also meant that he'd be meeting his Uncle Bryn soon.

Dylan finally said, "Well, boys, I've got to stop over at my mother's house and then head back to tell Gwen. I don't think she'll be disappointed this time."

After one more brief round of congratulatory back slaps, Dylan waved and headed for the doorway following Kyle.

Once outside, he grabbed Crow's reins and said, "Let's go tell my mother and then I can't wait to see the expression on Gwen's face."

Kyle thought that Dylan would mount his horse to get there more quickly, but he didn't and continued to walk alongside Kyle.

"Kyle, you sure saved my bacon. If I hadn't read that telegram and sent a confirmation reply, then I would have lost my badge and not known about the assignment to Denver."

"Wouldn't they just send another one if you didn't answer?"

"Not if Edgar Claggett sent a telegram telling them that I had left my badge on the desk."

"He'd do that?"

"He'd do it with a song in his heart. That reminds me. The main telegraph office is just a little out of the way, so we'll swing by there and I'll get that on the wires. I'm glad I didn't write a letter."

"Letter!" Kyle exclaimed, "In all the excitement, I forgot about the letter that they gave me when I got here. It was sent to me care of you at the marshal's office. I stuck it in my jacket pocket and it's still there unopened."

"Who would send you a letter and also knew you were coming here?"

"It has to be from the Neumans, a farm family that I stayed with for a week or so in Pennsylvania. There was an incident with a jealous beau that might have left them worried that he might have killed me."

"You'll have to tell me that story later. Did you shoot the man?"

"No, sir. I used my half-finished baseball bat that I was using as a walking staff, but I did get his pistol after I knocked him off of his horse."

Dylan glanced at Kyle and said, "Now, I've really got to hear that story. Hold the reins while I go inside."

Kyle took Crow's reins before Dylan hopped onto the boardwalk and zipped into the large telegraph office. Kyle was astonished at the number of wires that were being fed into the building. He'd seen other multi-line telegraph offices before in the larger towns he'd visited, but even the cities didn't have one this expansive. He guessed it had something to do with the Union Pacific but would have to ask Dylan if he remembered.

He still was irritated with himself for not reading the letter. He had only guessed the sender when Dylan had asked who could have known where he was going and why. He assumed it was Mister Neuman who had written the letter, but there was also the chance that it was from Lisa.

He'd never spent that much time alone with a girl before, and it had only been a few minutes. But after his initial discomfort, he discovered that he had enjoyed talking to her. *What if Lisa wrote the letter and pleaded with him to return? Would he leave his new family to go back to visit her?*

He doubted that it would be the right decision to leave again after just arriving. He was already becoming fond of his new family and it had only been a day. When he returned to his room, he'd read the letter and then make his decision. He hoped the letter was from Mister Neuman.

Dylan popped back out of the telegraph office just five minutes after entering and Kyle handed him the reins.

As they resumed their walk toward 12th Street, Dylan said, "Now, without going into the reasons for the confrontation, at least not yet. Tell me about how you managed to knock a man from a horse and get his pistol when all you had was a big stick."

Kyle had to set a starting point before he began, saying, "I knew that he was tracking me on the roadway, but he wasn't there when I looked, so…"

As Dylan listened, he was impressed with Kyle's rational thinking when most men he knew would have panicked or done something stupid. He'd even taken the time to cover his stacked belongings with a dark slicker to keep them from alerting the rider to his presence. When Kyle finally finished the abbreviated narrative, Dylan was even more convinced that the young man was an Evans.

"Those were all good tactical decisions, Kyle," Dylan said as they approached the house.

"I don't know what tactical means, Uncle Dylan. Everything I did just seemed the best way to avoid getting killed. I learned a lot when I almost got stabbed in the back during the early part of the journey."

Dylan tied off Crow and said, "Now, you have another story to tell me, but let's go and break the happy news to my mother."

———

As expected, Meredith was ecstatic when Dylan told her that he had accepted the assignment to replace Al Esposito for the second time but hoped that he didn't continue the habit and follow him to Kansas City.

"When will we move, Dylan?" she asked excitedly.

"I'll have to go there in the next few days to meet with Al and set things up. I'll send a telegram to him and Bryn letting them know that I'll be coming. While I'm gone, you, John and Gwen can start making the arrangements for the move. We can rent a house if we have to before we build our own. I'm sure with four square miles of land, Bryn won't mind us using an acre or two."

Meredith had never lost her big smile as she said, "Can I tell John when he comes home?"

"Of course, Mom. I need to ride back and tell Gwen now. By the way, we all have Kyle to thank for not letting me do one of the stupidest things imaginable. I've got to go."

Meredith kissed her son on the cheek before he turned and shook Kyle's hand and said, "Thanks again, Kyle. Go read that letter before you forget again. Maybe that girl doesn't want her beau anymore. You're probably better looking, too."

Dylan then shot out of the house as Meredith turned to Kyle and asked for two explanations: how he'd saved Dylan from the stupid mistake and why a girl would be writing to him.

Both explanations only took a few minutes, but after he told her that John was going to stay at the office for lunch, Meredith quickly donned her hat and bustled out the door, leaving Kyle alone in the big house.

He stood watching the doorway for a few seconds then turned and walked up the stairs to the second floor and entered his new bedroom where he finally removed the letter from his jacket pocket before sitting on the bed.

The handwriting didn't look feminine, so he crudely ripped open the first letter he'd ever received, at least courtesy of the United States Postal Service. The first was still carefully protected in his top dresser drawer and he had promised himself and his mother that he would keep it safe until the day he left this mortal plane and was reunited with her and finally meet Huw Evans, his father.

He breathed a sigh of relief that it was just a brief letter from Karl Neuman to make sure that he'd arrived safely. As Kyle had originally suspected, Mister Neuman was concerned that Michael Lowry hadn't killed him and buried him in a forest. There was no mention of Lisa at all and despite his relief, felt a twinge of regret. She was a pretty girl.

He then set the letter on his quilts, so he wouldn't forget to write a reply. He would write it now but didn't know where he could find paper and an envelope. He wasn't about to start snooping around in the house.

Kyle sat thinking about the news that Dylan and the entire Evans clan in Omaha would soon be moving to Denver and felt the same growing sense of curiosity and excitement that had driven him across the continent. It was the desire to see something he had never seen before and to do things that he never thought possible.

Until that terrible day in early June, all he'd expected out of life was to work as an unskilled laborer and probably die before he was fifty. He hadn't even thought it was likely that he'd marry and have a family. Now everything had changed.

He was still far too ignorant to really take on an important role, but he desperately wanted to learn. He suddenly felt the urge to make his Uncle Dylan and his grandmother proud of him. He'd always wanted to make his mother proud of him, but never had the tools or the opportunity to do anything exceptional for her, but now he had both.

———

Dylan had pushed Crow a bit as he climbed and descended the two hills before ascending the last rise to his home at the top of the third.

When he turned down the drive, he spotted the children chasing after Peanut who seemed to enjoy being the object of their attention in many of their games. He hadn't grown an inch since Dylan had ridden back with him from the ferry incident but hadn't seemed to age either. At least now he wasn't so scruffy as the children delighted in brushing him. He was surprised that Peanut didn't purr as they did.

They saw him riding toward the house forgot about chasing Peanut, then raced in his direction stopping just as he dismounted.

Lynn asked, "Why are you still wearing your badge, Dad? Didn't they take it?"

"No, sir. The big boss said that I was still a marshal and I had to go where he sent me without crying about it."

"So, we're going to Cheyenne City?" asked Garth.

"We'll be leaving in a couple of weeks, but we need to go and tell your mom."

Bethan took her father's hand before he climbed the porch steps and Alwen raced in front to open the door.

"Mom, dad's home!" he shouted.

Gwen was sitting on the couch with Brian on her lap and replied, "I can see that, Al. I'm right here and there's no reason to shout."

She then looked at her husband and made the same observation that Lynn had earlier and asked the same question, "Why are you still wearing your badge?"

Dylan dropped his floppy leather hat on the table then walked to the couch and sat down beside his small wife as their other children plopped onto the floor and Alba March entered from the kitchen.

"I just explained to our curious brood that the head of the service didn't accept my resignation and that I would accept the assignment."

Despite her efforts to hide it, he saw the disappointment in her brown eyes as she said, "When do we have to be there? Do we need to wait until the railroad gets there?"

"I hope not. From what I hear, the railroad won't arrive for at least another year or maybe two."

Gwen was confused and said, "But I thought they were supposed to get there before the end of the year."

"Oh," Dylan said as he stretched it out, "I can see why you would be confused, sweetheart. I guess I should have explained the other part of the telegram."

"What other part?"

"The part that ordered me to take over Al Esposito's spot in Denver. He's been reassigned to Kansas City and I have to take over by the first of September."

"You, you!" Gwen exclaimed as she sought to find an appropriate insult in the presence of the children who were already standing and bouncing as they cheered.

Dylan disarmed her outrage by kissing her furrowed brow and saying, "I'm sorry, Gwen. I was just going to tell you straight, but when Garth asked if we were going to Cheyenne City, I thought you'd have more fun hearing the news this way."

"Well, sir, I didn't have more fun. However, the news is so amazing, I'll forgive you for that extremely poor delivery. We're really going to be reunited with Bryn and Erin? I can't wait to see them again. Maybe we can get there before she delivers Grace Lynn. She's due near the end of August."

"Maybe we can. Mom was really excited about it, and I'm sure that John will be as well."

"What about Kyle? Did you even meet him?"

"I accidentally met him on the road when I had to stop Crow from trampling him. The similarity between him and Bryn was so striking that I knew in an instant who he was. He asked if he could come along with me to the office, and I wanted to talk to him anyway, so we chatted along the way.

"Gwen, Kyle found out about the new orders before I did. I had turned in my badge and didn't even bother opening the personal telegram that I was convinced was an acceptance of my resignation. I had crumpled it up and tossed it onto the boardwalk before the office, but Kyle grabbed it and asked me if I was going to even read it. Even then, I was so disgusted with giving up my badge because of that weasel who now sat in my chair that I told him to read it if he felt like it. You can imagine my reaction when he handed it back to me and told me that it wasn't what I thought it was."

Gwen smiled and asked, "I hope you told him that he'd be joining us in Denver."

"I'm not sure if I did, but I will when I see him again, just in case he hasn't figured it out yet. He's a remarkable young man, Gwen, and I think he'll be a real asset to the family."

"He is. It was a heartbreaking event that sent him to us, but I'm so happy that he's here."

"I sent a telegram to Denver already, so Bryn will know that we're coming. I'll go there in a couple of days and meet with Al Esposito to get a rundown on the office and the current cases and overall situation. I'll find someplace for us to live while we have our new house built and maybe I'll bring Kyle along so he can meet Bryn. John might want to join us so he can arrange for his own house to be constructed, too. By the time we leave Omaha, they'll probably be halfway done already."

"Mom can stay with us while you're all away, but don't stay too long. I want to be there when Erin has her little girl."

Dylan smiled then replied, "Your trick may not work, you know."

"Tell that to Bethan."

Dylan smiled at Bethan and their other gloriously happy children as they chattered about seeing Uncle Bryn, Aunt Erin and their cousins again. They seemed just as excited about seeing Katie Mitchell, who had been almost like a big sister when she had been their nanny before Bryn moved them all to Denver.

———

The family news of the Denver assignment was ripping through Omaha as Al Esposito received a second personal telegram from Washington.

He was in his office when it arrived and after the messenger left, he quickly popped off the seal and read the expected confirmation message.

"Well, I'll be damned!" he exclaimed to himself before he quickly rose and left the office.

The only deputy outside was Bert Willis, the youngest deputy marshal after Cal accepted the job as sheriff in Golden. That move still had Al worried even though they hadn't heard any bad news since he'd taken the job. He and Bryn both suspected that Cornbread Funk was just biding his time to let things cool off. Bryn had told Al that he'd make unrequested visits to Cal to keep a feel for the situation, but Cal was an affable sort and was skilled with his pistol but had a habit of acting before he thought.

"Well, Bert, you'll be the first one to know. I've been reassigned to the Kansas City office and have to be there by the first of September."

Bert was startled before he asked, "Who's taking over? Is it John?"

"Nope. They're sending in an experienced marshal. Does the name Dylan Evans sound familiar?"

"*Bryn's brother is coming here?*" he exclaimed.

"In the telegram I just received, the boss said that Dylan had resigned rather than take the Cheyenne City assignment, but he didn't want to lose a man with his experience and reputation. He had an opening in Kansas City, and my original request for assignment had been for that office, so he ignored the resignation and asked Dylan to take this job. I guess that's what delayed the confirmation in the first place."

"Do you think Bryn knows?"

"I doubt it. The timing wouldn't work, and he didn't say anything before he left this morning."

"How come the sheriff didn't go? It's in his county."

"It was theft of U.S. mail that triggered our involvement. There weren't any injuries and the thieves only stole the mail bag. It sounds like an amateur job because there probably isn't fifty dollars in that bag, and that's a generous estimate."

"Maybe they knew something that we don't."

"Maybe. But I've got to head over to the house to tell Jean that it's official. I'm really proud of her for not letting the word leak. I know she wrote a letter to her family in Kansas City letting them know, but I figured by now her friends would all be blabbing the news across the town."

"Well, congratulations, boss," Bert said as Al grabbed his hat and trotted out of the office.

———

Bryn had listened as his boss and then the stage driver who had described the pair of mail robbers as nothing short of idiots, but the motive for the theft bothered him. They hadn't even worn masks as they committed the robbery. The stagecoach wasn't part of a large concern like Wells Fargo, it was a shoestring operation run by three brothers in Denver that serviced two nearby towns. They only had two secondhand coaches and their teams weren't much better. The driver of the stage was the oldest of the three brothers and they couldn't afford to hire a shotgun rider. That had never been a problem for them before, but this time it had been.

Two men had just ridden from behind the stage just a few miles out of Schuler which was only ten miles east of Denver. One of them fired a warning shot, and because he had no shotgun rider, the driver had pulled the stage to a stop. There was no cashbox or anything else of value on the coach, and the two passengers on board were far from wealthy. They were an elderly couple who were making the trip to Denver to visit their daughter.

After the coach came to a halt, the driver put his hands in the air and the two riders ordered him to toss the mail bag to the ground and then told him to drive away. They hadn't even looked in the coach to steal from the passengers, nor had they even threatened the driver. He'd driven away, expecting them to follow, but when he glanced back, he'd seen them just sitting on their horses watching.

His description of the men and their horses was precise and damning as each of the men had unusual features and their horses would be easily identified.

One man was very large and wore a full beard while the other was much smaller, about average size, but had a head full of curly red hair. It was almost as if they were begging to be caught, and that was what caused Bryn to believe that they weren't amateurs or idiots. There was a motive for the crime that he hadn't discovered yet and he felt it was the key to finding them and avoiding being shot in the process.

He was approaching the site of the theft, and as he drew closer, he spotted something just off to the side of the roadway and soon identified it as the stolen mail pouch.

Bryn stepped down and picked up the mail pouch, expecting to find it empty, but it wasn't. He rummaged through the sack and estimated there were sixteen to twenty letters inside and none had been opened. He hung the mail pouch over his shoulder and then mounted Maddy again, stuffed the mail pouch into his saddlebag then headed for Schuyler, about thirty minutes ahead.

As he neared the town, he slipped his new Winchester from its scabbard and kept Maddy at a walk. He didn't bother looking down any longer as he assumed the two men were still in Schuyler. He didn't believe that they'd try to ambush him so close to town, but he wasn't about to become a victim of an erroneous assumption and kept his eyes scanning for any potential threat.

When he reached the main street, he pulled Maddy to a stop and searched the traffic on the road and the horses tied up at the hitchrails to see if he spotted their mounts. One had been riding a hairy nag with a mixed brown coat and the other had been riding a light gray animal with a black mane and tail. The driver had remarked that both animals should have been put out to pasture years ago.

He didn't spot the horses, so he nudged Maddy to a walk and proceeded down the street, looking down each of the alleys as he passed and scanning the open windows for a possible shooter.

Bryn was more than halfway into town and was the object of many townsfolk's interest as he walked his horse past them with his repeater in his hands, but his badge didn't raise that interest to the level of fear. It was as he passed the hardware store that he spotted the two horses tied up before The Watering Hole saloon. He should have been shocked when he recognized them but by this time, he wouldn't have been amazed if the two men flew out of the saloon riding winged cows. It was a bizarre case.

He slid his Winchester home then dismounted and tossed Maddy's reins over the hitchrail. Before he entered the saloon, he moved his badge to his shirt behind his vest then pushed his hat back on his head before he ambled through the batwing doors hearing them squeal in protest.

There were only six patrons in the place, and none of them paid the least bit of attention to him as he crossed the floor and headed for the bar. That alone was another surprise because he was sure that none of them recognized him and strangers always attracted attention in a small town.

He stepped up to the bar, ordered a beer and then after exchanging his five-cent piece for the amber glass of foamy liquid, he took a sip then turned and leaned on the bar. It didn't take long for him to find the two thieves who were engaged in a three-handed game of poker at one of the saloon's four tables.

As he sipped his warm beer, he studied the men and began to wonder if he had the boys who'd held up the stage. Both of the men matching the description wore pistols, but they seemed to be having a grand time as they joked and chatted while they played their card game. It was a Saturday afternoon, and they were behaving like ranch hands after getting their monthly pay.

After finishing his beer, he bought a second then after it was set before him, he picked up the glass and headed for the table. When he was close, he stopped then just watched at close range to attract their attention.

Less than a minute later, the smaller man asked, "Are you new around here?"

"Just passin' through. You mind if I join your game?"

"We're only playin' penny ante, but you can park it right there if you want."

HUW'S LEGACY

Bryn set his beer on the table, sat down then pulled thirty cents from his pocket before he had to reach into his other pocket and extract eight pennies.

After being dealt his five cards which was as bad a poker hand as he'd ever seen, he folded and let them all bet.

The big man folded as well then asked, "What brings you to Schuyler, mister?"

"I'm coming back from Denver after looking at some horses. I just bought a small spread over by Box Elder."

"I shoulda done that after the war, but I spent all my musterin' out pay on whiskey and women."

Kyle smiled and said, "That's not unusual. I saved mine, which is how I bought the ranch."

The hand had played out quickly then the shorter, redheaded man asked, "What outfit were you with?"

"The 2nd Iowa. I signed up in '61 but was sent packing after I took a Minie ball from one of my own pickets. It was my fault, though. How about you?"

"Me and Homer signed up with the 94th Illinois but didn't get to see much. We were at Vicksburg, though. They mustered us out at Galveston down in Texas, so instead of heading back that way, we moseyed out to Colorado lookin' for gold. We kinda struck out there, too. Now we're just doin' what we can to get by. We don't make much money, but not many folks do these days."

Bryn still couldn't match them to the crime. They just didn't seem the type. Then Homer unintentionally started the conversation that finally provided the mysterious motive for what they had done.

Homer laughed then said, "Elrod here didn't want to come along to Colorado, but I told him we could strike it rich out west and then we could return in style. He was planning on heading back and marryin' his girl and rubbin' her old man's nose in it, but that didn't work out. He kept writin' to her sayin' that he'd have a lotta money soon, even after we got here. He was kinda stretchin' the truth, too."

Elrod snapped, "Don't start bringin' that up now, Homer. Not today."

Bryn looked at Elrod and asked, "Why not today? What's different?"

Homer grinned as he replied, "Elrod don't wanna talk about it 'cause he made a fool of himself over that girl and he kinda took it too far yesterday."

Elrod groaned as Bryn asked, "What did he do?"

Homer was still having a good time embarrassing his friend as he replied, "Last night, after he poured out his heart to his girl, who ain't sent a single letter since we been here, he figured he'd prove how important he was and put his last twenty dollars in the letter before he posted it. When he asked me to pay for chow this mornin', I asked him where his pay went, and he told me. He already felt stupid for doin' it, but said it was too late. So, I told him to go see Pappy Linden and ask for his letter back, but it had already been picked up and the stage was rollin' outta town. We had to chase it down to get the letter and his money back."

Elrod dropped his head as the third player began to laugh, but Bryn asked, "Did the driver give you back the letter?"

"When we chased after the coach, I already figured he wouldn't do that 'cause he didn't know us from Adam. So, I just stopped the coach and took the mail pouch. We left it by the road so they could find it later and I made Homer buy us the beer when we got back."

"Didn't you know that it is a Federal offense to tamper with the U.S. mail?"

"Hell, we didn't tamper with nothin'! We just got Elrod's letter back and slowed the rest down a bit."

Bryn didn't bother showing them his badge or even commenting after that. He was sure that the rest of the mail was now in his saddlebag and there was no reason to arrest the two perpetrators.

He continued playing poker for another half hour losing every hand to either Homer or Elrod and thought he'd spent enough time in Schuyler.

"Well, boys, it's been a pleasure meeting you. I hope things work out for you boys and I was glad to hear that you weren't with the 52nd Indiana, or I wouldn't have been so friendly."

"Why not?" Homer asked as Bryn rose and pulled on his hat.

"Those boys began firing at our backs at Fort Donelson and I still haven't forgiven those Hoosiers."

The poker players laughed then Bryn gave them a short salute before leaving the saloon, mounting Maddy and after letting him drink at the trough, he headed back for Denver with another tale to tell. At least this one didn't involve gunplay. He was still concerned about Cal's situation in Golden and didn't believe that it would go away so easily.

———

It was late afternoon when he pulled Maddy to a stop before the office, stepped down and then entered. He was already smiling in anticipation of telling the story of the missing mail which was already in the hands of the Denver postmaster when he spotted a grinning Al Esposito stepping into the other end of the large front office.

"Wait until you hear this one, boss," Bryn said as he tossed his hat on the desk that was still occupied by Bert Willis.

Al preempted him by replying, "Hold on to that story, Bryn. I have much bigger news to tell you. I've been ready to bust waiting for you to come back."

"Well, you're the boss, so go ahead."

"I've been reassigned to the Kansas City and have to be there by the first of September."

Bryn was startled by the news but could see that Al was more than happy about it. Bryn and everyone else who knew Al understood that his wife, Jean, was from Kansas City and he'd been lobbying the big boss in Washington for the job.

"Congratulation, boss. I'm sure Jean is really excited about it."

"She is and so will you. I'm tickled that for the second time in my career, I'm being replaced by an Evans."

If he'd been startled before, he was shocked now. Bryn knew that he was an experienced deputy marshal, but still didn't feel ready to take over a large office like Denver.

"Boss, that would be a real honor, but I'm not ready," Bryn protested.

Al grinned and replied, "I'm sorry, Bryn. I just said it that way to get a rise out of you. Dylan will be taking over. He turned down the assignment to Cheyenne City then resigned, but the big boss didn't want to lose him, so he offered him this job."

"*Dylan's coming to Denver?*" Bryn exclaimed as Al handed him a folded sheet of paper.

"You received this telegram about an hour ago, and I'm sure that it's from him. I can't tell you how comforting it is to me to know that I'm leaving the office in his hands. I know how devastated he was when they appointed that idiot Claggett to take his place in Omaha."

Bryn nodded as his mind raced with the news and the thought of having his entire family back together again.

Finally, he said, "I'll write up my report tomorrow, boss. Essentially, a local in Schuyler sent a letter he didn't want delivered and stopped the coach to get it back. I dropped off the mail to the postmaster but didn't see any reason to charge them."

"I agree with you. Now go and tell Erin the good news. I bet that you're happy you didn't put that house you got from Peacock on the market yet."

"You're right about that and I imagine there will be more houses built on the Double EE, too."

Bryn was all smiles as he grabbed his hat and yanked it back on while trotting out the door.

Once he'd mounted Maddy, he opened Dylan's telegram and received more good news and one very confusing line before he turned Maddy onto the road and headed home to tell Erin.

Kyle was sitting at the kitchen table with his grandmother and John who had returned with her just thirty minutes after learning the news.

They were excitedly planning for the move to Denver, which they expected would happen before the end of August. And just as Gwen was hoping to arrive before Erin had the latest addition to the Evans clan, Meredith had also expressed her desire to be there before the blessed event. She knew that Bryn was concerned about Katie being the only other woman on the ranch and he was thinking of hiring a midwife soon to at least assist. If she could get there sooner, she could act as a midwife and bring her new granddaughter into this world.

"When do you think we'll be moving, John?" she asked.

"Well, I've got to put the house and business up for sale, and then we have to stay until they find a buyer. I'm sure that Dylan needs to go soon, but we can ask him to have a nice, but smaller house built nearby."

"Do you think we'll have a problem selling the salvage business?"

"Not at all. I think we can sell it faster than the house. I've told you about the offers I've had for it over the past year alone."

Meredith nodded then looked at Kyle and asked, "Are you going to wait for us to leave or do you want to go there with Dylan?"

Kyle was surprised by the question and asked, "Why would he want to bring me along? I only met him this morning."

"I'm reasonably sure that he'll ask. He'll want to spend some time with you so he can get to know you better and he'll want you to meet Bryn and his family."

"Do you really think so?"

"I know my boys, Kyle, and I'll be surprised if he doesn't."

Kyle still found it hard to believe that his newly discovered uncle would want to have him tag along. He had never ridden a horse and knew that it was at least five hundred miles to Denver. Yet the idea of another long journey intrigued him and the thought of seeing 'real' mountains only added to his excitement. He hoped that his grandmother was right, and that Dylan would ask him to join him for the trip. He wanted to meet his Uncle Bryn's family, too.

———

"Dylan and Gwen are coming here?" Erin exclaimed.

"He's going to be my new boss, but I worked for him before and it wasn't a problem."

"I can't believe it. I was excited to think that they would be just a hundred miles away, but this is so much better. Will they just buy a house or build a house nearby?"

"I should think he'd rather build. We certainly have the acreage. I didn't get to the second part of the news that my mother and John will be coming as well."

Erin was flabbergasted as she stared at Bryn then looked at Katie who was already smiling, knowing that she'd be reunited with Dylan and Gwen's children.

Then Bryn opened the telegram and said, "There's something else that he wrote that has me a bit confused. He wrote 'will be bringing Huw's son'."

"Huw? Didn't you tell me that he died in a mine collapse more than ten years before you lost your father and brothers?"

"Closer to eleven years now. I didn't know that he had any children but then, I was just a young boy when he died. Dylan said he'll be coming here in a few days, so I guess we'll find out the whole story when he gets here."

―――――

So, as the sunset closed out Saturday, the 27th of July, the wheels were set in motion for the much-anticipated Evans family reunion in Denver.

Kyle lay stretched out on his bed that night with his bat on his bare chest, letting the hard maple remind him of the journey that had brought him here. Before he turned out the lamp, he'd read his mother's letter again.

"Mom," he said softly, "you were right. My new family did welcome me warmly and more than that, they gave me purpose. My grandmother thinks that Uncle Dylan will ask me to go with him to Denver in a few days, and I hope he does. It's only half the distance that I traveled from Wilkes Barre, and I'll be riding a horse this time. I know that my butt will probably

250

feel like a rock, but it'll still beat walking. I can't wait to meet my Uncle Bryn now. Uncle Dylan said I looked just like him, but everyone else keeps telling me how much I resembled a younger Dylan. I'm sure that their brother, Huw, wasn't much different either. You can see them all now, Mom, so you'll know.

"I still have so much to learn, and I'll try hard to be the man that you always wanted me to be. If I can even come close to what Uncle Dylan has accomplished then I'll be satisfied, and I know you will be as well. It may not be as a lawman, but I'll find something. I know that I don't have to promise you that I'll never do anything to hurt anyone and I'll even avoid those gray areas. I may have a new family, Mom, but you'll always be the center of my life."

He closed his eyes then said a silent Lord's Prayer,before setting his bat slowly to the floor and letting himself drift to sleep.

CHAPTER 8

July 30, 1867

Kyle mounted the light brown mare from Dylan's stock back in Omaha and settled into the saddle as his uncle watched. She was a temporary ride and would be left with Bryn for his growing herd.

"Ready for a long ride, Kyle?" Dylan asked with a marginal grin.

"Yes, sir. I'm ready, but I'm not sure my behind is."

Dylan laughed then said, "Okay, let's head to Denver."

Kyle nudged the mare forward and had her at slow trot beside Dylan so they could continue their long conversation.

Ever since they'd boarded the train in Omaha, they had engaged in an almost non-stop dialogue interrupted only by sleep. The long train ride to Julesburg had taken longer than Dylan's trip east from the end of track because it was a passenger train.

During that first leg of the trip, they'd exchanged what would be classified as war stories even though neither had been in the actual war. Kyle had explained his two confrontations on his trip and then asked Dylan about his much more numerous adventures. Dylan had also talked extensively about Bryn, including how he'd won his Medal of Honor.

Now as they started their long ride to Denver, the subject shifted when Kyle asked him how he'd met Gwen.

Dylan was more than happy to tell the story beginning when he'd first spotted the small, pigtailed girl standing with the other women on the deck of the *Providence.*

As he talked, Kyle could see and hear the pleasure his uncle had when he spoke of his wife and after meeting her, he could understand why. When he'd gone to their home to pick out his horse, he could see the same joy in her face when she was with Dylan. He'd never seen such bonding before and was sure that was how his mother had felt about Dylan's brother, Huw.

When he finally finished, Kyle asked, "How did Uncle Bryn meet Erin?"

Dylan's explanation wasn't as animated, but his uncle's description of Bryn and Erin's relationship sounded much the same and he wondered how both of his uncles could have been so fortunate in their choices. Maybe it was just karma.

As they stopped for their first break to rest the horses, Dylan asked, "Can you show me how you use that club of yours? I had a hard time imagining how you could drive off two knife-wielding thieves and then dismount and disarm a rider with just a heavy stick."

"I'll be happy to, but you've got to show me how to use the pistol and the repeater you gave me, too."

"I'll do that. I was really surprised to see that you had a Smith & Wesson Model 2. Most men carry one version of a Colt or the other. Was that Lowry's pistol, the man you laid low with your club?"

"Yup," Kyle said as he slipped the bat from his bedroll.

He spent a couple of minutes working out the kinks and stiffness that was already causing him some discomfort before he grasped his bat and began his dance. He whirled, stabbed and swung the club in harmony with the waltz being played in his mind. He could almost hear the orchestra as he maneuvered across the ground and defended and then attacked imaginary opponents.

Dylan was impressed with the display and knew that Kyle had spent many hours of practice to reach that level of expertise.

When he finished after working up a good sweat, Dylan asked, "Why didn't you finish off Lowry? He was there to murder you and you could have done it without anyone questioning how it had happened. He had a pistol and you were unarmed. It would be a clear-cut case of self-defense."

"Aside from the fact that his father was a judge, I just couldn't do it. He had already lost his pistol when I smashed my club into his knee, so the threat was gone."

"But didn't you say he had the hammer back and was about to shoot you? Didn't that make you angry?"

"No. My biggest concern at the time was that he'd go back to his father and swear out a warrant for my arrest. So, I took his gun as proof that he had been the aggressor and once I did that, I warned him about going back to see Lisa Neuman. He said he was finished with her, and I believed him. Just to let you know, I did use your name as the threat. I told him that you were a United States Marshal and that I'd tell you what he'd done if he bothered her again."

"That's a good threat, Kyle. Did she write that letter to you?"

"No, sir. Her father wrote it and just wanted to be sure that Lowry hadn't killed me and buried me somewhere. I wrote a reply just before we left and told him that I'd be moving to Denver and if he had any problems with Lowry, he could send a letter to me there."

Dylan smiled and replied, "I don't think he'll cause you any problems, Kyle. Did he add anything about Lisa in the letter?"

"Nope. I was kind of relieved, to be honest. She was a pretty girl and I really liked talking to her, but I didn't want to go back to Pennsylvania," he said as he slid his bat back into its temporary home.

"You're heading the wrong direction if you did want to reach Pennsylvania, Kyle," Dylan said as he mounted Crow.

Kyle stepped into the saddle and replied, "I'm going in the direction that I want to go, Dylan."

Dylan nodded then they started their horses along the road again. He'd decided to get off the train in Julesburg, even though other stations further west were closer because there was already a good road all the way to Denver. If they'd stayed on the train any longer, they would have had to ride cross-country.

They also had a regular stagecoach service between the two towns now that the railroad was in Julesburg. It only made the run every other day, but it meant that when he had to move his family, they'd be able to ride in relative comfort. It also meant that there were two waystations between the two towns, but Dylan hadn't planned on using either just because of timing. The coaches moved at a faster pace than they would be riding, so they'd probably reach each one during the daytime rather than the evening. Even if they did decide to stop, they would more than likely not have any spare room after housing their paying customers.

Kyle had been somewhat uncomfortable when Dylan had told him to stop calling him 'Uncle Dylan' because he wasn't that much older than Kyle. The math was easy because of their birthdays. Dylan would be turning thirty in January the day before his eighteenth birthday. But even though he had been initially uncomfortable, he appreciated the more familiar use of his Christian name.

Dylan was well aware of the age difference but wanted Kyle to feel as if he was more of a brother than a nephew. He wanted to have Bryn do the same, and was sure that he would, especially as Bryn was almost four years younger than he was.

But even as they continued to talk as they rode, Dylan wondered about Katie Mitchell. Gwen had passed on Erin's concern about her younger sister, and nothing that Erin had done seemed to help. He glanced over at Kyle, who was talking about his lost friend, Lobo, and wondered if his arrival at the ranch might help with Katie. It wasn't a case of matchmaking because he knew that Katie was two years older than Kyle, but having a handsome young man living on the ranch might bring her out of her shell.

He just hoped that Katie didn't break his heart if he was attracted to her, which would be understandable. Katie was quite different from Erin, but she was still an attractive, vibrant young lady. He hadn't really thought about it before he'd asked Kyle to join him, as he'd just invited him along to get to know him better and to have him meet Bryn. But he supposed that it really didn't matter because he would have met Katie within a month anyway.

"How far are we going today?" Kyle asked as the sun reached its zenith.

"We'll get within twenty miles of the first waystation which is eighty miles from Julesburg."

"Is there any danger out here?"

"The Pawnee aren't happy at the moment, so we do have to keep an eye out for them, but they usually don't care about lone riders just passing through. Outside of that, we always have to be alert for highwaymen. It's not too bad out here in the open like this, but when we spot big obstructions like a small forest or even a hill or a ravine, keep your eyes open."

Kyle nodded and began scanning the horizons for potential danger. He doubted that he could fight off any Indians with his club but knew that Dylan had the reputation of being one of the best marksmen in the territory.

———

Dylan and Kyle found a decent, but not great campsite just before sundown.

As they unsaddled their horses, Kyle asked, "Did we miss the stagecoach?"

Dylan set his saddle on the ground before answering, "I think it left while we were getting our last-minute supplies. They wait on the train and then any passengers heading to Denver will board and off they go. We should see the northbound stage tomorrow."

"Are we going to make a fire, or will we have a cold camp?"

"I think it's better that we avoid letting anyone know that we're here."

"That's the same reason that I can't get any target practice until we get to Uncle Bryn's ranch, isn't it?"

Dylan was beginning to unload the pack horse when he replied, "That's it."

————

Forty minutes later as they ate their cold supper in the darkness of the new moon, Dylan asked, "Kyle, how do you want to be introduced? I know that the letter was addressed to Kyle Evans, but I'm guessing that your birth certificate lists you as Kyle Nolan."

"It does, so I guess that's what you should call me."

"Nonsense. I was just asking because I wasn't sure if you'd want to change your name."

Kyle was taken aback but asked, "Can I do that? I mean, wouldn't that cause some problems in the family?"

"No, it wouldn't cause any problems. If you'd like to officially be Kyle Evans, we can make that happen by just petitioning the court. It's a common procedure."

"Do you really think it would be okay? I'm a bit ashamed to have the name of the man who abandoned us and left my mother in such bad shape until I could go to work."

"I'd be proud for you to share my father's name. So, once we're settled in Denver, we'll do that, and I'll introduce you to Bryn and his family as Kyle Evans."

Kyle quietly said, "When my mother was told by the doctor that she had cancer and would die soon, she arranged for her burial. I didn't know about it until I had to tell him that she'd died. When I visited her grave just before I left Wilkes-Barre, I saw that her simple cross marker had her name as Bess Evans. It was her way of telling everyone that she was going to spend eternity with the man who should have been her husband."

Dylan just looked at Kyle in the starlight and tried to recall if he'd ever met Bess Nelson but couldn't. He would have been just a boy and was interested in boy things.

Kyle then said, "My mother's husband, Tom Nolan, picked out my name, Kyle, because he was Irish and liked the name. My mother didn't object, and because he didn't care about my middle name, she chose Hugh. I often wondered why she did, but it was spelled H-u-g-h, not the same as my real father. I think if she'd spelled it that way, he'd ask her why she chose such an obviously Welsh name."

"That makes sense, Kyle. I imagine she must have been worried for years that he'd discover that you weren't his son. It was only because he hadn't sired any other children that it came up at all. You probably wouldn't even be here if you'd had brothers or sisters."

"I thought about that and all of the other coincidences that brought me here, but there are so many that could have prevented it that I've stopped wasting the brainpower."

Dylan smiled and said, "One of those coincidences was named Lisa, wasn't it?"

"Not as much as you might think."

"Well, let's get some sleep. We have another long ride ahead of us tomorrow and two days after that."

"I hope they're as peaceful as today's was."

"So, do I, Kyle," Dylan replied before they headed to their bedrolls.

———

Dylan and Bryn were on the road again shortly after sunrise and less than an hour later, they spotted the northbound stage blasting along the road making an enormous dust cloud.

"We need to pull off the roadway, Kyle," Dylan shouted.

"I kind of figured that out, Marshal," Kyle yelled back as they shifted to the eastern side of the road.

The coach was moving at a high speed as it approached their standing horses when it began to slow.

Dylan looked up at the driver and shotgun rider as the stage drew near, knowing that they wanted to pass along some information, probably a warning.

The driver pulled back on the reins and the shotgun rider shouted, "We saw a Pawnee war party about an hour ago, right after we left the waystation. There were only six of 'em, and they were headin' north, so you boys might want to head back."

"Did they have any rifles?" Dylan asked.

"We didn't get close enough to check. Just thought you'd want to know."

The warning delivered, the driver snapped the reins and the coach began to roll.

After the dust cleared, Dylan didn't say anything, but nudged Crow into a slow trot and took the road as Kyle followed on his mare.

Once they were riding south again, Dylan finally said, "Keep your eyes open, Kyle. I don't think that six Pawnee would make up a war party. They were either a hunting party, scouts, or maybe they were scrounging. Whatever they were, we need to keep going."

"If we spot them, I'll do the smart thing and keep my mouth shut and ears open."

Dylan looked over at Kyle and grinned before replying, "That is definitely the smart thing to do."

"Can you talk to the Pawnee if we do run into them?"

"Not talk in their language, but I learned how to communicate with some basic sign language when I was with the Crow."

Kyle wondered how that worked when there was such a distance between the two tribes but hoped he wouldn't have to see it in action.

Ten minutes later, his wish was shattered when he spotted six Indians riding southwest of their position. He was sure that Dylan had seen them because he was looking in that direction, so he didn't say anything.

After a minute more of riding down the road, Dylan said, "Kyle, take off your gunbelt and hang it over your saddle horn. Act as if you don't see them."

"Okay," he replied as he began unbuckling the gunbelt.

Dylan didn't look at the Pawnee but then turned to Kyle and said, "If they start heading our way, I'm going to ask you to do something odd. Just get ready."

"Odd would be interesting, but nothing more, I hope," he replied with a grin.

"Did I tell you the story about Peanut?"

"Your little donkey back in Omaha?"

"Yup. I'd just arrested four thugs who'd taken over a ferry…"

As he talked, Dylan watched the Pawnee out of the corner of his eye to see if they were just continuing north or had shifted their direction toward them. It didn't take long to see the change and he counted eight warriors. He still wasn't sure if they were a war party or not, but the fact that they were coming in their direction made it irrelevant.

"They're coming, Kyle. They're about a thousand yards out, so we're going to stop, and I want you to dismount, take your club and walk off the west side of the road about thirty yards. When they get within fifty yards, start your exercise as if they aren't there. You can look at them, but the goal is to entertain and impress them. I'll be watching, but I won't have my Winchester drawn. A lot will depend on what kind of weapons they have."

"Okay."

Dylan was expecting at least one or two questions, but after Kyle's brief response, he turned Crow to the west to face the approaching Pawnee pulled him to a stop and folded his arms.

Kyle stepped down, slid his bat from the bedroll then strode across the western berm onto the empty ground.

Dylan watched and was surprised when Kyle simply stood with his club planted in the ground off to his right with his left hand on his hip. It was as if he was challenging the Pawnee to attack. Dylan hoped that they would just be more curious about what Kyle was going to do. He knew that he could extract his repeater and send his first shot out of the muzzle in less than ten seconds, but that could be a costly ten seconds for Kyle if he was wrong about the Pawnee's intent.

Kyle wasn't grandstanding to impress Dylan he was letting the Pawnee know that the bat was his only weapon and that he was confident that it was enough. As he watched them ride straight at him, he began to pick up more detail. They were wearing warpaint and three of them wore feathers in their hair. One had two, and he guessed that he was their leader.

He didn't see any rifles or pistols, but each man carried a bow and arrows, but none were nocked. They had tomahawks and knives at their waists for close combat, and if it came to a one-on-one confrontation at close quarters, he knew that he'd win. He just didn't know anything about how Indians fought other than the stories he'd heard and from the books he'd read. Soon, he'd learn firsthand.

When the Pawnee were about a hundred yards out, they slowed and began walking their horses toward Kyle. Their leader, Talking Raven, didn't understand why the white man was standing alone with his club while his partner was sitting on his horse with his arms crossed. He suspected that they were trying to draw them in closer before the man with the club pulled a pistol and the other one pulled his rifle. He could have just turned his warriors around and continued north, but it would have been an act of cowardice and that was worse than death, so he kept them moving.

Kyle continued waiting and had to keep from starting early as his heart began to pound against his ribs. He had to force himself to stay calm as the eight Pawnee drew closer. He'd picked out a small clump of bushes to act as his trigger point. It was probably closer to forty yards than fifty, but it was close enough.

As soon as they neared the bushes, Kyle lifted his right arm about a foot then slammed the knotted end of his maple bat hard into the dry Colorado soil creating a small eruption of dirt and dust.

Talking Raven thought it was the sign for the man on the horse to start firing and almost nocked an arrow, but then he and his warriors were all surprised when Kyle began the first steps of his waltzing exercise. The Pawnee war chief had them pull up more out of curiosity than concern as their sixteen brown eyes watched the white man.

Kyle began his moves as he always did with a wide, sweeping counterclockwise swing that ended when he thumped the ground and immediately rocked the bat into a cradling move and turned clockwise. He'd practiced the dance so often that it was second nature now. Each thrust, swing or tap to the ground was in rhythm and in perfect balance with the waltz he heard in his mind. As it always was, the three-quarter time dance was being hummed in his mother's voice which took his mind off of the imminent danger he now faced.

As he whirled and stabbed, part of him was on the floor in Wilkes-Barre with his mother in his arms as they danced. He knew that he was performing for eight Pawnee warriors under the Colorado sun, but the waltz in his mind kept him in step and kept him at peace.

For more than five minutes, the Pawnee watched Kyle and Talking Raven saw him as a brave warrior who was warning them of his skill with his weapon and challenging them to battle.

When Kyle finally reached the end of his abbreviated dance, he made one last flourishing twist then slammed the end of the bat into the ground and assumed the same position he'd held when he'd begun. He was sweating heavily and breathing hard, but he was satisfied that he'd done as Dylan had asked and stared defiantly at the Pawnee.

Talking Raven then said something to his warriors, pulled out his own small club, screamed his war cry and kicked his horse into a fast trot.

Kyle quickly drew his bat over his head into a fighting position and held it back, ready to strike. As the lone warrior raced toward him, he noticed that it wasn't a tomahawk that he held in his right hand, but what looked like a tomahawk without the deadly head.

Talking Raven charged straight at Kyle, ignoring Dylan but expecting him to be drawing his rifle as the man on the ground stood with his heavy club over his head.

Just as the Pawnee drew near on his right, Kyle dropped the bat's head off to the left side while still holding it behind his head. He could see the Indian's painted face clearly as he drew back his small club. Kyle was ready to swing, but something made him hold back. This wasn't like it had been with Michael Lowry because the Pawnee wasn't armed with a pistol, just that nasty-looking stick.

Talking Raven lifted his arm and as his horse charged past Kyle, rapped him on the shoulder with his stick then cried his victory as he whipped his mount back toward his fellow warriors who all acknowledged his courage.

Kyle watched him ride away and dropped his bat's knotted head to the ground again wondering what had just happened. The blow had been little more than a tap and he doubted if it would even leave a bruise. Yet when the Indian returned to his men, they all turned their horses north and simply rode away.

He watched them for another thirty seconds before he turned and began walking back to the road. As he did, he'd glance back expecting them to make a serious charge, but they kept riding north.

When he reached the mare, he slid his bat home then mounted as Dylan watched him with a big smile.

Once he was in the saddle, Dylan asked, "How did you know about counting coup?"

Kyle had pulled his canteen and was unscrewing the cap when he asked, "What's a coup?"

"You didn't know?" Dylan asked with raised eyebrows.

Kyle shook his head as he took a long drink of his warm, metallic-tasting water.

"Most Plains Indians believe that it shows more courage to just attack an enemy and touch him without being harmed than it is to try and kill him. They call it 'counting coup'. I think that the warrior who did it to you thought you'd challenged him with your club and the fact that you didn't have a pistol showed you to be a worthy opponent. The added threat of my being here with a rifle added to the danger."

"So, he had no intention of hitting me?" he asked as he capped his canteen and hung it back on his saddle.

"Nope. Well, that worked out better than I'd expected. Let's keep going. I hope that they didn't do anything to that waystation. We could use a hot meal before we press on."

Kyle just nodded as he nudged the mare forward to match Dylan and the pack horse. He'd learned a lot on this second journey already and much of it was about himself. The confrontation with the Pawnee was a bigger lesson than just understanding what counting coup was. It was the third time he'd used his bat as a defensive weapon, and each episode had been different.

The first was a defensive reaction to his inattention and almost got him killed. The second was a planned surprise attack to avoid being shot. But this one had required him to evaluate the threat, decide what would be the best outcome, then take the minimum amount of action to achieve that goal. It had all happened so quickly, but he knew what he had to do the moment he'd seen the stick in the Indian's hand.

He had no illusions and knew that he still had a lot to learn about almost everything but realizing that he had the capacity to adapt his methods to suit the need at the moment meant a lot to him. For the first time in his life, Kyle Hugh Evans believed that there was nothing he couldn't do if he put in the time and effort.

———

After an early lunch at the untouched waystation, they continued their journey southwest toward Denver in the scorching late July sun.

They kept a good pace with breaks to rest the horses and continued their conversation. By the time they pulled up for the night, they were more than halfway to Denver.

———

About a hundred miles south, Katie asked, "Have you figured out what Dylan meant in his telegram when he said that he was bringing Huw's son with him?"

Bryn replied, "I've spent quite a bit of time trying to figure that one out and nothing seems to work out right. I doubt if he's a fraud because Dylan can spot phonies a mile off. That leaves just a few possibilities, and none seem plausible."

Erin said, "It'll be an interesting story, and I wonder what he looks like. How old would he be?"

"Well, he couldn't be younger than seventeen. Huw died in that mine explosion on April 11, 1849. So, unless he magically sired a son after that, the latest he could have been born is January of '50. Correct me if my math is wrong."

"No, you're right. If he was older, wouldn't you already know about him?"

"Not necessarily. If he fathered the boy out of wedlock, which he obviously did, then the woman could have left Carbondale earlier than that."

"How old was Huw when he died?" asked Katie.

"He was seventeen. I was seven years old when it happened, and I remember my mother telling me and Dylan that night that it would never happen to us because our father had promised her that we would never go into that mine."

"How old was Dylan?"

"He was eleven, so he already knew about the promise because he'd been working in the pump house for years."

Erin then asked, "Do you think he looks like you or Dylan?"

"I have no idea, but we'll find out soon. They should be here in a couple of days."

"Then things will get very interesting," Katie said with a smile.

Erin looked at her younger sister and smiled back, not quite sure what she meant.

––––––

The third day's ride was uneventful, and they'd been passed by the stagecoach heading south and greeted a group of riders heading north along with two freight wagons. Dylan mentioned the Pawnee but didn't think they'd be a problem.

They stopped at the second waystation late in the afternoon, had an early supper and then continued on to get as close to Denver as they could before setting up their last cold camp.

"Are we going to the marshal's office first when we get into Denver?" Kyle asked.

"That's the idea. I don't know where Bryn's ranch is, just its general direction. It sounds big enough that it should be hard to miss, but I'd rather not wander around Colorado hunting for it."

"Why did he name it the Double EE?"

"For Erin. She was back in Omaha when he acquired the land and registered it at the land office to surprise her. He told me that he'd given up hope of ever getting his horse ranch because she was pregnant when Erin had literally spun him around and said to go west and find their new home. The brand is a pair of Es, so the sign reads that way, which some folks probably think makes it four Es, but he wanted Erin to see her initials when she saw the ranch."

"That's a nice story."

"It's the making of a man if he chooses the right woman. I have my Gwen and there were many times where she's been the one to steer me in the right direction, just like Erin has done for Bryn."

"How do you know if she's the right one?"

"Talk to her and listen. I was limited to just talking to Gwen for the first few weeks that I knew her, so I really didn't have a choice to do anything else. Bryn did the same with Erin, but for a different reason. Too many men get caught up on the outside and spend all the time talking about themselves to impress the woman. If you listen to what she has to say, then you'll understand her better. Just make sure that she's honest enough not to sit there and giggle and tell you how strong and handsome you are. If she expresses herself honestly and you still enjoy being with her, then you'll know soon enough."

"I did enjoy talking to Lisa Neuman, and she was pretty, too. I guess it really doesn't matter because I'll never go back there."

"Never say never, Kyle. You can never predict the future. In March, could you have imagined that you'd be spending the first of August in Colorado?"

Kyle grinned and replied, "No, sir."

"Then don't say that you'll never go back to Pennsylvania. It could happen. Maybe you'll go back there, marry that girl and become the governor."

Kyle laughed before saying, "Let's just say it's not likely."

Dylan grinned at his nephew and replied, "That's better."

_____

Kyle and Dylan were up early the next morning and were already on the road by sunrise, anxious to reach their destination which Dylan estimated to be another ten hours away.

"We'll be seeing more ranches and farm now that we're getting closer to Denver and we should see the town itself by early afternoon."

Kyle asked, "How many horses do they have on the ranch now?"

"I'd guess around forty to fifty. I don't know if Bryn has sold any yet or added any more mustangs. I'll be bringing our small herd with us when we move the families here later this month."

"Including Peanut."

Dylan grinned and replied, "Including Peanut."

_____

As Dylan had predicted, Kyle began noticing farmhouses and small ranches as they rode, and road traffic began to pick up after they passed through a small town that didn't seem to have a name listed anywhere. The road had been following the South Platte River since leaving Julesburg, but after leaving their campsite, it continued southwest while the river headed due west. There were still feeder streams that let them water the horses, so they made good time.

As they rode, Kyle's attention was drawn to the distant Rocky Mountains and he wondered just how tall they were.

He asked, "How far away are the mountains, Dylan?"

"Oh, about eighty miles or so, I'd guess."

"And they're still that big?" he asked in astonishment.

"Wait until you see them up close. Bryn's ranch extends into the start of the foothills, so you'll get a better idea from there."

Kyle was already planning on climbing one of the shorter mountains as they continued their ride southwest.

––––––

It was just early afternoon when Kyle pointed ahead and asked, "Is that Denver?"

"It's just the outskirts. We'll see the rest of the town soon enough. It's growing fast and Al Esposito thinks that once they build a railroad from Kansas City, the population will explode. He believes that will happen within a year or two and with a Union Pacific spur, it'll make Denver a railroad hub."

"How many deputy marshals does he have now?"

"Four, but he needs at least another two. I should say that I'll need another two. At least Colorado Territory is a lot smaller than Nebraska Territory was when I arrived."

"I can't believe it was that big. Even now, it's bigger than Pennsylvania."

Dylan nodded as he looked ahead, and Denver began to rise over the horizon. He hadn't been to Denver since it had been the territorial capital, and he already noticed changes, even at this distance. He imagined that he would find many more the closer they were to the city. He'd have to stop calling it a town. It was going to be a good place for him and Gwen to raise their children and they'd have the entire Evans clan nearby.

He turned to Kyle and said, "Thanks for making me read that telegram, Kyle."

Kyle just smiled back at Dylan before turning his eyes back toward Denver as it continued to expand across the horizon with the backdrop of the Rocky Mountains. He was even more impressed with the jutting peaks and couldn't imagine how high they were. Dylan had told him that they'd been slowly climbing ever since they left Omaha and would be a mile high when they arrived. He thought the tops of those mountains must be another mile or two higher.

He did notice that when he'd done his exercises that he'd tired sooner and was out of breath faster. Dylan had told him it was because of the altitude, but Kyle didn't understand why it made a difference and just took Dylan's word for it.

Less than an hour after first seeing Denver, they entered the city and the serious traffic began clogging the roads. They had to wind around wagons being loaded and buggies and carriages coming the other way along with a mixed bag of riders. No one seemed to pay any attention to them at all, which he'd noticed in other busy cities and towns along his journey to Omaha. The townsfolk in small towns all noticed strangers. Denver seemed to be a city of strangers.

They passed the large county courthouse then Kyle spotted the territorial capital building before they turned left and walked their horses down a side street.

Dylan then pulled up and only then did Kyle see the sign above an office that read United States Marshal Service, but it was two doors down.

Dylan waited as he stepped down and tied off the mare, then took off his hat and said, "I want to have a bit of fun, Kyle. I want you to put on my hat and walk inside. I'll wait outside the door to hear Bryn's reaction."

"What if he's not there?" Kyle asked as he accepted the unique flat leather hat.

"That's his horse tied out front. He must have just returned from some job."

"What will I say when I see him?"

"Play it by ear. I just want to hear what he does when he sees you."

Kyle looked at the floppy hat in his hand and then said, "Dylan, I know he's your brother and you want to josh him, but I don't want to make him think that I'm making fun of him the first time I meet him."

Dylan smiled took the hat back then said, "You're right, Kyle. Let's go and say hi to my brother. One of these days, you'll be able to josh him all you want and enjoy every second."

Kyle's relief was palpable as he smiled at Dylan before they stepped toward the open door.

Dylan expected that Bryn had anticipated his arrival and had asked Al Esposito for desk duty that day, so he wasn't at all surprised to see both Bryn and Al near the desk talking to a man who he didn't know.

Bryn's head turned away from Deputy Marshal Chet Caruthers, spotted Dylan then popped to his feet, came to attention and exclaimed, "Room! Ten-Hut!"

Neither Marshal Al Esposito or Chet Caruthers bothered snapping to attention but turned as Dylan and Kyle stepped across the office.

Dylan grinned at his younger brother as he said, "You're not in the army anymore, Captain Evans. A simple, 'welcome, your majesty', would have sufficed."

Bryn walked around the desk embraced Dylan and said, "I'm really glad to see you, Dylan, and even happier that you're taking over. Al is making us all work too hard. I'm sure that you'll let us slack off."

Dylan stepped back and replied, "Of course, I will…not," then turned and said, "Bryn, this is Huw's son, Kyle, who I mentioned in the telegram."

Bryn's focus had been on his older brother, but then he finally let his eyes shift to Kyle who was smiling at him.

Bryn blinked and then just offered Kyle his hand and as they shook, he said, "I'm pleased to meet you, Kyle. I'm sure that you have a lot of stories to tell me."

"I do, and I'm very happy to meet you too, Uncle Bryn."

"Unless you want to be less happy, call me Bryn. How old are you, anyway? My best guess before you arrived was that you were seventeen and would turn eighteen in January, although you do look older."

"Did you want to go for a date?" Kyle asked with raised eyebrows.

Bryn stepped back, scanned Kyle from head to toe then answered, "Um, how about the thirteenth?"

"Why the thirteenth?"

"It's my favorite number because everyone else thinks it's bad luck. How close was I?"

"As close as you can get. It's the twelfth of January."

"I should have asked you about your birthdate earlier, Kyle," Dylan said, "Gwen would have been impressed."

"Why?"

"Because my birthday is the eleventh of January and hers is the thirteenth. We've always celebrated a joint birthday on the twelfth. How's that for coincidence?"

"That is odd."

Al Esposito then stepped forward shook Kyle's hand and said, "Nice to meet you, Kyle. I'm Al Esposito and I'll be leaving this office for Kansas City in a few days after I give the rundown to Dylan. This character is Chet Caruthers and I don't know why the government pays him, but he's a deputy marshal."

After Kyle shook Chet's hand, Dylan said, "Al, I'll be back tomorrow, so we can start the transition and do the paperwork. Right now, Kyle and I need to get settled in."

"Sure. It's quiet at the moment and all we have is the usual subpoenas and statute deliveries. You have two other deputies at the moment because we just lost one courtesy of your brother. He can explain on the ride to the Double EE."

"Good enough. Can you show us how to find your horse ranch, brother?" Dylan asked.

"Let's go, Dylan. I have a lot more news that I need to tell you on the way."

As he turned to follow his uncles out of the office, Kyle appreciated that Bryn hadn't commented on how much he looked like Dylan, or even asked how he'd suddenly appeared out of the ether. He assumed it was because he trusted Dylan's judgement and he'd hear the whole story soon anyway.

They were soon mounted and heading west out of Denver toward the Rockies then before they reached the outskirts, Bryn had them turn south.

Kyle rode on Dylan's right and Bryn rode on his brother's left side while Bryn passed on the news.

As they passed a big house, Bryn pointed and said, "That's mine now. I didn't pay a dime for it, either. I was going to sell it, but now that mom and John are coming, I figured they may want to live there rather than out on the ranch."

"How did you get a house for nothing?"

"It's a long story, so I'll tell you later."

"Speaking of the ranch, I was wondering if you wouldn't mind giving up a bit of your four sections of land so I can build a house nearby."

"Um, that's another thing. In addition to the house, I was also given the adjoining twelve sections heading south."

Dylan's head snapped to his left as he exclaimed, "You own sixteen sections of Colorado?"

"I do, and you can put your house anywhere you want. Erin and I built our house and a smaller house for Flat Jack, our wrangler."

"How is Erin doing? She obviously hasn't had her baby yet or it would have been the first thing you told me."

"No, she's still heavy with Grace Lynn and I just hope that she doesn't have a baby with external plumbing. She's convinced that Gwen's method for having Bethan will work for her, too."

Dylan laughed then turned to Kyle and explained what Bryn meant before asking his brother, "How's Katie?"

"She's still a bit reclusive, but other than that, she's fine and seems happy to be at the ranch with Erin and our boys."

"Are mom and John excited about coming?" Bryn asked.

"More than you can imagine. John was getting a bit bored with the salvage business anyway, but mom really missed you, Erin, and her grandchildren."

"We missed her, too. When do you think they'll be coming?"

"She wants to be here for Grace Lynn's arrival, so I'm supposed to get the housebuilding started then return right away and bring everyone here."

"I'd feel more comfortable having mom here when Erin goes into labor. I know Katie's assisted in two childbirths, but she hasn't been the midwife yet."

"Why don't you have a midwife stay at the house?"

"Erin doesn't want to hurt Katie's feelings and says she's already had two babies and could probably do it on her own if she had to."

"Maybe Kyle could help," Dylan said as he grinned at his nephew.

Kyle shook his head, saying, "I can't even milk a cow."

Bryn and Dylan laughed as they left Denver and headed southwest toward the Double EE.

Dylan and Bryn continued to catch up as Kyle listened.

It wasn't long before Bryn said, "See the smoke ahead? That's from the cookstove. I'm sure that Katie is baking something special for your arrival."

Dylan replied, "I'm sure that Kyle is as willing as I am to eat anything that isn't moving."

"You always did like your steaks almost bleeding, Dylan," Bryn said before he laughed.

The ranch buildings soon appeared and then Kyle had his first glimpse of the herd of horses that were grazing in a large fenced pasture. He'd never seen so many horses before and began a count. Dylan had estimated that Bryn had about forty to fifty, but he soon passed sixty before he stopped counting. He was sure that there were more in the barn, too.

Ten minutes later, they entered the large barn and dismounted. As they began unsaddling their horses, Bryn noticed Kyle sliding his bat from his bedroll and asked, "What's that?"

Kyle replied, "It was supposed to be a baseball bat, but I turned it into a walking stick when I left Wilkes-Barre, and now I use it as a defensive weapon, too."

"You'll have to show me how that works," Bryn said as he set his saddle on a wide shelf.

Dylan removed Crow's saddle blanket and said, "He's pretty effective with that thing, Bryn."

"Maybe I should bring you along when I go to Golden next week to check on Cal."

"I'd like to help," Kyle said as he set his saddle on the shelf.

Dylan said, "It wouldn't hurt to have him along, Bryn."

"If you're not too out of sorts after that long ride, then I'd be happy to have you come with me, Kyle. It'll probably be on Tuesday or Wednesday, so you should be recovered by then."

"I'm not nearly as sore as I had expected to be. I'd never ridden a horse before I got to Omaha."

"Really? Well, after we get you settled, we can find a nice one for you to replace the mare my brother let you use. I have a few geldings that would suit you much better anyway."

Kyle grinned at the thought of having his own horse and judging by the amount of tack on the shelves, there was no shortage of saddles either.

They left their packs in the barn for the time being as Dylan and Kyle followed Bryn out of the barn and headed for the house. It was a large house, but only a single floor and as they crossed the open ground, Kyle looked at the small house nearby and wondered if that was going to be where he stayed.

As they approached the back porch, the door swung open and a very pregnant Erin stepped out of the house and said loudly, "Welcome to the Double EE, Dylan."

"Hello, Erin. This is Kyle, our surprise nephew from Pennsylvania."

Erin smiled at Kyle as they stepped onto the porch and said, "Welcome to you too, Kyle. I'm sure that you have an interesting story to tell."

"Thank you, ma'am. Not as interesting as some of the stories that Dylan told on the way here, I'm afraid."

"He's been known to exaggerate," Erin said as Katie appeared behind her.

Kyle wasn't sure who the young lady was because she was so much shorter than Erin and her red hair was a noticeable shift from Erin's reddish brown. They both had the same shade of blue eyes and shared some facial characteristics, but Kyle waited to be introduced to be sure.

Katie stared at Kyle for a few seconds stunned at the obvious resemblance to both Dylan and Bryn, but then smiled and turned back into the kitchen as Erin shuffled behind her, carrying her heavy natural burden.

Dylan, Bryn and Kyle entered the house that was filled with the wonderful aroma of whatever Katie had just taken from the oven.

Once inside, Erin quickly took a seat and said, "Kyle, this is my sister, Mary Catherine, but everyone calls her Katie."

Kyle smiled at Katie and said, "It's nice to meet you, ma'am."

She returned his smile and said, "We were wondering what you looked like and now that I see you, I can tell that you're an Evans."

"That's what they all tell me."

Dylan and Bryn glanced at each other before they hung their hats on nearby pegs and then began unbuckling their gunbelts. Kyle's gunbelt was still in his saddlebags since meeting the Pawnee because he hadn't had any reason to wear it.

"Where are my nephews?" Dylan asked.

Erin replied, "The big one is standing beside you, Dylan, but if you're talking about our sons, Mason and Ethan, they're both napping."

"I don't want to wake them, so let's get caught up quickly."

"It won't be that quick," Erin said as everyone joined her at the large kitchen table.

For the next twenty minutes, most of the conversation was about the family's move to Denver and Dylan taking over the marshal slot. After Mason appeared from the bedroom rubbing his eyes, it shifted to Bryn's family news and how he'd acquired all the land and the house in Denver. That quickly morphed into Bryn's confrontation and arrest of Sheriff Brown in Golden and the current sticky situation in the town that now required him to return, but this time with Kyle.

"I know I'm probably overly worried about Cal's ability to handle Cornbread Funk, but I don't think a man with that much to lose is going to return to just being a saloon and bordello owner. He'll look for a way to either get Cal to work for him or eliminate him," Bryn said.

Dylan nodded and asked, "What about you? Do you think he harbors a grudge against you?"

Bryn grinned and replied, "I'm sure he does, but Cal is in the town with him and is his first concern."

"Has he contacted you since he took over?"

"Nope, but that doesn't mean much. He's probably pretty busy with only one weak deputy. He said he was going to add two more, so maybe he's already hired one."

As they talked, Kyle kept glancing at Katie and tried to guess her age. Dylan had only said that she was Erin's younger sister but hadn't said how much younger. He was never good at guessing ages and she was harder than most. She could be anywhere from sixteen to twenty-two. He didn't think it mattered, but he was curious.

Katie, on the other hand, knew almost precisely how old Kyle was after Bryn had estimated the range of his birthdates. He had to be at least two years younger than she was. Just as Kyle believed, she didn't think it mattered, but it would be nice to have someone else to talk to who wasn't related. There was something that he'd said that did bother her. He'd called her 'ma'am', as if she was already a spinster and as much as she hated to admit it, the use of the simple form of address had stung.

———

After a long supper where Kyle again narrated his story, he and Flat Jack returned to the barn and moved his things into the only empty bedroom in the small house, lit the lamp then spent another half an hour putting everything away.

He and Flat Jack spent another two hours talking, and Kyle asked the old wrangler to teach him about horses because he was ignorant of the critters and just about everything else.

Kyle liked and admired his uncles, but he made an instant connection with Flat Jack not understanding that he had seen a real father in the tough fifty-year-old ranch hand, not the thoughtless man who'd abandoned him and his mother when he was six and not the real father he never knew.

That night as he lay on his bunk listening to Flat Jack's snores reverberate through the silent house, he was finally able to relax.

It had been a whirlwind since he'd arrived in Omaha and except for the almost serene journey to Denver, it seemed that he never stopped answering questions. He could understand why it was that way, but still hoped things would finally settle down now that he'd met all of the Evans.

————

"What do you think of our nephew," Bryn asked Erin as she wiggled around in a vain attempt to find a position that was remotely comfortable.

She finally settled on her left side looking at Bryn and replied, "I like him a lot. I know I'm prejudiced because he looks so much like you, but he's so polite and yet I could see the calm confidence in his eyes. I feel better knowing that he'll be around when you're gone."

"Flat Jack is here, Erin."

"I know, but he's usually out with the herd or out hunting for mustangs. Besides, he doesn't move so fast anymore. After hearing those stories, I think Kyle has unlimited potential."

"Dylan told me that on the way down here, they met up with a Pawnee war party of eight warriors, and he sent Kyle to stand about thirty yards off the road with his bat to show them his skill with the club as a weapon. He told me that Kyle had planned to use it as a baseball bat, by the way."

"He sent him out there by himself?" Erin asked in hushed surprise.

"He was close enough where Dylan could pull his repeater and they didn't have any guns. Anyway, what Dylan said that was most impressive was after Kyle did his exercise with the bat, which he says looks like a defensive dance, one of the warriors attacked Kyle with a coup stick. Kyle pulled his bat above his head in an attack position, but even as the Pawnee warrior thundered close, he just held the bat steady.

"The Indian rode past tapped him with his coup stick then whooped his victory and left. Kyle never swung his bat and Dylan thought it was because he knew the warrior was just counting coup, but he didn't even know what it was. That and the other stories that Kyle told about his other two confrontations on the walk from Pennsylvania, showed what an extraordinary man he is. He didn't panic and he didn't overreact to any of the threats. I've seen too many men, including deputy U.S. marshals, fire first and think second."

"You and Dylan don't," Erin reminded him.

"We're Evans men, ma'am, and so is Kyle. Dylan is going to have his name legally changed to make it official."

Erin then smiled and said, "That's good. When Katie marries him, then she'll be an Evans, too."

Bryn's eyes popped wide as he replied, "Where did you see that? I must have missed it."

"Oh, it wasn't much, but they were evaluating each other during supper, and it was probably just a young man and young woman thing. But I hope that Kyle can finally help Katie climb out of her pit. I'm not saying that they'll really get married or anything, but I just wish Katie didn't waste any more of her youth just out of fear."

"It could become a real mess around here if anything develops and then falls apart. He's two years younger than Katie, you know."

"I know, but he seems older than that and Katie has always seemed younger. Maybe it was because she was so shielded for most of her life because of the whole nun thing. All I know is that she's either got to get past it soon or she may as well become a nun after all."

"That, wife, would be a terrible waste."

Erin laughed then took Bryn's hand and laid it on her big bump.

———

In Golden, at the Ace High Saloon, Cornbread Funk was sitting in his office with the door closed to keep out the noise from the gambling tables. Across the desk from him was the former Jefferson County Deputy Arnie Popovich. Since being released from the storeroom he'd worked in the saloon as Cornbread's personal guard. It paid more than he'd earned as a deputy sheriff, but it didn't have the under-the-table payouts that more than doubled his salary.

He saw that new sheriff, Cal Burris, strutting around town acting all friendly with the citizens and even Chet Caruthers seemed to be more important now. When Arnie had been a deputy, Chet had been anchored to the desk and served as a jailer more than a deputy. Burris had even hired a new deputy to replace him, a veteran of the war named Iggy Justice. Arnie had laughed at the name but seethed inside.

But now the boss had called him in to have him do a very important job and it held the promise of a move up the ladder.

Kyle may have believed that Cornbread's focus was on Cal, but Cornbread had met him more than once to get a read on the man and thought he could be handled whenever he wanted. He thought the real threat lived on his ranch outside of Denver and when the deputy marshal said that he'd be coming to Golden periodically, Cornbread had to come up with a way to stop that from happening.

He'd devised an incredibly heinous plan that only a sick mind could have devised, but he had the man to do it, and it wasn't Arnie. Arnie would be just a supporting actor in the two-act tragedy, and Cornbread really didn't care if he was alive to take a bow at the finish. When it was done, he wouldn't have to worry about U.S. Deputy Marshal Bryn Evans any longer and could switch his attention to the new sheriff.

After Cornbread told Arnie what he expected him to do, Arnie was startled at first, but didn't say anything as he tried to picture the attack but hadn't heard most of the plan.

Finally, he said, "I don't think it's a very good idea, boss. I mean, that damned Evans is just too good with his guns."

"Yes, he is, but he also goes to work every day and that's why I want it done on a weekday. You can do this in just a day, and nobody would know it had anything to do with you."

"But it would bring the wrath of the new marshal and his whole office down on us, boss."

"If there aren't any witnesses, why would they come up here to look? You can make it look like some horse thieves went after his animals."

"But I never killed a woman before, boss. Kids are even worse."

Cornbread looked at Arnie, saw his vacillation and said, "I figured that, Arnie. I've already arranged for Bill Cargo to join you and he'll do all of the difficult killing and you'll just have to back him up and finish off that old wrangler. I'll pay you a hundred-dollar bonus for the job, too."

Arnie stared at the boss with wide eyes and said, "Carbo is here?"

"He's been here for a while and I've used him once before, but I need you to go with him because he's unfamiliar with the area. He's really good with those knives and it won't take but a few minutes."

Arnie leaned back and said, "If we get caught, all hell will break loose around here, boss."

"I know that and it's worth the risk. You'd better bring some extra clothes with you, so you aren't covered with blood when you get back. Then nobody will know you even left the town."

Arnie finally nodded and said, "Okay, boss. When do I meet Carbo?"

"When you come to work tomorrow, you'll meet him in the back room. Take your time to get everything right. Plan on going on Monday morning."

Arnie nodded, but wondered why they couldn't do it tomorrow.

CHAPTER 9

The next morning before Bryn went to the office, he and Dylan rode to a spot about four hundred yards west of the big house and Dylan marked off the location for the two houses that would be built in his absence. Even though Bryn had the house in Denver, he knew that his mother would want to live on the ranch with her grandchildren. Besides, it wouldn't be a big house, but it would be bigger than the house where Kyle and Flat Jack hung their hats. His new house on the other hand, would be even larger than Bryn's or their home in Omaha to accommodate his already large brood.

After Bryn and Dylan headed to Denver, Kyle and Flat Jack wandered to the big corral.

"Bryn said for you to pick out your own horse, Kyle. I'm not gonna say anything. I want to see which one you choose."

"It sounds like a test, Jack," Kyle said as he scanned the crowded corral.

Flat Jack grinned at Kyle and replied, "Kinda."

Kyle grinned back then Jack opened the gate and Kyle began his closer examination. There were a lot of horses in the corral and even more out in the pastures to the west. The ones in the roaming herd in the pastures were all green broke, and it was Jack's, and now Kyle's job to break them the rest of the way. Jack described the process last night and Kyle was sure that it would be a black-and-blue learning experience.

As he weaved among the big animals, Kyle took a few seconds to examine their hocks, flanks and shoulders. He checked the size of their chests and looked at their eyes when they turned to study him in return.

He wasn't looking for the handsomest horse, but as he studied each of them, he found that the sturdiest seemed to be the best-looking as well.

"Why do the prettiest horses seem to be the strongest, too?" he asked Jack as he ran his hands across the neck of a black gelding.

"Breeding does that. The best stallion gets to mate with the prettiest mare because she's got the best figure, at least for a horse, I reckon. It's the same with folks too in case you didn't notice. Your uncle Bryn married a fine filly in your Aunt Erin, and they have two fine lookin' boys already. I'll bet that the little girl she's carryin' about is gonna be a real head-turner."

"You haven't met Dylan's wife, Gwen, have you?"

"Nope. I guess you'll be tellin' me that she's a right pretty gal, too."

Kyle laughed and replied, "Yes, sir. She's very pretty and their children are all handsome, too."

"Well, then maybe you oughta hook up with Katie. She's a pretty young thing and you two would foal some mighty handsome young'uns."

Kyle turned to Jack and said, "Jack, I only showed up yesterday. Don't you think I should do something like work before I even think about seeing girls?"

"Maybe so, but I did the same thing, Kyle. When I was your age back in Ohio, I was all smitten by a girl named Harriet Longley. We were gonna get married and I know she woulda made me real happy. But I didn't figure I was ready yet, so I asked her to wait, and she did, too. She waited for two and a half years while I went about the business of learnin' the horse trade so I could get a good job.

"Then after I got the job, I wanted her to wait until I was settled in, so she waited another six months. Then her daddy said she'd waited too long and if I wasn't gonna marry her, she'd better find a man who would, so she up and married her second cousin who had been waiting to move in. I left Ohio when I heard she'd accepted him, and it took me a while to get over the mistake.

"Don't go makin' the same mistake, Kyle. If you find a girl that takes your heart, don't let her go. A regular time for courtin' is okay, but don't keep puttin' it off to try and make it perfect, because there ain't any such thing."

Kyle nodded then replied, "Thanks, Jack, but I think you're wrong about there not being anything so perfect. I saw it with Dylan and Gwen, and I'm beginning to see the same thing with Bryn and Erin. It may happen more often than you think. Maybe if you'd married Harriet, you would have had the same thing too."

Jack exhaled then grinned, smacked Kyle on the shoulder, and said, "Maybe so, but now you've gotta find your horse."

Kyle saw the flare of sadness in Jack's eyes, so he smiled then turned to the horse and said, "Let's go."

It took them another twenty minutes before Kyle spotted a tall, light gray gelding with a black mane and tail and four black stockings. He was as handsome a horse as Kyle had laid eyes on and wondered if he was available or was one of Bryn's or Erin's personal mounts.

He approached the gelding then as he touched its flank, the horse slowly turned his eyes to look at Kyle and just stared at him.

"Could I have him, Jack? I mean, I could understand if you, Bryn, or Erin would want him. He's spectacular."

Jack smiled and said, "You can have him, Kyle, and I've gotta tell you, he's the one I woulda chose for you. He's just three years old and can be a bit skittish, but I think you'll be able to handle him as long as you ask him to do things instead of tellin' him."

Kyle stroked his long neck as he said, "He sure has fire in his eyes, Jack."

"He's a keeper, that's for sure. Now, let's take him out of the corral into the barn and get him saddled," he said as he began putting a bridle on the gelding.

————

Once astride the gray, Kyle felt a sense of power emanating from the horse and as Jack watched, he trotted him out of the barn into the bright Colorado sunshine.

Kyle then nudged the gelding's flanks and he headed west, and soon passed the back of the big house where he saw Katie beating a small rug. He waved and she smiled back as she returned his wave with the rug beater in her hand.

He continued west for another five minutes before turning south, knowing that Bryn's land stretched for another seven miles or so. He and the gelding quickly developed a bond as they trotted away from the barn.

They reached the first of several big streams that flowed northeast from the nearby Rockies, and he let the gray drop his muzzle into the cold water as he scanned the landscape.

It was so much different than any other place he'd seen in his travels across the country. The heavily forested terrain of Pennsylvania had thinned into the hills of Ohio and had remained the same across Indiana before the hills began to get lower and the trees fewer.

Iowa had been a transition state that would turn into the Great Plains of Nebraska that he knew stretched north beyond the Canadian border. Trees were hard to find, but the land wasn't as flat as most people back East thought.

Now he was studying land with its own unique signature. The Rocky Mountains to the west dominated the view in that direction, but as they gave way to the nearby foothills, the pine forests began to take control. The melting snow that could still be seen in the mountains even in August provided the continuous cold flow of water that flowed across the rocky ground and eventually would reach the South Platte River.

He could understand why Bryn would love it here and hoped that he could make his own home somewhere close. He had never even considered the possibility until his talk with Flat Jack. He would be eighteen in January and maybe by then, he'd have a firmer idea of what he would do. But for now, he just sat on his new friend's back and admired the scenery.

It was his new friend that reminded him that they should start moving again when he tossed his head and nickered loudly.

Kyle laughed, and patted the horse's neck as he said, "Okay, Nick, let's head back."

As he wheeled the gelding around, he didn't realize that he'd given his horse his name. It had just popped out because the gray had nickered at him. Regardless of the reason, he liked the name because it reminded him of his mother who told him stories about St. Nick when he was young.

Christmas would have been just another cold winter day if his mother hadn't spent the night before telling him about St. Nick and the real reason that they celebrated the day. They never went to church, and he never missed it until he asked her one day when he was thirteen after a friend had asked why he didn't go to church.

She'd told him that her father had sent her away because, as he had told her, he was a 'good Christian' and she wasn't worthy of living in his house. Kyle hadn't pressed the issue at the time because he saw how sad it had made her. It wasn't until the very end of their time together that he knew the reason and finally understood why she had never remarried.

He and Nick reached the barn where he found Flat Jack waiting with a big grin.

"You two seemed to get along," he said as Kyle dismounted.

"He's a good friend, Jack. I name him Nick. Is that okay?"

"It's better'n most. I was hopin' you weren't gonna name him Boots or Socks. That woulda riled me some."

Kyle began unsaddling Nick as he replied, "Does he go back into the corral, or do we leave him in the barn now?"

"He's a family horse, so he gets to stay here. You can put him in the stall next to Katie's mare."

Kyle lugged the saddle to the shelf and after setting it down, he asked, "What's her horse's name?"

"She's Zoe, and she's a pretty lady, don't you think?"

Kyle approached the dark brown mare and asked, "The horse or her rider?"

Jack snickered then replied, "They're both pretty ladies, mister, but I was talkin' about her mare."

"I know, Jack. I was just having some fun. She is a handsome young lady. How old is she? And I'm talking about the horse."

"The mare is four and has only foaled once. Your filly will be twenty in September."

Kyle blushed in the shadows of the barn as he quickly replied, "She's not my filly, Jack. She's Erin's sister. That's all."

Jack was still smiling as he silently helped strip Nick.

————

Dylan had stopped at the construction firm that Bryn had recommended and spent almost two hours selecting the designs for the two houses and a large barn and corral. When he left, he was told that the crews would start work next Wednesday and would have the jobs done by the last week of September.

Dylan didn't mind the delay if it was done right, so he signed the contract and left a large draft before heading for the office. Bryn had offered him the use of the empty house in Denver, so he and Gwen would stay there while their new home was being built. John and his mother could stay at the Double EE and watch the construction while his mother anxiously awaited the arrival of Grace Lynn.

When he got to the office, he met with Al Esposito for another two hours before buying lunch with the entire office, including Bryn. Two of the deputies were out at the time, so the bill wasn't as large as it could have been.

After lunch, Dylan sent telegrams to Gwen and his mother letting them know that he and Kyle had arrived safely and that their new homes would be well underway when they arrived. He added a line to his mother's message that Grace Lynn still hadn't made her appearance.

———

Jack had shown Kyle how to shoe a horse, and after the instruction, watched as Kyle replaced the worn shoes on the buggy horse before they carried some hay out to the corral, then pumped the large trough full before heading into the small house for lunch.

Jack wasn't a very good cook, so Kyle took over the duties. He'd cooked for himself and his mother for the last few months, but his menu was limited. Still, Jack called him a master chef just for making two smoked pork sandwiches.

It was after the quick lunch that Jack said, "Dylan said that you could handle that club of yours like a knife blade. Can you show me?"

"Not in here. How about the barn?"

"Okay," he replied as he stood and wiped his hands on his britches.

———

Ten minutes later, Kyle was deep into his exercises as Jack stood near the barn door watching with approving eyes.

Kyle wanted to impress Jack and added a few flourishes that almost backfired when he came close to losing his grip, but the knob at the bat end stopped the slip and he was able to complete the maneuvers.

When he finished, he popped the knotted end to the floor, and smiled at Jack as the sweat rolled off his brow and soaked his bare chest and back.

"That was worth payin' a nickel for admission, Kyle," Jack said as he walked into the barn, "It was like you were dancin'."

Kyle leaned the bat against a stall and replied, "That's what it is, really. I was shown how to waltz by my mother, and I realized that if I hummed the music in my head, I could match my moves to the beat. It made the moves smoother and more effective."

"You practice every day?"

"Unless I'm busy. I'll do it in the afternoon in the barn until I can do it outside after sunset."

"Why?"

"I have to take off my shirt or I'll be washing it every day. Right now, sunset is too late, so I can do it in the barn. I don't want to embarrass Erin or Katie by practicing outside where they can see me."

Jack shook his head as he chuckled but didn't comment while Kyle let himself dry before he could put on his shirt.

Just two minutes later, as he slid his arm through the sleeve, he said, "I dry a lot faster here."

"It's drier air out here."

Kyle nodded then left his bat where it was as he and Jack left the barn to take care of the horses in the corral and continue his education.

––––––

In Golden, Arnie Popovich was in the back room at the Ace High talking to Bill Carbo about the job that they'd be doing on Monday. Two things had bothered Arnie when he met Carbo. The small hired killer seemed to know more about the job than he did, and the man himself.

Bill Carbo scared Arnie despite his size which was six inches and eighty pounds less than his. Carbo's cold eyes and reputation with his knife spooked him. Arnie didn't mind the thought of being shot but being sliced by Bill's razor-sharp blade gave him the willies.

Cornbread had offered Carbo a one-time payment of a two hundred dollars to help Arnie and Arnie thought that Carbo would have done it for nothing. He just enjoyed killing and it was that soulless flaw that had driven him to Golden.

He was hunted by the law in almost every state or territory west of the Mississippi and one or two on the other side of the great river. He'd arrived a few months ago and had been laying low until he'd recognized an opportunity and approached Cornbread to offer his services. He'd done one quiet job for the saloon owner that no one had even noticed, but this one was right up his alley.

As he stared at Arnie, Bill asked, "Why is he having us wait until Monday? That's four days away and we could get this done tomorrow."

"The boss said to wait to make sure that it's done right."

Bill continued to glare at Arnie sending chills up his spine as he said, "I could go down there and do this myself, Arnie. I could get that deputy marshal, too."

"No!" Arnie exclaimed, "We need to get this done so nothing points back at the boss. He doesn't want that entire marshal's office comin' here."

"Alright, but I still think we oughta go tomorrow."

Arnie relaxed but only barely as he began reviewing the plan. It really wasn't complex, at least the part that he understood. They'd get to the ranch which should be occupied by one old man, two women and children and simply enter the house and kill them all. Arnie knew that the deputy marshal's wife was pregnant, but he'd leave her to Carbo. He was already planning on leaving the children to the heartless killer as well, but he'd use the young sister before giving her to Carbo after he was done. He'd take care of the wrangler by himself while Carbo did his dirty work.

When they finished their killing, they'd ransack the house then open the corral gate and let the horses loose. After changing out of their bloody clothes, they'd simply ride back to Golden taking the road so they wouldn't leave a trail.

They'd leave early in the morning, get to the ranch around noon and should be back in time for supper.

————

During the supper at the Double EE, Dylan told them about the construction crews that would be starting on Wednesday, and that he'd be heading back to Omaha to begin preparations for the move on Saturday.

"Am I coming with you, Dylan?" Kyle asked.

"Nope. I'm not even riding Crow. I'm taking a stagecoach like a regular citizen. I want to get an idea of what it's like. Hopefully, we'll be returning in a couple of weeks. We'll have a freight company bring our things and I'll ride with them and trail our horses, so I may be here before they get here, but I could be later, too."

"Are you bringing the player piano?" Erin asked.

"Yes, ma'am."

"You aren't leaving Peanut behind, are you?"

"Now, Erin, you know better than to ask me that question. The boys would gang up on me in my sleep if I even thought about it and Bethan would just give me those sad eyes that always wins any arguments."

Erin laughed even as she glanced at Kyle who was sitting beside Katie, which was her doing.

Kyle had been uncomfortable when he found the only open chair to be the one beside Katie, so he'd been studiously ignoring her since they began eating. It was difficult because he could detect her light flowery scent even over the dominating aroma of the roast beef.

301

Katie hadn't been as uncomfortable as she'd expected when Kyle had taken the seat. Maybe it was because he looked so much like Bryn that it had washed away her normal skittishness. She may not have been uncomfortable herself but could almost feel his awkwardness as they sat just three inches apart at the crowded table.

After ten minutes of being ignored, Katie finally turned to Kyle and asked, "What did you name your horse, Kyle?"

Kyle turned to face Katie and as her blue eyes caught his hazels, he was momentarily forced into oblivion and couldn't remember the name at all.

After a tortuous five seconds, he stammered, "Um, I…I named him…" then asked, "Why don't you guess?"

Katie smiled and Kyle began to wonder if he'd soon forget his own name and almost missed her answer.

"Well, you wouldn't name him something as obvious as Boots, and I'm sure that you'd stay away from some of those horrible Gaelic words, so let me think."

She continued to stare and smile at Kyle suddenly enjoying making him so disjointed before she finally said, "How about Nick?"

Kyle stared back at Katie's laughing eyes and suddenly his discomfort evaporated as his own eyes closed to slits and he said, "You already knew that; didn't you?"

"Jack might have mentioned it after you rode off," she answered, her smile never leaving her face.

Kyle hadn't noticed that everyone else was watching them as he said, "I suppose that it's only fair because he told me Zoe's name, too."

"Then we're even, but it was fun; wasn't it?"

"Yes, ma'am. I'll admit that it was."

Katie's smile vanished when he called her 'ma'am' for a second time, and she quickly turned away to return to her food.

Kyle was startled when the suddenly enjoyable interplay had ended so abruptly, so he resumed eating wondering what he had said that was so offensive.

Erin knew immediately what the issue was because Katie had mentioned that she suddenly felt old when Kyle had called her 'ma'am'. She thought that her sister had understood that Kyle's background was the only reason for his use of the term, but now she seemed to have returned to a sulk.

She then smiled at Kyle and said, "Stop being so polite, Kyle. I'm sure that Mary Catherine wouldn't mind if you addressed her by her Christian name."

Kyle turned to Katie and asked quietly, "Would you mind?"

Katie took a split second to look at her sister before she turned to look at Kyle's incredibly innocent face and felt foolish as she softly replied, "Not at all. I do call you, Kyle, in case you haven't noticed."

"I didn't, but thank you for the privilege, Katie."

Her smile returned as she replied, "I'd hardly consider it a privilege."

Kyle then warmly smiled before saying, "I do, and if I call you 'ma'am' again then just smack me in the head to remind me."

"I'll take your advice, but I won't hit you as hard as I've seen Erin hit Bryn."

Bryn then said, "She has a longer reach than you do, Katie."

Erin was pleased with her intervention and snapped, "You're close to earning another smack, mister!"

With the brief but momentous interruption ended, the conversation resumed its previous happy chatter about the changes coming to the Double EE and Dylan's trip back to Omaha to retrieve the rest of the Evans clan.

———

After they returned to the small house, Flat Jack and Kyle played poker for a while, but not for a penny as Jack used it as another tool to improve Kyle's understanding of men.

As they played, Jack didn't mention Katie or Kyle's obvious sudden attraction to her but did make a few side comments about horse breeding and their mating habits.

Kyle ignored the obvious inferences as he tried to concentrate on the cards in his hand. He couldn't understand why Katie had suddenly affected him this way. He'd talked to her a few times since he'd arrived and hadn't been as flummoxed as he'd been at dinner. He knew that it had to be just an infatuation because Dylan had told him often that the only way he could really understand and love a woman was to talk to her openly and let her character reveal itself. He hadn't gotten into any meaningful conversations with her yet and suspected that his obvious attack of puppy love would fade soon.

After he blundered and tossed a pair of kings down to replace them with the seven of clubs and the three of diamonds, he vowed to put his mind straight and learn the game.

Jack knew that Kyle was playing so badly that there was no reason to continue the game but there was nothing else to do, so he dealt the next hand.

———

After putting Mason and Ethan to bed, Katie passed Erin's bedroom and entered her own, closing the door behind her. She undressed slowly as she let the recent memory of Kyle wash over her. It hadn't been as sudden or as surprising as it had been for Kyle because when she had first seen him, she'd been struck by how much he resembled both of his uncles.

She had pushed that similarity aside and tried to judge him as a young man and not as Bryn or Dylan's lookalike. She greatly admired both of her brothers-in-law, more for the way they treated their wives than their courage or attractiveness. She had to see Kyle as Kyle and not as another Evans even if he wasn't an Evans yet.

As she pulled up her quilt and slid onto the sheets, Katie knew that if she wanted to avoid becoming the spinster that had seemed her destiny, she'd need to talk to Kyle alone and at length. She knew that she'd never flirt or act coquettish because it wasn't who she was. She was honest with herself and knew each of her faults, and even though she'd worked hard to minimize the worst ones, her temper and her stubbornness, she knew they would always be there. Now she just hoped that Kyle would at least tolerate them.

———

Friday began with the family breakfast and was close to a mirror of Thursday when Bryn and Dylan left the ranch to go to the office while Kyle and Flat Jack headed for the corral. This time, they mounted and headed out to the western pastures to check on the other horses.

As he rode Nick away from the barn, Kyle's mind was already thinking of what he could do for his lifetime's work. In just a short time, he'd learned a lot about horses and other things from Flat Jack but wanted more. Dylan had told him on the first day that Kyle arrived that he had always wanted to be a lawman and Bryn wanted to raise horses but only after he'd seen the slaughter of the animals on the battlefield. Now Bryn owned a horse ranch but was still a deputy marshal which Dylan had said was his second calling.

Kyle didn't have a calling of any kind and smiled when he remembered Dylan telling him that Katie had been overjoyed to avoid being a nun because she didn't have the calling.

Jack yelled over, "Let's head over to the smaller herd over to the east," then turned his tall black gelding in that direction.

Kyle nudged Nick and he followed alongside Jack's horse that he'd named Darky at first, but Bryn had strongly suggested he just drop the 'y', so now he was just Dark. Jack sometimes slipped and called him by his original name but never when Bryn was around.

They reached the herd and rather than dismount, Jack began inspecting the animals from the saddle and started questioning Kyle about their condition.

He stopped beside a small brown mare and asked, "What's his situation, Kyle?"

"For one thing, he's a she, and she's carrying a foal."

Jack grinned and asked, "When is she gonna drop it?"

"Soon, I'd guess. Probably late September or early October."

"Close enough. You're gettin' better, Kyle."

Kyle then looked west to the Rockies and asked, "Have you ever gone that way, Jack?"

"Just up in the foothills. Bryn told me that he got this land from a feller named Peacock who bought it cheap because there wasn't any gold around and then seeded it with some dust and sold acre claims to a bunch of miners before they kinda let him know that they weren't happy."

"How come there's no gold? I thought it all came down in streams from the mountains?"

"Beats me. I just know it ain't here."

"Do you have any problems with prospectors still hunting around for it?"

"I've seen 'em on the western edge of the ranch down south a few times, but they don't stick around long."

"Does Bryn scare them off, or do they just leave?"

"Mostly, they just leave, but we've had to run off a few of the troublemakers."

"Are you any good with that repeater?"

"I'm okay, but Bryn is scary good with the pistol and his Winchester. He told me that Dylan is even better. How are you with that pistol?"

"Not very good, but I've only fired it eight times since I got it."

"Why don't you practice some? We sure have enough ammunition."

Kyle shrugged and replied, "I have my bat and it's served me well."

"Well, son," Jack said as he grinned, "It ain't gonna help if the other feller's got a pistol."

"It did once but to be honest, he didn't see me and I kind of ambushed him."

"You ain't gonna be that lucky again, Kyle. You should do some practice shootin'."

"Maybe," he answered before they turned south to check on the other herd that wasn't corralled.

As they rode south, Kyle knew that he should follow Jack's advice and learn to shoot, but right now the timing was bad because Bryn and Dylan were spending so much time together and he didn't want to bother Bryn.

Dylan would be leaving on tomorrow's stage to head back to Julesburg and Bryn would be at work, so he'd ask Bryn about the target practice on Sunday.

———

At the office, Al Esposito and Dylan signed the papers making him responsible if anyone came in and stole the office when they weren't looking then there was a small celebration at Al's house. Dylan could see how happy Jean Esposito was to be returning to Kansas City and she knew that he was just as pleased to be taking over the Denver office.

Dylan was pleased but one of his biggest concerns, aside from the almost perpetual shortage of deputies was when Bryn had told him about the situation in Golden when he had first arrived. Al had confirmed Bryn's beliefs and expressed the same concerns about Cal Burris's ability to deal with Cornbread Funk.

Dylan had told Al about Bryn's pending visit to Golden, probably on Tuesday because Mondays were always a hectic day in the office but didn't mention Bryn's decision to take Kyle along. That was his call now.

———

Dylan's last night at the Double EE for a month or so wasn't much different than the others and the talk was mostly about Gwen and his children's arrival with Meredith and John and Alba March.

Kyle hadn't avoided talking to Katie but hadn't said anything personal, nor had she. It was as if they were each waiting for the right time, which was exactly what they were doing.

———

Saturday arrived and after a hasty breakfast, Dylan kissed Erin, Katie and their children goodbye then shook Kyle's hand before shaking Flat Jack's.

It was shortly after sunrise when Dylan and Bryn left the ranch to make the fast ride into Denver to catch the morning stage.

Once they were gone, Kyle and Jack had to ride out to the herds again to rope a colt who would soon lose his stallion-ship. It wasn't a difficult or even an overly messy job, but Kyle had expressed his sympathy to the young horse and had automatically rammed his thighs together as a show of support.

"Does it hurt?" Kyle asked.

"I reckon it does, but I ain't about to find out," Jack replied as he stood.

Kyle let the colt's neck go and then walked with Jack back to their horses.

"You gonna do some practice shootin' tomorrow?" Jack asked as they headed for the barn.

"I was going to ask Bryn about it tonight."

"Well, if you do, I'll come along."

"So, I'll have two men laughing at me rather than just one."

Jack laughed as he replied, "I ain't sayin' that I won't snicker a bit."

Kyle grinned at Jack and was glad that he lived in the same house with him. There wasn't any tension, but there were moments of humorous insults which were usually spawned when Jack emitted large and loud volumes of gas from either end of his digestive system.

———

Dylan was sitting in the coach on the west-facing window across from a young couple who would be catching the same train that he'd be taking back to Omaha. They'd just been married and were excited about seeing her parents.

Surprisingly, Dylan hadn't heard her family's name before and that began a long conversation that helped pass the time as the coach raced northeast toward the first waystation.

The couple was surprised and pleased to know that he was a United States Marshal, and although Dylan didn't know her family name, the young lady had certainly known who he was and his reputation, so his presence on the coach helped to assuage her many concerns about making the long trip through Indian country.

———

At supper that evening, Kyle asked, "Bryn, I've only fired my pistol a few times and I wasn't very good with it. Can you help me to get better?"

Bryn set down his fork and asked, "What kind of pistol is it?"

"It's a Smith & Wesson Model 2 and fires a .32 caliber metallic cartridge."

Bryn broke into a wide smile and replied, "Dylan didn't tell me that piece of information, but it's what I shoot most of the time. Dylan was the one who gave me the pair before I left Omaha to go into the army."

"He told me that when he saw mine. So, can you help me?"

C.J. PETIT

"Of course, I can, and I'll do you one better. I have an old Henry that I don't use anymore that hasn't even been fired that much and you can have it. The one I took with me in '61 when I enlisted is getting pretty tired."

The Henry's faults had been described to him by Dylan on the long journey from Omaha but knew that it was the ancestor to the much-improved Winchester Model 1866 that was already becoming wildly popular.

"Thanks, Bryn. I promise not to try and grab the barrel when it gets hot, load it too quickly or at too steep of an angle."

Bryn laughed and said, "Dylan must have lectured you for a while about his new Winchester."

"Yes, sir."

Then Bryn said, "But don't stop practicing with that bat of yours."

"I'll always use it but maybe one of these days, I'll use it for its intended purpose to play some baseball. Maybe after Dylan's boys arrive, we can set up a baseball diamond."

"Now that sounds like fun!" Katie exclaimed.

Kyle turned to Katie and asked, "Do you want to learn to play, Katie?"

"I'd love to. I saw some boys playing a game back in Omaha and tried to understand the rules, but all I saw was them hitting a ball with a stick and running."

"Sometimes there aren't any rules, but the basic game is the same. One of these days, I'll tell you what happened in my last game back in Wilkes-Barre."

She smiled and said, "I suppose that you'll tell me that you won the game with one mammoth swing of your bat."

"Well, I did win the game, but it was hardly a mammoth swing. In fact, I thought I'd barely struck the ball, but things worked out and we won. It was our first victory over the boss's handpicked team, and it cost me my job. They claimed that I had cheated, but they just hated losing."

He'd barely finished talking when there was a general outcry for him to tell the story, and Kyle knew that once Katie had asked, he'd have to describe the action.

He started by having to explain the rules of the game, but knew that there would still be many questions, especially not understanding why the third baseman had to tag him with the ball, but he still started with the situation at the bottom of the ninth inning.

As he'd expected, he barely got one line done when someone would ask a question about the game, so what should have been a two-minute long tale soon stretched out to thirty minutes.

When he reached the point where the third baseman made his mental error, he explained the rule and that in the game's early years, the third baseman would have had to throw the ball at him and hit him to get the out. The concept seemed to tickle everyone's funny bone and resulted in Garth throwing the remains of his baked potato at Lynn and shouting, "You're out!"

By the time he reached the climactic slide into home, he was standing in the center of the floor mimicking the throws, catches and attempted tags as everyone watched. Even three-year-old Mason seemed entranced.

Then just as he pretended to be the catcher and spread his legs wide and stretched out with cupped hands toward the floor with his imaginary ball, Bryn shouted, "Run him down, Kyle!"

Kyle stood then looked at Bryn and said, "That's what everyone expected me to do, but he was an enormous man and I'd probably break a bone or two if I had and I'd still be out. So, I decided to slide between his legs and touch home plate with the winning run."

Katie excitedly asked, "Did you make it safely without being tagged out?"

"Yes and no. I started my slide and when I felt him ram that ball into my chest, I, um, well, I kind of made him drop it out of his hands and was called safe."

"How did you manage that if he was so big?" Erin asked.

"Well, I didn't try to knock the ball out of hands directly. I just made him forget that he had the ball at all because he found something else that was more important to him."

Erin looked at him curiously but Bryn began laughing as he said, "You kicked him as you went between his legs. Didn't you?"

Kyle just nodded and then shrugged his shoulders and returned to his seat beside Katie.

Erin and Katie had joined Bryn and Flat Jack in laughter as Kyle took a sip of his coffee before Erin said, "You won't teach Mason or Ethan to do that, I hope."

"I won't teach them, Erin, but boys learn to do those things because sooner or later, it happens to all of us. Just don't ask me about my own experience. I'm sure that Bryn can tell you his later."

Bryn looked at Erin with raised eyebrows and shrugged which almost ensured him that she'd question him when they were alone in the bed.

Katie then looked at Kyle and almost asked if he would tell her of his personal temporary tragedy later, but thought it wasn't the right time.

————

Later that night, as Dylan was resting at the first waystation, Flat Jack and Kyle talked about building a baseball field nearby and about tomorrow's target practice.

Kyle was just grateful that none of the discussion was about Katie or about his very real concern that she was going to ask him what had happened to him that prompted his answer to Erin's question.

————

The target shooting on Sunday afternoon was a revelation to Kyle, who learned quickly how much he'd done wrong.

Now he was learning from a true marksman and it wasn't long before he felt more comfortable with his pistol and even Bryn's old Henry. None of his shots were nearly as close as Bryn's but he did beat Flat Jack a few times. Jack blamed his less than perfect eyesight and his knobby knees for his performance.

After they finished Bryn showed Kyle how to care for the Henry and gave him a box of cartridges and a scabbard for Nick's saddle.

"Now you need to wear a real hat," he said as they walked back to the house.

"I don't like hats unless it gets really cold. I had one when I left Wilkes-Barre and I found that it blocked my vision."

"Okay, but when you need one, let me know and we'll go to Miller's Haberdashery instead of the emporium. They have a better choice."

"Thanks, Bryn."

Bryn then stopped and turned to Kyle and said, "I'll be heading to Golden on Tuesday. Do you still want to come along?"

"Yes, sir. I'd like to see the town."

"Hopefully, it'll just be a quick ride, a fast lunch after a talk with their sheriff then a ride back in time for supper."

"Do I bring my bat?"

"Never go anywhere without that thing. There were a lot of times that I wished I had a weapon other than a pistol or rifle. A knife is good, but when you're facing more than one man, it's not good enough. Your bat can fend off more than two if you manage it right and put them all out of commission without killing any of them. Maybe when we get back, you can show me how you use it."

"Okay, Bryn," he answered before they started walking again.

———

That night, Kyle disassembled the Henry and cleaned and oiled each piece before reassembling the repeater under Jack's watchful eyes.

After he reloaded the carbine, Jack nodded and said, "Good job, Kyle. You might even match Bryn or Dylan in a while."

"I doubt it, Jack. I'm just happy to figure out all the things that I was doing wrong."

"Better now than when you need it, Kyle."

Kyle grinned at Jack and said, "I don't think anything's going to happen around here unless some of those prospectors start trouble."

"You never know, Kyle," Jack said before he stood and headed for his bedroom.

———

In Golden, Bill Carbo was sliding the edge of his smaller blade across the stone slowly as Arnie watched from the other side of the small room.

When he finished, Bill held the knife in his right hand and lightly touched his left index finger to the tip and a drop of blood escaped onto the blade. He then wiped his blood across the bright steel with the bleeding finger and smiled.

"I'm ready, Arnie. When do we leave?"

Arnie stared wide-eyed at the blade which was the effect that Carbo had expected as he replied, "Tomorrow morning around nine. It'll take us about three hours to get to his ranch because we'll be taking the back trail around Denver, so nobody sees us."

Bill nodded as he stared at his red blade but didn't say anything.

Arnie then continued, saying, "We'll head outta town to the south and pick up the trail. If we keep heading south after it turns east, we should reach the back side of that ranch and the only one who could be out there is that old wrangler."

"He's not a problem. Even you can probably outshoot the gray-bearded bastard."

Arnie wasn't sure but he figured it didn't matter. If they did have to shoot him, then the sound might alert the women in the house but like Bill had just said, it's not a problem if they all started screaming before Carbo started his deathly work.

CHAPTER 10

Monday, the fifth day of August, arrived in spectacular fashion with a bright red sunrise spreading its rays across the Double EE ranch.

By the time it had been up for an hour, Bryn had kissed Erin goodbye, mounted Maddy and ridden down the access road before heading into Denver. With Dylan gone, the most senior deputy, John Knapp would be in charge. John was a meticulous recordkeeper and had little else to give him hope to become a marshal but at least he understood his limitation and was grateful to wear the badge without having to issue orders. The other two deputies, Chet Caruthers and Tom Shelton, were both older than he was but had less experience.

Al had done his best to improve the skills of his deputies, but they were always so busy with menial administrative tasks that he never had the chance. The fact that they were all married and had children added to the difficulty. Bryn was just glad that Dylan had arrived. He'd be able to hire two more deputies, and maybe lure Thom Smythe and Benji Green from Omaha.

Mondays were always an annoying paperwork catchup day and they rarely left the office except for a fast lunch. At least he'd be heading out to Golden tomorrow, so maybe he'd find some real lawman work there.

———

It was just when Bryn was stepping down from Maddy that Arnie Popovich and Bill Carbo rode out of Golden and soon picked up the start of the southbound trail.

Carbo wasn't talking as he visualized what he would do when he arrived at the Double EE, and Arnie was glad that he hadn't spoken. When he'd first heard Cornbread say that Carbo was joining him, he hadn't really understood the man that well. He knew that he was a cold-blooded killer, but even he hadn't realized just how demented the man was. His biggest concern now was that after blood lust had taken over Bill's mind, he'd turn on him.

––––––––

Kyle had worked with Jack all morning then after lunch in the small house, he asked, "What do we do this afternoon, Jack?"

"I was just gonna take a ride south and check for prospectors."

"Do you want me to come along?"

"Nah. If I find any of 'em, I just tell them that the landowner is a U.S. Deputy Marshal and they usually skedaddle. I haven't seen one for a while anyhow. I just like to ride by my lonesome sometimes and headin' that way is just an excuse."

Kyle laughed and said, "Well, I hope you enjoy your solitude. I'm going to head out to the barn in a little while and get my exercise done."

"I'd rather be ridin' Darky than doin' all of that sweatin'," he said with a grin before he stood grabbed his hat and left the house.

Kyle then got to his feet and walked to his room where he unbuckled his gunbelt and hung it over the bedpost. He sometimes forgot to take it off and then began his exercise before the pistol-filled holster bounced off his thigh reminding him that it was there.

He'd also started taking a towel with him to dry off more quickly, so after leaving his room, he opened the linen closet, removed a towel and draped it over his shoulder before leaving the house.

———

Arnie and Bill had passed the turnoff to Denver and were winding their way south toward the Double EE when Bill finally asked, "How much longer?"

Arnie was startled but soon replied, "Less than an hour, I reckon."

"Good, I'm getting too excited."

Arnie glanced at his temporary partner and felt that chill up his spine again. He reassured himself that in four hours, he'd be back in Golden and having a cold beer without Bill nearby. He also began to seriously think about backshooting the small man if he got the chance but only after they finished the job.

———

Kyle removed his shirt and hung it on the side slats of Nick's stall and grasped his bat's handle firmly.

He looked at his gray gelding and said, "Don't think I'm crazy or going to hit you, Nick. This is just exercise."

Nick didn't complain, so Kyle began his stretching exercises to loosen his muscles. He knew that he wasn't bulky like other strong men, but he recalled Lisa describing him as 'sleek' and was satisfied with that description.

He soon began the serious portion of his routine. He had broken it down into five sections, the stretching followed by a slow buildup that lasted about two minutes before entering the middle five or six minutes of whirling, thrusting and pounding that pushed him to his limits. When he felt his strength waning, he entered the fourth phase, a gradual slowing that lasted two minutes until he slowed enough to stop and rest. The rest would vary, but usually lasted three or four minutes before he dried himself.

As he matched his moves to the waltz in his mind, he didn't notice the blue eyes that were watching him from the edge of the barn doors. He was just so focused on his exercise that he was usually unaware of his surroundings.

Katie had seen him enter the barn with the towel and knew what he would be doing. She thought that this was an ideal opportunity to talk to him alone at last and get a better idea of who Kyle really was. She also admitted to herself that she would enjoy every moment as a voyeur.

Just the past few days talking with Kyle and listening to Erin as she talked about him had pushed away her concerns and had allowed her to make this bold move. She liked Kyle and after she had admitted it to herself, she'd decided that she would test her own mettle and spend time alone with him.

As she watched Kyle's muscles flex and bulge as he hefted the heavy shaft, she felt herself growing flush and reveled in the unexpected sensation. Yet even as she immersed herself in her newfound feelings, she was transfixed by the ballet that she was witnessing. This wasn't some violent banging that she'd pictured in her mind; it was artistic with smooth, flowing motion that she couldn't have imagined.

Kyle began slowing, yet still moved his feet with the same three-quarter time that he always used and soon planted his knobbed bat to the floor while he breathed heavily, and his sweat dripped to the barn floor. He was facing Nick when he was startled by the sound of a single person's applause from behind him.

He whirled around and saw Katie's smiling face as she clapped her hands and slowly entered the barn.

"That was beautiful, Kyle," she said before she stopped three feet before him and he set his club against the nearby stall.

Kyle was surprisingly not embarrassed to be standing in front of Katie without a shirt and covered in sweat, so he replied, "Thank you, Katie. I didn't know you were watching."

"I saw you enter the barn with the towel, and I wanted to see your exercise. Dylan told Erin about it and I was curious. It wasn't anything like I expected."

"What did you expect?"

"Oh, I guess I thought that there would be a lot more banging and violent moves, but it looked as if you were dancing."

Kyle was drying himself as he answered, "I was dancing. My mother taught me how to waltz and after I had to use the bat to defend myself, I realized I'd made too many mistakes that could have gotten me killed. So, I remembered the waltz and now I just play it in my head when I do my exercise."

Katie softly said, "I've never been to a dance. I don't know how."

Kyle replied, "I've never been to a dance either, Katie."

Katie's heart was pounding as she asked, "Could you show me how to dance, Kyle?"

"I'd love to show you, but when do you want to do it?"

"Right here and right now, if that's alright."

Kyle looked into her blue eyes and said, "Let me get my shirt on first."

"Okay."

Kyle then turned, tossed the towel onto the stall boards then grabbed his shirt pulled it on and began buttoning it as he returned to Katie.

"Um, I'm going to have to hold you, Katie."

Katie smiled and said, "I can't imagine that you could teach me to dance by mail, Kyle."

Kyle smiled took her small left hand in his right then placed her right hand on his left hip and put his left hand behind her waist, leaving a six-inch gap between them.

Katie's heart hadn't slowed as she looked up at Kyle and asked, "Now what do we do?"

"I'll start humming the waltz, then when you feel my hand pull yours slightly, just move your feet to the beat of the music. It goes like this," he said before he began humming the opening bars to the waltz.

"Are you ready, Katie?" he asked.

"Yes," she whispered as she felt his warmth even with the gap.

He began to hum and soon, she felt his hand tug slightly, and she stepped off. She thought it would be difficult, but she'd watched Kyle when he'd exercised and soon matched the rhythm of his movements with her own. He was taller than she was, but it didn't seem to matter as they waltzed across the barn floor.

Kyle was astonished that his first dance with a girl who'd never danced before was going so smoothly, but it felt as if Katie wasn't even there because she was moving so gracefully.

That sensation of not recognizing her presence soon evaporated when after a minute of sliding across the barn floor, they began drifting closer together and by the time they'd reached the midway point of the long waltz, Katie was pressed against Kyle and he almost missed a step.

Kyle was finding it difficult to recall the next note as he felt Katie but only his constant repetition prevented that obvious mistake.

For two more minutes, Kyle and Katie danced and when Kyle finally ended his waltz vocalization, they continued for another silent minute before they slowed to a stop.

When they were standing together in the barn, Kyle slowly lowered his right hand and joined his left hand behind her back as she dropped her left to his waist as they looked at each other.

Kyle quietly said, "The waltz is over."

"I know," she whispered.

"Is this okay?"

"Yes."

"This is all new to me, Katie."

"It is to me, too."

"We need to talk a lot more now."

"I think that's a good idea."

Kyle knew that it was time to end the dance that would soon follow the waltz and stepped back.

He was about to ask what she'd like to talk about when he heard hoofbeats coming from the west and he initially thought that Jack was returning early but there were two horses making the sound. He felt his neck hairs bristle as he concentrated on the sound.

"Who is it?" Katie asked quietly as she turned to look through the barn doors.

"I don't know, but it's not Jack."

Katie started to walk to the house, but Kyle grabbed her arm and whispered, "Stay here, Katie."

Katie saw the shift in Kyle's eyes and knew that he was concerned about the incoming riders, so she backed into the barn as he released her arm.

He didn't see the riders yet, but he headed into the barn and snatched the only weapon that was nearby, his half-finished baseball bat.

———

When the two assassins rode onto the Double EE, they'd been surprised to see two houses, but decided to ignore the smaller house because if anyone was inside, it would have been the wrangler, and he didn't matter.

But the house did distract Arnie as they walked their horses closer to the big house. He didn't want to be surprised by a rifle shot from the wrangler.

Bill had his eyes focused on the house that was just fifty yards away while Arnie slid his pistol from his holster still glancing at the small house as they passed the barn.

———

Inside the house, Erin was sitting with Ethan on her lap talking to Mason as he played with his carved horses. She was in a cheerful mood as everything seemed to be coming together. The rest of Bryn's family would soon be here, Grace Lynn would soon be in her arms instead of making it difficult to maneuver, and Katie had at last shed her cocoon and was out in the barn talking to Kyle. She couldn't imagine anything spoiling her day.

———

Kyle had the bat firmly in his right hand as he stood near Katie toward the back of the barn with their eyes focused on the bright sunshine past the barn doors.

Katie wanted to ask Kyle what to do but understood the need for silence.

Kyle watched as the two riders walked their horses past the barn and headed for the house. He didn't know who they were, but the fact that they'd come from the wrong direction was enough to convince him that they had evil intent. He didn't know if they were disgruntled prospectors or some of Bryn's revenge-seeking outlaws, but it didn't matter, he had to stop them.

He then turned and whispered to Katie, "Watch from the barn. If they get past me and get into the house, run to the small house and get my pistol from my bedroom. Do you know how to shoot it?"

"Yes."

Kyle nodded then stepped quickly to the barn door, stopped and looked toward the house. The two men were almost at the back porch, and he knew he had to act now, or it would be too late.

He dropped the head of the bat to the ground and instead of rushing out across the wide gap to the house, he began to limp forward using the bat as a cane.

He wasn't sure it was a worthwhile ruse if they just decided to shoot him, but Dylan had told him one thing on their ride south that now became a critical piece of knowledge. He'd said that most men tried to shoot their pistols too quickly and invariably would miss their targets. That was especially true when they were on horseback, and Kyle was hoping that he was right as he gimped his way closer to the men who were preparing to dismount.

Even as he made his way slowly across the yard, he noticed that the big man had his pistol drawn, but the smaller man didn't.

Arnie was staring at the small house when Bill asked loudly, "Who's that?"

Arnie whipped his head toward the barn and spotted Kyle hobbling toward them and replied, "I think he's that damned Evans! He ain't supposed to be here!"

"Well, you'd better shoot the bastard. He's not wearing a pistol and he must be hurt, so you don't have to be afraid of him anymore."

Arnie took a second to glare at Bill and snap, "I'm not afraid of him!"

———

Kyle heard the exchange and realized that his resemblance to Bryn had marked him as his uncle, which he might be able to use to his advantage if he could get close enough.

He was just fifty yards away now and was thinking of dropping the invalid act and rushing the two men who were still in their saddles when everything changed.

———

Arnie suddenly turned his horse toward Kyle cocked his pistol and started his gelding at a trot while Bill Carbo watched and grinned. He may not be doing the killing but watching a man die was almost as good.

Kyle was momentarily stunned when he saw the big man whip his horse around and head right at him as he tried to aim his pistol.

It was in that brief two or three seconds that his mind cleared, and he saw his opening. He ignored the pistol entirely as the rider bounced on the horse and the revolver's muzzle bounced with him.

He picked up his bat and just held it level in his hands for two heartbeats as the big horse thundered towards him then when he was twenty yards away, he quickly lifted the bat above his head and brought it to his left as the rider fired.

Kyle didn't care where the bullet went but he knew it hadn't hit him as the rider cocked his hammer for a second shot but was just ten yards away.

As Arnie took his second shot, he watched as Evans swung his bat and didn't think it mattered as he cocked his hammer and slowed his horse.

Kyle put all of his strength into that one swing knowing that he wouldn't get a second, and when the heavy maple knot hit the rider's leg right below the knee, he felt the bat shudder as it struck solid bone.

Arnie screamed in pain as his pistol fell to the ground his lower leg shattered by the blow.

Even as the bat rebounded from the hit, Kyle maintained his balance and twirled counterclockwise until he faced the house and squelched the urge to sprint toward the second man. He needed to make him believe he had an advantage, so he returned the bat head to the ground and resumed his fast, limping gait toward the second rider.

Bill Carbo's grin disappeared when he had heard Arnie's scream, but he was far from afraid or even worried as he stared at the gimpy deputy marshal.

Kyle was just thirty yards away as he watched the smaller man dismount and slide two knives from his belt, so he slowed to regain his breath. The man wore a pistol, but it was still in its holster which meant that he had greater confidence in his skill with his knives than he did in his Colt and that made him more dangerous.

Bill kept his cold glare on Kyle while he flashed his blades in the sunlight with practiced moves as he stepped closer then stopped when he was six feet away.

"You think you can beat me with that stick, Evans?"

Kyle had his bat level with the head pointing at the man as he replied, "It's all I have. You have a pistol and two knives."

"I don't need the pistol. I'll kill you with my blade and then go into the house and kill that pregnant wife of yours and all your kids and then I'll take my time with that young sister of hers before I kill her. Does that make you mad, Evans?"

Kyle knew that it wasn't an idle threat just by watching his cold, lifeless eyes but simply replied, "My name's Kyle Nolan. Bryn Evans is in Denver at the office."

"Is that so? Well then, this should be easier. I hear that Bryn Evans is a hard man to kill. Are you hurt or something, Nolan?"

"You'll never know, will you? I could be faking an injury just to have an advantage."

Bill shook his head and replied, "I saw you leave the barn and you're bluffing."

As Arnie still wailed in the background, Kyle said, "Why don't you just get on your horse and take your noisy partner with you back to wherever you came from and leave us alone?"

"And let you bring the whole marshal's office down on us? I don't think so."

Kyle knew that his time was growing short and any advantage he might have had was almost gone.

"Well, what if…" Kyle began then in one action, swung his bat backwards like a pendulum then took one long stride forward and rammed the bat into a stunned Bill Carbo's chest.

It was a bit short of the mark, but the head of the bat popped Bill Carbo's chest knocking him back a few feet. He stumbled but recovered quickly and swung the knife in his right hand as the tip barely reaching Kyle's left forearm.

Kyle didn't even feel the razor-like blade as it sliced through his shirt and skin, but knew he still had a dangerous foe in front of him. He still had a firm grip on the bat and even as Carbo was completing his arcing slice after cutting his arm, he began his clockwise spin letting the heavy bat's weight help him build speed as he pirouetted.

Bill Carbo, immediately after his initial slicing motion was preparing to stab Kyle with his other knife when he realized that his victim was already moving and started to step back to avoid being hit by the heavy stick as it whistled toward him.

But Kyle was making the best use of his long arms and Bill Carbo didn't have enough time to avoid the rushing bat. He knew it was about to hit, so he instinctively brought his right arm up to prevent it from hitting his head just as the bat arrived, forgetting that he had his sharp knife in his hand.

The bat head slammed into Bill Carbo's elbow, shattering the joint and shoving the tip of his knife into his neck.

Even as Bill began to scream in pain from his fractured arm, the knife cut deeply into his neck severing his carotid artery before slicing the front of his throat making his screech suddenly diminish to a gurgling whimper as he crumpled to the ground.

Kyle didn't know what had happened and was preparing to strike the man again when he realized that there was no need. He was shocked to see blood spurting out of his neck and had to step away as Carbo writhed in pain and tried to staunch the flow of blood with his left hand. It was pointless and just fifteen seconds after the deathly blow, Bill Carbo lay motionless on the ground.

He then turned to take on the big man who was still moaning and crying on his horse when Erin stuck her head out of the kitchen door and shouted, "*What happened, Kyle?*"

"I don't know yet. Go back inside for now and I'll stop by in a few minutes."

Erin knew that she had to care for her children including Grace Lynn, but she loudly asked, "Is Katie all right?"

"She's fine."

Erin was relieved and returned to the house wishing that Bryn was home.

Before Kyle could reach Arnie, Katie exited the barn and picked up his pistol from the ground and waited for Kyle to reach her.

When he arrived, she handed him the gun and asked, "Is he dead?"

"Yes. I've got to get the other one down before he rides away."

"I'll go and tell Erin what happened."

"Okay," Kyle replied before he turned and walked toward Arnie.

Arnie hadn't even watched Bill Carbo's death as he'd had his eyes closed and tried to shut out the incredible pain he suffered from his right leg. He hadn't even thought of riding away as the very idea of a jolting ride with his shattered leg would have been unbearable.

It was only when he felt his horse moving again that he opened his eyes and saw his assailant with the reins in his hand and leading his horse toward the barn. He stared at the top of Kyle's head and wished that there was something he could do but was helpless.

After Kyle led the horse into the barn and tied him off, he turned to Arnie and said, "Well, mister, you're in a lot of trouble. Your partner bragged about what he was going to do before he died, and I imagine that when my Uncle Bryn hears that you were planning on killing his wife and children, he's going to have you hanged."

Arnie blinked and said, "You ain't Evans?"

"No, I'm his nephew, Kyle. Now I'll get you down from that horse and give you some whiskey for the pain, but that's not going to happen until you tell me who sent you here."

"Nobody sent us. It was Bill's idea and I was just comin' along to protect him."

"If that's your story, then you can just stay in the saddle until Bryn returns and you can tell it to him. He should be home in a few hours."

His throbbing leg was now of primary importance to Arnie as he quickly replied, "You can't leave me here! It was Cornbread Funk who ordered us to come here and do this."

Kyle had heard enough of the story to give Arnie's new claim some validity, but he wasn't sure if it was completely honest. But he knew he had reached his limits on what should happen next and that the one person who should handle it was in Denver.

He set his bat aside transferred the Colt New Army to his right hand and said, "Alright, I'll help you down but if you try anything, I'll shoot you with your own pistol."

"I won't try nothin'. Just get me down."

As big as Arnie was, getting him out of the saddle wasn't going to be easy, but Kyle made a quick splint of small boards and used some pigging strings to keep them in place. With his broken leg reasonably secure, he helped to lift his right leg as he swung it over the saddle and waited with his left foot in the stirrup while Kyle walked around to his side as Arnie began a long string of cursing.

Kyle supported his injured side as he stepped down then once he was on the barn floor, Kyle helped him to the pile of hay and lowered him onto his back.

As Kyle began to bind his wrists with more pigging strings, Arnie asked, "Why are you doin' that? I ain't goin' anywhere."

Kyle didn't answer but then bound his ankles as well. He wanted to be sure that he wasn't going anywhere even if he tried to roll away.

When he finished, Kyle asked, "What's your name, anyway?"

Arnie was about to refuse to answer the question but knew it didn't matter because Evans knew who he was, so he muttered, "Arnie Popovich."

Kyle nodded then turned and untied Arnie's horse and led him out of the barn as Arnie shouted, "Where's the whiskey?"

Kyle turned at the barn doors and replied, "We don't have any," then left Arnie as he began a new string of curses.

He tied off Arnie's horse before doing the same to the other man's animal realizing that he never asked the name of the man he'd killed other than Arnie calling him Bill. After tying off the horse, he walked to the dead man's bloody corpse and dragged it away from the house all the way to the west side of the barn that was in shadow.

He then unbuckled and removed the gunbelt and set it aside before he began going through his pockets. He found a wallet in his inner jacket pocket, but all it contained was currency. Granted, it was a sizeable amount, over a hundred dollars, but it didn't tell him who the man was. He finally figured he'd leave it to Bryn to find out then stood left the gunbelt and wallet on the body and began walking back to the house to talk to Katie and Erin.

———

Inside the house, Katie had finished telling Erin what she'd witnessed, including the chilling plot that the smaller man had described to Kyle.

When she'd finished, she asked, "Did you recognize either of them?"

"No, but I'm sure that Bryn will when he gets home."

"I've never seen anything like that before, Erin. Kyle only had his bat and even then, he didn't race out there. He pretended he was crippled and used the bat like a cane. The big man began shooting at him, but Kyle didn't even duck. Then he had to defeat the second man who had two knives. I was terrified when he left but then as I watched, I began to believe that he would prevail and wouldn't be hurt at all."

"He was cut on his left arm, Katie."

Katie hadn't even noticed and quickly asked, "Are you sure it wasn't blood from the dead man?"

"No. It was his. I saw it dripping from his fingers. I don't think he even noticed it."

Katie turned to look out the open doorway but didn't see Kyle.

"Should I go and help him?"

"I'll get some towels and you start pumping some water. I'm sure that he'll be here shortly."

"Okay," Katie replied before each of them rose from the table.

———

It was when he'd been making the splints that Kyle realized he was bleeding. He'd pulled back his blood-soaked sleeve and saw the three-inch long slice across his forearm. It wasn't very deep, but it was still bleeding, so he walked to the shelf, rummaged for the cleanest rag he could find and wrapped it around his arm. He then rolled his sleeve over the temporary bandage to hold it in place. It wasn't the best solution, but it should help until it was fixed properly.

As he walked back to the house, he wasn't concerned about his arm nearly as much as he was worried about Erin. He hoped the shock of what had just happened didn't trigger the early arrival of Grace Lynn. He may have been in a deadly fight but wasn't ready to help Katie deliver her baby.

When he stepped onto the porch, Katie popped out of the kitchen looked at his arm and said, "Get in here and let me clean that up, Kyle."

Kyle smiled and said, "Yes, milady."

"Milady?" she asked as he entered the kitchen.

"I didn't dare risk calling you 'ma'am' again."

Despite all of the recent terror that she had just witnessed, Kyle's joking reference to her sensitivity about her age made her smile.

Erin was sitting down at the table with Ethan somehow wedged onto her lap and Mason sitting in another chair as Kyle was guided to the sink.

Katie used her shears to cut away the sleeve above the elbow and then after it was removed, she gingerly unwrapped the dirty cloth.

"Couldn't you have used anything cleaner?" she asked as she dropped it into the sink.

"That was the cleanest one I could find."

Katie examined the wound and said, "You'll probably need stitches, Kyle."

"Are you going to do it, or do I have to go and see a doctor in Denver?"

"One of us is going to have to ride into Denver to tell Bryn anyway. How are you feeling?"

"I'm okay. Just a bit tired after that second exercise. If you'll clean it up, I'll take one of their horses into town and tell Bryn and he can tell me where I can get this fixed."

"Alright."

As Katie cleaned the wound and then began to wrap a clean towel around his forearm, he watched her face and felt as if their private dance had just been a dream even though they'd waltzed across the barn floor just minutes earlier. He still wasn't convinced that Katie was the one because they still hadn't spent much private time together and hadn't talked like Dylan said they should. But if she wasn't the one, he would always treasure their barn dance.

Katie gently tied off the towel with strips of cloth before standing back to admire her handiwork then turned to Kyle and asked, "Are you going to go to Denver now?"

"Not yet. I'd rather wait for Flat Jack to get back just in case."

Erin said, "You don't have to wait, Kyle. Bryn will be back in a couple of hours and I have my pistol."

Kyle nodded then said, "I left the big man tied up in the barn. He said his name is Arnie Popovich if that rings a bell."

Erin tilted her head and replied, "It does sound familiar, but I can't place it exactly."

"I don't know the dead one's name, but it doesn't matter. I'm sure that Bryn knows. I'll just take Arnie's horse into Denver because I won't have to adjust the stirrups."

Erin smiled and said, "Thank you for saving my children, Kyle."

Kyle returned her smile and replied, "Don't forget about Grace Lynn, Erin."

She rubbed her bulge and said, "I never forget about her."

Kyle nodded then smiled at Katie before turning and leaving the house.

As he mounted Arnie's horse, Katie appeared in the doorway and waved.

He waved back and said, "Thank you for the dance, Katie."

"It was the happiest few minutes of my life, Kyle."

He smiled once more at Katie then turned the horse to the east and set him at a trot down the long access road before heading north to Denver.

As he rode, he tried to think of the motive for the two assassins to arrive on the Double EE. They had to have known that Bryn was in the office and the small man had said that he was going to kill everyone, including the children. *What would drive anyone to commit such a heinous act?* He was sure that it had something to do with whatever had happened in Golden.

He expected that Bryn would be riding to Golden immediately after he checked on Erin and his children. Kyle didn't know if he'd be bringing another deputy with him, but still wanted to go. He hoped that Bryn wasn't so furious with Cornbread Funk that he didn't let his rage overpower his good judgement.

Dylan had told him that Bryn was as good as they come in law enforcement, but even the best men could be sent into an unmanageable fury when they find that their families have been threatened. Maybe that was this Cornbread's whole plan in the first place. Send the two assassins and if they were successful, so be it. But if they failed or succeeded then he'd expect that United States Deputy Marshal Bryn Evans would be paying him a visit and wouldn't bother watching out for an ambush in his haste to find retribution.

Kyle knew he was operating beyond his expertise, but it was just a matter of common sense, assuming that Arnie hadn't lied about Cornbread being behind their attack.

He had Arnie's horse at a fast trot and soon reached the outskirts of Denver before turning down the street to the Office of the United States Marshal.

After he pulled the horse to a stop then dismounted and tied him off, he trotted across the boardwalk and then slowed as he entered the office but didn't see his uncle.

"Where's Bryn?" he asked Deputy Bert Willis who was at the desk.

"He's in talking to our temporary marshal. What's the problem?"

Kyle replied, "Not much," as he walked past the desk while Bert stared at his sleeveless left arm that was wrapped in a towel.

He didn't knock on the doorway but just turned at the threshold and said, "Bryn, I need to talk to you."

Bryn turned saw Kyle's wrapped arm then said, "Okay. Is it private?"

"Yes."

Bryn turned back to Acting Marshal John Knapp and said, "I'll be back in a few minutes, John."

"Okay. This isn't important anyway."

Kyle then turned and began walking back down the hallway as Bryn strode behind him wondering what had happened. The bandage on Kyle's arm concerned him that something might have happened to Erin, so he was already anxious as they stepped onto the boardwalk.

Once outside, Bryn turned and quickly said, "Before I tell you anything, I want you to know that Erin and everyone else on the Double EE are all just as perfect as they were when you went to the office this morning."

"*What happened, Kyle?*" Bryn exclaimed.

Kyle then began a concise narration of the events and as he spoke, Bryn felt his anger grow with each word but knew he had to contain it, or he could create a second disaster.

"I left Arnie Popovich tied up in the barn with a broken leg and moved the second man's body to the west side of the barn."

"Do you know who the second man is?"

"No. I forgot to ask Arnie, but figured you'd know him. He called him Bill."

"He only used knives when he had a pistol?" Bryn asked with raised eyebrows.

Kyle nodded then said, "I've got to get this sewn up. Where can I go?"

"I'll take you to Doctor Bedard's office and then I'll have to come back and tell John what happened before I go back to the ranch."

"Bryn, are you going to go to Golden right away?"

Bryn thought about it and replied, "That might be the best time to go because Funk won't know if they succeeded or not, so he won't have time to set up an ambush."

"But what if that was his plan all along? What if he sent them just to get you angry enough to rush to Golden and he'd be waiting?"

Bryn was annoyed with himself for not thinking of it himself but nodded and said, "You're right, Kyle. That's just the kind of thing he'd do. Maybe if we head there tomorrow, he won't be ready."

"They came from the northwest corner, Bryn. Is there a back way around Denver?"

343

"I haven't noticed it, but I can follow their tracks and find out. Let's get you to the doctor first and get that wound sewn up. How long is it?"

"About three inches, but it's not very deep at all."

Bryn nodded then said, "The office is two blocks away on this side of the street," before stepping off in that direction.

———

Kyle was surprised that he was finished being treated before Bryn finished talking to Acting Marshal Knapp, which had been extended to an office meeting with the other two deputies.

By the time Kyle entered the office with his newly bandaged arm, they were still in the meeting and he was just in time to hear John Knapp tell Bryn that he could call the shots on this operation, but it appeared that he wasn't finished.

Bryn had been chomping at the bit ever since he'd left Kyle at the doctor's office, and John's incessant need to act like the boss had pushed his patience to the breaking point.

Kyle announced his presence by asking, "Bryn, could you escort me back to the ranch? I'm feeling a bit woozy after the sixteen stitches the doc used on my arm."

Bryn nodded then said, "I've got to leave, John."

"Of course. Good luck with Cornbread."

Bryn waved, grabbed his hat and then followed Kyle back out the doorway.

"Where's Nick?" he asked as he finally noticed the horse Kyle had used.

"He's in the barn. I used Arnie's horse because he was still saddled."

"Well, lead him around back and I'll saddle Maddy."

After he untied the borrowed horse, Kyle followed Bryn through a side alley and then spotted a small barn.

"You're really not woozy, are you?" Bryn asked as he tossed his saddle blanket over Maddy's back.

"No, sir. That was a mild exaggeration, but I didn't want to wait around and figured that you didn't either."

"I was ready to toss my badge if he didn't shut up. John can be a good guy but he's a stickler for paperwork and now that he's in charge, he's enjoying the power."

"Am I still coming with you to Golden?"

"Only if you don't think you're up to it with that arm."

"I'll be fine. It just stings a lot."

Bryn set his saddle on Maddy then turned and said, "Kyle, in the short time that I've known you, you have impressed me more than any of those deputy marshals in the office. You may not be a good marksman yet, but your quick thinking and sound decision-making mark you as an exceptional man. What you just did at the Double EE is nothing less than what I would have expected from you."

Kyle blushed at the praise but replied, "Thank you, Bryn. That means a lot coming from you. I'm honored to come with you and promise to help when I can and learn even more."

Bryn grinned as he tightened the cinches and said, "Dylan thought the same thing about you, by the way. Let's get back home."

Kyle mounted quickly and soon they were riding west until they reached the southbound road and picked up the pace.

"What do we do with Arnie?" Kyle asked loudly over the pounding hooves.

"We'll take him to the county jail later and bring that body back with us to the morgue. You said that you found a wallet on him with a lot of money?"

"Over a hundred dollars, but I didn't count it. It's on the body with his gunbelt."

"You didn't check Arnie's pockets when you tied him up?"

"No, sir. I knew he didn't have any weapons and thought that once I was done stopping them, it was up to you about what do to do after that."

"That was a good call, Kyle. Maybe I should have Dylan make you a temporary deputy marshal when he gets back."

"I'm still too ignorant and too young, Bryn."

"You have time, Kyle."

Kyle watched the landscape roll past as they spotted the Double EE on the horizon and he wondered what he should do until Dylan returned with his family. He enjoyed working with Flat Jack, but he'd felt a surge of satisfaction when he realized that he'd protected Erin and the children, not to mention Katie. Whatever he decided, he thought that it had to be something that mattered.

————

When they returned to the Double EE, they found Flat Jack standing guard near the front of the house and returned his wave when they headed down the access road.

As they dismounted, Jack stepped down from the porch and said, "Sorry I wasn't here to help, Bryn."

"It's okay, Jack. Kyle took care of the problem. I'm going to talk to Erin for a little while then I'll have a chat with Arnie Popovich. Have you checked on him?"

"Just to make sure he wasn't goin' anywhere. He asked me to bring him some water, but I kinda forgot."

"You are getting old, Jack, so that's understandable," Bryn said as he stepped onto the porch.

Kyle then took the horses' reins and followed Jack as they walked to the barn.

"Katie was tellin' me how you took out those two bastards, Kyle. I think she's mighty proud of ya."

Kyle ignored Jack's comment about Katie and said, "It was close, Jack, and that small bastard's knife was so sharp that I didn't even feel it cut me. Did you pick up his knives, gun and wallet?"

"Yup. I left 'em in the house with Erin to give to Bryn. I figure they might be evidence or somethin'. Is he headin' to

Golden to make that Cornbread piece of manure pay for sendin' them here?"

"Yes, sir. We'll be heading that way tomorrow using the back trail that they must have used. Do you know about a trail from the northeast corner?"

"There's a trail that runs from Golden along the foothills that was used by prospectors, but it didn't come this far because the gold ran out in between."

"They must have used that trail to get here."

They entered the barn and ignored Arnie's loud pleas for water in between his groans and curses as they unsaddled the two horses.

As they removed the tack, Kyle asked, "Did you already unsaddle the other one?"

"Yup. He's in the corral where he's meetin' his new friends. What is Bryn gonna do with that noise over on the hay?"

"We're harnessing the wagon and bringing him and the body into Denver."

"Okay. If you'll roll out the wagon, I'll go and grab a couple of horses."

"Okay," Kyle replied before following Jack, but stopped in front of the wagon as Jack left the barn.

With his fresh stitches, Kyle had to use just his right arm and his legs to get the wagon into the sunlight before dropping the harness onto the ground.

When Jack arrived with the horses, Kyle said, "Jack, I need to go and change my shirt and get my pistol. I'll be back in a few minutes."

"I shoulda been more thoughtful about your cut, Kyle. Go ahead and I'll have this thing ready to go in a few minutes."

Kyle waved and began walking to their small house and wasn't at all surprised when Katie bounced out of the back door and waved. He stopped and returned her wave as she trotted towards him. He knew he was staring at her as she moved and suddenly their dance in the barn seemed much less like a dream. She may have been smaller than Erin but as she jogged closer, he was reminded just how well-formed she was.

She slowed down and without either of them saying anything began stepping by his side as he resumed his walk to the house.

After opening the door and letting Katie enter first, Kyle left the door open and walked to his bedroom where he began unbuttoning his ruined shirt.

Katie plopped onto his bed and asked, "How is your arm?"

"It's a bit sore, but not too bad. The doctor said it looked as if it had been cut by a scalpel and not a knife."

"When Jack brought those knives into the house, Erin and I both were in awe of how sharp the blades were. I think you could shave with either of them."

"I don't doubt it," he replied then as he pulled on his clean shirt he asked, "Did you hear what he said before we tried to kill each other?"

"Yes. I told Erin, too. He was going to use those knives on all of us; wasn't he?"

"Yes, he was. You didn't see his eyes, Katie. They were cold, lifeless eyes without an ounce of human compassion. I swear the man would have enjoyed doing it, too."

Katie shivered at the thought before she asked, "Were you afraid, Kyle?"

Kyle stopped buttoning his shirt and looked out the window while he let the memories return then said, "I didn't have time to be afraid, Katie. I had to come up with some way to stop them, so my mind was too busy. The whole thing only took a couple of minutes."

"I know, but I'll admit that I was terrified when I saw you standing there with your bat while that man charged at you and began firing. After you stopped him, though, I knew that you'd be able to stop the second man."

"I was lucky with both of them, Katie. The first one was firing too quickly from the back of a horse, so he missed. The second one thought I was lame, and he would be able to avoid anything that I did with my bat. If he'd pulled his pistol, I wouldn't have stood a chance and then, Miss Mitchell, I would have been afraid."

Katie smiled then said, "I don't think you would have been afraid, Kyle. You would be thinking of ways to stop him even then."

Kyle turned and said, "I guess we'll never know."

"Bryn said you'll be going with him to Golden tomorrow."

"I am and I'm glad to be going. I need to learn so much more, Katie."

"He also said that he asked you if you'd be a temporary deputy marshal when Dylan returned. Are you going to do that?"

"I don't know yet. I still have a lot to think about."

"When you come back from Golden, we still need to talk."

"I think we can talk for a little while because Bryn wants to have a chat with the man in the barn before he and Jack load the body and Arnie onto the wagon."

Katie nodded then patted the bed next to her, so Kyle stepped over to the bed and sat down leaving an appropriate two feet of open air between them.

"What do you want to talk about, Katie?"

"We don't have a lot of time right now, but can you tell me about your mother?"

Kyle nodded then said, "Her name was Bess Ann, and it wasn't short for Elizabeth. You know the story about how I came to exist and come here, so I'll just tell you about her. She was the center of my life and I barely remember the man she married. It's just as well anyway, I suppose. We didn't have anything, and my mother did domestic jobs and took in sewing and any other way she could earn a few pennies just to keep us afloat.

"I always wondered why she never remarried because I thought she was the most beautiful woman in the world. When I was nine, I decided that I had to leave school, so my mother didn't have to work so hard. She argued with me, but I took a job at the Vulcan Ironworks in Wilkes-Barre as a floor boy who did all sorts of nasty chores. I didn't earn much, but it was enough to help us survive. I gave her my pay each month and she would thank me as if it was a fortune.

"The winters were bad in that small house because we usually only had each other for heat, but I knew that others had it even worse. She taught me each night from borrowed books, so I would keep learning, even though I thought I'd learned enough by the third grade. She taught me other things too, like the dancing and how to be courteous and never to judge someone before you get to know them. It's hard for a boy to learn those kinds of things, but I had to listen to her because she was my mom and I could never disappoint her."

Kyle exhaled as he looked at the floor and continued, saying, "When she began having stomach pains that wouldn't go away, I had to talk her into seeing the doctor. She didn't want to spend the money, so it took a while. When the doctor told her that she had a stomach cancer and there was nothing he could do, I was crushed. I expected her to be depressed and lifeless, but she wasn't. She seemed to accept her fate and was still the happy and wonderful person she always was. Looking back now, I think what let her find her peace so easily was that she knew that she would soon be reunited with Huw after all those years."

"She'd be proud of you, Kyle," Katie said softly.

Kyle lifted his eyes to her blues and replied, "It's what drives me, Katie. I always want to make her proud."

Before either could say anything else, they heard Jack shout, "We're ready to go, Kyle."

Kyle smiled at Katie then stood and walked out of the door and headed out of the house where he found Bryn waiting on the driver's seat and Jack standing off to the side.

As he stepped off the short porch and clambered onto the wagon to sit beside Bryn, Katie stepped out and said, "We'll talk more when you get back, Kyle."

"Okay."

Bryn smiled and said, "Goodbye, Katie."

"Bye, Bryn. Goodbye, Kyle."

Kyle waved to Katie and said, "Bye, Katie," before Bryn snapped the reins and the wagon lurched away.

As soon as it began rolling, Bryn said, "Do you know who you killed?"

"No, sir."

"His name is Bill Carbo and he's one of the most wanted men in the entire country. He started killing people when he was just fourteen and at last count had murdered over thirty. We're not sure how many he really killed because he operated at night most of the times or didn't leave any witnesses. What marked him as different from the routine murderer was that he always uses knives to dispatch his victims. He carried a pistol, but rarely used it. I'm not even sure he could hit the side of a barn at fifty feet."

"How was he able to avoid capture for so long? Why wasn't he caught?"

"He has no distinguishing characteristics and he keeps his knives under his jacket. I wouldn't be surprised if he hasn't walked into a few sheriff's offices just to tweak their noses. He moved around a lot too, which is why so many jurisdictions are looking for him. I guess that's why he eventually wound up in Golden."

"When he stood in front of me with his knives, I noticed how lifeless and cruel his eyes were, but I had no idea he was that evil."

"Well, he was and that means, Mister Evans, that you'll probably be getting a significant reward after we send out the notices of his death. That notice will also let a lot of folks sleep peacefully knowing he's gone and provide a semblance of justice to the families of his victims."

Kyle hadn't given one thought about any kind of reward, but it did add to his sense of satisfaction when Bryn said that the families of victims of Bill Carbo's knives would feel some measure of satisfaction for what he'd done.

Arnie tried to keep from rolling on the wagon's bed as it rocked along the rough road and almost regretted telling the lawman about Bill Carbo, but not quite. He was now more concerned about his own future if he had any. He wasn't sure that he'd be hanged for just riding with Carbo and also thought that Cornbread might exert some of his influence to either bribe the jury or even break him out of the county jail. He didn't think for moment that he was expendable.

———

On the road east of Golden, in the same spot where Sy Hartman and Joe Utz had attempted their ambush, a lone shooter stood on the rock scanning the road. He'd had to drop down a few times since he'd set up to avoid being spotted by passing traffic, but he still hadn't seen the deputy marshal that Cornbread had told him would be coming before sunset.

HUW'S LEGACY

Elwin Hatcher wasn't a typical assassin. He had no war experience and no instruction. His father was a farmer as was his father's father back in Germany. He'd grown tired of working the fields in Kansas and had just left the farm when he was sixteen. He'd gone to Kansas City and done manual labor until he'd earned enough to buy a pistol. From there, it was just progression until now just six years later, he was a skilled marksman with both his Winchester and his Colt.

He'd been in Denver when Cornbread has his initial troubles with Bryn Evans and expected that sooner or later, he could make some money from the saloon owner, but didn't rush to Golden. He wanted to let Cornbread stew in his humiliation for a while. When he did ride to the town and talked to Funk, he expected that the man would ask him to take out the deputy marshal, but he discovered that he already had a plan in the works to deal with Evans, but that his services would be appreciated to execute the second part of that plan – literally. Now as he waited on the enormous flat-topped boulder, he was beginning to wonder if his target was going to arrive.

Elwin took a long drink of water from his canteen as he looked east. It was getting late and he doubted that the deputy marshal would make his appearance today. He stoppered the canteen and set it down before taking a seat himself.

He pulled out his pocket watch and estimated he had another two hours of daylight before he headed back to Golden. He'd enjoy Cornbread's offer of female hospitality for the night and then return tomorrow.

———

"That wasn't as bad as I'd expected," Kyle said as the wagon rolled out of Denver.

"That's because we were dealing with Sheriff Wheeler of Denver County and not my office. All they get is a report, but the jailing of Arnie and the rest falls to the county and the sheriff is a good lawman. And before you ask, Golden is in Jefferson County and he doesn't have jurisdiction."

"I already knew that, Bryn."

Bryn laughed and then before he said anything else, Kyle's stomach growled loudly enough to be heard over the creaking wheels and the eight hooves pounding the rocky roadway.

"Hungry?"

"I forgot about lunch."

"I can't imagine why," Bryn said then added, "Erin tells me that Katie went to visit you in the barn just before those two arrived."

"She did. She showed up and watched my exercises. I didn't know she was there until I was finished."

"And?" Bryn asked with raised eyebrows.

"Um, we talked and then I showed her how to dance."

"Maybe you can show Erin after Grace Lynn is born. We'll have that player piano in Dylan's house after it's built."

"I can do that if you promise that you'll let her teach you."

Bryn laughed and replied, "It's a deal, Kyle."

Kyle was pleased that Bryn hadn't made a big deal of his barn dance with Katie and just moved onto another topic that was much more immediate, tomorrow's ride to Golden.

"When are we leaving for Golden?"

"Early in the morning. It's normally a three-hour ride but taking that trail might add another hour or so. We'll need to keep our eyes peeled for an ambush, but I don't know if Cornbread even knows about the trail. If he set up an ambush for me, it'll most likely be on the main road."

"Couldn't you just ride behind the stagecoach?"

"We could, but I want to be able to get into Golden without anyone knowing that we're there. Once we get there, I'll notify Sheriff Burris, who used to be a deputy marshal in our office, and then we'll find Cornbread and arrest him for conspiracy to commit murder."

"Does he have protection in his saloon?"

"Probably, but we'll be ready for them."

"What happens to the saloon after we arrest him?"

"That's Jefferson County's call. Why did you ask? Are you thinking of becoming a saloon owner?"

"No, sir. I was just trying to understand how the law operates."

"That's the best answer you could have given, Kyle."

Kyle nodded but didn't answer as they approached the access road to the Double EE.

The sun was setting behind the Rockies as they reached the barn and Jack quickly took control of the horses as Bryn and Kyle climbed down.

"I've got it from here, Bryn," Jack said before he led the team and the wagon away.

"Thanks, Jack," Bryn shouted over the wagon's din before he and Kyle headed for the front of the house.

———

After a big supper that finally satisfied his rebellious innards, Kyle said goodnight to the family smiled at Katie then left the house to get some much-needed sleep before tomorrow's confrontation.

Bryn had told him to wear his gunbelt but to bring his bat, which had surprised Kyle because this would be in a closed space where he didn't believe it would be effective.

As he entered the house, Jack met him in the front room and said, "Your stuff is in your room, Kyle."

"What stuff?"

"You know, your stuff from the fight with those two killin' bastards. Bryn said you get their horses and gear, too. The horses are in the corral and the tack is on the shelf in the barn."

"Do I have to give up Nick?"

"Nope. He's yours and always will be."

"He's a good horse and he rode smoother than Arnie's."

Jack was all grins as Kyle stepped past him and entered his bedroom. On the bed was Bill Carbo's wallet, gunbelt and knives. Bryn had cleaned both blades and had taken the sheaths as well, so they wouldn't slice through any more of Kyle's hide even accidentally.

Kyle sat on the bed and took out what appeared to be a much thicker wad of cash than he'd found the first time. He correctly guessed that Bryn had combined it with what he had found on Arnie when he searched him.

He pulled out the bills and began dropping them onto the bed as he counted. When he finished, he had three-hundred and sixty-five dollars on the bed. He stared at the treasure and couldn't believe it. When he'd left Wilkes-Barre, he had a little over eighty dollars and after the donation from Michael Lowery, it had ballooned to over a hundred and forty. He still had sixty dollars left even after buying the train ticket to Denver. *What would he do with all this money?*

He was going to toss the wallet away because it belonged to the hated Bill Carbo, but then realized that it didn't matter. He'd still keep the pistol and knives just as he'd keep the horses and gear. So, he refilled it with the currency then walked to his drawer and removed his remaining cash, stuffed twenty dollars into his pocket then the rest went into the wallet.

After dropping the bulging wallet into the drawer, he returned to the bed and examined the pistol. It was a Colt, but he didn't know the model number. He did notice that it had a much bigger barrel than his Smith & Wesson, but used percussion caps, so he'd need Bryn or Jack to show him how to load it.

He moved the pistol and the knives to an empty drawer before leaving his room to talk to Jack. He was sure that Jack was dying to hear what had happened from the one who had actually done it.

He wasn't wrong and Jack listened to Kyle's tale with wide eyes and when he finished, Jack said, "You made it sound like it was all luck, Kyle."

"It was mostly luck, Jack. If they'd been smart, they could have killed me without a problem."

Jack grinned and said, "But they didn't 'cause you were smarter. That took a lot of sand to go out there hobblin' like that knowin' that they were gonna come at ya."

Kyle still didn't believe that he'd done anything heroic. He was sure that either Dylan or Bryn would have done the same thing and so would Flat Jack. They all would have probably done a better job and not been sliced either. He just happened to be there at the time.

As he turned in that night, he wondered if he'd be just as lucky tomorrow. It wasn't as critical as Bryn would be there and he'd be running the show, but he wanted to see how a real lawman handled the situation.

————

Erin looked at her husband and said, "Katie said that he didn't hesitate at all. When he tells the story, it sounds like one of yours or Dylan's. You repeat the important facts without embellishment or braggadocio. You just act like it wasn't important or dangerous. If anyone had the slightest doubt that he was an Evans, then this would be the final piece of proof."

"Dylan said the same thing about what he did with the Pawnee. I'd rather have him with me than any of the other deputies tomorrow. I know I can depend on him to keep his head."

"How about you, husband? Will you be able to keep your temper after you see the man who ordered this horrible thing?"

"It'll be difficult, but I'll manage. Did I tell you that it was Kyle who suggested that we wait until tomorrow to go there? I was ready to ride as soon as we returned, but that might have been a disaster because I was already so furious. I'm better now."

"Did he tell you about his dance with Katie just before they showed up?"

"He did, but I didn't ask too many more questions. I didn't want to make him feel bad, at least not until he's more comfortable around Katie."

"I'm simply astounded by how much he's affected her. I can't recall her being so bouncy and happy since before she was told she was going to be a nun."

"Maybe she found her true calling with Kyle."

"I hope so. I'm still astounded that she seems so, well, normal with Kyle. When I saw her leave the house to go to watch him in the barn with a smile on her face, I was so happy for her. I hope that they can make this work. I'd hate to see her or Kyle with a broken heart."

Bryn kissed Erin then rubbed her swollen tummy as he stared at the bump and asked, "When will you come out to visit, Grace Lynn?"

Erin laughed and replied, "If you felt that kick, it's her way of saying she's perfectly warm and happy where she is."

"Well, maybe she is, but the rest of us are anxiously awaiting her arrival. Then a few weeks later, I'll have my skinny wife back."

"I've never been skinny, mister."

"I know, but compared to this watermelon anything less than two hundred pounds would seem downright svelte."

Erin laughed and smacked him on his head before kissing him and then trying to get comfortable before closing her eyes.

————

Dylan looked out at the passing prairie and was pleased with the trip back so far. The coach had arrived on time and he'd only had to wait two hours to catch the train. Tomorrow morning, he'd be arriving in Omaha and then they'd begin the move in earnest. He'd sent telegrams to his mother and Gwen before leaving Julesburg, so they'd be expecting him. He knew that John and Gwen had already started the moving process but was curious to learn how far along they were.

He smiled when he thought of seeing Gwen and the children again and hoped that his mother was able to be in Denver when Grace Lynn arrived.

CHAPTER 11

Even as Dylan was stepping down from the train in Omaha to be greeted by John, his mother, and his entire brood, Bryn and Kyle rode out of the Double EE following the trail left by the two assassins.

As they kept a slow trot, they didn't talk even this far from Golden just in case Cornbread had realized that his attempt had failed and had sent another assassin to finish the job.

———

Cornbread had word of the failure the evening before from one of Sheriff Wheeler's deputies who had also let him know that Deputy Marshal Evans would be coming to Golden the next morning. He had been well paid for the information but hadn't been in the jail when Bryn dropped off the prisoner who needed medical attention. He was going on hearsay and didn't know about Kyle and even the deputy who was on duty who had told him about Bryn's plan didn't know about the route that Bryn and Kyle would be taking.

After the deputy left the office to go upstairs to spend a night with one of his higher end prostitutes as part of his reward, Cornbread sent a note to Elwin Hatcher to let him know that it was definite that his target would be arriving before noon. He was in a good mood despite losing Arnie and that spooky assassin.

———

His new assassin had reached his previous ambush location and after bringing his horse behind the rocks, he climbed onto the same flat boulder and looked to the east. The morning sun made it almost impossible to see anything, so he returned to his horse and waited. He was aware of the first failed ambush and wasn't about to make the same mistake. He'd watch for any signs of the lawman and once he spotted him, he'd just drop down behind the rocks and listen. When he heard the horse pass, he'd stand up on the rock behind the big boulder and take his shot. He had never needed to take a second.

It was a pleasant morning and the cool morning air was welcome after a string of real scorchers. He was ready and now he just needed his target to arrive.

———

Bryn and Kyle were about halfway to Golden and had reached the old trail which made travel a little easier. They still hadn't talked but kept their concentration on their surroundings as they drew closer to the town.

Before they'd gone, Bryn had explained what he expected to find when they got to Golden and much of what would happen depended on Sheriff Burris. Bryn hadn't met his new deputy and hadn't been impressed with the one who was left over from Sheriff Brown's aborted time in office.

Kyle's bat jutted out from his bedroll as Nick carried him around the rocks and trees that provided excellent cover for an ambush. His eyes searched each obstruction for movement, but never spotted anything more suspicious than a squirrel stealing nuts from his diligent brother.

An hour later when they were getting close, Bryn pulled up and waved Kyle over.

When Kyle stopped, Bryn said, "I'm pretty sure we'll see Golden in about half an hour. If they're waiting for us, they'll be on the eastern road but far enough from town so no one will see them. The last time, they almost had me when they were waiting behind a big cluster of rocks and boulders about three miles out."

"How far east of Golden are we now?"

"About that. Jack didn't remember exactly where the trail exits, but you can reach it from the south edge of the town. I want to check to see if anyone's waiting for us on that road. I'd hate to have them come up on us from behind."

"How do you want to do it?"

"I'll take the lead and I want you to drop back about fifty yards. Keep your eyes open and if you see something that I miss, shout a warning. If I stop, then you stop."

"Okay."

Bryn nodded then started Maddy at a slow trot again as he pulled his Winchester from its scabbard.

Just ten minutes later, Kyle saw the edge of Golden to their west as the trail split and Bryn kept going straight.

———

Elwin had almost shot a stranger who rode past him until he noticed that the man had a full gray beard as he looked down his sights. He snickered as he lowered his Winchester and released the hammer. Traffic had been building up, but it still hadn't presented a problem.

———

Bryn finally spotted the main road as he watched an older man ride past. He waved at the rider, who waved back, probably relieved that the man wasn't going to shoot him.

He then slowed Maddy to a walk as he glanced west toward Golden, then let his eyes arc toward the east taking in the details as the panorama rolled past.

When he reached his two o'clock position, he stopped his scan and focused on the same set of rocks that the last ambushers had used. *Surely, they wouldn't use the same spot again!* He continued to stare at the spot and then saw a horsetail whip through the air behind a boulder.

Kyle had stopped fifty yards back but couldn't see what had attracted Bryn's attention.

Bryn couldn't figure out how the assassin could be there and still hit his target. If he was down with his horse, he'd have to be listening for hoofbeats, but if the rider was moving at even a medium trot by the time he could climb into position and take a reasonably accurate shot, the target would be close to the maximum effective range of a Winchester. He didn't remember the rock that he'd used as a seat for hogtied Joe Utz after his failed attempt.

Elwin Hatcher was using that same rock as a lift to get him above the boulder where he'd make the shot rather than climbing all the way onto the rock.

Even with that memory lapse, Bryn was sure that there was a shooter behind that rock and wanted to take him alive if possible. So, he released his Winchester's hammer and slipped it back into the scabbard before stepping down and tying Maddy's reins to a young pine.

He pulled his pistol cocked the hammer and began walking toward the flat boulder about sixty yards away. He stopped before reaching the road, checked for traffic then stepped quickly to the other side and kept walking north as he started winding through the wide collection of rocks and boulders.

His eyes were still looking east and only had occasional glimpses beyond the rocks when there were spaces. He glimpsed down as he walked to keep his approach as quiet as possible and as he cleared one ragged-edged rock, he saw the back end of the horse and knew that he was getting close.

Kyle had seen Bryn enter the rocks and wished that there was something he could do to help but knew that Bryn was stalking a back shooter and needed to be quiet and avoid distraction. Waiting like this was much worse than actually being part of the action, but he knew it was what Bryn needed.

Bryn cleared the next boulder and smiled when he spotted his would-be assassin sitting on a rock. He didn't recognize the man, but it didn't matter. He was just fifty feet away and had nowhere to run.

Bryn brought his Smith & Wesson level and set the sights on the man before he shouted, "Stand up and put your hands in the air!"

Elwin was shocked by Bryn's shout and rather than pop to his feet, he turned his head to see who had made the demand and spotted Bryn with his pistol pointed right at him.

Most men would have thrown up their hands and prayed that they didn't get shot, but Elwin Hatcher wasn't just any man. He quickly estimated the odds at fifty feet with a pistol and thought he'd have better odds with his rifle. Even if he lost, it would be a better way to die than by a hangman's noose.

Bryn shouted again, "I'm United States Deputy Marshal Bryn Evans! This is your last warning! Stand and put them in the air! Now!"

Elwin slowly rose from his rock then as he acted as if he was about to put his hands up, he dropped behind the rock and grabbed his Winchester as Bryn fired.

His .32 caliber bullet almost instantly crossed the fifty feet of light Colorado air without losing much energy, but Elwin's surprise move had given him that precious fraction of a second, so when the bullet arrived, it caught the outer edge Elwin's left upper arm, not his chest which had been Bryn's target.

Bryn fired again to keep the outlaw's head down then moved slightly to his left to avoid getting hit with the Winchester's .44.

Elwin ignored the pain in his left arm as he cocked his hammer and set his sights on the space where Bryn had been. He held his fire until he had a target but thought that he was in the better position because he knew that the deputy had no way out other than to go past that gap in the rocks where he'd fired. It was now a waiting game and Elwin knew he'd win. He had a canteen and plenty of ammunition and doubted if Evans had either.

Kyle had heard Bryn's shouts and then the two shots before silence reigned as the gunsmoke wafted in the still mountain air.

He sat on Nick for almost a minute but with no more movement, he suspected that they were in a standoff and he knew that Bryn had a limited supply of cartridges, so he decided that he had to actively help now.

He dismounted, tied off Nick on the same small pine then pulled out his bat and began walking toward the roadway. He knew where Bryn had entered the rocks and that the gunsmoke had come further east of that spot, so he suspected that the shooter was somewhere in the big rocks in that direction.

Kyle then quickly crossed the roadway but instead of heading into the rocks, he turned east until he reached what looked like the end of the cluster. There was a big flattened boulder that would be difficult to climb, but he slid his bat onto the surface and then had to boost himself onto the boulder where he lay flat on his stomach to listen.

Bryn was angry at himself for not putting the man out of commission with that first shot. He knew what a bad situation he'd made for himself when he looked to his left and realized that that way was blocked and decided that it wouldn't hurt to shout to Kyle to ask him for help.

He bellowed, "Kyle! I'm in trouble and I need you to take my Winchester and go around the boulders so we can surround this bastard!"

Kyle almost shouted that he was already here but didn't have the rifle when Elwin shouted, "Well, ain't that too bad, Evans. I ain't fallin' for that old trick, either. I'm gonna wait you out and then I'll kill you."

Kyle was startled that the voice was so close just on the other side of the rock. That also meant that he was too close to use his bat. But as he lay on the boulder, he began to think that maybe it had a different use.

He slipped his pistol from his gunbelt and slowly cocked the hammer then took a deep breath before he slid a few feet forward and spotted the back of the horse standing behind the biggest rock. That limited the location of the shooter, so he slipped his left hand around his bat and slowly slid it forward in front of him as he wriggled his way closer to the edge.

Bryn didn't expect Kyle to answer him but thought that if he kept the shooter talking, Kyle could find him easier. He didn't know what the visibility was on the other side of that big boulder that hid the horse, and he wanted to give Kyle every advantage he could.

He shouted, "I'm not bluffing, mister! Even now, my brother is coming up behind you with my Winchester and you'll realize your mistake soon enough."

Elwin took a quick glance at the only open space behind his horse, didn't see any movement and yelled back, "If he's really there, Deputy, then he's either slow or stupid. Probably both if he's your brother."

Kyle had an almost exact location on the man now and gradually began to rise to his knees. He still couldn't see the man, but as he began to slowly stand, he finally found his target and as it turned out, the bat wouldn't have to be used as a distraction after all. He didn't swing it but used his left hand to toss the bat at the top of the shooter's head.

Elwin was still enjoying having Evans under his control when the lights went out.

Kyle watched the bat strike and then bounce off the shooter's head before he toppled off to the right and lay still.

"He's down, Bryn!" Kyle shouted as he slid down from the boulder and onto the rock that had been hiding Elwin seconds earlier.

Bryn was relieved to hear Kyle and even as he began scrambling through the crevice, he wondered how he'd managed to take the man out without gunfire. He suspected it had something to do with his bat, but still couldn't figure it out.

Kyle quickly stripped the gunman of his pistol and set it aside before picking up his repeater then heard Bryn say, "You're a sight for sore eyes, Kyle."

Bryn picked up his bat and said, "After I heard you shout and then two shots, I waited for something else to happen. I thought you'd call me if you got him, but when you didn't, I figured you were in trouble, so I came to help."

"You can tell me about it after we take care of this bastard."

Bryn holstered his pistol then dropped to his heels to check his pockets and only found a wad of cash and some silver. He handed it to Kyle, who stuffed it into his pocket then as the man began to moan, Bryn tied his ankles with pigging strings and rolled him onto his stomach on the sharp, rocky ground. He then made a quick bandage out of Elwin's right sleeve to stop the bleeding.

He'd just finished binding his wrists when Elwin awakened and asked in a confused haze, "Where am I?"

"Right now, you're tied up behind some boulders, but you'll either hang or spend a few decades in prison soon enough."

The fog cleared and Elwin snapped, "I had you!"

"Sorry to disappoint you, mister. What's your name?"

"I'm not telling you a damned thing!"

Bryn stood looked at Kyle and asked, "Have you ever hit a man in the crotch with that nasty club of yours, Kyle?"

Kyle grinned and replied, "No, sir, but I'd sure like to see what happens when I do."

"You've broken legs with that, haven't you?"

"Well, one was a leg. The other one just lost a knee."

Elwin heard the exchange and squealed, "You can't do that! You're the law!"

"I am," replied Bryn, "but Kyle here is a civilian, and if I turn my back, I can't control what he does."

"My name is Elwin Hatcher and Cornbread Funk paid me to kill you."

Bryn looked at Kyle and said, "Well, I think it's time to visit Cornbread," then dropped his eyes to Elwin and said, "We'll pick you up later, Elwin."

As Elwin began to complain, Bryn and Kyle clambered over the boulder and Kyle had to pass the bat and the two Winchesters to Bryn after he dropped to the ground near the road.

Five minutes later, they were mounted again and riding down the back trail heading into Golden and soon passed the back of the Ace High saloon before Bryn pulled them to a stop behind the Jefferson County jail.

They dismounted and walked down the alley between the buildings and popped out into the sunshine again before stepping onto the boardwalk and heading for the jail.

When they entered the sheriff's office, newly hired Deputy Sheriff Iggy Justice looked up from the desk and asked, "What do you fellers want?"

Bryn asked, "Where's Sheriff Burris?"

"He and Jimmy rode outta town a little while ago 'cause some old geezer said he heard gunfire out east."

"Alright, Deputy, tell him when he gets back that United States Deputy Marshal Bryn Evans is going to the Ace High to arrest Cornbread Funk for conspiracy to commit murder."

Iggy's eyes popped white as he said, "You're gonna arrest him?"

"If he's lucky," Bryn replied before turning around and with Kyle right behind him, they left the office and turned back east along the boardwalk.

"How do you want to handle this, Bryn?" Kyle asked as they stepped along at a fairly slow pace.

"The place should be almost empty on a Tuesday afternoon, so we shouldn't have to worry about anyone but the bartender and any bodyguards he may have hired. You need to have your bat in your left hand so you can keep your right free in case you need to use your pistol. We'll stop before we get to the saloon, release our hammer loops and then we go into together and I may want you to get everyone's attention with your bat, so get ready to make some noise."

"Alright."

As they approached the western end of the big saloon, Bryn came to a stop then after he and Kyle pulled their hammer loops free, Bryn moved his badge from under his brown leather vest to the front then turned to Kyle, who had the bat's strap around his left wrist and a firm grip on the handle.

"Ready?" he asked.

"Ready," Kyle replied.

Bryn took a breath to try to calm his smoldering rage at the man who'd ordered the cowardly assassination of his family rather than confront him then started for the batwing doors.

Kyle walked beside him and as they entered the saloon, he realized that he'd never been in one before but now wasn't the time to laugh about it.

As Bryn had expected, the large barroom and gambling floor held few patrons, fewer than eight, and only two of them turned to look at the newest customers.

Bryn knew where he was going and as they passed through the large room, he pulled his pistol and pointed it at the bartender and said, "Come out from behind the bar and take a seat."

The barman glared at Bryn but grudgingly shuffled around the end of the long bar as Bryn and Kyle continued to walk and Kyle pulled his pistol, expecting that he'd be left behind to keep an eye on the bartender.

Bryn then said, "Make sure they behave, Kyle. This won't take long."

"Yes, sir," Kyle replied as he shifted away from Bryn then stopped and put his back against the west wall where he had a good view of the entire saloon.

Bryn reached the bar, then turned down the short hallway to Cornbread's office and was surprised that there wasn't a guard at the door. He assumed that there was one inside, so he didn't slow down as he quickly opened the door and even before it slammed against the wall, he stopped and had to use all of his willpower to keep from putting a bullet between Cornbread Funk's stunned eyes.

He had been talking to a man Bryn recognized and who was more shocked than Cornbread to see Bryn, if that was possible.

He looked at the man sitting across from Cornbread and said, "John, I want you to slowly remove your pistol with your left hand and drop it on the floor. Funk, you place both of your palms on the desktop and don't you dare move. You know that I'm using every bit of my willpower to keep from shooting you where your fat ass is planted, so don't give me any excuse to pull my trigger."

Denver County Deputy Sheriff John Coleridge had just come downstairs to pick up the bulk of his reward for the information he'd provided, and the last person he expected to see was Bryn Evans. But he wasn't about to try anything with that muzzle just five feet away, so he reached across with his left hand, released his Colt's hammer loop and just for a moment thought he might be able to get a decent grip and use his left hand, but that didn't last long. He'd have to cock it and knew that he'd never get the chance, so he just dropped the heavy pistol to the floor.

After the Colt thumped onto the polished wood, Bryn looked at Cornbread who was glaring at him from behind the desk, but had both hands splayed across the desktop.

"What's your real name, Funk?"

Cornbread replied with just a hint of pride, "If you think you can spell it, it's Mortimer Roland Alphonse Harold Funk."

Bryn didn't react to the fancy name as he replied, "Mortimer Funk, you are under arrest for conspiracy to murder a Federal officer and several other charges of conspiracy to commit murder."

"I'm not going anywhere. You can't prove anything, Evans."

"Don't be stupid, Mortimer. Of course, I can. I have one of your assassins in jail, another one tied up east of town, and now, I have your pet deputy sheriff here. I'll bet he'll tell his boss anything to keep out of prison."

Cornbread visibly deflated as he realized that his last card had been played and had come up useless.

Bryn then said, "I want both of you on the floor on your bellies. Mortimer, you come around the front of the desk and lay beside John."

John Coleridge rose from the chair dropped to his knees and slowly prostrated himself on the floor as Cornbread walked around the desk and joined him.

Kyle hadn't seen anyone move since Bryn had entered the office, but had listened to the arrest, so he wondered if he should leave the saloon floor to help bind the two men. As it happened, he didn't have to make the decision when Sheriff Cal Burris and Deputy Sheriff Jimmy Gabbart entered the bar and spotted Kyle with his pistol.

Before the sheriff could draw his gun, Kyle loudly said, "Bryn is in the office and just arrested Cornbread. Do you want to take over out here, Sheriff?"

Cal hesitated, then asked, "Who are you?"

"I'm Kyle Evans, Bryn's nephew. He asked me to help him with the arrest."

"Oh. That explains what Elwin Hatcher said when we found him tied up outside of town. He said that two men jumped him, but that didn't make any sense because his horse was tied up behind the rocks."

"He was supposed to ambush Bryn, but Bryn found him first."

"He's good at that. You go and help Bryn and I'll join you. Jimmy can keep an eye on this crowd."

Jimmy Gabbart pulled his pistol as Kyle and Cal both holstered theirs and headed for the office.

"What's with the club?" Cal asked as they reached the hallway.

"It's supposed to be a baseball bat, but I use it as a walking stick, too."

Bryn had pulled some pigging strings from his pocket when he heard Cal's arrival, so he just waited until he and Kyle reached the office.

He handed the pigging strings to Kyle, who set his bat aside and began to bind the wrists of the two prisoners as he turned to Cal Burris.

"I arrested Cornbread for conspiracy to murder and John Coleridge is facing the same charge."

Cal looked down at the man on the floor and asked in surprise, "John?"

Deputy Coleridge didn't look up or reply but closed his eyes as Kyle finished trussing him up.

"Did you bring his assassin back to town?"

"He's in the jail. Are you taking him back to Denver?"

"Yup. I'm taking all three of them back. Do you know what that bastard paid two men to do, Cal?"

"Besides trying to shoot us when we came to arrest Sheriff Brown?"

"Not those two. He sent the ex-deputy and a killer named Bill Carbo to murder my entire family. They were going to kill Erin and my children, Cal!" Bryn exclaimed with vehemence as his held back rage exploded.

Cal was stunned at the magnitude of the crime and was in awe of the man who had still just arrested the man responsible rather than emptying his pistol and his Winchester into him.

"Thank God you stopped them."

"I was at the office, Cal. Kyle stopped them. He put Arnie Popovich out of action with that baseball bat of his while Arnie was shooting at him from his horse. Then he used it to fight off Carbo and was able to kill him."

Cal looked down at Kyle who was tying Cornbread's wrists and asked with raised eyebrows, "He killed Carbo with that club? Where did Cornbread find that bastard? Everybody and his brother are looking for him."

"He was hiding out in Golden and he offered his services to Cornbread. Anyway, I've got Arnie in jail in Denver and with these three joining him, I think you'll have a better town now. What you and Judge Fletcher do about his two saloons is your problem."

"I'm glad you got him, Bryn. Let's get them to jail and you can tell me everything over lunch."

Bryn nodded then he pulled John Coleridge to his feet while Kyle wrestled the heavier Mortimer Roland Alphonse Harold Funk to his.

———

After a long, informative lunch, Bryn and Kyle left Golden trailing three horses with their heavily bound passengers and started the three-hour ride to Denver.

Once clear of Golden, Kyle asked, "When will their trail be held?"

"I'd guess in about a week or so. It's a Federal charge, so we have to get a Federal judge in from Kansas City. I'll send a telegram to Dylan to let him know and then another to the judge's office."

"Can I be there in the courtroom for the trial?"

"You have to be there, Kyle. You'll be subpoenaed as a witness."

"I hadn't thought of that. I've never been in a courtroom before."

Bryn looked over and grinned as he asked, "You've never been arrested?"

"No, sir. I couldn't afford to get arrested. My mother needed my pay."

Bryn replied, "Sorry, Kyle. I was just having a little fun."

"I know. I'm just a bit nervous about having to testify. Is it hard?"

"Not at all. Just tell the truth. But there is one thing that is of paramount importance when you're sitting in the witness stand?"

Kyle smiled and asked, "Don't pee on the chair?"

Bryn laughed and said, "No, but that's number two...or maybe number one. But the most important thing to do is never say too much, even to the prosecutor, who'll be on your side. Just answer the questions as succinctly as possible."

"Why?"

"So that you don't say something that they can twist into sounding completely different. I did that once and the defense attorney made it sound as if I had been the one who was guilty. The prosecutor explained my error after the trial, as if I hadn't realized my own blunder."

"Okay. I'll keep my answers short."

"Good. Now tell me what you're going to do with all that reward money you'll be getting."

Kyle hadn't really thought about it at all. He was still in awe of the cash he had in his dresser drawer back on the Double EE.

"What should I do with it? I already have more money than I ever thought possible."

"The first thing you need to do is open a bank account in Denver and deposit what you have already. Then as those rewards start coming in, you deposit those."

"How do those rewards work?"

"When a wanted man is captured or killed, the law agency sends out telegrams to the ones who offered the rewards. It's on their wanted posters. What's really odd about Bill Carbo is that he had so many that they had two different wanted posters. It'll take a few weeks, and some of those who offered the rewards will balk and ask for proof, but most don't especially when the notice comes from the office of the United States Marshal."

Kyle had no real use for the money at least not now, so putting it all in the bank sounded like a good idea. As they trotted along, he thought about the many changes in his life and not just the big ones. He'd been in a saloon and would soon be opening a bank account and even testifying in a big trial. It was as if he was a different person entirely and maybe he was.

_____

They arrived in Denver in late afternoon and stopped at the Denver County jail.

Bryn said, "Kyle, keep an eye on our prisoners while I go and talk to Sheriff Wheeler. I don't believe he'll be very happy to learn that one of them is his deputy."

"Okay, Bryn," Kyle replied as he watched Bryn dismount.

It wasn't five minutes later before Sheriff Quentin Wheeler and two deputies exited the jail with Bryn and Kyle could see the outrage on the sheriff's face.

As his deputies pulled Cornbread and Elwin Hatcher from their horses, Sheriff Wheeler stood beside John Coleridge's horse and screamed a storm of insults and epithets at his deputy before yanking him awkwardly from the saddle.

Kyle finally stepped down and followed the lawmen and their prisoners into the jail. They spent another twenty minutes as Bryn told Sheriff Wheeler what had happened and listing the charges against each man.

After leaving the jail, Bryn stopped at his office and told Acting Marshal Knapp an abbreviated version of the arrest.

Despite John Knapp desperately wanting more information, Bryn simply said that he had to send a telegram to the Federal judge in Kansas City and left the office before John could start badgering him.

———

They arrived at the Double EE as the sun was setting and both were feeling the physical effects of the long and emotionally straining day.

But when they stepped down before the house, Erin opened the door smiled at Bryn and he felt his exhaustion wash away as he stepped onto the porch and gave her a warm kiss and a hug.

"I'll take care of the horses, Bryn," Kyle said as he took Maddy's reins.

"Thanks, Kyle."

Erin looked past Bryn and said, "Supper in ten minutes, Kyle."

"Thank you, Erin," Kyle replied as he led the two tired horses to the barn.

Jack exited the small house and soon reached Kyle then took Maddy's reins as he asked, "What happened, Kyle?"

Kyle began the story that continued while they unsaddled the two horses and was still talking when they left the barn.

Supper was accompanied by another long conversation about the last two days' events and the upcoming trial and as much as Kyle wished he could have stayed to talk to Katie, he walked back to the small house with Jack and within ten minutes, he was sound asleep.

———

Dylan walked into the house and after a quick kiss from Gwen, he sat at the table and waited until she and the children were seated before pulling out a sheet of paper from his pocket and unfolded it.

"I received a very long telegram from Bryn before I left Omaha."

"Did Erin have Grace Lynn already?" Gwen quickly asked.

"No. It was something very different and very frightening. He said that yesterday, two assassins rode onto the Double EE while he was at work and were going to kill his entire family and Katie. They'd been sent by a saloon owner in Golden for Bryn's interference in his criminal activity."

Gwen asked in shock, "How did he stop them?"

383

"He didn't find out about it until later. Kyle injured one and killed the really bad one with his bat. The one he killed was named Bill Carbo, and he was one of the sneakiest killers in the country. He used knives and usually worked at night. I don't know how Kyle was able to pull it off, but he did. Then Bryn and Kyle went to Golden the next day, stopped another assassin then arrested the saloon owner and brought them to Denver for trial."

"But everyone is okay?"

"Yes, ma'am. This telegram must have cost him a fortune to send, but I know that there's a lot more to come. I'll tell mom and John tomorrow when we meet with the buyers and then I'll send a reply."

"I'm glad that everything's coming together so quickly. I can't believe that we found buyers for our house so fast."

"Neither can I, but I'm not complaining, Mrs. Evans. Now let's eat and we can talk about the move."

Garth then said, "I hope I see some of those Indians, Dad."

Dylan smiled and replied, "Maybe you will."

———

The next morning, things around the Double EE began to shift in a much more pleasant direction as the construction crews returned for their second day of work. Kyle was impressed with the men as they seemed to swarm around the worksite but was pleased that it was more than four hundred yards away from the big house. After the attack, he felt wary of any men near the house.

Work around the ranch still had to be done, but Kyle found that his recently sutured left arm wasn't much help as he and Jack needed to add to the stock of firewood. When the pile reached a certain point, they'd roll the oldest of the big pine logs that had been harvested in the spring before and then had to cut the trunk into the correct lengths before splitting them on a large stump behind the barn.

Kyle felt guilty as Jack did most of the work, knowing that he wasn't as strong as he used to be, but like most men, he refused to admit it. Kyle was still able to handle the other end of the two-man saw and then toss the split logs onto the wagon for transport to the houses.

After lunch, they rode out to check the herd and discovered a new foal that had arrived early. Jack inspected the young filly and pronounced her healthy before they headed back to the house.

The foal's birth was the biggest news to tell Bryn that evening over the dinner table, but he told them that Federal Judge Robert Porter would be arriving on the 14th of the month and the trial would be the following day. He also had received a telegram from Dylan, who had expressed his outrage and apologized for not being there but then added that things were going faster than they'd expected and that they'd probably be leaving in the middle of the month.

"So, when will they arrive?" Erin asked.

"Five days after they leave, but Dylan is going to be showing up after that because he'll be driving a wagon with the freighters and he'll have Lynn, Alwen and Garth with him, too. He said that the stage just wasn't big enough for the entire family."

"Will your mom make it here in time for Grace Lynn's arrival?"

"That, my love, is up to Grace Lynn. I just hope she's patient enough to wait."

Erin smiled and said, "Not if she's got enough Irish in her. She'll be stubborn enough to leave when she's ready and won't wait another second."

Kyle smiled then glanced at Katie and found her blue eyes looking at him as she asked, "Do you want to walk over to Dylan and Erin's new house to see how it's going?"

"I'll help you with the dishes and then we'll go. Is that okay?"

Before she could answer, Bryn loudly said, "No, no, Kyle. Don't start doing things like that. Pretty soon Erin will have me changing diapers."

Erin laughed and said, "Like you haven't washed dishes or even changed those nasty nappies already."

"I was just trying to protect my young brother, Erin."

Katie then said, "Well, I for one, thank you for your offer, Kyle."

"You're welcome, ma'am."

Kyle watched Katie's eyes after he addressed her as 'ma'am' and was pleased that they lost none of their sparkle as she rose with her plate.

Kyle stood and after Bryn picked up Ethan and shooed Mason down the hall as Erin waddled behind them, they

386

cleared the table and soon were standing close to each other as they washed the dishes.

"How's your arm?" she asked.

"It's a bit sore, but not too bad. I did feel bad not being able to help Jack with the log-splitting earlier, but it should get better soon."

"Bryn said that you got him out of a real jam yesterday in Golden."

"I wouldn't have been able to help at all if Bryn hadn't kept the guy talking so I knew where he was. What I did was easy. Bryn did the hard part."

"You sound just like him and Dylan. Did you notice that he called you his brother?"

"Yes. He did yesterday at the saloon. I guess it's because I'm too old to be a nephew. Nephews are little boys like Mason and Ethan."

"I think it's for a different reason, Kyle. You've only been here for a couple of weeks and you've saved his family and then helped him when he needed it. He probably thinks that a nephew sounds too distant, but a brother is real family."

"Do you want to know something odd?"

"Of course. I'm a first-class gossip."

Kyle grinned at Katie before saying, "From almost the moment I met Dylan, I thought of him as a brother and then I felt the same way when I met Bryn, and it wasn't because I looked so much like them either. I felt as if I knew them, the way they thought and the things they believed. The odd thing, though is that I feel like Flat Jack is like a father to me. He tells me things each night that make me think. We have fun over there too, but Jack is a very good man and I'm proud to call him my friend."

Katie put a plate in the drying rack and said, "None of that is odd at all, Kyle. I think it's wonderful."

Kyle handed her the cutlery and after she set them in the basket, he dried his hands then handed her the towel.

The sun was setting over the Rockies in its usual spectacular display as Kyle and Katie began walking south toward the construction site.

"What was your life like, Katie? I know that you were supposed to be a nun."

Katie wasn't hesitant to talk about her life with Kyle, and as they stepped across the rocky ground, avoiding the bigger stones, she told him of the initial excitement when she was just a girl followed by the growing disappointment as she grew older.

She told him how her parents lectured her when she had expressed her reservations and told her she would go to hell if she refused to enter the convent. She finished her long narrative when she reached the exciting day when Father Duffy had told her that if she didn't have the calling, she shouldn't be a nun and wouldn't go to hell. It was at that meeting that he'd asked her if she wanted to join Gwen at the Evans home.

"Then I was a nanny for Gwen and Erin when Bryn bought this ranch and I came here with them. I'll admit that I've been a bit annoying to both of them because I didn't see any young men and Erin kept trying to get me to go to socials."

"Why didn't you go? Was it because you couldn't dance?"

"No. It was because I was uncomfortable with the idea of being alone with a boy and having to get involved with the expected romance."

"Oh," Kyle replied then after a brief pause said, "but you don't seem that way to me."

"That's because I'm not afraid anymore. You did that, Kyle. Just like you said that you feel as if you knew Dylan and Bryn right away, I felt just as comfortable with you. When we had our impromptu waltz in the barn, it was like magic to me. I felt alive and whole as I've never felt before. I wished we could have danced in that barn for hours."

Kyle looked at Katie and asked, "May I have this dance, Miss Mitchell?"

"I would be delighted, Mister Evans."

They had to move a few feet to a less cluttered area before they faced each other and placed their hands for the start of the waltz.

Kyle began to hum the melody then with the deep red of the Rocky Mountain sunset behind them, they began to whirl across the ground.

There may have been fewer rocks on their rustic dance floor, so they weren't free from trips or stumbles yet they continued to dance even after Kyle finished humming just as they had in the barn.

When they finally slowed, Kyle again let his hand slide to Katie's back as they stood motionless in the growing darkness.

It was such an incredibly romantic setting that Katie was sure that Kyle would give her that previously feared first kiss. She looked up at his face just inches from hers and felt her heart quicken and her breath grow rapid and shallow.

Kyle did want to kiss her, but he felt so awkward. He'd just reached the point where he was comfortable with Katie and was worried that she might think he was taking advantage of her. So, after another thirty seconds, he took his hands from her waist then took her right hand.

Katie was disappointed, but then they began walking south again toward the new house. It had been so close that she began to wonder if what she had finally dismissed as unimportant was important to Kyle.

Without fanfare, she said, "I'll be twenty in December, Kyle."

Kyle glanced her way and asked with a smile, "Is that a hint for a nice birthday gift?"

"You know why I told you. It's why I got upset when you called me 'ma'am. It made me realize how old I was already, and I'm more than two years older than you."

"I knew that, Katie. But even though you're older in years, you look younger and I look older, or so everyone tells me. Even if that wasn't true, our age difference doesn't matter to me at all, but if you believe that it's too important for us to continue down this path of exploration, then let me know now."

"Are you sure that it doesn't matter? What about that girl in Pennsylvania?"

Kyle had to think about it for a few seconds before he asked, "Which girl in Pennsylvania? I didn't know I had a girlfriend."

"The one you met on the farm."

"Oh, you mean Lisa Neuman. I knew her for just a few days and we barely passed a few words. I don't even know how you found out about her."

"Dylan mentioned her when he was here."

"Well, Miss Mitchell," he said as he lifted their clasped hands, "this is the first time I've ever held hands with a young lady and I'm not planning on holding anyone else's. That is unless you tell me that our age difference really bothers you so much."

Katie smiled at Kyle and replied, "It won't anymore. I promise."

"Good. Now that we have that settled, where do we go from here?"

"I have no idea. We're both real amateurs at this, aren't we?"

"Yes, ma'am, but I think we can learn as we go."

"I do have the advantage of an older sister who has already given me several pointers."

"Then I guess you'll have to take the lead in this dance, Miss Mitchell."

Katie stopped, pulled his hand around her waist and pulled herself against him as she looked into his eyes and said, "If you insist."

Kyle put his other hand behind her small waist and felt her hand on the back of his neck and then she pulled his head down toward her as she stood on her tiptoes and looked up. Kyle took the hint then bent down and their lips met for the first time.

For each of them that first kiss was a revelation. Aside from the surprising wetness, it was the sudden release of unexpected passions that almost made Katie pass out.

Kyle felt her knees weaken and broke off the kiss, expecting he'd have to keep her from collapsing.

"Why did you stop?" she asked breathlessly.

"I thought you were going to faint."

"I don't care," Katie replied before she kissed him again.

Kyle and Katie remained locked in their tight embrace for another six minutes as they kissed and enjoyed each second of their newfound urges.

Katie had been waiting for this moment since they'd shared the dance and wasn't disappointed. Erin had been telling her about the thrill of passion since they arrived in Denver trying to get her to change, and now she understood what she had been missing. She didn't regret the delay because she knew that she could never feel this way about another man. Only Kyle would ever release her passion and she wanted to unleash his.

When Kyle had to use all of his willpower to keep his hands from touching Katie in places that he thought might make her believe he was a sex fiend, he separated slightly and smiled at her. He still thought that they needed more time.

"I think we should be heading back, Katie."

"We haven't been to the new house yet."

"I don't believe that was our intent when we left anyway."

"It wasn't, but I was trying to lure you even further away."

Kyle laughed and then pulled her along as he began to head back to the house.

As they slowly stepped along Kyle said, "Katie, I have a confession to make."

"You're going to tell me that you're going back to Pennsylvania to see Lisa?" she asked with a grin.

"You know better than that. It's just that, well, when we were kissing and I felt you close to me, I kind of...I kind of wanted to, um, I wanted to...touch you, but I didn't want you to think I was a pervert."

Katie almost giggled but replied, "I would never think that of you, Kyle. Oddly enough, it was exactly what you were thinking of doing that had prevented me from going to socials."

"But if we go for a walk again and kiss, which we know is going to happen, will you tell me to stop if I touch you where I shouldn't? I'll stop right away."

"Why would I ask you to stop? When you had me in your arms and I felt you close against me and we were kissing, I wanted to feel your touch. I know that's probably a shock to you, and it was to me when Erin explained it to me.

"I thought she was making it up, but she seemed to be so happy when she told me and all of the other things, I knew that she had felt that way. I just never thought that I could. I was still afraid of even having a man hold my hand that I couldn't imagine letting him touch me in more exciting places, but now I understand."

"I feel like a schoolboy, Katie. That's embarrassing for any male my age."

"Didn't your mother talk to you about girls?"

"She did, and once I got past the 'yucky' stage that all boys feel, she mainly talked about how to respect girls and to talk to them. She said that the rest would follow naturally, and I guess she was right. But what she told me about respecting girls was always the most important thing to me, and that's why I asked."

"She didn't tell you that girls enjoyed it?"

"No. I guess she didn't want me to think she was a wicked woman."

"I hope that doesn't make me a wicked woman."

"It doesn't, and it wouldn't have changed my opinion of her at all."

They reached the house and stepped onto the dark porch. Before she opened the door, Katie stood on her tiptoes and kissed Kyle then turned opened the door and went inside.

Kyle stood motionless on the porch for two minutes letting the memory of their walk establish a strong foothold in his mind. He had learned so much from Katie during that walk, and expected he'd be learning from her for the rest of his life.

As he stepped down from the porch and headed for the small house, he had no doubt in his mind that Mary Catherine Mitchell was the one.

CHAPTER 12

The next morning at breakfast, neither Katie nor Kyle said a word about the walk but didn't have to as it seemed as if everyone at the table understood that there had been a massive movement in their relationship. Kyle began to wonder if even Grace Lynn knew about it.

But that change didn't mean work didn't need to be done, and after Bryn headed for the office, Kyle and Jack returned to their duties of maintaining the ranch and the critters that inhabited it.

The afternoon was interrupted by a violent thunderstorm that rolled out of the Rockies and spawned gale-like winds that threatened to take down the new construction.

After it had passed as quickly as it had arrived an inspection of the site and the ranch revealed little damage, but one of the mares had run into a ravine and broken two legs, which meant she had to be put down. Jack took care of it with his Henry before he covered the carcass with coal oil and set it ablaze.

Once the fire was gone, he and Kyle shoveled sand on top of the charred remains. The reason for the apparent cremation and burial was to reduce the likelihood of any big predators coming onto the ranch and going after one of the young colts or fillies.

———

Over the next few days, Kyle and Katie walked each night, weather permitting, but Kyle still avoided touching Katie. Now he was more worried about himself and what any boost in his level of excitement might have. Katie may have said that she wanted him to touch her, but he was sure that she didn't want what would result if they got carried away.

But lack of touching aside each of their walks was filled with conversation and discovery. They found they shared the same sense of humor and beliefs that each felt was critical to simply getting along.

————

In Omaha, the Evans and the Wittemores were wrapping up their stay in Nebraska. The houses and the salvage business were all sold, and the freight company was scheduled to arrive on Monday, the twelfth of the month, to pack the things that they'd take with them. It was already Saturday, so they all had a busy weekend ahead of them. The freight company estimated that between the two houses on the Evans' place and the Wittemore's home, they'd need three large wagons in Julesburg, but their agent there claimed that he could handle twice that.

Dylan had John then purchased tickets on the morning train for Tuesday and arranged for the transport for a dozen horses and one tiny donkey. Dylan also bought his own freight wagon and would use four of his horses as the team.

Sunday night, as Dylan and Gwen lay close to each other in bed, Gwen said, "It's going to feel strange not coming up that hill or seeing the Missouri River in the distance."

"When you see the ranch and the Rocky Mountains, you'll be impressed."

"I know. It'll be nice to see Bryn, Erin and the boys again, too."

"Gwen, will you miss your sisters?"

"I'm almost ashamed to admit that we've all just grown apart."

"Was it because of Arial?"

"I'm not sure. I know that Arial only makes small talk when I see her, and I think that Dona sides with her because she lives so close by. My mother, of course, is even more so because she married her father-in-law. But I don't really know why Megan and Meredith have stayed away."

"Maybe that's my fault, Gwen. Maybe not directly, but Mark had that run-in with the deputy sheriff and seems to blame all lawmen and he and Oliver were always tight."

"You might be right. The last time I did talk to Meredith, she mentioned something that Mark had said about you that wasn't flattering."

"Well, we'll have the packers arriving early in the morning and then we'll be moving into the Martin House until we load up the train. I'm sure the hotel will appreciate having our traveling circus stay in their rooms."

Gwen looked down at little Brian, who was sleeping quietly for the moment and said, "Maybe the rocking of the train will let him sleep better."

"Maybe," Dylan said then asked, "Can you think of some special way to spend our last night in this bed? At least while it's still in this house?"

"I was wondering how long it would take for that idea to pop into your head."

––––––

Monday was as chaotic as imaginable when the freight wagons arrived, and the crews began to pack the marked items for shipment. As they worked, Gwen and Alba had to keep the children from getting in the way while Dylan and John began putting bridles on the horses except for the four that would pull the new freight wagons and put their remaining saddles on the rest. Peanut just watched the hubbub and wondered what the silly humans were doing.

Dylan and John led the horses to Omaha and left them with in the enormous Union Pacific stockyard with their shipping tags attached to their bridles leaving Peanut alone in the barn for the time being.

Once that was done, Dylan walked to the marshal's office and said his farewells to his deputies while his replacement stayed in his office pretending not to hear what was going on just twenty feet away.

He'd left Crow in the barn behind the office, so once he saddled the gelding, he headed south again to see how the packing was going.

When he turned onto the drive, he was impressed to see two of the wagons already fully loaded and spotted the player piano on the second wagon.

As he pulled up to the front porch, he had to step aside as two men lugged out a large and apparently heavy crate before he entered the house.

"All set?" Gwen asked as she stepped through a half empty parlor.

"They're ready to go. How are things going here?"

"Faster than I had expected. I think they'll be done in another hour."

"I think they want to get everything on the night train rather than have to put it in a warehouse for a day. Everything should be there when we arrive in Julesburg."

She handed Brian to Dylan and said, "Be careful, he just had his after-lunch snack."

Dylan opened his mouth to make the almost obligatory comment about Brian's nutritional source, but Gwen held up a finger and said, "Not a word, Marshal."

He grinned as he lifted his four-month-old son to his shoulder and waited for the burp.

―――――

It was late in the afternoon when Dylan snapped the reins and the four horses lurched the heavy freight wagon forward. The bed contained some of the personal items that they didn't want to risk losing along with Lynn, Alwen and Garth, who would be riding the wagon with Dylan from Julesburg. Bethan rode in the bed comforting a nervous Peanut. Cari was sitting with her mother and Alba March, who had Brian in her arms. It was a crowded wagon that turned south onto the road to Omaha.

As they rolled down the hill, every eye except Dylan's was looking back at their home as it slowly melted into the landscape.

Dylan hadn't looked but felt the same tug in his heart that he knew each of his family had. It was the only home any of the children had known, and the place where he and Gwen had started their life together. They'd be happy in their new home on the Double EE, but they'd never forget those wonderful days on their hill.

———

The next day, as the train pulled out of Omaha to make its long journey across the Plains, the older children were all excitedly bouncing on their seats as they pointed at different buildings as they rolled past.

Dylan looked at Gwen and said, "In another hour, they'll be bored and fall asleep."

"I hope so. Some of the other passengers look like they want to throw them all off the train."

Dylan smiled then moved his United States Marshal badge to the outside of his jacket.

———

As the rest of the Evans clan hurtled across the vast emptiness of central Nebraska, the Colorado Evans family was sitting down for their supper.

"How did that happen?" Katie asked before she cut into her roast chicken.

Bryn replied, "They all started pointing fingers at each other to avoid walking up the gallows. It started with Arnie Popovich, who had just returned from the doctor's after having his leg repaired because Kyle had broken it almost in two. He asked how to avoid getting hanged and was offered life in prison if he testified against Cornbread. He was the first to roll and was going to testify that Cornbread had sent him and Bill Carbo to kill everyone on the Double EE while I was at work. Then when the prosecutor told Elwin Hatcher about it, he took the same offer. When he interviewed Cornbread, he was angry when he was told of their betrayal, but the prosecutor thought he was still too smug as if he knew he'd get off anyway. Now with the two men he'd hired to murder willing to testify against him and Kyle's testimony, he knew that Cornbread had no chance at all, yet he seemed confident about his acquittal.

"He knew that he couldn't have bribed the Federal judge coming in from Kansas City, so that meant he must have arranged for someone to bribe some of the jurors. So, he told Mortimer that the judge would be bringing twelve men with him to make up the jury and that took all of the starch out of Funk's sails. He broke down and began to beg to avoid the noose. The prosecutor said he'd think about it and left him in his cell to dwell on it."

"Was that true about a jury coming with the judge?" Katie asked.

"Of course not. It was a bluff, but I guess Cornbread was too afraid of being hanged to call it. Then after letting him stew for a while, the prosecutor talked to me about it because I'd have to approve any plea bargains, and I agreed if the prosecutor thought that Mortimer's information was worthwhile."

"Was it?" Kyle asked.

"He listed all the officials he'd been paying off, tossed Deputy Coleridge into the fire and even gave them the names of the moonshiners who provided him with his liquor. It was enough for me to agree to the plea bargain, so there won't be a trial that needs a Federal judge. It's a county problem now.

Kyle and I will still have to testify at John Coleridge's trial. He was the low man on the totem pole and may hang for conspiracy to commit murder by telling Cornbread that we were coming."

Jack asked, "Why'd you let that Cornbread off the hook, Bryn? I woulda thought you'd wanna see him hang."

"He's getting a life sentence that he'll spend in the territorial prison. I don't think he'll make it a year. Those men inside those walls are the worst kind and even they won't tolerate someone who ordered the assassination of a pregnant woman and her children. It won't be long before he realizes that he'd be a lot better off if he'd taken that walk up the gallows steps. He won't find any protection from the guards either."

"You're right, Bryn. That's a lot worse, I reckon."

Bryn nodded then looked at Kyle and said, "Your rewards are beginning to come in, Kyle. Do you want me to bring them home with me?"

"No. Keep them there until they finish, then I'll open that bank account as you recommended."

"You didn't ask how much it was."

"I know. I suppose I should be excited to get all that money, but I'm not. I guess that makes me a bit odd."

"I'll give you that. Most men would do damned near anything for a hundred dollars or even ten dollars for that matter. But odd doesn't mean bad, Kyle. Money is necessary to provide for our families. It's what's let us build our homes and put food on the table. Men who focus their lives on just getting more money miss the real treasure in life."

"Amen to that," Erin said as she smiled at Bryn.

Kyle nodded then felt Katie's hand slide onto his under the table. He slowly flipped his hand over and held hers firmly as he turned and smiled at her.

Bryn then said, "Okay. Enough philosophy. Kyle, the trial for John Coleridge is tomorrow morning at ten o'clock, so you don't have enough time to meet with the prosecutor. You can come with me to the office in the morning and I'll explain everything to you on the way."

"Okay. I remember the biggest rule about not saying anything more than I have to."

"Good. Remember your second rule, too."

Kyle laughed and said, "I can't promise anything."

Bryn grinned at Kyle as they finally returned to eating and Kyle released Katie's hand.

———

That evening as they walked, Kyle had to explain the mysterious second rule for a witness that set Katie into a serious case of the giggles.

They had found a better outside place for their sunset dances nearer to Dylan and Gwen's growing house, making for a smoother waltz which they now ended with a long kiss.

But each walk was still mostly about talking and learning about each other. Neither hid any secrets or tried to mask any faults or insecurities which made the conversations both long and intense. They still managed to poke fun at each other and as they grew even more comfortable being together, they found that just walking in silence was almost as valuable.

Bryn's mention of the rewards had put Kyle's mind in motion about his future. He knew that he'd have enough money now to set up a household for Katie, but still didn't know how he could provide for her. He didn't want to stay on the ranch as a wrangler but wouldn't legally be an adult until January. It was the only real obstacle he could see to a future with Katie. He hadn't had to talk to her about it because he was sure that she understood the issue.

But now as they waltzed in the light of the setting sun, nothing else mattered. He had Katie in his arms, and he was happy.

———

It was exactly 10:18 the next morning when Kyle was called to the witness stand. After taking the oath, he sat in the still dry witness chair and began answering the prosecutor's questions as succinctly as possible.

He had to point to the accused to identify John Coleridge as the man in the office with Cornbread. The defense attorney didn't ask him a single question because he hadn't been in the office when Bryn entered.

After Kyle sat down and Bryn replaced him on the stand, the prosecutor asked his questions and then sat down. The defense attorney began making the case that Deputy Sheriff Coleridge was there of his own initiative to unearth evidence which would link Mortimer Funk to attempted bribery of Denver County officials. It was a weak line of defense, but it was all he had. He tried to get Bryn to admit to that possibility, but Bryn simply replied, 'no'. He asked the same question three more times with increased volume and received the same quiet reply.

After Bryn returned to the witness bench beside Kyle, a still angry Sheriff Wheeler took the stand and was eager to testify that Deputy Coleridge was a disgrace to his office. He then read Cornbread's statement saying that he'd paid the deputy for information.

Kyle watched the entire trial as if he was in a classroom. He learned a lot about the rule of law as the process unfolded. When the jury left the courtroom to deliberate, many of the spectators left, but he stayed to wait the obvious verdict.

Bryn turned to him and said, "This won't take long. Did you see the looks on the jurors' faces?"

"They seemed either angry or disgusted, sometimes both."

"And that was before they heard Quentin read Cornbread's affidavit. They were ready to hang the poor bastard after that."

"Are they really going to hang him?"

"I don't think so. The jury will come in with their guilty verdict and then Judge West will hand down the sentence. I don't even think he'll give him life in prison. He'll probably get ten years."

"Why?"

"The judge knows John and probably understands why he did it. It doesn't negate the damage he could have caused, but if you step back and look at it, he really didn't have that big of an impact. That shooter was going to be there anyway, and all John did was to confirm that I was coming and that I had you with me. I guess we're lucky he didn't know about the trail."

Kyle nodded just as the bailiff entered the judge's chambers and two minutes later, the bailiff called the court back to order and everyone stood as Judge Ronald M. West entered his courtroom and took a seat at the bench.

Everyone sat as the jury filed back into the box and sat down. The judge asked for their verdict and the foreman announced the expected 'guilty on all charges'. The jury was dismissed, and a hangdog John Coleridge was asked to stand.

Kyle had been wrong about the ten-year sentence, but not by much. The judge sentenced the ex-deputy to five years at hard labor at the territorial prison, banged his gavel, adjourned the case then rose and left the courtroom.

As his recent fellow deputy sheriffs led John Coleridge from the courtroom, Kyle watched him leave before he and Kyle joined the rest of the crowd and began to leave.

While they shuffled toward the open doorway, Bryn said, "If John survives those five years, Kyle, he's going to come out of there a very different man. He'll be angry and a lot more violent. We need to be ready when he walks out of the prison in August of '72. He'll probably have made some nasty friends by then too."

Kyle glanced at Bryn and saw the serious concern in his brown eyes and understood the reason. He'd almost lost Erin and his children a few days ago and the idea that Coleridge or anyone else may try it again was now very real.

That five-year sentence now seemed excessively light, but there was nothing either of them could do about it.

"Are there any other outlaws that you've arrested that might try to start trouble for you, Bryn?"

"There are a few that I put away that weren't happy with me, but the difference with John is that he knows me reasonably well, and I'm the only one he can blame for what happened."

"Why would he blame you? He's guilty and has to know what he did."

"Most men like to blame others for their bad decisions. It's human nature. But let's not worry about it. Are you heading back to the ranch?"

"Yes, sir, unless you need me for something else while I'm here."

Bryn stopped causing an accordion-like effect behind him before he pulled Kyle aside and said, "Let's go see Judge West."

Kyle thought he was going to ask the judge to change the sentence, so he nodded then followed Bryn as they wound through the thinning crowd and then headed for the judge's chambers.

Once outside, his clerk smiled and said, "Hello, Bryn. You did a good job in there. Do you need to see the judge about something?"

"Yup. Can you have Kyle here fill out a form to legally change his name?"

"Not a problem," the clerk said as he pulled out his bottom drawer and flipped through a few sheets before finding the one he wanted and slipped it free.

Kyle felt a rush almost like the one he'd felt when he first kissed Katie as the clerk dipped a pen into his inkwell then turned the form around and handed Kyle the pen.

Kyle glanced at a grinning Bryn before he smiled then began filling out the form. It was pretty straightforward which was a departure from most government forms and simply required him to write his current name, date and place of birth, and his new name.

As he wrote Kyle Huw Evans on the last line as his hand trembled slightly, and he hoped it didn't look too much like Erans. After making sure that that the 'v' didn't look like an 'r' or any other letter, he slid the form back to the clerk then gave him back his pen.

The clerk reviewed the form, then looked up at Bryn and asked, "He's a relative?"

Bryn nodded, rested his right hand on Kyle's left shoulder and replied, "He's my brother."

The clerk smiled at Kyle and said, "You're a lucky man, Kyle Evans," then blew on the form stood and said, "I'll be back in a minute."

He picked up another blank form, walked to the heavy oak door, rapped three times then went inside, returning just two minutes later. He then sat behind his desk, copied Kyle's form onto the second then handed the first one back to Kyle.

"You are now officially Kyle Huw Evans."

Kyle accepted the sheet then slowly folded it before turning to Bryn and in a choking whisper, he said, "Thank you, Bryn."

Bryn shook his hand and replied, "You saved my family, Kyle. I'll forever be in your debt."

"No, you won't, Bryn. Brothers never owe each other anything."

Bryn smiled,then smacked Kyle on the shoulder and said to the clerk, "Thanks, Fred."

Fred just nodded as he pretended to be blowing his nose with a handkerchief that covered his eyes.

Kyle and Bryn then left the judge's offices and crossed the courtroom.

As they walked, Kyle asked, "Bryn, what does it take to be a lawyer?"

"A lot of study and usually a few years clerking for a practicing attorney. Why? Are you thinking of becoming a shyster?" he asked followed by a light laugh.

"Never mind. It was stupid to even think about it."

Bryn wished he hadn't made light of his question, so he said, "I'm sorry, Kyle. I shouldn't have joked about it. It's not a bad ambition to have, if you think that's what you'd like to do."

"It's okay. It doesn't matter. I only had three years of schooling, so I shouldn't have asked."

"President Lincoln had almost none at all and learned everything from his mother and books. He became a great trial attorney and you know what he did after that. You're a smart and level-headed man, Kyle, and if you want to try that route, we'll all support you."

They reached the boardwalk and stopped before their horses when Kyle asked, "Bryn, what about Katie?"

"I know Katie cares very much for you, Kyle. What do you want to know?"

"If I decide to try this, I won't be able to, um, do anything about us until I become a lawyer and that could take five years. I know she's already worried about becoming twenty soon and I won't even turn eighteen until January. Can I have her wait that long? Will she even want to wait? She already told me that she's no longer afraid of being around men, so what if she decides to see someone else while I'm studying?"

Bryn said, "Let's sit down on that bench, Kyle."

Kyle nodded then walked with his brother to the bench and took a seat.

"I know you didn't ask about the rewards, but even though the highest single reward was two-hundred and fifty dollars, there are so many that the total came to an incredible $4,250. Nobody could believe it when we added it up. They're trickling in, but even if some refuse to pay, you'll have well over three thousand dollars. That's more than enough to keep you going for a while and if you decide to follow that path, you'll get paid as a law clerk. I know two good attorneys in Denver and I'm sure that they'd be very pleased to have an Evans clerk for them."

Kyle then asked the question that had nagged at him since he'd first seriously thought about Katie.

"Katie told me that she's not afraid of men anymore, and even though she told me she didn't care, I sometimes wonder if she's just settling for me because I'm here."

"I don't think so, but why not take Katie to the big social to celebrate the last day of summer if you still have a concern?"

Kyle nodded and replied, "That's a good idea."

"Alright. We have that settled. You and Katie can just let things run their course while you begin studying for the bar. You'll need to order the books before you do anything else. If you become Kyle Huw Evans, Esquire, then I'll know that Denver will have an honest attorney."

"Thanks, Bryn. I'll head back to the ranch and talk to Katie. When is the social?"

"Around the middle of September, but I don't recall the exact date."

Bryn rose and said, "I hope this all works out for you, Kyle."

Kyle looked up at Bryn smiled and replied, "I think it'll all be okay."

Bryn gave him a short salute then turned mounted Maddy and headed back to the office while Kyle remained sitting on the bench.

For five more minutes, he sat and thought about everything that Bryn had told him; about becoming a lawyer and his future with Katie. The two dreams were now tightly linked and of the two, he was more concerned about the law. His small doubts about Katie were just that, but he wanted her to be sure. His confidence in his own ability was the big doubt, but he knew that he had to try or spend the rest of his life wondering.

Kyle finally stood, mounted Nick and trotted west before turning south to the Double EE.

———

When he returned to the house, Erin, Katie and Jack all asked about the trial during lunch and Kyle provided a blow by blow description of the process and the surprising five-year sentence. He didn't pass along Bryn's concern about John Coleridge's potential as a threat when he was released and left that for Bryn to tell or keep to himself. He did tell them about his new name and showed them the judge's signed order making it legal, which ignited happy congratulations from Erin, Katie and even Jack

After lunch, he helped Jack geld another poor prince then they moved a good amount of hay to the corral.

When they finished, Jack headed back to the house and Kyle began his exercises. He'd missed a few days because of his injury and didn't want his skills to lapse, not after that deathly confrontation with Bill Carbo. As he spun, thrust and swung his bat in his waltz rhythm, he tried to repeat that fight to see where he'd made his first mistake that had almost cost him his arm. The stitches would have to come out tomorrow, so he thought they had healed enough by now.

He knew that he'd been too far back and his thrust that should have caused the knife fighter to drop his weapons had just popped him enough to knock him back a couple of steps. As he grunted and sweated, he tried to picture the cold eyes as he'd begun his stabbing motion and then saw his mistake. It wasn't much, but as he had stared at the evil monster, he'd begun to say something, expecting the killer to wait for him to finish the sentence. But it was his own eyes that had betrayed him. As he had locked eyes with him, just before he began his lunge and swinging motion, he'd narrowed his eyes just enough to warn Carbo that he was about to strike.

He put that revelation back into his mind as he continued his workout. He'd talk to Bryn about it and ask how he could avoid it in the future, even though he hoped it would never be necessary again.

Kyle began slowing and as he turned toward the barn door, he wasn't at all surprised to see Katie standing in the center of the wide opening watching him with her arms folded. He didn't stop but continued his routine of slowing down gradually until he finally popped his bat's knobby head to the floor and stood facing Katie as the sweat poured across his exposed skin.

"What, no applause?" he asked as his chest heaved, and he gulped air between the words.

Katie laughed then stepped into the barn as she replied, "Only when I'm surprised, Mister Kyle Huw Evans."

Kyle smiled then asked, "Could you sit down, Katie? I have something I want to talk to you about. Two things, really."

Katie nodded noticing the sudden serious tone then walked to the work bench stool and took a seat while Kyle walked behind her. She wondered what he would tell her that had him so concerned.

He set his bat against the work bench then as he dried himself with a towel, he said, "When I was in the courtroom watching the trial, I was impressed with the order and the way that the law was being processed. I learned a lot in that one hour, Katie, and I asked Bryn when we left about becoming a lawyer. I didn't think it was possible with my three years of schooling, but he pointed out that President Lincoln had no schooling at all. He said I had to study hard and then clerk for a lawyer for a while before taking the bar exam. What do you think?"

Kate was relieved by the question and replied, "I think you can do anything you choose, Kyle. If you decide to be a lawyer, I'm sure that you'll be a good one."

"Thank you, Katie. That means a lot to me. It'll mean that for about five years, I'll be studying the law and working in Denver as a clerk."

Katie was startled and slowly asked, "Five years?"

Kyle saw her reaction and quickly replied, "I know it sounds like a long time, and it is to me, too. But Bryn told me that with all the rewards I have arriving I'll have well over three thousand dollars in the bank and when I'm a clerk, I'll get paid, too."

"Why is that important now?" she asked quietly.

"Because I was worried about those five years, Katie. I didn't want you to have to wait. What that means is that we don't have to wait that long. We can just let things progress just as wonderfully as they have been."

Katie sighed and said, "I thought you were going to ask me to wait, and I'm not sure I could. Each night after our walks, I help put Mason and Ethan to bed and watch Erin and Bryn together. I want that, Kyle. I want that with you."

"I want the same thing, Katie, but I want you to be sure."

"I am sure."

"Then will you come with me to the big social next month? I've never been to one either, so it'll be a new experience for both of us."

Katie quickly exclaimed, "I can't, Kyle! Please don't make that a condition for our future."

Kyle was startled by her reaction then said, "You said you weren't afraid anymore, Katie."

"I'm not afraid of you, Kyle, but I don't know if I'd tolerate some strange man dancing with me. Please don't make me go."

Kyle sighed then pulled over an empty flour barrel sat down and took her hands.

"Katie, I would never do anything to hurt you or see you hurt. If you don't want to go, then neither will I. We can spend the night together and have our own social in the barn. Okay?"

Katie visibly relaxed before she said, "Thank you, Kyle. You probably think I'm a weak, silly woman now, but I can't face it."

"We all have things that scare us, Katie. I was just worried that sometime in the future, you'd regret not meeting other men. You're an attractive, well-figured young woman who would attract any man's eye. Doesn't that happen when you go into Denver?"

"I don't go very often and when I do, I don't look at the men. I keep my eyes down. It's one of my many flaws, Kyle."

"You never looked down from the moment I saw you, Katie."

"And I never will as long as you're with me," she said as she squeezed his hands before she asked, "What scares you, Kyle?"

"Getting sliced with a sharp blade. I don't mind getting hit with something, even a bullet. But the thought of being sliced open just gives me the willies."

"But you faced that deadly knife fighter even after he'd cut you."

"I had to beat him, Katie. I didn't even know that he'd sliced my arm, either."

"So, it's alright if we don't go to social? Really?"

"Really. Now as long as we're here in the barn, would you honor me with the next dance, Miss Mitchell?"

"I am the one who will be honored, Mister Evans," she replied as she stood.

Kyle rose then took her hand and led her to the center of the barn, and before he placed his hand on her waist, he realized that he hadn't put on his shirt.

"Give me a second to get my shirt on."

Katie gripped his hand put her hand on his naked skin and said, "No, this is fine."

Kyle smiled at her put his hand on her waist and began humming the *Blue Danube* before they began their slow waltz across the floor.

Katie was incredibly happy knowing she wouldn't have to wait for even a year now. She knew that he turned eighteen on the 12th of January because it was the day between Dylan and Gwen's birthdays, which had created quite a stir. Next year, she thought, she might be an Evans as well.

———

"Where are we now, Mom?" Bethan asked as she looked out of the stagecoach window.

"We're almost to the first waystation where we'll spend the night."

"Oh. Can you see Dad anymore?"

Gwen replied, "He's already too far away to even look. He'll probably keep going after we stop, but they'll make camp along the road."

"It looks like west Nebraska out here," John said as he looked out the window with the dust flying past.

"Dylan says that it changes remarkably the closer we get to the mountains."

Cari then exclaimed, "It's dusty!"

"I know, dear, but we're moving very fast and that means you'll see your cousins very soon."

"And we'll see Uncle Bryn and Aunt Erin, too?"

"Yes, sweetheart. In just two more days."

"Good."

Meredith smiled at her youngest granddaughter and still hoped that she'd get there before Grace Lynn arrived.

———

Nine miles behind the stagecoach, Dylan was driving his new freight wagon at the back of three fully loaded wagons

417

carrying the Evans and Wittemore furnishings and crates. They were making better time than he'd expected and had actually rolled out of Julesburg before the stagecoach left the depot.

He had his two Smith & Wesson pistols at his waist, a Winchester leaning on the driver's seat between him and Lynn and both of his Henrys stored on the bed right behind him. His second Winchester was in the footwell of the wagon. None of the boys' legs were long enough to let their feet to reach it, so he didn't believe he was mistreating the new weapon. He had a box of .44 cartridges and another of .32s in the footwell beside the Winchester. His old Colt Dragoon, Walker and other pistols were stored in one of the cases.

He knew it was probably overkill, but the freighters all appreciated his presence even though they each had a rifle and a pistol.

Dylan had been surprised that the boys didn't get bored with the trip after the first hour or so, and even now were still chatting continuously about small critters that they'd spotted or odd bits of landscape.

"Do you think we'll see any Indians, Dad?" Lynn asked as he looked up at his father.

"Maybe. I don't think they'll be a problem, though."

"Did Uncle Kyle really just stand there with his bat while that Indian rode right at him?" Al asked.

"Yes, sir. I was ready to pull my Winchester if they looked like they started to aim their bows, but their warrior chief just raced his horse all by himself. I thought your Uncle Kyle was going to hit him with his big bat, and that might have started a ruckus, but he didn't. He let the warrior smack him with his coup stick and then just watched him ride away."

"Wow! That must have been scary!" exclaimed Garth.

"Not to your Uncle Kyle."

"Is he really our uncle, Dad? Mom said he was our cousin."

"She's right, but he's so much like a brother to me and your Uncle Bryn, that I think he's closer to an uncle."

Al then excitedly said, "He stopped those men from killing Aunt Erin and everyone else, too!"

"That's what your Uncle Bryn said in that telegram. I can't wait to hear the details when we talk to him. I can't see how he could have beaten an evil man like Bill Carbo with just that bat of his."

"But we're still going to play baseball when we get there, aren't we?" Lynn asked.

"Kyle said he was going to build a baseball field on the ranch, and if he does, I'm sure that you'll all get to play."

"Will you play, Dad?" Al asked.

"We'll see," Dylan said with a grin as he continued to scan the horizon ahead.

He didn't expect another confrontation with the Pawnee but having four heavily loaded wagons rolling across the open plains was almost a handwritten invitation for some of the unsavory men that traveled the west. Many of them were dissatisfied railroad workers, and the further they were away from those tracks, the better he liked it.

With the dry weather and packed roadway, he estimated that because of the extended daylight even with breaks for the horses, they could make sixty miles a day. If they could manage to keep this pace, they might only be a day behind Gwen's stagecoach when they arrived in Denver.

He had a large pannier of food and a full water bag in addition to four canteens. They weren't going to build a campfire at night, but the boys seemed to relish the idea of camping out in the wilderness, so that wasn't a problem.

Dylan had already talked to the lead driver and they'd set up a night watch as the heavy wagons couldn't afford to leave the road and risk being stuck in the soft soil. Pulling off to the side to let the stagecoach pass had caused a delay to get the heavy wagons back on the hard surface, but it would be much worse if all four wheels were off the road.

———

It was getting toward sunset and the wagons were still rolling when Garth, who was standing on the seat and looking back pointed and said, "Somebody is coming back there."

Dylan turned around and saw a dust cloud on the horizon, but no riders. It was barely visible in the fading light, and as he watched, the dust cloud began to settle and then disappeared.

Lynn smacked Garth on the shoulder and said, "There isn't anybody back there!"

"I saw them, Lynn. I'm not lying." Garth replied defensively.

Dylan said, "Lynn, leave Garth alone. I think he's right. Whatever made that cloud didn't want to be seen."

Alwen asked, "Are they outlaws, Dad?"

"I don't know, Al. It could be some folks traveling to Denver like us and just pulled over to camp for the night."

The boys were all kneeling on the rocking driver's seat as Dylan turned his eyes to the front. This could be trouble. Someone could have tracked them from Julesburg knowing that they'd have to stop a good twenty miles from the waystation and couldn't move the freight wagons off the road. They'd be a sitting target.

———

Ten minutes later, the wagons pulled to a stop, so Dylan set the handbrake told the boys to stay put then clambered to the ground with his Winchester and headed for the lead wagon where the other teamsters were meeting.

As he approached, they all turned to look at him and the lead driver asked, "Did you see a dust cloud back there a while ago? Joe here swore that he did, but I couldn't see anything behind us."

"I saw it too, and I don't think it was made by any innocent travelers, either."

"We lost a wagon a couple of months ago and never saw it again or the two men who were driving it either. I knew both of those boys and they were as honest as you can be."

Dylan glanced back at the darkening roadway then said, "I don't like the idea of an unknown danger coming up at us from behind. I don't want to give them any advantage either. They know where we'll be and probably that I have the boys with me. I imagine they've been following at about five miles behind us all the way from Julesburg."

"What do you want to do, Marshal?"

"I've got all my horses back there and most have saddles. Do any of you have any experience with those repeaters?"

"We all do, but Buddy here is the best shooter."

"I only want one man to come with me and we'll ride about a mile or so back down that road then dismount. I don't think they'll be that close because we couldn't see them when we stopped. We tie off the horses, cock our rifles and walk as quietly as possible. We should hear them before we see them."

He then asked, "Buddy, have you been in a gunfight before?"

"I served with the 15th Michigan at Shiloh and a few other places. I guess you could call that a gunfight."

Dylan smiled and said, "Then you and my brother, Bryn, should swap war stories. He was at Shiloh with the 2nd Iowa."

"I heard stories about those boys."

"Alright, Buddy, grab your rifle, and we'll start walking. The rest of you boys set up behind the horses and spread out. If you hear shooting, get ready in case any of them make it past us. If you see someone, just yell, 'Peanut!' and either me or Buddy will shout back, 'Donkey!'. If you don't get that reply, then you have a target."

"Why 'Peanut' and 'donkey'? Buddy asked.

Dylan grinned then replied, "It's a funny story. I'll tell you about it when we get back. Just keep my boys safe."

"We'll do that, Marshal," the lead driver replied before they returned to their wagons to get their repeaters.

Dylan then walked back to his wagon and leaned on the front left wheel as he looked up at his three boys and said, "Boys, I need you to be quiet and brave now. I'm going to ride back down the road with one of the teamsters to make sure that whoever created that dust cloud isn't a problem. Okay?"

"Okay, Dad," they replied in unison.

Dylan then placed his right foot onto the step, hoisted himself halfway and shook each of his sons' hands before stepping back down.

Buddy trotted up behind Dylan then they walked to the trailing horses. Dylan pointed out a tall dark brown gelding for Buddy to use and told him to tighten the loose cinches before he tried to mount as he separated Crow from the trail rope. After he tightened Crow's cinches, he stepped into the saddle and waited for Buddy to mount then they began walking the horses back down the road.

"Is Dad going to get them?" Garth asked as they all stared at their disappearing father.

"Dad always gets the bad men," Lynn said proudly.

Alwen added, "They'll be sorry for trying to pick on us."

———

There was going to be a full moon tonight, but it hadn't risen yet as Dylan and Buddy walked their horses toward the unknown riders. Estimating distance at night was bad enough, but with few landmarks, it was even more difficult. Dylan was making up for it by ignoring distance and just going by time.

Since he and Buddy began to move, he started a silent count. He estimated that the horses were walking about three or four miles per hour, so a mile would be fifteen to twenty minutes. He decided that they'd dismount when he reached a thousand.

The sound of the steel-shoed hooves striking the hard dirt soon made Dylan change his mind. He thought that the sound would carry too far, so he suddenly pulled Crow to a stop and stepped down.

Buddy halted his horse dismounted then walked over to Dylan and whispered, "Have we gone a mile already?"

"Maybe half that, but those hooves were making too much noise. We'll walk the rest of the way."

They walked their horses off the eastern edge of the road and tied them off on what barely qualified as a stick with branches before returning to the road.

As they walked, Dylan kept looking at the eastern sky, wondering how much longer it would be before the moon popped over the horizon. If it came too early, then it could be a disaster.

They walked slowly and after another forty minutes, Dylan finally began to hear the distant sound of human voices. He looked over at Buddy, who was already looking at him and pointed at his ear. Buddy nodded and they continued to walk.

As they drew closer, the voices grew louder and more distinct, but it wasn't until almost ten minutes had passed that they could distinguish individual voices and understand what they were saying.

The conversation confirmed Dylan's suspicions as they drew closer.

———

"When do you wanna go, George?"

"I figure they'll be sleepin' in another three hours or so."

"Y'all are just wastin' time. I say we just sneak up on 'em right now, while they're eatin'."

"That almost cost us last time, Willie. We wait and then we just take 'em."

"What if they put out a guard?"

"Then we shoot him first. They had kids with 'em, so I figure they'll just toss their guns down if we tell 'em that we're gonna shoot the kids."

"Aw, Bobby, I don't wanna kill no young'uns."

"Then don't worry about it. We can leave 'em out here in their skinny white birthday suits."

———

There was loud laughing and giggling as Dylan and Buddy finally picked up their shadows in the starlight.

By the different voices, Dylan had guessed that there were four of them and now that he could make out individual forms, that estimate was confirmed, He assumed that none had their pistols out of their holsters, but he motioned to Buddy to split up a few yards so they could cover all of them in case any tried to break away into the night.

His Winchester was cocked as he estimated the range to be about sixty yards from their cold camp. Buddy was now fifteen yards off to his right and when Dylan stopped, he waited until Buddy glanced back at him and held up his hand.

Buddy then held his position brought his Winchester to bear and waited.

Once he was sure that Buddy was ready to fire, Dylan set his sights on one of the shadowy figures and shouted, "Marshal Dylan Evans! Put your hands in the air where I can see them!"

Not one of the outlaws paid any attention to his warning as they felt that the night gave them enough protection. Each of them scrambled to his feet and reached for their pistols.

Dylan fired at his selected target then shifted one step to his right as Buddy fired. He fired his second shot as he saw two of them draw their pistols and stepped to his right again as he cocked his Winchester.

One man fired and Buddy immediately fired as the muzzle flare illuminated the shooter. The last man then turned to fire at Buddy just before Dylan fired his third shot and he watched the fourth outlaw drop.

The acrid smell of gunsmoke filled the night air as Dylan shouted, "Are you okay, Buddy?"

"Yes, sir!"

"Stay put for a minute."

"Okay."

Dylan listened to the assorted groans and moaning from the campsite and watched to see if anyone was moving away. After another minute, he began walking the last sixty yards with his Winchester still cocked and pointed at the four men. It didn't take long to find them spread across the ground, two on their backs, one on his stomach, and one curled in a ball.

"Okay, Buddy! Come on in!"

Dylan then stepped closer and kicked each of the bodies that were silent before rolling over the only one who still moaned.

Buddy arrived and Dylan said, "This one isn't going to last long. Let's get the gunbelts off of them and see who the hell they are."

"Okay, Marshal."

By the time the search was done, the only survivor joined his comrades in death, and they had found a total of $45.15 on the four men which Dylan handed to Buddy but hadn't discovered any identification at all. Their horses were still saddled a few feet away, so they walked to the animals and searched their saddlebags, but only found the expected essentials, although one did have a folded Confederate battle flag. Buddy stared at it then tossed it to the ground and spit on it before he and Dylan put their gunbelts into the saddlebags.

"What will we do with their bodies?" Buddy asked.

"They're far enough off the road that nobody will see them, so we'll just leave them there and let the critters have their fill. It's the only good that men like that ever do in their lives."

"Sounds good to me. I sure didn't want them to sully our wagons."

They checked the horses made sure the cinches were tight, then each mounted one, took the reins of a second and rode out of the campsite.

As they rode to get their own horses, Dylan was pleased that he'd stopped that bunch of killing thieves. This road needed to be safe for those stagecoaches like the one that was carrying his family.

———

Back at the freight wagons, all eyes were looking back down the roadway as the moon appeared and sent its soft light across the prairie. It seemed like daytime as the eyes of the five teamsters and Dylan's three sons peered into the night.

"I think Dad got them all," Garth said.

"Me, too," echoed Lynn.

"Will he be bringing more horses with him?" asked Al.

Before either of his brothers could answer, they spotted two riders leading four horses in the distance.

"It's Dad!" Garth shouted.

The teamsters cringed when he'd yelled, but just stared at the approaching riders.

When they were within hailing distance, Dylan shouted, "Donkey! Buddy and I are coming in!"

The five men grinned as they began to walk forward, and the Evans boys waved wildly over their heads at their returning hero, who just happened to be their father.

———

As Dylan added the new horses to the long trail rope, the teamsters began setting up the camp as they grilled Buddy on what had happened.

"Come with me, boys," Dylan said as he lifted Peanut from the back of the wagon, set him on the ground then untied both trail ropes from the back of the wagon.

He led the horses off the road to the thick prairie grass near a tiny creek and let them graze as the boys waited.

"How many were there, Dad?" Al asked.

"Four, but they didn't want to give up, so they went for their guns. They stood still and just tried to shoot, which made it seem like target practice. Do you know how stupid it was for them to even think about stealing the wagons?"

Lynn then asked, "Why? There's a lot of stuff here."

"Yes, there is a lot of valuable items in those wagons, but there are also seven armed men. They must have seen me board the wagon with all of the guns, and even if they managed to sneak up on as at night, it was likely that at least one or two of them would be killed. Do you think what's in those wagons is worth dying for, Lynn?"

"No, sir."

"The only thing worth dying for is family, boys. If you want to die for a cause, like your Uncle Bryn had done, then that's alright, too. But no one ever seems to care if you die except your family."

"Thank you, Dad," Alwen said.

Dylan looked down at his nephew and asked, "Why would you say that, Al?"

"Because it made me feel better."

"Me too, Dad," Lynn said before Garth agreed.

Dylan scrubbed each of the boys' heads then said, "Let's head to the camp and get some supper and forget about danger for a while."

Each of the boys then smiled and as they passed the small grazing donkey, patted him on his back and said, "Goodnight, Peanut," then walked with their father to join the teamsters.

As Dylan walked with the boys, he was almost startled when he recalled that only Garth was his natural son. Lynn was conceived when Gwen had been briefly sham married to Burke Riddell in Fort Benton and Alwen was Colwyn's son. They'd formally adopted Alwen before they left Omaha, so he was legally his son, and he and Gwen had never treated Garth any differently than Lynn or Alwen. He regarded each of them as his son and knew that Gwen did as well.

Yet as he looked at the boys as they trotted past him to beat each other to the campsite, he noticed the distinct physical difference between Lynn and the two boys with Evans blood. His behavior was the same, but Dylan hoped that the difference didn't create problems for him when he was older. Alwen knew that he was really Dylan's nephew, but Lynn had no idea of his true parentage.

He finally threw aside the idea and joined the boisterous crowd as they began preparing their cold supper.

CHAPTER 13

August 17, 1867

Bryn and Kyle were sitting outside the stage depot when the thundering sound of the coach's team announced its arrival as it entered the main road.

They stood and headed for the edge of the boardwalk then watched the horses slow and then stop as the driver pulled back on the reins.

Bryn then walked to the coach opened the door then held out his hand and said, "Welcome to Denver, Mrs. Wittemore."

Meredith took his hand and stepped down as John exited behind her. Bryn hugged his mother then as he shook John's hand, she embraced Kyle.

The next one to exit the stage was Bethan who really bounced out rather than step outside. She squealed and leapt into her Uncle Bryn's outstretched arms as Kyle stepped to the doorway and took Brian from Alba and then helped her down to the boardwalk.

He gave Brian back to his nanny then plucked Cari Lynn from Gwen and held her in his left arm while he assisted Gwen's exit.

"I swear, I'll never be able to sit down again," Gwen said as she arched her back and stretched.

Meredith then asked Bryn, "Erin hasn't delivered yet, has she?"

"No, Mom. She's waiting just for you."

"Good. Where will we be staying?"

"Tonight, you can all rest in my house in Denver. Kyle and Katie made sure it was clean and the pantry was stocked, so you'll be able to relax."

"Can we walk there?" asked Gwen.

"Yes, ma'am. It's about three blocks from here on a side street."

John looked around and said, "This is bigger than Omaha."

"Yes, sir, and it's growing even faster. When they get a railroad in here, it'll explode."

Kyle said, "I've got a buckboard, so I can take your luggage to the house. Do you want me to take Brian and Cari with me, Gwen?"

"That would be marvelous. Alba, can you go with Kyle?"

"Of course. I'm too stiff to walk anyway."

———

Twenty minutes later, everyone had been moved into the house that Bryn had been given by Jim Peacock. It was late in the afternoon and rather than spend hours catching up, Bryn and Kyle made their farewells and said they'd be back in the morning to bring them out to the ranch to meet the newcomers to the Evans clan and to inspect their unfinished homes.

———

It was midmorning the next day when Kyle drove the rented carriage out of Denver heading for the Double EE. Bryn was inside continuing the almost non-stop monologue that had begun when they entered the Denver house.

The current plan was for John and Meredith to stay at the big house while Gwen stayed with the children in the Denver house with Alba and wait for Dylan to arrive. That housing arrangement wouldn't change until the two new houses were completed and furnished in about another three or four weeks.

After he pulled the carriage to a stop by the front porch and set the handbrake, Kyle clambered down to help with John and Meredith's luggage as the carriage began to empty.

Erin, Katie and Flat Jack were all waiting on the porch, and not surprisingly, the first person out of the carriage was Meredith, who hurried up the stairs and embraced Erin but refrained from rubbing her bulging tummy.

Gwen then stepped up the stairs with Brian in her arms while Alba held Cari's hand and Bethan held her sister's other hand as they climbed the four steps.

Bryn and John helped Kyle with the luggage and brought them into the parlor where the Denver Evans cousins were reunited with their Omaha cousins and met their newest cousin, Brian.

After setting the luggage down, Gwen walked over to Kyle and asked, "Could I talk to you for a minute, Kyle?"

"Yes, ma'am," he replied and followed her back out onto the porch, wondering what she needed so soon.

Once he closed the front door, Gwen said, "Kyle, I know this is just silly talk, but I'm worried about Dylan and the boys. They should be about thirty or forty miles behind us, and it probably won't make any difference, but could you ride out there to meet them on the road, just to make sure they're safe?"

"Of course, I will, Gwen. I'll saddle Nick and leave right away. Jack or Bryn can drive you back to the house. Is that where Dylan can find you?"

"Yes. Thank you, Kyle. And I can never thank you enough for what you did to save Erin, Katie and the children. I know that when mom heard the story, she wanted to shoot that last one even if he is in prison. We're all so very grateful."

Kyle simply replied, "Well, I'll get going. I'll tell Katie first, though."

Gwen hooked her arm through his, then opened the door as she said, "She's a very lucky girl, Kyle."

Kyle blushed as they entered the house then when Gwen released his arm, he caught Katie's eyes and walked towards her.

She had Brian in her arms and smiled when he approached and she said, "Isn't he a beautiful baby? I'm sure that Grace Lynn will be just as pretty when she arrives, too."

"I'm sure that she will, Katie. Gwen asked me to head out on the road to meet Dylan and the boys just to make sure they're safe, so I'll be gone for a day or two. I just wanted to let you know."

Katie didn't even think of raising an objection. She could understand Gwen's worries, especially in light of the recent violence at the ranch.

She said, "Come back as soon as you can, and you'll owe me two dances when you do, sir."

Kyle grinned and replied, "I owe you more than two dances, Katie," then surprised Katie and anyone else in the room who was looking their way when he leaned across Brian and kissed her before turning and leaving the parlor.

Katie watched him leave and then turned her eyes to Erin who was talking to Meredith, but still smiled at her. She'd obviously been watching the scene as she listened to her mother-in-law.

––––––

Kyle stopped at the small house and packed some food into a sack that should last him for the day if he didn't find them then filled a canteen with fresh water and snatched his Winchester before leaving the house heading for the barn to saddle Nick.

Ten minutes later, he trotted out of the Double EE and headed north. Forty minutes after that, he left Denver behind and had Nick at a medium trot. It was a Sunday, so there wasn't as much traffic as usual, so Kyle pretty much had the roadway to himself.

––––––

After the takedown of the four highwaymen, the freighters picked up the pace as if there were more coming. It wasn't intentional, but there seemed to be a sense of urgency now.

They were still about seventy miles out of Denver when they began that morning and by noon, they'd cut that distance to fifty. They'd have to stop when they were about twenty miles out, but that meant they'd arrive in the early afternoon the next day.

The boys had been excited when they saw the Rocky Mountains and as they drove southwest each passing mile made them appear even larger.

"They'll be a mile high when we get to Uncle Bryn's ranch!" Garth exclaimed as he rocked on the driver's seat.

"I'll bet they're two miles high!" yelled Lynn from the bed.

Dylan laughed and said, "We're already a mile above sea level right here, boys. Some of those peaks reach almost three miles into the sky."

"Wow!" exclaimed Al from the back of the wagon bed as he rubbed Peanut's fuzzy head.

Peanut had his own reserved spot on the wagon with a pile of hay for him to snack on and had finally learned not to poop in the wagon and would wait until they stopped unless he wanted to express his dissatisfaction.

Dylan had been a bit worried about one of the mares who was heavy with foal when they left Omaha and had almost sold her rather than bring her along, but Gwen was fond of the young lady, so he'd added her to the trail rope. He still checked on her condition whenever they stopped, but she seemed to be doing well. He'd still feel better when she was in the corral at the Double EE and under Flat Jack's care.

It was late in the afternoon when the lead driver shouted back, "We got a rider comin' from the south!"

Dylan looked that way and saw a small dust cloud and a lone rider. He wasn't concerned at all, so he turned to the boys and said, "It's okay. He's just one man and he's probably heading to Julesburg to catch a train."

"We're not scared, Dad," Lynn said from behind.

"I know that none of you are, Lynn. You're all brave boys."

Dylan continued to watch the rider for no other reason than there was nothing else to attract his attention.

In the lead wagon, Joe Lindell was wound a bit tight after the incident with the four outlaws and pulled his Winchester from the footwell and cocked the hammer while he stared at the rider, who was about a thousand yards away.

––––––

Kyle had spotted the wagons before they'd seen him but didn't bother waving yet. He was just glad to find them so soon, and happy to be able to give Nick a break when he reached Dylan. He had asked a lot of his equine friend today and even though he'd stopped for a break and let him drink and graze, he knew that he'd used a lot of energy.

When he was about four hundred yards away, he twisted around and slid his bat from his saddlebag. He wanted to identify himself to Dylan, not realizing that Dylan was in the last wagon and didn't have the best view because of the dust.

After sliding his hand through the wrist strap and getting a firm grip on the handle, he lifted his bat over his head.

Joe Lindell had seen Kyle pull the bat and from that distance and with the glaring afternoon sun in his eyes, mistook it for a Winchester. When Kyle raised it above his head, he was certain that the rider was ordering them to stop and would probably have confederates hidden nearby. Once that belief was firmly established in his mind, there was no turning back.

In the last wagon, Dylan saw Kyle hold the bat in the air and exclaimed, "I think that's your Uncle Kyle, boys!"

Everyone's attention was on the approaching rider, so no one paid attention to what Joe was doing.

Joe watched the rider approach with the rifle still held in the air and even though the range was too far, he wanted the outlaw to know that they were armed, so without a hint of his intentions, he quickly brought his repeater level, aimed high and pulled the trigger.

Kyle was smiling until he saw one of the teamsters pull his rifle and aim it at him. He was so stunned by the move, that he still had his bat in the air when the man fired. He felt as if time had stopped as the flash of light from the muzzle reached his eyes and was soon followed by the billowing cloud of gunsmoke.

He couldn't understand why they were firing at him and instinctively dropped his bat in front of his face to protect himself. The chances were almost nil that the .44 would come anywhere near him at this range when fired from a rolling wagon at a moving target. But that miniscule possibility arrived when he felt his bat pop back toward his face then bumped against his forehead.

No sooner had Joe fired than the lead driver, Happy McFarland turned and yelled into his ear, "What the hell are you doin', Joe? Drop that thing!"

Joe stared at the approaching rider and replied, "He's got his rifle out, Hap!"

"That ain't a damned rifle. Now put yours down and hope he doesn't shoot you when he gets here."

Joe looked at the rider, who'd lowered whatever it was then slowly set his Winchester back in the footwell.

Kyle let Nick keep moving as he turned his bat around and discovered a .44 slug buried in the hard maple. It probably didn't have enough energy left to punch into his head, but he wasn't sure. It could have hit his eye and that would have killed him.

He lowered the bat, but just hung it off to the side as he slowed Nick and pulled off to the east side of the road away from the shooter before he pulled to a stop to wait for the wagons.

Dylan had been as stunned as everyone else in the wagons when Joe had quickly fired but was relieved to see that Kyle hadn't been hit. He really wanted to have a talk with Joe Lindell when they stopped. The boys were all still staring with wide eyes at Kyle as he sat on his horse.

When the first wagon reached Kyle, Happy said, "I'm really sorry, mister. My idiot friend here was kinda trigger happy after a run-in we had with some highwaymen the night before last."

"It's alright. I can understand that. I'm Kyle Evans, so I'll just head on back to see Dylan and the boys. Can you hold up until I can get my horse tied off with the others?"

"I'll do that, and thanks for not gettin' so riled."

Kyle smiled gave him a short wave then started Nick at a walk as he passed the other wagons.

When he reached Dylan's, he stepped down with the bat still hanging from his wrist then said, "Howdy, Dylan. Gwen asked me to ride out here to make sure you and her boys were safe."

"You're not turning around and riding back, are you?"

"She didn't say that. I think she just figured I could come out here to help. I'll tie off Nick and then join you up there."

"Go ahead."

Kyle led Nick to the back of the long line of horses, attached his reins to the extended trail rope and noticed the foal-filled mare before heading back to the front of the wagon.

After watching Kyle climb aboard, Hap McFarland started them rolling again.

"We were all watching you coming closer and were shocked when Joe fired at you. Luckily, he didn't come close, but that was a stupid thing to do."

"He didn't miss, Dylan," Kyle said before lifting his bat and showing Dylan the buried bullet dead center in the thick end.

The boys all stared at the back of the .44 as Dylan whistled and said, "That's a one in a million shot, Kyle. Luckily, you had it off to the side."

Kyle glanced at the boys before he replied, "Yes, sir. I was lucky about that," then set the bat on the footwell.

Dylan then said, "Tell me about what happened on the Double EE."

"I thought you might want to know about that, Marshal Evans. Well, I was in the barn exercising with my bat as I did every afternoon, when…"

The boys congregated as close as they could as Kyle told the story. Even though Dylan knew from Bryn's telegram that Kyle had stopped the two assassins with his bat, hearing how the confrontation with the two killers happened, blow by blow, was still startling. Bryn narrated the story factually without embellishment or leaving out any details because of the young ears that were listening. He even included what he and Katie were doing in the barn when they arrived.

He shifted to the ride to Golden with Bryn to arrest Cornbread and having to stop another attempted ambush on the way and ended the story with the trial of ex-Deputy Coleridge and Bryn's concerns when he left prison in five years.

Naturally, as soon as he ended the tale, the boys wanted to see his scar from the knife fight, so he rolled up his left sleeve to display the still-red scar.

"Lordy, Kyle! You have been busy since I left you there. I'm glad that I did, too. I can't imagine the tragedy that would have happened if you hadn't been there."

Kyle didn't reply, but then Dylan began asking questions about the new construction followed by some about Kyle's obvious interest in Katie.

Kyle didn't mind talking about Katie because he valued Dylan's opinion as he'd known Katie a lot longer than he had.

He told Dylan about their long talks and his one lingering concern.

"You're worried that she hasn't met any other young men and that she might find one that she prefers to you. Is that it?"

"Not so much that I'm worried about losing her as I am about making her regret never having had the choice. She's adamant about not going to the social next month and I'm certainly not going to drag her out of the house to take her against her will."

Dylan thought about it for a minute then said, "I'll see if Gwen has an idea. She always seems to find a way. Did I ever tell you that she hired Erin just because she knew that Erin was a perfect match for Bryn after the Arial heartbreak?"

"She did that on purpose?" Kyle asked in surprise.

"I didn't find out about it for a long time, and I'm not sure if Bryn knows yet. I'm not going to say anything, and neither will those three young men listening to this story right now. Will they?"

After receiving a chorus of 'no, sirs' and 'no, dads', Dylan said, "I don't think Bryn would care one bit now anyway. So, you're thinking of becoming a lawyer?"

"Yes, sir."

"It'll take a lot of work, Kyle, but I think you're up to it. It would be great to have an attorney in the family."

Kyle smiled and said, "I was surprised when Bryn took me to the judge's office to have my name legally changed. If you look at the form, you can see how shaky my handwriting was when I wrote 'Kyle Huw Evans'."

"I'm a bit jealous that I didn't have that honor, Kyle, but I'm glad that Bryn took care of it."

"Can you tell me about the problem with the highwaymen that the teamster told me about?"

"It wasn't much because those four made too many mistakes, but what happened…"

———

Three hours later, they pulled up for the night and after Joe Lindell practically slobbered at Kyle's feet in apology, Kyle shook his hand and said it was just a mistake and he wasn't upset.

It was their last night on the road, so there was almost a party-like atmosphere in the camp as stories were told and some were invented, but they passed the time and the boys felt accepted when some of the teamsters accented their stories with ribald humor and their father didn't object.

———

As she lay in her bed that night, Katie couldn't help but feel worried about Kyle, knowing he was riding alone across empty land that was only inhabited by Indians. When she began to imagine that Kyle may not return, she examined her own behavior and regretted not agreeing to go to the social because of her almost nonsensical fear.

She understood why he'd asked and spent a long time in self-examination wondering if she wasn't being selfish by not going and defying her weakness. Before she finally drifted off to sleep, Katie decided that she'd tell Kyle when he returned that she'd go to the social with him. He would be her only dance partner that night, but she would go just to show him that she had no doubts.

———

It was in mid-afternoon when the four heavy wagons entered Denver the next day, and three of them headed for the warehouse where they'd store their cargo until they were brought out to the new house along with the new furniture that Gwen and Meredith would have to pick out.

Dylan had given each man a gold eagle that morning, even Joe Lindell, who felt guilty as he accepted the coin, but not guilty enough to refuse it.

As they turned toward the warehouse, the drivers all waved to the Evans crowd who waved back before they continued along the main street and headed for Bryn's house where Gwen and the rest of Dylan's family waited, including Alba.

When they pulled up, Kyle let Dylan and the boys charge into the house while he waited on the driver's seat. He was anxious to get back to the Double EE and see Katie again to tell her the story. He'd already decided to tell her where the bat had been when it took the bullet meant for him because he was sure that if she asked, he couldn't lie to her. He knew that she'd be able to tell in an instant because she seemed to be so adept at reading his eyes.

On the day's long ride, he'd told Dylan that he needed to find a way to be able to read men better, and Dylan had surprised him when he quickly answered, "play a lot of poker."

He explained that it was the best way to get an idea of what men are thinking as long as the other players weren't professional gamblers.

Dylan exited the house, and after Kyle climbed down from the driver's seat, Dylan said, "Let's get most of that stuff into the house. I'll keep Crow and another horse here, and you can take the rest with you to the Double EE."

"What about Peanut?"

"He'll go with you."

"Okay, let's get this thing unloaded."

————

It took almost an hour to empty the wagon, but Kyle didn't have to wait to open the crates, so he climbed onto the wagon and was rolling south as the sun touched the tops of the Rockies.

He turned onto the access road less than an hour later as the sunset was in full swing and headed for the corral.

No one was outside as he passed the house and soon reached the corral. He lifted Peanut to the ground then began stripping the horses that were saddled including Nick and set their tack in the back of the wagon.

After all of them were barebacked, he led the long string of horses to the corral opened the gate then one by one, he removed their bridles and let them loose to join the rest of the herd.

He finally left the corral and dropped the trail rope and bridles in the back of the wagon then unharnessed the team and led them into the corral.

With all of the horses put away, he looked down at Peanut and asked, "Do you want to go into the barn, Peanut?"

The donkey looked up at him then snorted, trotted away and turned into the open barn doors. Kyle doubted that he understood the question but wasn't sure.

He then began picking up Winchesters and Henrys before carrying the five repeaters, one of which was his to the small house then as he was about to set them on the porch before opening the door, it swung open and Jack grinned at him.

"We didn't figure on seein' you back so soon. My hearin' must be bad 'cause I didn't hear you and all those critters goin' past."

Kyle said, "I guess nobody heard me, Jack. Let me get these guns put away."

Jack stepped aside as Kyle entered the house and asked, "Where'd you get so many?"

"Dylan had a run-in with some highwaymen the first night out of Julesburg. You can guess what happened to them," he answered as he set the guns on the couch.

"Anybody hurt besides the ones that shoulda been?"

"Nope. Dylan and the boys are in Denver with Gwen."

"You hungry? I was just headin' over for chow."

"I'll join you, but I need to get cleaned up first."

"I'll put those repeaters away while you do that."

Ten minutes later, Jack and Kyle strode across the yard to the big house and even fifty yards away, Kyle's mouth began to water when he picked up the aroma of roasting beef.

When they entered the kitchen, Meredith and Katie were at the cookstove, Erin was sitting down with Mason and Ethan while Bryn and John were already standing.

"You're back!" Katie exclaimed before she dropped her whisk and hurried to Kyle.

She didn't worry about anything as she threw her arms around him and kissed him as if he'd just returned from a voyage around the globe.

Kyle was pleasantly startled by his welcome and didn't understand what had prompted it.

Katie released Kyle then stepped back two feet and said, "I was worried that you might run into Indians or outlaws."

"I only found Dylan and the freighters, Katie. I left Dylan and the boys with Gwen back in Denver and left their horses in the corral."

Bryn stood behind Katie and asked, "Are they all right?"

"They're fine. They did have a problem with four highwaymen the first night, but it wasn't a problem for very long."

"You can tell us about it during supper," Bryn said before he turned around to take his seat.

Katie then whispered, "Are we going for our walk later?"

"I've been looking forward to it."

Katie smiled then returned to the stove to start loading up the plates while Kyle took his customary seat waiting for her to sit beside him.

The supper was filled with conversation about what Dylan had told him, but Kyle didn't mention the bizarre welcome he'd received when he found the wagons. He needed to talk to Katie first.

———

After supper, Kyle and Katie left the house holding hands as they walked south toward the new houses that finally looked like houses.

Before Kyle could tell her about the bullet in his bat, Katie asked, "Kyle, will you take me to the social next month?"

Kyle looked at her and asked, "Why do you want to go, Katie? I'm not going to take you if it will make you upset."

"I know that you're concerned that I might be settling for you because I haven't met any other men, and I don't want you to ever believe that. I know I'll be uncomfortable, but I want to go. I need to go, Kyle. I can't keep behaving like this."

"Are you sure, Katie?"

"Yes."

"Well, we have three weeks or so before we have to go, so if you change your mind, let me know."

Katie sighed and replied, "I will, but I'm determined to do this. If you can face down two killers with your bat, then I can certainly handle facing men on the dance floor."

"Alright, Katie. Speaking of my bat…"

Katie listened as he told her what had happened as he approached the wagons and then she asked, "Where was the bat when it was hit?"

"In front of my face. The bullet had lost most of its punch at that range, but it would have hurt."

Katie should have been horrified but somehow having Kyle's hand in hers softened the imagined impact of his answer.

They reached their designated rural dance floor and as he placed his hand on her waist, Katie said, "I guess this is practice now."

"It will be practice for the rest of our lives, Katie," Kyle said before he started humming the waltz.

———

The next day, Dylan brought Gwen and the entire brood to the ranch for an Evans family reunion and to examine the construction of their new home.

After that first day on the ranch, things began to settle down on the Double EE and in Denver. Dylan officially took over the office as Gwen converted the Denver house to their temporary home.

Meredith and John stayed at the Double EE and the Evans matriarch hovered over Erin as her time grew closer. Katie was grateful that she was there because it gave her more time to other chores and to prepare her dress for the social. She'd never really concerned herself with her appearance and wanted to look her best at the event.

Kyle continued his daily exercises and was beginning to add some weight with the steady diet but didn't notice it. He and Katie never missed an evening walk and dance which always ended with a kiss followed by several encores.

———

August 29, 1867

It was in mid-afternoon. Bryn was at work and Kyle was out in the west pastures with Jack and the herd when Erin called to Katie from her bedroom. Grace Lynn had decided it was time to make her grand entrance.

As Katie put pots of water on the stove and started the fire, Meredith began preparing Erin in the bedroom.

Katie then walked out to the back porch and rang the dinner bell that really only served as a warning bell and let its loud clanging echo across the pastures before she returned to the house and hurried to the bedroom with armfuls of towels.

Erin had been through this twice before but this one felt different and she didn't think it was because the baby was a girl. There was something wrong and she started to worry, even as she grunted with the powerful contractions.

Meredith and Katie stood beside the bed and could see the troubled look on her face behind the pain.

"It'll be fine, Erin. Soon, you'll be holding little Grace Lynn in your arms," Meredith said as she touched Erin's sweating face.

"I'm worried, Mom. Something's not right."

"That's how I felt with your husband, Erin. I thought there was something amiss, but I soon saw my little pink son and knew he was perfect."

Erin managed a smile at her mother-in-law as she said, "He is still perfect, Mom."

Katie wasn't sure if Meredith had told her that just to reassure her or not, but at least it took Erin's mind off the baby for a few moments.

Kyle trotted into the kitchen and soon understood the reason for the summons when he heard Erin's cries from the bedroom.

He walked quickly to the open doorway then stopped at the threshold before asking, "Do you want me to get Bryn?"

Meredith replied, "No. He'd only get in the way and he'll be home in two hours anyway. He'll be here long before Grace Lynn arrives. I need you to help mind the boys."

"Okay," he replied before walking down the hallway to find Mason and Ethan.

Ethan was still crawling, but Mason was an almost-three-year-old explorer who could be anywhere. The key to finding him was to find Ethan who would be trying to track down his elusive older brother.

He found Ethan peering under the bed in the next bedroom, then heard giggling from under the bed but didn't bother disturbing them. He just sat down and watched Ethan as Erin's cries and loud grunts echoed from the adjoining room.

He didn't know much about childbirth, but he thought that they lasted for a long time and this seemed to be happening quickly. She'd only been in labor for an hour or so now.

Mason finally popped out from under the bed and as he started walking toward the doorway, Kyle picked him up and plopped him onto the bed beside him.

"Who is crying?" he asked.

"Your mom is having a baby sister for you and Ethan, Mason."

"Why is she sad?"

"She's not sad. It just hurts for ladies to have babies, but they're really happy after they get to hold them."

"Why?" he asked as he looked at the wall between the bedrooms.

"We'll never know the answer to that, Mason, because we're men and we can't have babies."

"Why not?"

Kyle laughed as he plucked Ethan from the floor and replied, "Your dad will tell you why when you're a big boy. Okay?"

"Okay. How long is she going to cry?"

"I don't know that either. It could be a long time, though."

Mason was obviously dissatisfied with Uncle Kyle's lack of knowledge, so he stopped asking questions.

———

By the time Bryn rushed into the house after hearing Erin from the back porch, Kyle was feeding Mason and Ethan in the kitchen as Jack fixed dinner and John assisted.

"How is Erin?" he asked excitedly as he hung his hat on a peg and removed his gunbelt.

"She's doing fine."

"How long has she been in labor?"

"Almost three hours now. I offered to come and get you, but I was overruled."

"It's okay. I'd probably just get in the way."

Meredith heard his voice, so she left Katie to watch over Erin and exited the bedroom to talk to Bryn.

"How is she, Mom?"

"She's fine, but she keeps saying that there's something wrong or different. I don't understand why she's so convinced because everything seems so normal. She's moving along very quickly, but that's not unusual for a second or third child."

"How much longer before we meet Grace Lynn?"

"I'd say another three hours. Why don't you just try to relax and get something to eat. I'm sure that whatever Jack is making will be tasty and filling."

"Thank you for being here, Mom," Bryn said before his mother smiled then returned to the bedroom.

———

After eating their supper, putting the boys to bed and serving both Katie and Meredith when they were able to sit down, the three men shared coffee.

The sun had set, and Erin's cries grew louder and more frequent and Erin's conviction that something was wrong only added to Bryn's concerns.

As a way to keep Bryn's mind off his worries, Kyle brought out a deck of cards and invited Jack, John and Bryn to play some poker.

————

An hour later, in the lamplit birthing room, Erin knew that it was time and began to push for all she was worth as Meredith encouraged her and Katie pressed cool damp cloths to her face.

"She's coming!" Meredith exclaimed, "Keep pushing, Erin!"

Erin was still worried but kept squeezing her muscles to let Grace Lynn take in her first breath. She desperately wanted to hear her daughter's loud wail as she announced her arrival in good health. Hours earlier, she'd begun to think that her little girl would be stillborn when she tried to think of a reason for the difference between this birth and the other two.

Meredith saw the baby's head emerge and guided the rest of the baby free and pulled it onto a blanket.

Before the baby had a chance to cry, Erin asked in panic, "Is she okay? Is she okay?"

Meredith smiled as she lifted the child who began to cry then replied, "He's a beautiful baby boy, Erin."

Erin was so relieved that he was alive and well, but disappointed that he wasn't Grace Lynn.

Then after cutting the umbilical cord, Erin suddenly grunted again and automatically pushed harder than she had before.

Meredith was holding the newborn in her hands then looked down before quickly exclaiming, "Katie, hold the baby!"

Katie took two rapid steps to the foot of the bed accepted the squirming infant and then heard Meredith exclaim, "I see another head, Erin! Keep pushing!"

Erin almost started laughing as she pushed despite the overwhelming pain. She finally understood the reason it felt so different. Grace Lynn had arrived with a brother.

Just two minutes after seeing the baby boy, Meredith held Grace Lynn Evans in her hands and laid her onto a towel. They only had one baby blanket and the firstborn had usurped it for his own use.

Erin was absolutely exhausted but incredibly content and fulfilled as Katie and Meredith laid her two babies onto the crook of each of her arms.

"They're both so beautiful!" she whispered.

"You just stay there and admire your new babies, Erin. I'll clean up here while Katie gives the good news to your husband."

"Thank you, Mom. And thank you, Katie."

Katie smiled down at her older sister then left the bedroom and walked out to the kitchen.

She thought that they'd all heard Meredith's exclamations, but when she entered the room, Kyle quickly stood and asked, "Is Erin all right? Is Grace Lynn healthy?"

Katie smiled and replied, "Erin is fine and as happy as you can imagine. Grace Lynn is a beautiful little girl."

"When can I see them?"

"Um, in a little bit, but I think you should sit down first."

"Why? Is something wrong?" he asked as he sat down.

"No, but we found out why Erin thought that something was different. You now have Grace Lynn and she brought her brother along with her. Erin had twins."

Bryn's eyes went wide and asked, "She had another boy, too?"

"That's what brothers are, Bryn. I'm going to go back now and help mom with the cleanup and then she'll come and get you when she's ready."

Bryn stood then hugged Katie and kissed her on the forehead before letting her return to the bedroom.

He collapsed on the chair then looked at Kyle and Jack as they both grinned at him.

Bryn said, "Twins. That's a surprise."

Kyle slid the king and queen of hearts across the table and said, "Why don't you keep these as a memento. I'll get a new deck."

Bryn snatched up the cards and slid them into his shirt pocket before saying, "I'm glad I built too many bedrooms in this house."

"You and Erin are catchin' up to Dylan and Gwen, Bryn," Jack said before he snickered.

Bryn just smiled and finally relaxed.

———

Twenty minutes later, he was ushered into the bedroom to see Erin and their new children.

As he took a seat next to his tired but happy wife, he leaned past the closer baby and kissed her gently before sitting back and saying, "I guess Grace Lynn didn't want to be alone while she waited."

Erin softly said, "We need a boy's name now. We never even thought of one for some reason."

Bryn said, "I think Kyle is a good name."

"I was thinking the same thing. We owe him so much."

Bryn looked over at Katie and asked, "Can you have Kyle join us, Katie?"

She nodded then left the room returning with Kyle just a minute later.

As he slowly stepped into the room holding Katie's hand, he looked at the two babies and Erin's smiling face and was in awe that she could appear so happy after going through that ordeal.

Bryn looked at Erin and nodded then she raised her eyes and said, "Kyle, we'd like to name our son after you. You are the reason that he's here now and why I'm able to have the joy of seeing him and Grace Lynn."

Kyle was astonished at the honor but replied, "Thank you, Erin. It means a lot to me, but if it's alright with you and Bryn, can you name him Huw? I'm sure that would make my mother happy."

Meredith was close to tears when Erin had asked Kyle, but her eyes flooded with his reply. It had been almost two decades since she'd heard that devastating news of her firstborn son's death and now, she'd delivered the newborn son who would carry the same name. It was as if a circle had been completed and at the center was the young man who had made that thoughtful request.

Bryn replied, "You are an extraordinary young man, Kyle," then turned and gently kissed his newborn son's forehead.

"Welcome to the world, Huw Lynn Evans," Kyle said softly, then stood and kissed his daughter's forehead and said, "We're happy to meet you, Grace Lynn Evans."

He didn't sit again knowing that Erin needed her rest, so he and Kyle left the room and headed back to the kitchen then Kyle and Jack continued to the small house.

Katie was exhausted when she finally crawled into bed just after midnight but as tired as she was, she had a difficult time falling asleep. She'd assisted in two other childbirths, but Erin's was different and not just because she had twins. She had been almost as worried as her sister was throughout her labor and when Huw Lynn finally arrived, she shared her sister's joy and disappointment until Grace Lynn made her appearance. It was such an emotional journey that finally ended with Kyle's request.

But more than that, it was the first time she'd been present at a birth since she'd fallen in love with Kyle and committed herself to their future. She'd entered the bedroom with Meredith worried that watching Erin endure the extended pains of labor would push her back into her old fears and force her to deny Kyle. That fear had only escalated along with her concerns for Erin as the labor progressed. It was only when she saw Erin's face as she and Meredith laid her newborns into her arms that she felt that fear dissolve into the ether. She saw Erin's loving eyes as she looked at her babies and then at Bryn and instead of letting her fear return, it shattered it into non-existence.

Katie realized that this is was her future and now, she wanted it more than anything she'd ever hoped for before.

———

Over the next two weeks before the social, Kyle and Katie continued their walks and moved their dances onto the parlor floor of Dylan's new house that was nearing completion.

John and Meredith's smaller house wasn't as small as the second one on the Double EE with four bedrooms, an office, and a large kitchen and parlor, but Dylan's was of necessity, much bigger, with eight bedrooms, an enormous kitchen, parlor and dining room and a large office and library.

It was just two days before the social that the whole housing plan underwent a major modification.

After everyone was seated at the dinner table that Thursday evening, John looked at Kyle and said, "Meredith and I have made a swap with Bryn and Erin. We're going to live in the big house after Dylan moves his family into their new house rather than move into the new house on the Double EE."

Kyle asked, "Why are you telling me, John?"

"Because it's your new house, Kyle. Meredith and I both are very happy with the idea of living in the city, so we can walk to the stores like we did in Omaha. I guess we were spoiled. We didn't know that Bryn even had the house until we arrived. So, rather than leave the new place empty, we want you to have it. You may need it soon."

Kyle quickly looked at Bryn who was smiling then turned to see Katie's equally surprised face.

Kyle said, "I was planning on asking Bryn if could build a house myself soon, so I guess that I'm supposed to say something like 'I can't accept it', but I'll just say thank you, John and Mom. It's a very generous thing to do."

He reached across the table shook John's hand and rather than walk around the table, he shook Meredith's hand as well.

Finally, he turned his eyes back to Katie but didn't know what to say.

Katie knew what she wanted to say but not here and not now.

With the offer of the house accepted, Bryn then said that Dylan wanted him to have the four horses and tack along with the repeaters and pistols from the highwaymen claiming that he couldn't take them as a U.S. Marshal, but he could dispose of them at his discretion.

———

That night as they walked south a little earlier than usual, Katie asked, "Was the gift of the new house a hint by John and mom?"

"I think all of them were behind it, Katie. It makes sense, though. I do know that mom would rather live in a city and the house is nice, too."

"I'm not complaining, Kyle, but I think it's a bit premature. We have the social on Saturday and I might fall in love with some handsome young gentleman."

"How do you know that I won't be smitten by some bosomy young lady who catches my eye, Miss Mitchell?"

"Because if I see some big-chested floozy letting you gaze down her cleavage, I'll show you mine and you'll forget all about her."

"Don't think that I haven't thought about your, um, features."

"Features? Really, Kyle? Is that the best you can do?"

"If you must know, men have at least twenty-two substitute nouns for women's breasts and none of them are exactly repeatable in female company. There's one that a boy I knew in the ironworks used that I've never heard before or since."

"And can you tell me what it is, or will I be offended?" she asked with a grin.

"You won't be offended because it doesn't sound like anything. He called them 'meegles'."

Katie started laughing and they had to stop walking as she bent over when her laughter overtook her mobility.

Finally, she stood wiped her eyes and muttered, "Meegles? Now that is odd."

"So, impressively meegled lady, are you at all concerned about the social?"

"Some, but I'm a lot better now."

"Why?"

"Watching Erin have Huw and Grace was nothing less than a revelation to me. In a way, I'm looking forward to the social to prove something to myself."

Kyle smiled at her as they reached their new house walked through the front entrance and were soon engaged in their waltz.

———

September 14, 1867

Kyle helped Katie down from the buggy and took her arm as they walked toward the big hall. Other couples and many single men and young women were filing in already and Kyle felt a bit of anxiousness as the climbed the steps.

He had been awed when he first saw Katie in her new dress and had tripped over the rug in the parlor as he stared at her.

Katie had been enormously pleased to see his reaction, and almost started giggling when he stumbled but held it to a smile. She still had butterflies in her stomach as she walked up the steps with Kyle but steeled herself for what lay inside the big building.

When they entered the building, they left their coats on a long table then walked into the dance hall and Katie felt as if every male eye in the expansive room was staring at her but knew that they weren't. She fought the urge to look down as they crossed onto the dance floor and then turned left to a row of chairs.

As Katie sat down, she forced herself to scan the room looking at the young and some old faces. A few were looking at her and Kyle but most, she noticed belonged to other young women and some were quite attractive.

She knew that she had to avoid feeling inadequate and revisited Kyle's reaction when he saw her in her new dress. It was that recent memory that bolstered her and when the band began to play an unfamiliar tune, she thought that Kyle would wait for a waltz, but he didn't.

He stood took Katie's hand and said, "This will be our first dance that isn't a waltz, Katie. All we can do is fall on our faces, like I almost did in the parlor."

Katie laughed then took his hand and stood. The music wasn't in the same rhythm as the waltz but it wasn't difficult to match their steps to the new time as they watched the other couples.

They stayed on the floor for two more dances before they returned to their seats and had barely had a chance to sit when a short young man dressed in a nice suit and wearing a gold chain across his vest stepped close and asked Katie if she would like to dance.

Katie glanced at Kyle then took a breath and stood. She had something to prove not only to Kyle, but to herself as well.

Kyle watched as the man put his hand behind Katie's back and felt a twinge of jealousy spark inside him. As he kept his eyes on her, he didn't notice the young lady taking Katie's seat beside him.

After he lost Katie and her partner in the crowd, he sat back and heard a light cough on his right then turned and saw a very pretty young lady smiling at him with her big brown eyes.

"Do I know you?" she asked.

"I don't believe so, miss. I've only been in Denver for a few weeks."

"You remind me of someone, though. What's your name?"

"Kyle Evans."

"I'm Ann Forrester. It's nice to meet you, Kyle."

He smiled and replied, "It's nice to meet you too, Ann."

She was obviously waiting for him to ask her to dance, but the tune was nearing its end and he expected to see Katie sailing back across the floor, so he asked her something inconsequential.

"Have you lived in Denver very long?"

"No. I was born in Kansas City, but my father was transferred here two years ago. He's a banker. What do you do?"

"Right now, I'm just helping my uncle at his ranch. I haven't made any plans yet."

The music stopped and Kyle looked at the dance floor but didn't see Katie, so when they struck up the next song, he turned back to Ann and asked, "Would you like to dance?"

"I thought you'd never ask, Kyle," she replied as she stood.

After she took his hand and he placed his hand on her waist, they began to swirl around the dance floor, and he knew it was rude to ignore her especially as she seemed to want to push her bosom through his chest. But he only glanced at Ann as he scanned the passing dancers wondering where Katie had gone.

She was wearing a white dress with a blue sash, but so were many other young women. It was almost two minutes into the dance when he finally spotted her red hair and saw her smiling at the short young man, and he felt his stomach drop.

He lost interest in the dance, but still waited for the music to stop before he thanked Ann for the dance before hurrying to the chair and sitting down in a huff. He felt like an idiot for asking Katie to come to the social and it had backfired on him in the worst way.

He knew that he couldn't leave but kept his eyes down as the band began another tune, and as luck would have it, it was the *Blue Danube*. He almost started laughing at the irony as he stared at the polished floor knowing that Katie would be sharing their waltz with someone else.

Then gentle fingers tapped him on his shoulder and as he looked up, he saw Katie smiling down at him as she asked, "Will you honor me with our waltz, kind sir?"

Kyle stared at Katie for a couple of seconds before standing and taking her hand and starting to slide across the dance floor.

Once they'd set themselves in motion, Katie softly asked, "What's wrong, Kyle?"

"Nothing. I'm okay."

"I thought that you'd be happy that I danced with someone else."

"I am. I'm very happy."

"You don't sound happy to me, Mister Evans. Now, out with it! What's wrong?"

Kyle sighed and answered, "I thought you'd come back after one dance, but then you didn't, so I danced with a different girl so I could get on the dance floor and find you. Then when I did, you seemed so happy to be dancing with the other man, I thought that I'd lost you."

"Why would you think such a thing?"

"You seemed so happy. You were smiling at him as you danced. What else could I think?"

"Do you know why I was smiling at him? During that first dance with him, I listened to him as he talked constantly about how important he was and how much money his family had, and I was uncomfortable. Then when he asked me to dance with him again, and he renewed his sales pitch because that's what it was, I realized that I could not only let another man touch me, but that I could judge him. It was then, Mister Evans, that I began smiling, not at him, but at the thought that

I had already found the best man I could ever hope to find. The man who has me in his arms right now."

Kyle felt as foolish as he'd ever felt in his life then as he looked down at Katie as they floated across the dance floor, he looked into her sweet blue eyes and quietly said, "I love you, Katie."

"I love you, Kyle. And thank you for taking me to the social."

"Will you marry me two days after my birthday?"

Katie smiled and replied, "So it doesn't fall on Gwen's birthday?"

"Yes, ma'am."

"I can't wait. It'll be like a second Christmas."

The long waltz continued for another two minutes then they left the floor and with no more reason to stay, they exited the hall and were soon driving the buggy back to the Double EE.

As they rolled south, Katie was snuggled in close to Kyle when she asked, "So, did the girl you dance with have big meegles?"

Kyle laughed then replied, "She let me know they were there when she pressed against me. She was wearing a corset, so I thought she might impale me."

Katie laughed and couldn't wait to talk to Erin if she was still awake. Feeding two babies seemed to keep her tired all the time, but Meredith's constant attention made her life much easier.

When Katie had mentioned Christmas, Kyle realized that this would be the first Christmas when he had the money to buy nice gifts, time to arrange for everything and most importantly, a large family to add that special meaning to the already special day.

He was still thinking of what to do when they turned down the Double EE's access road.

"May I tell them, Kyle?" Katie asked as they rolled toward the house.

"Of course, you may. I'll just tell Jack. He's been dropping hints that I should ask you for some time now, almost after the first week."

"Really?" she asked, "That long?"

Kyle smiled at Katie as he pulled the buggy to the front of the house and after stepping out didn't have to go to the other side to help her exit because she was in the middle. He held her hand as they stepped onto the porch then before he opened the door, he kissed her goodnight.

Katie then said, "You make my toes curl."

Kyle reached for the doorknob and replied, "I won't say what you do to me, Katie."

Katie laughed then walked through the open door before Kyle trotted back down to the buggy and drove it to the barn.

When he finished unharnessing the buggy, he walked to the small house and when he passed over the threshold, Jack looked up at him from his book and asked, "Well? Did you ask Katie to marry you?"

Kyle closed the door and shook his head as he grinned at Flat Jack and said, "I don't know why you would think that, Jack, but yes, I did."

Jack whooped threw down his book and trotted over to Kyle and wrapped his arms around him as he said, "I'm really happy for you and Katie."

"Thanks, Jack."

Jack let him go then said, "Now, tell me how it all happened."

Kyle removed his jacket and gloves then set them on a chair and proceeded to tell Jack the rather unusual circumstances that led to the proposal.

————

The news of the proposal reached the Denver Evans the next morning when Bryn rode into town to tell Dylan and Gwen. Neither was surprised by the news and Bryn asked Gwen if she was somehow behind it, but Gwen protested her innocence, at least in this one.

That morning, Kyle was in the barn shoeing Katie's mare, Zoe, when Peanut walked into the stall and stared at him.

Kyle grinned at the sight, but as he stared at the diminutive donkey standing in front of the scattered hay on the floor, he had an inspiration.

After Zoe had her new set of shoes, he left the barn and went out to the corral to find Jack to tell him what he wanted to do.

When Kyle finished, Jack nodded and said, "I think we can do that, Kyle, but we're gonna have to figure out where we can do it."

Kyle smacked Jack on the shoulder then said, "We'll find someplace. It's finding what we need that might be hard."

"Not for me, it won't."

Kyle was already getting excited and it wasn't even October yet.

———

On the 23rd of September, the freight wagons arrived from Denver with the first of two loads for the Double EE's new houses. John and Meredith's things that were now not being sent to the new small house were already in the Denver house.

The next day, Gwen, Katie, Meredith and Alba began putting the final touches on the two houses and on the 26th of the month, it was time to make the move.

The horses had already been transferred to the new barn and corral, and Kyle had moved his things out of the small house to his new home. One of his few purchases for the place was a gun cabinet for his repeaters and pistols. He also made a wall mount for his bat, realizing that it could never be used in a baseball game anymore.

Not surprisingly, Katie moved in with Gwen and Alba moved in with Erin. It had been Gwen's suggestion, of course. She thought that with the colder weather approaching, it would be more difficult for Kyle and Katie to spend time together.

But what moving into his own house meant to Kyle was that he now had a place to begin his project. Jack could come over to help, but this was going to be his gift.

He also ordered his law books which were delivered on October 10th. He now had to balance his studying with working with Jack and his project, but none of it cost him time with Katie.

They avoided being alone in his house because it was too much of a temptation, but they still used his new parlor for their nightly dances and would invite Jack or Alma over to sit before the fire and enjoy some coffee and act as chaperones.

Dylan was whipping the Denver office into shape and hired two new deputy marshals that met his standards. One of the old ones quit in a huff, but he wouldn't be missed.

Thom Smythe and his wife and son arrived on October 23rd after having a falling out with Marshal Claggett. He'd wired Dylan and asked if he still had a slot available and Dylan had replied that if he didn't, he'd make one.

Kyle's project was coming along smoothly and at the end of the month, Jack came through with what Kyle had thought was the difficult part.

There was a serious incident in Golden in the middle of November that almost cost Cal Burris his life when he was shot twice in an attempted bank robbery. He'd shot one of the four outlaws before he was hit, and another before he took the second shot. By then, the remaining two raced out of town heading east and were trailed by a posse who caught up with them halfway between Denver and Golden. One of the members of the posse was killed and both outlaws died in the gunfight. Cal would be bedridden for a few weeks but wouldn't have any impediments after he'd healed.

The first snows arrived in late November and the winds howled from the Rockies making work more difficult, but it had to be done.

The first two weeks of December were surprisingly mild, and Jack and Kyle took advantage of the lull to bring the herds into the small box canyon on the west end of the property, about two miles south of the Double EE ranch house. They used Dylan's heavy wagon to bring a full load of hay to the canyon and knew they'd have to make a few more trips in the winter. Both barns had their lofts packed with hay and the piles of firewood were stacked high in preparation for the snow and cold.

———

December 24, 1867

Kyle and Jack had worked in the late hours putting the finishing touches on the project before returning to the small house.

That night, rather than return to his house, Kyle stayed with Jack to make sure that they hadn't missed anything and after their review, Kyle poured them each a fresh cup of coffee and took a seat.

"Well, Kyle, I'm kinda impressed with it."

"I am too, Jack. Can I ask you something?"

"Sure."

"Katie mentioned something to me yesterday and I was wondering if she knew something that I didn't."

"Ladies always know what's goin' on before us."

"So, when she said that you were thinking of courting Alma, she was right?"

Jack stared at the mug in his hands and replied, "Maybe. She's a real nice lady, Kyle, and if we were to get together, it wouldn't change much."

"I hope it works out for you, Jack. You could use some female companionship after all this time."

"Thanks for not makin' fun of me, Kyle."

"I could never make fun of you, Jack. I respect you as the father that I never had."

Jack smiled at Kyle but knew he couldn't reply without embarrassing himself.

————

Christmas morning dawned with only four inches of snow on the ground and by ten o'clock, the entire family was gathered in Bryn and Gwen's home. They had both fireplaces roaring and two heat stoves helping to keep out the chill as the children anxiously awaited their chance to open their gifts from the enormous pile that filled the corner of the room.

Kyle had bought appropriate toys for each of his cousins, even baby Huw and Grace Lynn. He had found something nice for Gwen, Erin, Meredith and Alma, but it had been much easier to buy manly gifts for Dylan, Bryn, John and Jack. Katie's gift had been easy to think of, but difficult to find.

When all the gifts had been opened and appropriate thanks offered to the giver, Kyle waited until most were opened before he sat beside Katie and handed her a long, thin box.

Katie smiled at him and carefully peeled back the wrapping paper and once she saw the box label, she laughed then turned and kissed Kyle before saying, "This is perfect, Kyle. Can we try it later?"

"That's why I bought it, Katie."

"What is it, Katie?" Erin asked.

"It's a roll for the player piano. It's the *Blue Danube*."

As everyone smiled at the couple, Kyle took Katie's hand, then stood and said, "I have a special gift for the entire family, but you'll all have to dress warmly because it's out in the barn."

Jack knew what it was, so he said, "I'll stay here with the little ones."

Each of them donned jackets, hats, gloves and galoshes before Kyle led the parade out of the house and walked with Katie to the barn.

As they followed the path through the snow, Katie asked, "Can you tell me what it is?"

"Nope. I don't want to ruin the effect."

Katie was curious as they reached the barn and Kyle grasped one of the door handles before turning to the assembled family.

"Merry Christmas, everyone!" he announced then swung the door wide.

As they filed into the barn, their eyes grew wide as they stared at his creation.

The children were more excited about who was there as much as what he'd worked so hard to build.

Katie said, "It's beautiful, Kyle. Did you build it?"

"With some help from Jack, including finding her."

What mesmerized everyone was a life-sized creche carved out of boards and painted before draping them with cloth. But what Kyle had expected to be difficult to find and Jack had managed, was standing off to the side and in the manger itself.

Peanut looked back at the humans all gaping at them and didn't care. Beside him was a tiny jenny that was still taller than Peanut, but in the manger was a very young donkey that was no bigger than a Texas jackrabbit.

"Is that Peanut's baby donkey?" asked Garth.

"No, sir. Jack found the lady donkey for me a couple of months ago and she'd just had her foal. We've been keeping them in the loft for a while now. He's a boy, and it's up to all of the Evans boys and girls to decide on a name."

"What about his mother?" Bethan asked.

"I already gave her a name because it seemed right."

Katie was smiling as she asked, "What's her name?"

"Hazel."

There was just a moment's pause before a rippling laughter passed among the adults before Alwen asked, "Why is that funny?"

Gwen replied, "Because she's Peanut's wife and so, she'll be Hazel Nut."

The children joined in the laughter before they all approached the creche to welcome Hazel to the family.

After they returned to the house, it took over an hour of deliberation before the children arranged themselves before Kyle and as Lynn counted down, they shouted in unison, "Wally!"

Kyle grinned at them and replied, "That's a perfect name for him. Well done!"

There were smiling faces all around before they all headed into the dining room and kitchen for their overflowing Christmas feast.

———

That night, Katie and Kyle went to Bryn's house and after installing the paper roll in the piano, they began their dance. This time, Bryn and Erin, then Dylan and Gwen joined them on the floor and a new Evans family tradition was born.

———

January 14, 1868

Kyle and Katie stood before Judge West and Kyle couldn't believe that he had so many good things happen to him since he'd left Wilkes-Barre. He had a real family now and a new name. He had a house and soon would share it with his wife who still could make his heart melt just by smiling at him.

Before the judge began the ceremony, Kyle said a private 'thank you' to his mother for setting him on this path.

The first thing that he'd done after depositing all of his reward vouchers and cash was to wire fifty dollars to Doctor Turnbull in Wilkes-Barre expressing his wishes to have a proper headstone placed on his mother's grave.

On the new headstone, he asked for the following inscription:

Bess Ann Evans
Oct 11, 1838 ~ June 3, 1867
Cherished Mother of Kyle Huw Evans
And
Loving Wife of Huw Lynn Evans

Now as he stood with Katie's hand in his and listened as she vowed to love, honor and cherish him forever, he knew that when his time came to meet his father and be reunited with his mother again, he'd be either waiting for Katie or she would be waiting for him. Then he and Katie would watch over their children, their own legacy to the world.

EPILOGUE

In May of that year, Kyle began clerking for Robert L. Barr, Esquire. He knew that he still had much to learn, but he threw himself into the job and the attorney was very happy with his performance and willingness to listen.

By then Katie was already in her fourth month and Gwen and Erin were both expecting again as well.

Jack and Alma had married in March and as Jack had told Kyle not much really changed on the Double EE.

A month after that, Katie received a letter from her brother Ryan in Omaha who asked if he could join them in Denver, so after receiving Bryn's permission because it was still his ranch, Kyle had sent him a hundred dollars for the trip. He arrived just before Kyle began clerking and stayed with Kyle and Katie for the time being, but John Wittemore understood that the newlyweds would need their privacy, so he and Meredith financed the building of another small house for Ryan's use and he moved out in June.

Ryan took over Kyle's position with Jack and seemed to enjoy working with horses, which also gave Kyle more time for study.

Another change on the Double EE that summer was the new baseball field that Kyle built near the small house. He bought two baseballs and a bat, and Katie sewed three bases out of stuffed canvas while Kyle cut out a home plate. Each

Sunday, weather permitting, the whole family would be on the field learning the game and making monumental blunders that were more fun than playing it right.

Katie delivered their first child on October 22nd, a little girl they named Bess Lynn, but Gwen returned to the Evans tradition and had a boy they named Conway Lynn on December 2nd. Erin had another daughter they named Emily Lynn just nine days later.

————

Kyle made steady progress in his studies and what he learned in the law office and in the courtroom. He also spent time with Dylan and Bryn asking questions about criminal law to get a practical understanding of its application.

The long-awaited railroad arrived in 1869 and soon Denver was connected not only to Kansas City, but to quickly growing Cheyenne in Wyoming Territory. The expected explosion in the city's population was realized and it appeared as if new buildings grew overnight like mushrooms.

On April 11, 1872, less than four years after starting as a clerk, Kyle Huw Evans passed his bar exam and became a practicing attorney at the age of twenty-two.

At his swearing in ceremony, Katie stood with six-week-old John Lynn in her arms while Meredith held eighteen-month-old Colwyn and Alba stood with Bess Lynn as they watched Kyle take the oath.

Filling the first two rows of the courtroom was the rest of the Evans clan.

And after he lowered his right hand and shook Judge West's hand, Kyle turned and faced his family as they all applauded Colorado's newest attorney. Kyle then stepped beside his loving wife and couldn't avoid the tears that streaked down his face as he saw the love in each of his family members' eyes and felt as lucky a man who had ever walked on God's earth.

He knew that there would always be difficulties ahead because that's the way life is, but he was even more confident that his family would always be there for him and he would be there for any of them.

For a boy who walked out of Pennsylvania with no family to call his own, this was the greatest blessing of all.

BOOK LIST

1	Rock Creek	12/26/2016
2	North of Denton	01/02/2017
3	Fort Selden	01/07/2017
4	Scotts Bluff	01/14/2017
5	South of Denver	01/22/2017
6	Miles City	01/28/2017
7	Hopewell	02/04/2017
8	Nueva Luz	02/12/2017
9	The Witch of Dakota	02/19/2017
10	Baker City	03/13/2017
11	The Gun Smith	03/21/2017
12	Gus	03/24/2017
13	Wilmore	04/06/2017
14	Mister Thor	04/20/2017
15	Nora	04/26/2017
16	Max	05/09/2017
17	Hunting Pearl	05/14/2017
18	Bessie	05/25/2017
19	The Last Four	05/29/2017
20	Zack	06/12/2017
21	Finding Bucky	06/21/2017
22	The Debt	06/30/2017
23	The Scalawags	07/11/2017
24	The Stampede	08/23/2019
25	The Wake of the Bertrand	07/31/2017
26	Cole	08/09/2017
27	Luke	09/05/2017
28	The Eclipse	09/21/2017
29	A.J. Smith	10/03/2017
30	Slow John	11/05/2017
31	The Second Star	11/15/2017
32	Tate	12/03/2017
33	Virgil's Herd	12/14/2017
34	Marsh's Valley	01/01/2018
35	Alex Paine	01/18/2018
36	Ben Gray	02/05/2018
37	War Adams	03/05/2018

38	Mac's Cabin	03/21/2018
39	Will Scott	04/13/2018
40	Sheriff Joe	04/22/2018
41	Chance	05/17/2018
42	Doc Holt	06/17/2018
43	Ted Shepard	07/16/2018
44	Haven	07/30/2018
45	Sam's County	08/19/2018
46	Matt Dunne	09/07/2018
47	Conn Jackson	10/06/2018
48	Gabe Owens	10/27/2018
49	Abandoned	11/18/2018
50	Retribution	12/21/2018
51	Inevitable	02/04/2019
52	Scandal in Topeka	03/18/2019
53	Return to Hardeman County	04/10/2019
54	Deception	06/02.2019
55	The Silver Widows	06/27/2019
56	Hitch	08/22/2018
57	Dylan's Journey	10/10/2019
58	Bryn's War	11/05/2019
59	Huw's Legacy	11/30/2019
60	Lynn's Search	12/24/2019
61	Bethan's Choice	02/12/2020
62	Rhody Jones	03/11/2020
63	Alwen's Dream	06/14/2020
64	The Nothing Man	06/30/2020
65	Cy Page	07/19/2020
66	Tabby Hayes	09/04/2020
67	Dylan's Memories	09/20/2020
68	Letter for Gene	09/09/2020
69	Grip Taylor	10/10/2020
70	Garrett's Duty	11/09/2020
71	East of the Cascades	12/02/2020
72	The Iron Wolfe	12/23/2020
73	Wade Rivers	01/09/2021
74	Ghost Train	01/27/2021
75	The Inheritance	02/26/2021
76	Cap Tyler	03/26/2021

77   The Photographer   04/10/2021
78   Jake   05/06/2021
79   Riding Shotgun   06/03/2021
80   The Saloon Lawyer   07/04/2021

Made in the USA
Middletown, DE
28 December 2022

20589702R00286